Julia.

Julia.

MELANIE MARTINS

Melanie Martins

VAN DEN BOSCH SERIES

BOOK FIVE

Melanie Martins, LLC
www.melaniemartins.com

First published in the United States by Melanie Martins, LLC in 2023.

ISBSN ebook 979-8-9861626-7-6

ISBN Paperback 979-8-9861626-8-3

Printed and bound by CPI Group (UK) Ltd, Croydon, CR0 4YY

This is a 1st Edition.

DISCLAIMER

This novel is a work of fiction written in American-English and is intended for mature audiences. Names, characters, places and incidents are either the product of the author's imagination or used fictitiously. Any resemblance to actual persons, living or dead, is entirely coincidental. This novel contains strong and explicit language, graphic sexuality, and other sensitive content that may be disturbing for some readers.

To all my dear readers, thank you.

READING ORDER

While you don't need to have read the *Blossom in Winter* series to start this book, we recommend the following order to get the very best reading experience:

Blossom in Winter series (Petra & Alex's story)

1. Blossom in Winter
2. Lured into Love
3. Lured into Lies
4. Defying Eternity
5. Happily Ever After: Part 1, 2, 3, and 4

Van den Bosch series

1. Roxanne.
2. Andries.
3. Elise.
4. Dan.
5. Julia. (You are here)
6. Sebastian.
7. Hannah.
8. Johan.

PROLOGUE

Sebastian

I had my doubts about this hunt and whether it would at all quiet my racing thoughts, but the embrace of the natural world around me is a welcome surprise. Thoughts of Julia—and all the joy and complications which accompany her—are finally quieted somewhat as I walk beside my father and the other men we have invited along with us for the hunt. We are in Hungary in search of a red deer, but more importantly, to woo this group of potential partners. Some carry their rifles and follow us with the ease of experienced hunters, while others are more in awe of the setting as a whole.

We had set off into the forest just after dawn, where the trees tower above us, and the underbrush is thick and dense. The sun filters through the branches, casting a gentle glow upon the forest floor, where the leaves crunch and rustle beneath our boots.

It's been an uneventful hunt thus far, but I personally don't mind. The air is crisp and cool on my face, and I feel the moisture in the air as the sun burns off the grass's morning dew. It's quiet, aside from the sounds of the men next to me. Luckily, they are aware enough not to scare away any potential prey and only speak in hushed whispers.

As the day progresses, the woods come alive with a symphony of sounds: the chirping of birds, the rustling of leaves, and the occasional snap of a twig, which sets everyone on the edge of anticipation. My eyes scan the surrounding trees, looking for any sign of movement or life, but the colors around us are blending together to create a natural camouflage, concealing the creatures that dwell within.

Occasionally, a flash of bright red or brown, indicating the presence of a deer, captures our attention, but they are elusive, disappearing into the underbrush as quickly as they appeared. But we are close, and the energy of the group is rising.

We walk quietly through the woods, our footsteps muffled, when suddenly we come upon a small herd of red deer grazing in a clearing—their majestic forms silhouetted against the background lit by the late afternoon sun. My heart beats faster as I watch the deer, hands tightening around my rifle. I slide a glance over to my father, who shakes his head once, and I allow my grip relax. We had agreed to let the businessmen make the kills if possible, so they could go home with a positive memory of the trip, and therefore, our company.

I'm probably a better shot than all of them, but this isn't about my skills, so reluctantly, I keep my rifle at my side as the rest of the group stirs to life. Everyone looks at them with a mix of awe and excitement, the eyes of the non-hunters are wide with anticipation while the true hunters take their positions and raise their weapons, ready for the kill.

Slowly and carefully, they take aim at the deer, trying to minimize any disturbances to the herd. There are about half a dozen deer from my count, and there is no way that we will be able to tag them all. Once the shots ring out, it's unlikely we'll be able to take any other groups by surprise, so I hope the shooters make it count.

With an enormous 'crack', the sound of the rifles echoes through the forest, and a few of the deer fall to the ground, their bodies limp and still. The others in the herd scatter, fleeing for safety, their powerful legs carrying them swiftly through the dense underbrush. We watch as they disappear into the forest, their forms becoming fainter and fainter until they are gone from sight.

"Good show!" Dad announces, laughing as he claps the successful shooters on the shoulders and shakes everyone's hands. Where tense energy had blanketed the group at first, it is all celebration now.

The men who have managed to shoot the deer approach them cautiously, their eyes still fixed on the surrounding woods. The deer's bodies lie still and peaceful, and once the hunters give the go ahead, the staff we brought with us move to collect their prizes for cleaning while the rest of us make our way back to my uncle's estate for a post-hunt meal.

As the deer are collected and we gather in a small group to discuss the rest of the day—heaping an obnoxious amount of praise on the men we hope will work with us in the future—there is a commotion coming from the woods behind us. At first, it almost sounds like an animal running through the trees towards us, but it quickly becomes apparent that it's a member of my Uncle Leopold's staff on a small ATV, skidding to a stop and rushing over to my father.

The young man is breathless, as if he's run the entire way to us instead of coming on a vehicle, and he reaches into his pocket and pulls out a mobile phone that, bizarrely, looks to be still connected to a call as he hands it to Dad.

"Mr. Van den Bosch," the staff member gasps, his body almost shaking as he stands in front of my dad. "We have an urgent call for you."

I can tell Dad is about to complain about the interruption, but he seems to notice at the same moment I do how pale the young man is. My father takes the phone and walks a few feet away to take the call in private, but it's no use. Everyone's attention is on him.

"What's the meaning of this?" I snap at the young employee, who flinches.

"Well, I-" he stutters, "I think—"

But he doesn't get to finish his thought. Dad doesn't make much sound as the news hits him, but we all watch as the mobile slips from his fingers and he sinks to his knees here in the undergrowth. He's shaking so hard that by the time I make it over to him—so quickly that I don't even remember moving—I can hear the leaves crackling under his knees.

"Gone…" he whimpers, cradling his head in his hands, his eyes shutting tight. "Dear God, they're gone…."

Heart now galloping, I snatch the phone off the ground, putting it against my ear. "This is Sebastian. Who the hell is this and what the fuck is going on?"

The person on the other line takes a second to collect themselves before answering. "It's Willem, Sebastian."

"Willem?" The fact that it's my family's attorney and one of Dad's most loyal friends on the other side of the line gives me pause, making it somewhat even worse. For this call to be an emergency, something terrible must have happened. I feel panic setting in as I continue observing my distressed father, who remains on the ground just as before.

I collect myself and clearing my throat, I ask, "What's going on?"

"I don't know how else to say this, Sebastian, but…" he stops mid-sentence, as if reconsidering his words, before sighing loudly.

"Willem, speak!"

"Your mother and siblings have been killed in an auto explosion. It was, ah… your vehicle, I believe, and the explosion occurred before they were even able to leave the estate." Willem inhales slowly, letting his words crash into me. "Sebastian, I am so, so sorry–"

I hang up the call, fisting the small phone in my hand until my arm is quivering and I hear the faint cracking of the plastic casing. I throw it back down to the ground before I can break it irreparably, emotions hitting me like claps of thunder, one after the other. I can see Dad from the corner of my eye, now with his forehead touching the earth and his hands fisted in his own hair, but it's like he's a million miles away from me, not mere inches.

I stumble away until I can lean on a nearby oak, my hand pressed over my heart, which I think may explode in my chest just like my car did with almost everyone I've ever loved inside of it. Rage hits me first, but by the time I'm against the tree, it's fled, leaving a gaping chasm of grief that I can't even begin to process. It's hard to even take a breath.

Mom… Adriana… Freddie….

And then, the worst thought of all.

My car… my fault.

Freddie had asked so many times in the past to drive it, and I'd rejected him just as many, but this last time I had given in. Maybe it was the pressure of being asked so many times, or maybe it was because my mind was elsewhere, but I for some idiotic reason, agreed, and that simple agreement had gotten them all killed. The truth of it all is glaringly obvious—someone had meant to kill me, the heir to the Van den Bosch estate, but instead had wiped out everyone else in the family.

What a cruel fucking twist. I wish it was me… God, how I wish it was me.

My mind is still blank besides pain as my uncle arrives in a flurry on his own ATV, running to my father and immediately going to his knees next to his brother, wrapping him in an embrace the likes of which they haven't probably shared since they were children. Leopold rocks my father back and forth with his arms around him, and having one of the few members of his family left there with him, Dad breaks out of the haze of shock and begins to sob in huge, heaving gasps. I watch, distant and numb, feeling my phone vibrating in my pocket while everyone else starts circling the newly widowed man, without knowing what to say or do.

Oh, that's right. Everyone probably thinks I'm dead. I guess I should answer. I pull my Blackberry out, not even bothering to look at the screen. It isn't until Julia begins to speak, on the other line, that I realize I haven't even said anything since accepting the call.

"Sebastian?" she asks, her tone thick with panic. "Sebastian?"

"Julia," I reply woodenly, and she lets out an enormous sigh of relief.

"I'm so glad you're okay," she gushes before relief turns to sorrow. "But, oh God, Sebastian… your mom! Your siblings! I just heard. Are you…?"

"I'm not okay, no," I tell her, knowing what she's about to ask. "Physically, sure."

"I don't even know what to say… Sebastian…." I hear her little hiccup of a sob, and it annoys me. Why is she crying? She didn't even know them.

"You don't need to say anything. I'm hanging up."

"Wait!" she calls, and I stop with the phone halfway off my ear to hear what she has to say, watching my uncle try to coax my father to his feet. Dad looks like the walking dead. Around us, the businessmen hover like flies, unsure where to land as this all plays out.

"I-" Julia stumbles before finding her words, "I'm here for you, Seb. No matter what you need, no matter what time, I'm always here for you."

I allow myself a second to consider laying in her arms while all my angry grief spills out of me, but it isn't feasible. Dad is incapacitated, barely able to stand, and it's all going to fall to me. Everything… and I have to be ready for it. There is no time to mourn the way I want to.

Then, I consider something awful. If whoever rigged my car to explode was trying to kill me, that means other people in my life are at risk, too. The few people left that I care about, that is, and first and foremost of those people is sweet Julia.

"Stay home," I demand, my heartbeat in my throat as I try steadying myself. "Stay near your mother and don't go out in public alone for a few days, okay? Listen to me, Julia, because I can't lose you, too. I just–" to my shame, a sob sticks in my throat like a sticky ball of dough, refusing to move, and I know she's heard it. "Just keep yourself safe," I finish.

"I will," she promises. "But Seb–"

"We'll talk when I'm back," I interrupt, my eyes on my dad as he tries to stand again on his two feet with the help of my uncle. "For now just… fuck, Julia, all I need from you right now is to stay safe."

There's so much more I want to tell her, though. I want to tell her I love her, even if it sounds crazy, and that knowing she's alive is the only thing keeping me centered as the world crashes down. I realize she hasn't said anything in return since I finished speaking, not even goodbye, so I call her name, but no one answers.

"Julia?" I repeat once more. And yet, despite my insistence, there is nothing but silence from the other side of the line. My heartbeat quickens as panic settles in. "Julia?!"

With a jolt, I shoot up in bed, hand pressed over my racing heart as I suck in desperate breaths of cool night air. It was a nightmare…that same damned nightmare I've been having for two decades now….

I look over to the other side of the bed, and it's empty.

Again.

Throat dry as the desert, I reach over and turn my bedside clock to face me in the dark. It shines 4:02 am…too early to really be up, but too late to go back to sleep.

Fuck it. May as well start the day. It's not like I'm going to be able to sleep now, anyway.

After splashing cold water on my face and brushing my teeth, I head back to the unmade bed and pull my iPhone out from the bedside table, unplugging it from the charger. I don't usually sleep with it next to the bed, but with Julia gone, I'm not taking any chances of missing her call in the middle of the night.

There's nothing from my wife, though, just a single text from Alex, my brother-in-law.

Alex: *Hey man, everyone was at the rehearsal dinner except you and the kids. What's up?*

I sneer. I have no doubt Alex knows what's up, but I bet everyone figures he has the best chance of getting a response from me. Might as well give the people what they want, then.

Sebastian: *I wasn't going to attend that shit-show. No reason to bother with it. I'll see you afterward.*

With it being so early, Alex doesn't answer, and I find myself wishing he would, just for the distraction. It's so tempting to try and call Julia, just to hear her voice after the awful dream, but I know she won't answer. She hasn't in days. So, with the past on my mind so heavily that I can't think of anything else, I shrug on my robe and head to my study.

There, in a locked drawer in my desk, I find what I'm looking for—a photo album. The only visual reminder of those awful weeks I keep, just for times like these when I need to remind myself that I survived it and made a life for myself despite the tragedy.

I consider myself as having lived two lives; one before the explosion, and one after. I flip through the album pages and look at the photos of the man I was before. They are pictures of Dad and I before the hunting trip, happy and carefree. It's hard to imagine either of us ever being that young.

Just a few pages later, though, is me in my second life. The one I'm still living. The pictures I'm looking at were taken at the funeral for my family, but there is one that sticks out among the others. It's one of Julia and I at the cemetery, and it makes my heart ache more than ever. Her hand is holding my arm tightly as if she's afraid to let me go, desperate to keep me by her side, and I can't reconcile it with her absence now. I brush a finger on her beautiful silhouette, letting out a sigh.

With everything we had to fight for, and to fight through, how come you are so ready to give up on me now?

22 YEARS AGO…

CHAPTER 1

Sebastian

I take a deep breath and stand in front of my father's bedroom door. It's just a slab of wood I remind myself as I feel the brass knob under my fingertips, but it feels like a vast, uncrossable wall. I feel like shit even telling Dad that it's time to leave, but as much as I'd like to let him stay home and avoid all the heartbreak that is yet to come, I know it isn't feasible. We both have to say goodbye, and as shallow as it is, we also have to make an appearance for the press. A show of unity for whoever did this to us… to whoever has broken my father irreparably.

It's the day of my mother's and siblings' funeral, and although it's been a week since the incident, we're still struggling just as much to cope with this new reality as we were initially. But I know that I have to be strong for what's left of my family—my father especially. With a deep breath, I knock, pushing the door open without waiting for a response. I can hear a faint rustling sound coming from inside, but no response comes, even when I call out. Slowly, I walk through the room and find my dad standing by the window, lost in thought. His eyes are red-rimmed, and he looks like he's aged ten years in just seven days. His skin, once tan with health, looks paper-thin, now permanent frown creases pulling at his mouth.

"Dad," I say softly, trying to get his attention. "Everyone is waiting for you. We need to go to the cathedral."

He doesn't turn around, and I can see that he's lost in his own world. I take a step closer and reach out to touch his shoulder, and he jumps under my touch, but still says nothing.

"Dad, are you okay?" I ask, my voice shaky with emotion.

He turns to face me, and I can see the pain and sadness etched on his face. "How can you ask me that?"

I flinch. "Sorry. It's just a habit I guess. Of course, you aren't okay. I'm not either, but we still have to go."

"That's right," he says bitterly, steadying himself on his cane. "Even our mourning is on someone else's schedule." His voice might be barely audible, but the anger it carries is not. I remain observing him as he takes a long breath, his eyes going to the floor before flicking back on me. "After the funeral, we have to meet with Willem and his team."

I feel a surge of frustration at his words. Today is about saying goodbye to Mom and my siblings, not dealing with lawyers and paperwork.

"Dad, we don't have to do that today. We can take care of it tomorrow. Today isn't about anyone but us."

He looks at me for a long moment, and I can see the conflict in his eyes. "Who did this? Who could go as far as planting a bomb in your car to kill you?"

The change of subject is rapid, but not altogether unexpected. "We'll find out, Dad, I promise you. We have men already on it." I know it's not good enough, but I just don't have the answers that he wants yet. "We have to go, we're running late."

"Fine," he mutters as he turns from the window, his once strong and commanding presence now weakened by grief and age. He leans heavily on a walking cane, refusing my offer of help. "I can manage," he says firmly, his voice strained.

How is this the same man that was just walking through the forest with me only a few days ago, carrying a hunting rifle? It's almost as if he died that day, too. Or at least most of him.

After a nearly silent car ride, we make our way to the cathedral, the somber atmosphere of the day heightened by the presence of security personnel, their watchful eyes scanning the crowds for any potential threats. Somehow, it doesn't make me feel any safer. In fact, it just leaves a terrible heaviness in my chest, thinking about why exactly all this is necessary.

The ancient, majestic cathedral stands tall, usually serving as a beacon of hope and solace for those seeking refuge from the storm of life, but for me, it's the last place I want to be. I take a moment to look around and take in the place, trying futilely to put myself in the right mindset. The high ceilings and ornate walls are decorated with intricate carvings and paintings, depicting scenes from the Bible, and the pews are arranged in neat rows, with cushions for comfort. Beneath my feet, the floor is made of smooth, polished stone.

The light filtering through the stained glass windows casts a warm glow over the space, which is full of people I recognize, but I'm just too numb to acknowledge them one by one. As the sunlight streams through, the colors dance and shimmer, casting a kaleidoscope of hues on the walls, floors, and faces of the mourners.

The altar at the front of the cathedral is grand and imposing, with a marble surface and tall candlesticks on either side. Above it, a large crucifix hangs, reminding us of the sacrifice that was made for us. The space around the altar is adorned with floral arrangements, some appropriately subdued whites and pale yellows, while others bloom in garish designs that feel inappropriate.

There are three caskets, of course, each made of a glowingly pale wood, polished to a mirror sheen. I can't look at them, even though I know they are all but empty.

Explosions don't leave much to bury. The thought makes stomach acid rise in my throat.

The air is heavy with the scent of burning candles and incense as I look out at the sea of faces, seeing tears streaming down a great many cheeks, and hear the occasional sniffle or sob.

"We have to walk, Sebastian," Dad says in a low voice at my side, and it's now that I notice that he's shaking with the effort that it takes to stand. How long have I been standing here, in a trance?

"Sorry," I mumble, putting a steadying hand on his arm as we make our way down the aisle. I see members of the families my dad has business with among the distant relatives that have decided to attend, and they are all eager to offer their condolences and support. But my dad remains stoic and unyielding, his focus fixed on the task at hand–surviving the day.

Finally, the ceremony begins. The mournful notes of the organ fill the air as the choir members' voices blend in perfect harmony, but the beauty is lost on Dad and I, sitting in the front row, all too close to this awful reality. The priest's words are supposed to offer comfort and reassurance, reminding us that although our loved ones are gone, they will always be with us in spirit, so why doesn't it feel that way? I don't feel them with us… not at all.

Fuck, I really don't want to be here.

A few people speak—aunts, uncles, and friends—but I tune them all out, focusing on the speech I have to make in just mere minutes. I'm the last one supposed to speak, and I know that what I have to say will be what everyone remembers most. The lone survivor who was supposed to die instead… it's a role I never imagined I would have to take on.

People speak for what must be hours, the shuffling, unsettling energy of the crowd clueing me in despite time sliding by for me, but once the last speaker descends the podium and it's my turn, everyone goes quiet.

Steeling my resolve, I stand, straightening my suit and taking a deep breath as I walk the three stairs to the podium. It would be so easy to pretend to lose my nerve and leave, all the words I've practiced never being spoken, but Mom and my siblings deserve so much more than that. Decided, I look out at the crowd, feeling a surge of determination.

"Thank you all for coming. I'm sure it comes as no surprise to you that this is the hardest day of my life, but everything I'm about to say is important." Everyone's eyes are round and fixed, and there is an eerie silence in the room.

"I need to tell all of you something," I say, my voice firm. "The media has already reported this, and I'm sure it was glaringly obvious to most as soon as it happened but…" the crowd stirs, murmurs moving over the pews, and I lick my lips before continuing. My mouth has never felt drier. "I was the intended target of the explosion. Not my mother, not my brother or sister. It was me they were after."

The murmurs in the crowd grow louder, and I can see the shock on some of their faces and grim acknowledgment on others. But I don't falter. I continue, my voice steady.

"But let me be clear. Whoever did this will be brought to justice. We will not rest until they are held accountable for their actions."

I take a moment to compose myself before speaking again. Having the truth out in the open before continuing helps me feel like a weight has lifted from my shoulders, but it provides no relief from the sorrow. It would be effortless to give in and break down right now, but one look at my father, his face set like stone, forces me to collect myself.

"I know this comes as no surprise to anyone that has lost someone they love, but I have wished it was me in that car a million times over this last week. I would have sacrificed myself for any one of them, and the loss of all three of them… well, it's unimaginable. Unfathomable, and at the same time, all too real. During this time, the most painful part of my life, I wish I could turn to my mother, but she is gone. My beautiful mother… Heraldina. She was the most loyal and kind woman I have ever known. She was always holding her head high, no matter the adversity, and her love for us was always so crystal clear. She never showed weakness in front of us, even when my siblings and I were driving her mad, and as an adult, I can now see how much willpower that must have taken."

There are nods in the crowd, some people tapping their eyes with the corners of handkerchiefs.

"And my sister, Adriana," I continue, my voice cracking slightly. "She was just like my mother, but less composed. Fiery, even." A few people chuckle, nodding in agreement. "She dreamt of being an architect and had even started planning a new estate for our family, even bigger than the one we have. Of course, she planned her own wing, and it was the grandest of them all, and we teased her for it. Looking back, I wish we had just built the damned thing right away, exactly the way she wanted. Adriana deserved it all."

My throat tightens as I think of my younger brother. This one is the hardest of them all, because it was my acquiescence to him that set this whole tragedy into motion. "And of course, Freddie. He loved cars and had begged me to let him drive mine when I was out in Hungary. I had always said no, until… that day. The day I regret more than anything else in my life." I swallow hard, the sea of people in front of me blurring as unwanted tears fill my eyes. "He insisted so much, and I gave in," I admit, my voice barely above a whisper, the microphone the only reason anyone can even hear me at this point.

My words stick in my throat, and for a moment in time I think I really am going to have to flee the stand, but as I struggle to speak, my gaze flickers up and I see Julia walking inside the cathedral, standing at the end of the aisle. My heart aches to see her, her hands smoothing down the front of her black dress and honey-colored hair pulled back, she's so pure that she doesn't belong in this house of death. Seeing her, though, gives me the strength to continue. I don't want her to see me falter.

"But their deaths will not be in vain," I proceed, my voice rising and echoing off the ancient stone walls. "Whoever did this clearly doesn't know what we're capable of. The Van den Bosch family will not sit silently by while the ones we love are killed in cold blood. No matter how long it takes, we will find the murderers. I give you all my word."

I turn my attention to my dad, who is sitting in the front row, his face etched with grief. I give him a small nod, silently telling him that we will get through this together. And with that, I step away from the podium, feeling a sense of resolve wash over me. We will find justice for my family, even if it's the last thing that I ever do.

Adrenaline is coursing through my veins as I move back to my seat, but my speech signals the end of mass, and the rest of the crowd begins to stand and mingle as they make their way toward the door. There will be a short pause before we go to the cemetery, and I want to use it to speak to Julia, to tell her that she doesn't have to be here, but my father grabs my sleeve and there is no way I can leave him now in his time of need.

"You shouldn't have spoken of revenge like that," he tells me as I sit down on the pew next to him again. "You're just putting another target on your back. There's a chance that whoever planted that car bomb would lay low or even be satisfied after what happened and leave us be, but if you go around screaming that we're out for blood, then we will never know peace, son."

"I know that you're right in some ways, Dad, but I'm never going to know peace either way, and at least if I find justice then I know whoever did this didn't win. I want them to suffer like we have, don't you?"

Dad shakes his head, leaning forward on his cane, hands wrapped around the marble knob. "I don't want revenge, Sebastian. I feel almost nothing now. Aside from the love I have for you, my son, I am wholly empty inside. Please don't be rash."

I refuse to believe that my father would really rather that I leave this travesty alone. "Soon you won't be thinking like this. You'll be angry, like I am, it will just take some time. So I'm not going to make you any promises right now. Let me help you up, we need to get to the car."

People want to speak to us as we exit the cathedral, but I brush them off, only looking for Julia as I assist my father outside into the sunlight. It seems almost inappropriate that it should be such a beautiful day, but at least we won't be laying my mother, brother, and sister to rest under a dreary sky. Mom always loved the sun.

Julia is nowhere to be found, and there is no time to search for her further, so I usher my father to the waiting car with curses running through my mind. I'll have to call her later and apologize for not being able to speak with her, but that will come after a stiff drink or ten once this all is over.

The drive to the cemetery is another silent one. Most of the business acquaintances that were at the mass have since departed, and it's only family members traveling in a somber caravan to their burial site. We trail behind three black hearses which carry so many parts of my heart, at least in spirit. Dad's jaw is set so stiffly that I'm afraid his teeth will shatter, but I don't mention it. I can't… if I open my mouth, I'm afraid nothing will come out but sobs, and that's the last thing my father needs.

The cemetery is a peaceful and serene place, nestled in the rolling hills of green grass and wildflowers. The entrance is marked by a simple wrought-iron gate, which opens onto a winding path lined with towering trees, the line of cars following it at a crawl. We step out of the car and are immediately greeted by the warm sun on our skin while the sound of leaves rustling in the gentle breeze provides calming background noise, the total antithesis to the storm raging in me.

The cemetery where our family plots reside is well-maintained; the grass is neatly trimmed. Clean ivory headstones are scattered throughout the landscape, each one marking another soul's final resting place. Some are adorned with flowers and personal mementos, while others stand tall and alone

Among the rolling hills covered in green grass, dotted with clusters of trees and colorful wildflowers, are the three empty plots for Mom, Adriana, and Freddie. The priest is already there, awaiting us, while the caskets hover above the empty holes in the safe grip of the casket lowering systems. My stomach rolls at the sight.

It's early in the day, and the sky is cloudless as our extended family surrounds us. To me, their grief seems shallow compared to mine and my father's, and it makes me feel immensely lonely, even surrounded by all these people.

The priest's final words for my mother and siblings are just a buzz in my ears. It isn't until the caskets are finally below the earth that my father breaks, his once-strong shoulders shaking as he cries silently, and I wrap my arms around his shoulders giving him some comfort.

It's now that I see Julia is here, too, on the edge of the crowd, watching my father and I as tears stream down our faces. I hate that she has to see us like this, but no person on earth would deny me such an expression, especially not Julia.

Uncle Leopold joins Dad and I at the edge of the graves as we say our final goodbyes. Words feel meaningless here, but I do my best, telling them that I love them and will miss them for the rest of my life. Dad's goodbye is much simpler, but it hurts my heart tenfold for its brevity.

"I'm sorry, my dear. I love you. Please forgive me."

Once Dad is finally ready to turn away from his wife and other two children for the last time, I leave him with Leopold and excuse myself long enough to find Julia. Pain is searing inside me like a brand, but I still can't just let her leave without speaking to her. I need at least a moment with her.

I find her on the outskirts of the crowd, looking so out of place while remaining a welcome comfort to my soul. Wordlessly, we embrace, and it's the first moment of calm I've had in days. Still, I know it can't last, and I take her by the arm, walking her behind one of the small mausoleums so we can talk away from everyone else.

"Julia," I start, voice rough. "You shouldn't be here. I told you to stay safe."

"Of course, I should be here," she replies, shocked. "I want to be here for you. You don't have to cut me out of your life just because you're going through hell, you know. We can go through it together."

"Together?" I scoff, my head shaking at the idea. "For what, exactly? Whoever did this," I wave my hands back toward the graves, "isn't going to stop until I'm dead, Julia. I really like you. You're a sweet girl, but–"

"But you think you are too dangerous for me?" She plants her hands on her hips stubbornly, fixing me with her gaze. "Is that what you think?"

I pinch the bridge of my nose in frustration as I gather my thoughts. "I will only bring you pain and suffering, and you don't deserve that. Plus, my dad needs me more than ever. Willem has already been dropping hints that I might need to take over the company sooner rather than later. I'm..." I pause mid-sentence, searching for a better way to tell her the rest. "Fuck, Julia. I'm just not the right guy for you."

"I don't agree with that–" she starts, but I interrupt her.

"My mom and siblings just got killed for fuck's sake," I blurt out, louder than I planned, and Julia flinches. "God knows what else is going to happen, and staying with me will only put you in harm's way. I refuse to let that happen."

Julia considers it but shakes her head. "What if I stay around as a friend? I can't just go home when you're here in this state. Let me be here for you Sebastian, please."

I open my mouth to deny her again, but before I can speak Willem walks around the corner of the mausoleum, looking embarrassed to have to interrupt Julia and I. He's flanked by two security guards, which look annoyed that I have given them the slip.

"Seb," Willem starts, his voice solemn. "I'm sorry to interrupt, but we have to make that meeting with your dad, remember?"

I don't look at Julia as I respond, afraid that just seeing her will change my mind. "Of course. I'm coming now. Can you, ah… give us a second?"

Willem nods and departs, but the security guards hover around. Resigned to being shadowed by them, I turn back to Julia and pull her into a hug, which she enters willingly, wrapping her arms around my neck. She smells so sweet, so comforting, that it's difficult to let her go. "I'll get you a car, and you'll go home, alright? Tell your mom I send her my regards."

She tilts her chin up, meeting my gaze as I keep her close to me. "I'm not going home. I will wait for you at your place, but I don't want to go home."

Here in the sunshine, stubborn and gorgeous, dressed in all black but still looking to me like spring incarnate, I want her more than anything else in this moment. I want to sink into her and forget all of this, lose myself in her soft skin, but… it can't be. Not now, at least, and if I have her at my place not only will she be in danger of being harmed by the murderers, but I also don't know if I'll be strong enough to resist taking her to bed. So I brush a stray strand of hair off her forehead and kiss her there instead of her sweet lips, whispering in her ear. "Home, Julia. I will come to see you there, I promise."

"When?" she demands.

"When the time is right."

"And when exactly is–" Julia tries to ask, but the funeral photographer must have heard us speaking, and appears, camera at the ready.

"I'm so sorry to disturb you but can I get a photo of the two of you? It's for the family album," he asks, and I nod, grateful for the excuse to end the conversation with Julia before she wraps me around her finger and has me doing her bidding unconsciously.

I loop my arm around her waist, the feeling of her body next to mine the only pleasant thing I've felt today, second only to the kiss I planted on her forehead. Once the picture is taken, the two of us smiling faintly, I take her hand in mine and walk her toward the waiting line of cars. One is empty, idling, as a small group of relatives decide to ride home together to share their grief, and I open the door to help Julia inside the empty vehicle. She chews her bottom lip, looking up at me through her lashes, and I see annoyance flash in her eyes before she acquiesces and climbs into the backseat. I want to kiss her goodbye, but so many people are watching us now that I don't dare, so I close the door on the silent Julia and finally go to find my father.

He's already in our vehicle, once again composed and blank, tapping his fingers on the head of his cane.

"Sorry, Dad," I tell him, trying to sound light as I slide in beside him and shut the door. "I didn't mean to keep you waiting."

"Hmm," he responds wordlessly, turning to look me over for an uncomfortably long time before his eyes snap forward again. He might not have said a word, but I know exactly what he's thinking.

In silence, the chauffeur turns the engine on and the car hits the road. With the ride being just as quiet as the one we took to the cathedral, I turn my gaze out to the window, trying to avoid the inevitable.

"I didn't know you were so close to the oldest Van Dieren daughter."

My stomach sinks, knowing all too well this remark would be coming, but I brush it off. "I'm not close to her. We're just friends."

Dad barks a laugh, the first in days, but there is no humor behind it. "Friends, eh? A man in his thirties and a nineteen year old girl? Seb, I wasn't born yesterday."

"We get along, Dad. That's all."

"Is Margaret okay with you just… 'getting along' with her daughter?"

I can feel my face getting red. This is the last post-funeral conversation I expected to have. "Come on, Dad, can we just drop it?"

"No, I don't think so." He looks back at me now, his expression serious. "That girl is still in college, Sebastian."

The reminder of our age difference hits me like a ton of bricks, causing my stomach to tighten. "She is, but—"

Dad isn't in the mood to let me speak, though. "Then *you* have to be the one to drop it, son. You're thirty-three for fuck's sake."

"She is a friend, Dad. A friend!" My temper rises to meet his and looking him in the eye, I add, "I've never done anything inappropriate with Julia, do you understand me?"

Dad shakes his head as if he doesn't believe a word coming from my mouth, and his tone is rueful. "Enough excuses. Find yourself a woman who is your age, not a barely legal one." He pauses, as if thinking about his next words. "You do know what kind of woman her mother is, right? You're putting us in a very delicate situation here. If Margaret finds out—"

"That's enough," I snap, fisting my hands as I try to regain my composure. "Margaret isn't gonna do anything, because—and I repeat—there's nothing between us."

"I'll say this one more time." Dad lays a hand on my shoulder, and despite how annoyed I am, I let him. "I wasn't born yesterday."

CHAPTER 2

Sebastian

The car pulls around the circular driveway of the family estate, but to me, it doesn't feel like home anymore… just a place for us to exist. No matter how I feel, though, we've got to have this meeting, even if it leaves a bad taste in my mouth to do so while still dressed in our suits from the funeral.

Inside, I expect Willem and the other lawyers under contract to the family, but I freeze when I see that the conference room is actually full. To my surprise, the rest of the company board is waiting for us, seated with paperwork and pens in front of them as if this is any other work event, and not the horribly serious situation that it actually is.

My astonishment quickly turns to anger. How could my father be so insensitive to jump back into business right after burying his wife and children? Talking with the lawyers about inheritance and the state of the business going forward is one thing, but Dad treating this afternoon like just another day at the office pisses me off. I'd be angry for him, except something tells me that he's the one that planned this gathering.

"What the hell is going on here?" I ask, my voice raised in frustration as we make our way in.

"Sebastian, please calm down." Dad tries to maintain his composure as he hobbles to the seat at the front of the table. "We have an important matter to discuss."

I take a deep breath and try to compose myself as I pull my chair to his right hand side, where I've always sat since I joined the board. "What kind of important matter?"

"The future of the company," my father replies, gesturing towards the board members.

I glance around the room and see the middle-aged men nodding in agreement. They're all looking at me expectantly, waiting for me to say something.

"I don't understand," I proceed, my confusion mounting. "Why are we talking about the future of the company *now*? Shouldn't we be taking some time to grieve and process what's happened?"

Dad lets out a long sigh and looks at me with a mixture of sadness and determination. "I'm afraid we don't have that luxury." He pauses for a beat, his face deepening. "My health has clearly gotten worse, and I can no longer handle the stress of running the company." He sounds rather embarrassed to admit it, which is quite understandable coming from someone who was almost in perfect health only a few days prior. "You'll have the entire board to guide you, but I think now is the right time for me to step down."

"To step down?" I repeat his words, a frown forming on my forehead. "What does that mean?" I might be looking around the table for an answer, but no one seems to be in a hurry to give me one.

My eyes finally land on Dad again, who after being silent for way too long, blurts out, "I need you to take over… as CEO."

What? I force myself to keep my composure, but I can hardly believe what I'm hearing. Dad wants me to take on this responsibility at a time like this? I'm about to decline and tell him to appoint someone else, someone more experienced than me, but as I look into his tired, brown eyes, I can see the sincerity behind his words, and if I'm not mistaken, the fear he has that I won't accept the job. He's not doing this for himself, but for me and the rest of the company. It hits me like an arrow to the heart to know that my father is worried, even at a time like this, about leaving me a worthless business to take over and not the successful conglomerate that he runs currently.

"I don't know if I'm ready for this," I tell him, my voice unsteady. "Not that I don't think I can do it, but the timing…. Dad, we should both take some time off. This is ridiculous."

"I know it's a lot to take on." He pats my hand resting on the table, his voice gentle. "But you've been training for this your whole life. You have the skills, the knowledge, and the passion to lead this company forward."

I glance once more around the table, still trying to process what's happening. The board members are all stiff, some of them looking at me with nothing but apprehension at my dad's decision. Finally, one who seems rather empathetic of my situation speaks up.

"Sebastian, we understand this is a difficult time for you," he says, his tone kind and reassuring, "but there's absolutely no one else your dad trusts more than you to take over the company. You are young—and that is true—but you have been with us since your time in college and have proven over and over again that you can get the job done."

"We believe you're the best person for the job," the man sitting right in front of me adds, sounding rather convincing and sure of himself. "We'll do everything we can to support you and help you succeed as you adjust to your new position. I know that it will take some time for you to reach your full potential because of what you're going through right now, but we all still believe you're the best fit—your father included."

I take a deep breath and nod. It won't be easy, but I know I have to step up and take on this new challenge. After all, if Dad really believes it's the right time for him to step down, then I've got to trust him on this. But now that means my family's legacy and the livelihood of so many employees are resting on my shoulders. I just wish that I hadn't been so blindsided by all of this. I fully expected to be taking over sooner rather than later, but I had assumed that Dad and I would have time to talk about all of it in private first.

"Alright," I mumble, still reeling from the shocking news. Then, my eyes on Dad, I say, "I'll do it. But I need some time to think and plan."

"Of course," he replies, a small smile on his face. "We'll give you all the time you need."

As the meeting comes to a close, and everyone starts raising from their seat, I feel a sense of trepidation. This is a huge responsibility, but it's also a huge opportunity. It's always been my destiny to take over the company and lead it into the current era, but I never expected it so soon. Maybe in another decade, but definitely not so soon. I'll have to succeed, there is no other choice for me, but how much of myself will I lose in the process?

In a daze, I sign the documents that are pushed in front of me, smile for the picture, and my dad and I end up shaking hands while he says how proud he is of me. Then it's time for the board members to do the same, and they all—one by one—shake my hand, congratulating me on my new role. We take some more pictures to commemorate the occasion, but all I can think about is the weight of this new responsibility and how the excitement of taking over as CEO will be forever tainted by the death of my mother and my siblings in my memory. It isn't like this would be happening if they were still alive. Just two weeks ago, I was sure that Dad would be the head of the company for many more years to come.

"Now, let's have some lunch," my dad announces as the board members file out of the room. He then turns to me and lowering his voice, he adds, "It's a big responsibility, but I know you're up for the challenge."

"*What choice do I have, Dad?*" I think, but keep my mouth shut. The last thing my father needs right now is to feel even more guilt than he's already experiencing. I can feel the weight of my new responsibilities pressing down on me as I give him nothing but a worried frown.

Dad places a hand on my shoulder, bringing me back to the present moment. "Sebastian, I know this is a lot to take in, but I have faith in you. You've been working towards this your whole life, and I believe you're ready for it."

His words are supposed to be comforting, but they only serve to heighten the pressure that's building inside of me. I know that I have big shoes to fill, and I can't afford to make any mistakes, or I risk losing the faith that the board has in me. This is going to be an incredibly delicate time.

When Dad realizes that I'm done talking about it for the moment, he rises to his feet with some effort, and shuffles out to make his way to the luncheon. I don't follow, sitting alone and trying to process everything that's happened over the past few days. My mother and siblings are gone, and now I have to take on the role of CEO of the family company. What an awful fucking day. I really thought that stepping into my father's position would be a happy occasion.

When the butler knocks on the doorframe sometime later, letting me know that everyone is waiting for me to begin eating, I give up on having any more private time and go to join Dad, our guests, and the rest of the board in the formal dining room. I sit at the luncheon and try to keep my composure while the guests chatter on about their condolences and memories of my mother and siblings, but all I can think about is the pain that's consuming me. I try to push it down, to be strong for my father, but it's near impossible. I spend my time pushing the food around on my plate, looking at everyone in their mourning attire, and feel like jumping out of my skin.

I'm so ready to be done with all of this that it's almost a welcome distraction when the family doctor approaches me, his expression grave. Tapping me on the shoulder, the older man tells me that he'd like to see me in the adjoining study if it isn't too much to ask. My father is frowning at us, but I politely excuse myself and follow the doctor out of the stifling luncheon, not at all worried about missing the meal. I've never had less of an appetite in my life.

I escort the doctor to my dad's study, offering him a drink once we get in, which he refuses. I make my way to the bar trolley while he remains standing in the middle of the room.

He then frowns as he watches me pour myself a double shot of whiskey. "Have you found yourself drinking more than usual?"

I slide him a stoic glance. "I didn't think you pulled me aside to talk about my drinking problems. I thought we were discussing my father?"

The doctor sighs, adjusting his frames on his nose. "Yes, fine, you are correct. There's no easy way to put this, Sebastian, but if your father doesn't start taking the antidepressants I've prescribed him, I'm not sure that he will make it more than another month. The nurse told me he has been adamant in not taking his medicine."

"What do you mean?" I ask, my voice thick with worry. "Is he really that bad?"

"I'm afraid so." He gives a step in my direction, pondering his next set of words. "Your father's mental state has deteriorated significantly since the incident. He's been struggling to cope with the grief and hasn't been taking care of himself properly. If he doesn't start taking care of himself, his condition could deteriorate rapidly."

"How can someone die from depression?" I ask him in total disbelief.

The doctor looks at me with surprise, as if I should know the answer. "It's not the depression itself that kills, Sebastian," he responds, before heaving a long sigh. "It's the lack of will to live. Your father may be ready to give up, and we need to do everything we can to prevent that."

A lump forms in my throat as I think about the possibility of losing the last person in my family. "I can't lose him too, not so soon after the others," I grit out, taking a long drink of the whiskey in my hand.

The doctor leans forward and places a reassuring hand on my shoulder. "I understand how hard this is for you. But you need to be strong for your father now. He needs your support more than ever."

I nod, taking a few deep breaths to steady my emotions. "I'll do whatever it takes to help him," I say firmly, determined to be there for my father in his time of need. "Thank you for letting me know, doctor."

"It's my pleasure," he replies before his eyes flicker to the now nearly-empty drink in my hand. "Just remember to take care of yourself too. It's important to stay strong for your father, but you also need to prioritize your own well-being."

I ignore his last comment and proceed, "I'll watch over him and make sure he gets the help he needs. I'll also make sure he takes his medicine."

The doctor nods, a small smile settling on his lips for an instant before hitting me with a serious expression. "I'm sorry that you have to face all of this alone, Seb, but you're strong. You'll get through this."

We talk a while longer, even though I'm itching for the man to leave so I can get myself a refill without his judging eyes. He tells me that he's assigned my father a live-in nurse who will stay out from under our feet most of the time, but will be here to help with his mobility while also ensuring that he takes his medications and isn't alone to do anything to harm himself—whether on purpose or not—when I'm not home.

Finally, he leaves, and I pour another heavy gulp of whiskey into my glass before gathering my strength to go out and finish the damn luncheon. A funeral, becoming the CEO of the family company, and now finding out that my father is at risk of committing suicide....

Jesus Christ, will this nightmare ever end?

***

I close my eyes as I stand outside of my father's bedroom door while the nurse hovers behind me with his medication in a small paper cup. I told her that I needed to be the one to speak to him before he takes his first dose, knowing that even in his weakened state he has enough willpower to steamroll this poor nurse, but now I find myself reluctant to even begin the conversation. Nevertheless, it has to be done. I steel myself and knock. I know my father can be stubborn at times, but this is a matter of life and death according to the doctor, and I just can't swallow any more death without losing myself completely. When he doesn't answer, I push the door open and walk into his barely lit room, only to find him sitting in his armchair, staring absently into the void.

"Dad, we need to talk," I announce as I close the door behind me.

He flinches at my voice, pulling him back to the real world. He then turns his head in my direction, looking at me with empty eyes. "What is it, son?"

My stomach drops at his tone, and I inhale and exhale slowly knowing this won't be an easy chat. I walk a few more steps toward him, and once I stand in front of his chair, I squat down to be at his level. Eyes to eye, I deliver the news as calmly as I can. “The doctor says you need to start taking antidepressants,” I announce, causing Dad to immediately sigh in annoyance. “He thinks your mental state is deteriorating, and if you don't get help, you might not survive.”

Dad looks shocked at first, as if he’s been caught, and it makes my heart skip a beat. So he really has been thinking about killing himself?

But Dad quickly recovers and scoffs, head shaking dismissively. “I don't need any pills to fix my problems. I can handle this on my own.”

“Dad, it’s not about handling it on your own,” I reply, anticipating his behavior. “It’s about getting the help you need to recover. You’ve been through so much, and it’s okay to ask for help.”

He looks away from me, staring out the window that stands ahead “I don’t want to take those pills. They’ll just make me feel numb.”

“But Dad, they could also make you feel better,” I tell him earnestly. “And honestly, I’m not going to give you much of a choice. If you don’t take the pills, then I don’t know if I can take over the company. If I’m going to do that for you, then you need to take the pills for me.”

He doesn’t respond for a long moment, and I fear that he won’t budge. But then, finally, he looks back at me with a defeated expression.

“Fine,” he mutters. “I’ll take the damn pills since you’re so willing to let my life’s work go to shit if I don’t.”

Relief floods through my body, and I reach out to grip his shoulder in comfort. "Thank you, Dad. I know it isn't easy, but I need you with me. Okay?"

He doesn't respond, but he pats my hand, which is still resting on his shoulder, a few times before returning to looking out the window at our estate once more. It's a small victory, but it's a start.

Out in the hallway, I tell the nurse that she's good to go, and finally make my way to bed. I've got a headache pounding at the base of my skull from all the alcohol I've been drinking throughout the afternoon and evening, but it's been long enough that I'm starting to sober up. It's entirely unpleasant, though.

A hot shower chips away the pain in my head somewhat, but once I crawl beneath the sheets of my bed, I can't seem to find any peace. The house feels like it's full of ghosts, everything reminding me of the family that I was forced to bury this morning, and when I close my eyes, I swear I can hear them all talking and laughing on the other side of my bedroom door. It's all keeping me awake, and I know I can't stay here in this empty house with all these memories hunting me down.

Before I know it, I jump out of bed, dress in sweatpants and a sweatshirt, walk through the silent halls to the garage, and head to one of our cars. As I turn on the engine, it takes me less than a second to figure out where to go.

I then hit the road, heading to the Van Dieren estate. It's almost 10 PM, and the decision is reckless, but by now I'm totally sober, and I'm unbearably restless. The only thing that doesn't break my heart when I think about my new reality is being with Julia, so, almost unconsciously, I can't shake the feeling that I need to talk to her face to face.

When I pull up to the Van Dieren's estate, the black metal gates standing tall—and closed—in front of me, it becomes crystal clear in my mind that I should've just called her to talk. But now that I'm here there is no turning back. So once I stop the engine, I pick up my cell phone and call Julia.

"Hey...."

"Hey," I greet back, my heart speeding up at the simple sound of her voice. "Um, I'm outside. Can I come up?"

"What? Seb, it's late. Is everything okay?" she asks, concern evident in her tone. "I expected to hear from you during the day."

I open my mouth to speak, but nothing seems to come out. Closing my eyes for a moment, I lean against the headrest and say, "I just need to talk to you. Are you available?"

"What's going on?" Her concern keeps growing.

"I'm, uh...I'm in front of your gates," I repeat. "Can you let me in?"

"Like... now?"

"Yeah," I answer, my voice small and filled with shame as I realize it might have been a terrible idea after all.

There's a long pause before she finally speaks again. "I think it's best I come out. Wait for me there."

I oblige and find myself spending the next few minutes alone in my car, memories of my siblings and mom haunting me again. I try to focus on something else, but all I can think of is their screams as their bodies succumbed to the explosion. In a jump, I exit the car to stretch my legs and breathe some fresh air.

Why is Julia taking so damn long?

As I stand by the car, my eyes on the gates, I let my thoughts go to her and the time we spent together. She is someone precious, someone so special that I know on a cellular level that I'm not good enough for her… but I'm also not strong enough to let her go, not when she's all but begging to be here for me during the worst period of my life. Julia is a bright light. And right now, I feel like I'm drowning in darkness.

Finally, the small door beside the gates open with a creak, and Julia emerges, the street light giving me a clear view of her silhouette. She looks so lovely with her silk robe wrapped around her body, hair spilling loose over her shoulders, still damp from the shower. As she gets close enough to me, I reach out and pull her into a hug, and it takes everything in me not to break down. I desperately want to tell her everything—about my father's condition, about how I'm taking over the family business, how I'm struggling to keep up with everything, and how the thought of her is the only relief I get from it all—but as I look her in the eye, I don't say a word. It isn't fair to her. I know Julia would listen to my words with an open mind and heart, but she's still so damned young, and the severity of the things I'm going through right now are probably too crazy for her to really process. Even now, I find myself wanting to protect her in every way possible.

It doesn't take her long to pick up on my silence, though. "What's going on?" she asks, searching for an answer in my gaze.

I open my mouth to speak, but close it as I take in our surroundings. Staying here outside in the streets isn't the best place to have such an important discussion, so instead I invite her inside the car.

Julia gets in and sits beside me, her body turned towards mine, and gives me a few more seconds to gather my thoughts.

"Seb, what's going on?" she asks again, this time reaching over to take my hand in hers.

My attention turns to her wide-open eyes and I take a deep breath, trying to find the right words.

"Nothing. Everything," I utter, my voice barely above a whisper.

She gives my hand a gentle squeeze. "What happened?"

"I can't tell you everything yet, Julia, but having you here is helping."

Her smile is soft but turns regretful. "I'm here for you, Seb, but I only have a few minutes. I wish you would have called earlier…."

I wish the same, but every minute of my day has been occupied with terrible, stressful things, and this is the first second I've even had to escape and see her. Julia runs her small thumb over my knuckles, and that's when I decide to take a chance and ask her the question that has been on my mind for a while now.

Looking at her beautiful face, I ask, "Do you like me, Julia?"

Her eyes widen in surprise at my query. "Hm? What do you mean?"

I clear my throat and repeat my question. "Like do you enjoy my company despite our age gap?"

She chuckles at the odd question, but after a moment of hesitation, she answers. "I do, yes. Very much so." And then she turns the tables on me. "And you?"

I feel a weight lifting off my chest as I say, "I… I do too. But…" my tone turns serious, dissipating the sweetness of the moment, "my dad isn't too happy about it."

Julia chuckles again, and the sound unwinds even more of my tension. "Well, if that makes you feel any better, my dad has no knowledge of your existence, so we're zero for two on the dad front."

I knew Lord Hendrik and Lady Margaret were no longer together, but what's surprising, though, is that Hendrik wouldn't stay in contact with his bright, lovely oldest daughter. "Don't you ever call him?"

Julia waves her hand dismissively. "Sometimes, but Mom would be quite furious if she knew I was talking to him. Better to not complicate things by bringing you into the conversation as well."

"Speaking of your mother…" I continue, this time more carefully. "Does she know about us? I mean, does she know we're more than friends?"

Julia cocks her head to the side, worry creeping in. "To a certain extent…" she says, her voice trailing off. She then chews her bottom lip, fiddling with the controls for the heated seats of the car, clearly hoping I won't press the issue.

The scent of her shampoo and the warmth of her presence fills the cabin of the car, and I consider pursuing more enjoyable things with her, but I need to know more about Margaret. I reach out for her hand, shifting her focus back on me. "What does she know, exactly?"

"That you mean a lot to me," she announces, her eyes meeting mine finally. "Much to her chagrin, I assure you."

I can't believe it. Margaret Van Dieren is aware of our blossoming relationship? Nothing that Julia could have said would have surprised me more than this fact. "I assume she already hates me, then."

"You assume correctly," Julia says, but then she leans across the center console until she is invading my space. The proximity makes me uneasy in the most pleasurable of ways, but her next words make my heart race. "But that doesn't mean I give a damn about it."

Our eyes meet, and the temptation to kiss her is strong. So fucking strong. It'd be all too easy to close the distance between us and feel the softness of her lips yielding under mine, but I resist. I reach up to stroke her cheek instead, allowing myself the pleasure of her silky skin beneath my fingers. "I want to meet your parents before going any further."

Julia's eyes had gone hooded at my touch, but my words make them pop right back open. "Are you serious?" she asks, her tone coming off nearly offended.

I nod. "Why not? I don't want to hide this," I tell her, looking deeply into her eyes. My voice goes gruff as I try to convey the depth of my emotions. "I don't want to treat whatever we have as some sort of dark secret that we have to be ashamed of. You deserve to be in the light, Julia."

Julia looks at me, searching my face for something. Her expression is unreadable for a moment before she responds. "Fine," she utters with a sigh, her tone guarded. "But Dad isn't going to fly to Amsterdam, let me tell you right away. He's gone and can't come back."

I feel a pang of concern at her words, and I'm especially worried about what it could mean for our future together. "Why can't he travel?"

Julia just shrugs, her eyes dropping. "It's got to do with Mom. That's all I know. It's not like either of them would ever talk to me about it."

My mind races with possibilities as I try to figure out what it could mean. But my focus quickly shifts to finding a solution. "I'll speak with your mom, then," I tell her, pressing her hand in mine. "I want her to know that my feelings for you are serious and true."

Her mouth drops at my announcement and she fixes me a stare. "You want to meet Mom? Oh gosh, I don't know about that...."

Dad had warned me that Margaret isn't one to mess around with, but hearing it come from her own daughter is different. The idea of me meeting her mother obviously has Julia on edge, which raises alarm bells in my head, but I remind myself that she's worth any obstacle. "She can't be as scary as my dad," I say with a laugh, trying to lighten the mood, but Julia just frowns at me. I feel a shiver of trepidation run up my spine. "Can she...?"

Julia doesn't respond, so lost in thought that she jumps when her phone starts ringing. She checks the caller ID and sighs. "I have to go. I'll see what I can do about setting up that meeting, but you can't rush me. It isn't going to be easy."

I nod in understanding, a comfortable silence settling between us before we exit the car at the same time. I walk around to her side and open the small door beside the main gates for Julia, to which she rewards me by giving me a hug that lasts longer than would be considered appropriate by anyone else. This is Julia, though, and I hold her to me as long as she will allow, the press of her body against mine sweet and comforting. *And frustrating*, I think sardonically as my manhood twitches in my pants.

Watching her leave makes my heart pound with uncertainty—especially as I realize that she's rapidly becoming painfully important to me. I'm well aware that I'm way too old for her, but on the other hand, I won't let anything stand in the way of us…even if it means facing her formidable mother. I'm determined to find a way to make this work, to show her that I am committed to her and our future together.

My life has been shrouded in a darkness so heavy I thought I'd never be able to shirk it, but five minutes with Julia Van Dieren and I'm reminded that she is light incarnate. I'll never be able to let her go, and that knowledge makes my heart tight in my chest.

CHAPTER 3

Julia

As I stand on the front porch, I linger at the door for a long moment, knowing that once I go back inside, the magic of the moment with Sebastian will be over. I just want to hang onto it for a little while longer. But it's late, and if I take much longer, either Mom, Stuart—the butler—or some other staff member is going to come looking for me, so I step inside and close the door as silently as possible behind me.

With my heart still soaring, I feel like I'm on cloud nine. I can't believe that we finally admitted our feelings for each other. I try to discreetly go up to my bedroom, but as soon as my foot hits the first step, I hear a voice behind me.

"Miss Julia, finally! Your mother wishes to see you in the salon," Stuart informs me, his tone always so prim and proper, and I groan internally, thinking about what exactly Mom wishes to say. There's no avoiding it, though, and I need to come to terms with the idea that she knows what I was just doing outside. I can't hide it forever.

The petit salon is warm and cozy, with a fire burning brightly in the fireplace, crackling and suffusing everything in an orange glow. My mother is sitting in an armchair, her expression stern as she swirls the amber liquid in her glass. As soon as she sees me, her gaze returns to the fireplace and she slowly gives a gulp of her whiskey. "Did you finally end that relationship once and for all, Julia?"

Her tone is colder than ice, but it's her question that gives me pause and makes me feel uneasy. I find myself lost for words as I consider several answers. "I, eh, I don't know—"

"Don't insult me by playing dumb," she snaps, still not bothering to look at me.

My heart sinks. I know where this is going. "Fine. *No*, I didn't end it. And I won't," I tell her firmly, trying to stay composed.

Mom lets out a sigh and finally turns to face me. She looks annoyed, but stubborn, both of which is normal for her. "For God's sake, Julia, that man is obviously a pervert, and you're falling right into his trap." Her eyes flutter briefly shut before she heaves a long sigh, considering her next set of words. "I thought I raised you to be smarter than this." The disappointment in her voice is enough to bring tears to my eyes. "You won't see that man again. Are we clear?"

Tears threaten to fall, but I refuse to back down. "I love him, Mom. He's everything to me, and he just lost his family…" I trail off, feeling a lump form in my throat.

"I won't allow it," she interrupts, her tone rising. "My decision is final."

I feel my frustration starting to build, and when the tears actually do start to fall down my face, I brush them away before Mom can get the chance to see them. Why can't she just see how much Sebastian means to me?

"He even wanted to meet you. Don't be like this," I plead, hoping to find some common ground with her.

"To meet me? Oh, how convenient..." she scoffs, raising from her seat, her laughter cruel.

My anger starts to boil. How can she be so dismissive of Seb's pain? "He just lost his siblings and Mom. How can you be so indifferent towards him?" I ask, my heart stuck in my throat. "What if you were gone and someone was treating me this way?"

She ignores my pleas for understanding, seeming to already be convinced that she's right and that I'm absolutely wrong. Nothing short of usual. She turns to face me, pulling her shawl over her shoulder. "Sebastian is not the one for you, Julia. He is too old. He knows it, and yet he still had the audacity to come over and ask you to be with him. He has no manners, no honor, nothing!"

"That's not true! We just spoke, that's it," I snap back, feeling my frustration rising. "Neither of us did anything wrong!"

My mother shakes her head. "You already lied to me once. Why would I believe you now?"

Tired of her bullshit, I stand my ground and decide not to cave in. "I don't owe you an explanation, I'm not a baby anymore," I remind her just as fast.

"I know that." Mom pauses, her attention drifting to the fireplace as she ponders something. "And I also know that you could have met a fine young man at that ball, but instead, you wasted the entire time with him."

"It's Sebastian that I want," I tell her, my voice steady. "And you won't change my mind." And with that, I storm out of the room, my heart heavy with the weight of my mother's disapproval.

As I walk away, I can feel my resolve hardening. I won't let anyone stand in the way of my love for Sebastian. Mom might not believe that what I feel is real, but it is, and she's just going to have to accept that one way or the other.

With nowhere else to go, I simply make my way to my bedroom, throwing myself down on my bed with a thump and rolling onto my back, pressing the heels of my hands into my eyes. Why does the first thing to make me happy in such a long time have to piss my mom off at the same time? I know she loves to make my life difficult, but this is taking it to the next level. I'm an adult, it's ridiculous that she still thinks she can control me this way.

I reach beneath my head and rummage around under my pillow until my hand finds the cold rectangular item that I have hidden there. Pulling it out, I hold it up to look at, feeling my heart go soft. Right now, this picture of Sebastian and I dancing at the ball is my most prized possession. I trace our figures with my fingers, mind drifting back to that night and those first few thrilling minutes when we got to know each other.

Remembering the way he held me on the dance floor makes me feel flush, and I can almost sense the heat of the photograph in my hand. The colors swirl around in a blur of emerald, sapphire, and gold. A laugh escapes me as I remember how I had almost backed out of going to the ball that night. If I hadn't gone, I'd have missed meeting the man of my life.

The way his hand felt on my waist, his fingers intertwining with mine, the way his eyes locked onto mine, all of it felt like a dream. I never believed in love at first sight, but with Sebastian, it felt like the stars had aligned.

I glance over at the clock on my bedside table, realizing it's been nearly an hour since I've been back in my room, and I've been lost in memories this entire time. I take one last look at the photograph and tuck it back under my pillows, hoping that no one will find it. As much as I love Sebastian, I know that my mother is furious that I'm still seeing him. I can't imagine how irate she would be if she found a framed picture of the two of us in my bed.

But I can't help it. Every time I think of Seb, my heart swells with love and longing. I know that he's not perfect, but to me, he is everything.

SIX WEEKS EARLIER...

***

The knocking on the frame of my bedroom door continues, unrelenting, no matter how long I ignore it.

"I know you're in there, Julia," Mom protests, her resolve just as strong as before. She then twists the handle once more as if it would open by magic. "Let me in."

Gosh! Why did I even bother to come back home for the weekend? I have finally started college and settled into a small, but cozy apartment in Amsterdam, and yet, Mom somehow managed to convince me to spend the weekend here. What a mistake!

Tired of her insistence, a long sigh escapes me before I get up and unlock the damn door for her. "Fine, come on in, then!" I say loud enough as my mother enters my bedroom, interrupting my studying session.

When she sees me laying on the bed, book open in front of me, her neutral expression turns into a scowl. "Are you really not ready yet?" She's eager to take me to yet another society ball, but I couldn't care less and rejected her invitation just like I did for the previous ones.

"Mom, I really think that this event will be a waste of my time. I don't know anyone going."

Planting her hands on her hips, she gives me a scathing once over before stomping to my closet to go through dress options. "One more reason to go!" she snaps over her shoulder as she does so. "You will make some new friends."

"You know I don't care about making friends. I have plenty of friends back in Amsterdam, and I have got a lot of studying to do," I counter.

She begins plucking dresses from the closet, laying each choice over her arm as she goes. “Darling, it’s Saturday night, and I promised everyone I’d be there with my eldest daughter at my side.”

“You did that, not me. I didn’t make a single promise,” I huff, but I can’t ignore her when she gingerly sits on the edge of the mattress and stares down at me until I look up at her.

Her expression turns more genuine, making her almost seem like a kind and caring person. Almost.

“It would mean so much to me, Julia,” she pleads, looking at me with hopeful eyes, and it breaks me down. These soft moments from my mother are so rare that I’m helpless in the face of them.

“Okay! You win!” I relent, knowing that there’s no point in arguing with her any longer. “But it’s the first and last one I go to.” Mom nods in agreement, and I can’t help but exhale louder at it. “Now leave me alone so I can get ready to go to this stupid event.”

With a quick smile, my mother lays her choices of dresses on the bed next to me and finally leaves, giving me a chance to breathe now that she’s acquired her victory. Nothing that she’s picked out would be my first choice, but I quickly get dressed in a pale pink gown, adorned with delicate lace and pearls. It's not my favorite dress, but it will have to do. It’s not like I want to start another argument with her by going against her outfit wishes, as well.

Mother is waiting for me in the foyer once I finish my hair and makeup, opting for a natural, subtle look and soft curls. It was the best I was able to do with such short notice, considering that I’ve been trying to avoid the topic of this ball all day. Lady Margaret, though, looks flawless as always, in a dark turquoise gown and her hair pinned back to draw attention to her gracefully aging, perfectly made-up face.

"You look gorgeous, darling," she coos, adjusting the neckline of my dress and patting me on the cheek. "I was really hoping that you would pick this dress."

"Of course you were," I mutter, letting her take me by the arm as we walk out to the waiting car together. Her grip is gentle, as if she's just a doting mother wanting to be close to her daughter, but I know all too well that Mom always has been all about appearances above all else.

As we arrive at the estate where the ball is being held, my heart sinks at the sight of the grand stairs leading to the front entrance. With my car window lowered to get some fresh air, I can hear the music and laughter from afar. Everyone moves around like a fish in the ocean, knowing exactly what to say or do, except me who can't help but feel awkward about the whole ordeal. But Mom is determined to show me off to society—maybe as a little revenge for having spent the whole summer away from her—and make me one of them, so I'll just have to put on a brave face and follow her lead.

It's dark now, but the outdoors are lit up by antique gas light fixtures lining the driveway and walkway up to the main entrance. Our driver lets us out right at the front, while a valet opens the door for us. I take a steadying breath, looking over at my mother, copying the way she holds herself so I won't look completely ridiculous. I've done these sorts of events before, but despite what everyone tells me, it fails to get any easier. It's all just pomp and circumstance to me.

Inside, the ballroom is stunning, with crystal chandeliers illuminating the room and golden accents adorning the walls. The sound of a live orchestra fills the air, and it's impossible not to feel a sense of awe as I look around the room, no matter how cynical I'm feeling inside. The guests are all dressed in their finest attire, with men in sharp suits and women in flowing gowns, and Mother seems to hold the attention of them all.

"They're looking at you," she whispers, pulling me closer as we stroll. "I made a big deal about bringing you, so it's been a source of anticipation to see my reclusive daughter, who just happens to be one of the most eligible bachelorettes here, too."

"How on earth did you think that having people look at me would make me anything but uncomfortable?" I hiss, but Mom ignores me, greeting her friends and acquaintances like tonight is the highlight of the year for her. It's certainly not, but she puts on a good show, I have to admit.

My mother leads me toward the DeVries family, the first guests we see. I force a smile and exchange pleasantries with them, trying my best to make conversation, but my mind wanders, and I can't help asking myself why I even accepted to come here. I should be studying, not wasting my time at these frivolous events. Mom, on the other hand, is ecstatic. She's always been obsessed with these types of events and fits in perfectly. I often feel like I'm just a pawn in her game of social scheming.

After the DeVries, I meet a few young men that Mom insists I speak to, smiling on cue and laughing politely at their jokes. One, a redhead named Tom, even goes as far as to kiss my hand, which makes me shudder unconsciously. I see my mother frown, watching me out of the corner of her eye as she speaks to others, but I refuse to feel apologetic.

Tom seems to be filled with unwavering bravery as he straightens his shoulders, and, looking me in the eye, proudly asks, “Would you honor me with a dance, Miss Julia?”

Oh gosh! Alarm bells ring in my head at the awful request. The last thing I want is to be dancing with a total stranger.

“Um, I…” I glance around, trying to find a plausible excuse to decline without upsetting the young man. “Maybe later. I’ve got to go to the restroom.” And with that, I turn on my heels and disappear among the crowd.

I might have excused myself to go to the restroom, but in reality, I’m just looking for any place where I can be alone for even just a moment. The ballroom and adjoining areas are all packed full of guests, and it’s impossible to move around without being noticed.

I stop in front of a gold-framed mirror I find in a quieter hallway and observe myself briefly—my honey-colored hair is loose and falls in soft waves down my back, framing my glowing skin, and I’m wearing the silk dress with intricate lace detailing that Mom had chosen for me. The dress hugs my curves in all the right places, and I feel elegant and sophisticated. Yet, despite how stunning I look, I can't shake the feeling of unease that has been plaguing me since we arrived. After all, I know no one here and the thought of having to stay and dance with Tom—or anyone, really—isn’t helping.

I try to run outside back to the car, but the crowds of guests make it impossible. I feel trapped and suffocated by the loud chatter and forced smiles. I get back inside, hastening my pace as I search for a quieter part of the house. I try to open a few doors, only to find them either locked or just as busy. I continue walking down the hallway, turning left, and getting farther and farther away from the ball. Finally, another door comes to view, and this time, as I twist the handle, it opens with ease. I smile in victory and step in. As I take in my surroundings, the only place I can find solace in seems to be an antique library. I close the door behind me and start roaming around, grateful for the peace and quiet. My eyes wander around the impressive floor to ceiling built-in bookshelves that surround me. A spiral staircase giving to a second floor for more books stands at the end of the room, and a majestic mahogany desk lies on my right with a lamp bathing the room in a soft orange glow. Without thinking twice, I take off my heels, which I hate wearing, and let my bare feet walk over the Persian rug in the direction of the closest shelves. I start exploring them, my attention drawn to a row of leather-bound books with golden, embossed letters, to which I run my fingers over the spines. I feel like breathing again in this vintage atmosphere. It's peaceful here, away from the noise and crowds of the party outside. The perfect refuge to stay in until Mom is ready to leave.

"Isn't the party to your liking?"

My solitude is short lived as I flinch at the intrusive voice coming from behind me. My mouth gasps open as I spin around, startled, and find myself face-to-face with a tall, fit man across the room, dressed casually in jeans and a gray crewneck sweater, sleeves rolled up to his elbows. His piercing brown eyes lock onto mine, and I can't seem to look away.

"I'm sorry, do I know you?" I manage to ask, my voice barely above a whisper.

He flashes a warm smile, and I feel my heart skip a beat.

"I don't think so, no." I can hear the amusement in his tone, and I'm not sure what to make out of it. "You are?"

I clear my throat, trying to steady my nerves. "Julia," I reply, trying to sound confident, despite being literally caught in a room I have no business to be in.

We stand there for a moment, looking at each other. Then, in silence, the mysterious man starts moving around the room, picking up books and placing them back on their shelves.

"I-I'm sorry," I stammer, unsure what to do or say next. "I don't do parties. My mom forced me to come."

He nods sympathetically as he puts another book back in its place. A dark-brown lock of hair falls on his forehead causing him to run his fingers up to brush it aside. I can't help but smile at the gesture, finding it oddly enticing.

"Oh, I'm sorry about that." His eyes are fixed on the shelves, before falling back on me. "I assume you'd prefer to hide in here until the party is over?"

Not sure if he's being sarcastic or not, but I nod in agreement, following him as he moves to another section of the room. "I would. This was the first room I entered and, um, it was empty." Before I can explain myself any further, I stop mid-way and notice something odd. "Wait—why aren't you dressed up? Aren't you a guest?"

"Not really…" he trails off, fixing me with a stare and a side smile.

It's impossible not to notice how at ease he is in this room, as if it's his own personal sanctuary.

My jaw drops as the answer hits me and I do my best not to appear too embarrassed. "Oh gosh! I'm so sorry, is this your house?"

"My dad's," he answers casually. "But I suppose I'll inherit it one day."

I feel myself blushing as I apologize again, trailing behind him as he walks to another shelf. "Mom didn't tell me where we were going...."

He chuckles softly, and I notice how his laughter seems to fill the room. "Well, you are at the Van den Bosch estate...." His gaze holds mine as he takes a step closer to me—close enough that I can smell his cologne. Spice and sandalwood. The air circulating around us intensifies and my heartbeat starts pounding so hard inside my chest that I wonder if he can hear it. His closeness doesn't leave me indifferent, and I think I'm doing a terrible job at pretending otherwise. "I'm Sebastian, the oldest of the bunch, but you may call me Seb."

He extends a hand to shake mine, and I find myself hesitating for a moment before taking it. As our hands touch, though, an unpredictable jolt of electricity runs through me, but I do my best to keep it unnoticed.

"Does Julia have a last name?" he asks, an ounce of amusement tickling his lips.

"Van Dieren," I reply, feeling slightly more at ease. "Which I assume you know everything about."

"Not *everything*, no. I didn't know Hendrik and Margaret had such a charming daughter."

I smile in response, feeling a sense of comfort around him. "That's because I never attend any of your balls."

The corners of his mouth twitch into a grin at my answer. "Until now."

I feel my color deepen at the sound of his warm voice, so I breathe slowly in and out, doing my best to keep my cool. "Until now."

The way his dark-brown eyes pierce mine causes a rush of heat to bloom over my body. And I know deep inside my core that the longer we stand here, looking into each other's eyes, the worse it will be. I've got to do something. "So, um, Sebastian, why aren't you dressed up if you are hosting this party?"

My question is enough to break the spell between us, and Sebastian straightens his posture, averting his gaze. "I'm not hosting, my parents are. I'm just avoiding it as much as you by staying here in peace and reading."

I nod, my eyes wandering to the shelves of books surrounding us. "And what were you reading?"

"A financial audit of the company." His answer comes totally unexpected, causing my eyebrows to raise in surprise, and noticing it, he adds, "I work with my dad at Van den Bosch Industries."

"That sounds great," I find myself saying, trying to keep the conversation going.

Seb shrugs, unimpressed. "Not really, but it's alright. He's very passionate about the company and that's the only way I get to spend quality time with him." He turns towards the shelves, eyes scanning over the spines of the books, before he places the last book he's got in its place.

I continue admiring his face and how handsome he is, his face like a rough-hewn work of art that I can't get enough of. There's a dark aura around him that I can't quite place, and it only makes me more curious about him.

"And you?" His question is enough to pull me back to reality.

"I'm studying law," I say simply.

He raises an eyebrow, intrigued. "At Amsterdam Law School, I presume?"

I can't help but nod, quite impressed by his knowledge of the city's universities. "Yep."

"To become a lawyer?"

"Judge, actually."

"Oh, ambitious. I get now why I'd never seen you around."

I laugh nervously, feeling my heart flutter. "I go out, though, just not with Mom to her society events. I spend the week in Amsterdam. I've got a flat there."

I immediately regret sharing that last detail, but before I can backtrack, Sebastian surprises me by closing the small space between us, and, almost instinctively, reaches out and tucks a loose lock of my hair behind my ear. I watch him in total awe as he does so, and manage to take slow breaths through the nose, despite the hammering in my chest.

"Really? That's quite interesting." His voice low and husky isn't helping to steady it either. Gosh, I barely know this man. Why is he having such an impact on me? "I spend the week in Amsterdam too. Maybe we can see more of each other there." His eyes lock onto mine again and my throat goes dry as I lose myself in his gaze.

I can't believe what I'm hearing. Is he really asking to see me again?

"I'd love that," I manage to pull the words out.

My heart feels like it's about to burst, and I notice his eyes slowly darting down to my parted lips. "I'd love that too." One small move from him or me and we could literally kiss.

His presence dominates the air surrounding us and if I keep myself so close to him, I'll literally combust. *Shit! What's wrong with me?* Armed with some supernatural self-control, I take a step back, bringing some much-needed distance between us, and say, "Well, um, I should get going. Mom must be looking for me." Then clearing my throat, I straighten my posture, and take another step away, turning slightly towards the exit. "See you in Amsterdam, Seb."

"Sure," he utters, his eyes still fixed on me. "Have a great evening, Julia."

I wave at him, doing my best not to look utterly embarrassed that I was almost leaning in to kiss a total stranger. But it's hard to resist someone with such a striking face. As I leave the library, though, my mind is still racing with thoughts of our chat. The way he looked at me, the way he tucked that lock of hair behind my ear, so soft and gentle...it all felt surreal, magical even.

Walking down the hallway, I find myself frantically searching for a bathroom to check myself. As soon as I spot one, I rush inside and lock the door behind me.

I'm mortified to see that my face is as red as a tomato. Gosh, I must have looked like a complete fool in front of him. I splash some cool water on my face, hoping to calm down the flush in my cheeks. Then I take a deep breath and steel myself, ready to face the ballroom once again. I just hope Mom is almost done and we can head home soon.

As I step back out into the grand hall, it's not hard to find Mom from afar talking to a few other guests. I approach them with trepidation.

"Ah! Julia, here you are!" Mom exclaims, her tone welcoming as her gaze lands on me. "Come here and get to know everyone a little better."

I force a smile and introduce myself, but my mind is elsewhere. I keep glancing around, hoping to catch a glimpse of Sebastian, but in vain. Just as I'm about to ask Mom when are we going home, she waves over the redheaded man I had met earlier and he approaches us, his eyes twinkling. *Oh gosh! Not him!*

"Tom, how lovely to see you again!" Mom goes and interlocks her arm with Tom's, bringing him closer to me. "Darling, Tom was actually looking for you."

"Really?" I ask, feigning interest.

Tom seems a bit embarrassed as he pulls a tight smile. "Yes, um, in fact I was telling your mom how much I'd love to dance with you before the ball ends, but I couldn't find you."

Before I can even open my mouth and speak, Mom does it first. "Well, Julia is here now and she'd be delighted to dance."

I've never hated Mom more than I do now. I force myself to smile and accept his invitation, despite wanting nothing more than to just leave the damn ball once and for all.

Tom shows me his arm and I hold it, making our way to the dance floor. As we walk together, I try to ignore the sick feeling in my stomach. Tom is perfectly pleasant, but I'm just not interested. Every second feels like an eternity as we shuffle around to the slow music. The closeness of the dance makes me quite uncomfortable, and I cannot wait for this to be over.

Finally, the song ends and I breathe a sigh of relief. But before I can escape, Tom holds me by the wrist and says, "Let's dance to this next song, please, it's one of my favorites."

I can feel my heart sinking at the thought of enduring another slow dance with him. But just as I'm about to reluctantly agree, I hear a voice behind me.

"I think the lady has had enough, Tom. Thank you."

Recognizing the voice, I spin around to see the one and only Sebastian standing tall and imposing right there, dressed in a sharp tuxedo. My heart nearly hurdles into my throat as I stare like he is some sort of Adonis. He holds out a hand to me, and without hesitation, I take it. As he leads me away from Tom, and onto another part of the dance floor, I can feel everyone's eyes on us, but it's like I'm walking to heaven and everything else fades away.

As we get in position, my heart keeps racing, and my mind goes into overdrive. I can't believe that I'm here, about to dance with Sebastian and feel his body close to mine. As he places a hand on the small of my back, it sends shivers down my spine, and I feel like I'm walking on air.

It's all too easy to notice the way his eyes meet mine. They seem to see right through me, making me feel exposed and vulnerable, yet, at the same time, I feel so alive.

As we move to the music, I feel myself getting lost in the moment. It's as if the world around us doesn't exist, and all that matters is the two of us while we move in perfect harmony.

I can feel his breath on my neck as we sway back and forth, and I can't help but fantasize about what it would feel like to kiss him. *Gosh! Again?* I try to push the thought out of my head, but it keeps creeping back in.

As the melody intensifies, he pulls me in for a dip, his arms tightening around me. I'm not sure if it's the music or the way he's holding me, but I feel like I could stay like this forever. My heart's pounding as Sebastian pulls me closer, but I don't protest, liking the warmth of his body way too much.

"Why did you step in?" I ask, breaking our quiet silence. "Maybe I was having fun with Tom."

There's a hint of amusement in his voice as he says, "If your face was any indication, I'd say you were very far from it."

Blood rushes to my cheeks, and I find myself flushing at his words. "I was, um, just thinking about the music, that's all."

"The music? Really?" He pulls me even closer, causing me to gasp.

"What are you doing? Everyone can see us!" The worry in my tone is evident, but Seb holds my chin up, forcing me to hold his gaze.

"Was it really the music you were thinking about?" he asks, his eyes burning into mine.

I feel my resolve crumbling under his scrutiny. Breaking eye contact, I lean to his ear and say in a whisper, "I'm afraid what I was thinking about will remain a secret." I can't help but inhale his cologne, trying to bury the smell in my memory.

"If I tell you a secret, would you share yours with me?" he asks, looking me again in the eye.

I notice how much we have slowed down our pace, and at this point, we are moving just the bare minimum to keep up appearances.

Feeling my heart pounding in my chest, I play along and murmur a quick, "Maybe."

He leans slightly closer to my face, causing my lips to part at the proximity. "I came down here looking for you. And when I saw you dancing with someone else… I had to step in." His voice is low and intimate, and my heart flutters at the sound of it. "Now tell me, Julia, what were you thinking about?"

I'm lost in his gaze, completely under his spell. The only thing right now that I'm thinking about is to kiss him. To close the tiny space left between us and feel his lips press against mine. As if he could read my most intimate thoughts, his gaze lingers around my face until they stop on my lips. I know he wants me as much as I want him.

I open my mouth to speak, ready to confess everything to him, but before I can utter a word, we're interrupted by a loud female voice.

"Ah, Julia! There you are!" I turn around to see who is calling me and notice a lady, around the age of my mom, walking towards us. "I'm sorry to interrupt the dance, but your mom is getting tired, and she wants to go home."

"Now?"

"Yes, dear. Now."

I look back up at Sebastian, and he cocks an eyebrow at me. I don't want to leave this moment, but my mother's friend has broken our bubble of intimacy and is now working her way over to pull me out of his arms. The rest of the ball filters back into my consciousness—the noise, hustle, and bustle of it all, hundreds of different conversations going on all at the same time while I had been pretending that Sebastian and I were all alone. I feel my face flush with embarrassment, slowly letting go of him and allowing my hands to fall to my sides.

"I'll see you soon, Miss Van Dieren," Sebastian murmurs, quietly enough that only I can hear it, and takes my hand to brush the lightest of kisses over my knuckles before releasing me. It makes me shiver, but I don't have much time to parse through the feelings as my mother's friend clears her throat impatiently.

I take one last look at Sebastian, the first man to ever attract and fascinate me, and sigh, turning around and following the other woman out of the ballroom. It takes an insane amount of willpower to not turn back and gaze at him one more time. But as he said so well, we will see each other soon.

***

There is an obvious, palpable awkwardness in the car as our driver takes Mom and I home. I haven't seen her since the dance with Sebastian, and it's all too clear that she isn't happy with me. I'm having a difficult time figuring out why, though. I mean...didn't she want me to mingle and dance? As the Van den Bosch estate fades away, Mom breaks the silence, causing a knot to form in my stomach. I know she's going to ask about Sebastian, and I'm not sure how to answer.

"How come Sebastian van den Bosch was dancing with you?" Her tone is as incriminating as an FBI agent inquiring about a potential suspect.

"I don't know. He just came out of nowhere, I guess. Don't worry, he was a total gentleman," I tell her, trying to sound nonchalant.

Her eyes narrow. "Did you meet him before?"

"No," I say breezily.

It doesn't fool Mom, though. "Don't lie to me, Julia."

"I didn't. I met him there," I insist, hoping she'll believe me.

But Mom looks worried and stern as she thinks something through. The sternness is normal, but it's rare that I see her genuinely worried.

"What?" I ask, leaning forward to see her face better. "What's wrong, Mom?"

"I don't want to see you again with that man. Are we clear?"

The question makes me feel defensive almost instinctively. "Mom, it was just a dance. I don't know him any more than I knew the other men there."

"I'm just warning you. Sebastian shouldn't have danced with you in that way. It was very inappropriate."

My mouth falls open. "Inappropriate how, exactly?"

"Everyone was staring in shock at how close to you he was. That man is thirty-three. Did you know that?"

I shake my head, feeling a little foolish for not realizing it sooner. Of course, people would disapprove of it from the age gap alone. But at the same time, I find myself replaying every detail in my mind—the way he looked in his suit, the way his dark hair fell on his forehead, the way he smelled. It was all so intoxicating. With a quick shock, I realize that I don't care about his age… not at all. So I shrug and tell her, "No, I didn't know that, but he didn't do anything that I didn't like."

Mom's laugh is cruel and mocking. "Oh, you. Stop being silly. He's a pervert, don't you see? I can smell men like him coming from miles away. You are a beautiful woman, but still very young," she lectures me, and I bristle at the way she speaks to me as if I'm some sort of idiot.

"I'm turning twenty in a few months," I remind her, feeling a little indignant.

"Precisely. You are way too young."

When she doesn't continue, I let the conversation die, looking out the window and watching as the lights of the homes and city go by, thinking about how I can't wait to get out of this dress and go through the night in my mind at my own pace.

As we drive home, I begin to feel conflicted. Mom is right about one thing… Sebastian being thirty-three and me being nineteen really is quite the age gap, but things like that aren't so uncommon in our world. I think Mom is only so cautious because I'm her daughter, and she wouldn't think twice about an interaction like Sebastian and I's dance if we had been anyone else.

There is just something about Sebastian that draws me to him, though, something that makes me want to know him more. I know I shouldn't get involved with him, but a huge, loud part of me feels so curious.

Thinking about his hands on my waist during the dance makes me blush again, and I make sure that I'm fully turned away from Mom, because I'm sure if she sees me, she will know exactly what is on my mind. Maybe we should have really kissed in that library when we had the chance. Gosh, I should've been more daring….

CHAPTER 4

Julia

I tap my pen on my open, yet empty, notebook, trying to pay attention to what the professor is telling us but failing miserably. This is so odd for me that it's hard to come to terms with. Getting into Law School was one of my biggest dreams and now that I'm finally here, sitting in the auditorium and attending to a lecture about Law and Morality I'm having a hard time being fully invested in class. My treacherous brain only has one thing floating around in it—Sebastian van den Bosch.

I need to get through this day, no matter how hard it is. But my thoughts keep drifting back to him, the way it felt as we danced… it's like my mind is in a haze, unable to think about anything else.

Suddenly, Gabi's voice snaps me back to reality. "Hey, Julia, wake up!" she says in a whisper, nudging me in the side. "What's going on with you today? You've been out of it since class started."

I try to shrug it off, but Gabi is insistent. "Come on, spill. Did something happen at the ball?"

I bite my lip, knowing that I can't keep the truth from her forever. "I danced with someone," I fess up, feeling the heat rising on my cheeks. "And it was, uh, a lot more enjoyable than I expected."

Gabi grins, her eyes lighting up with excitement. "Who? Do I know him?"

I hesitate for a moment before answering. "It's not something I'm totally comfortable talking about yet."

But to my surprise, she seems genuinely thrilled. "You won't be able to keep it from me forever, but honestly I'm just shocked and happy that you had a connection with something other than a book for once."

I shake my head and huff at her comment, but she's right—my romantic life is as dry as the desert of the Sahara. Though if I'm being honest, no boy has ever been of interest to me. Until now....

Once the class is over, we gather our things and leave the lecture hall, heading onto the campus concourse. Gabi doesn't pressure me for my crush's identity anymore, but she doesn't waste time asking for all the details about the ball, especially the dance I keep replaying in my thoughts. I feel myself blushing even harder, but before I can say anything else, Gabi points to something behind us.

"It looks like that guy is heading our way," she says in a whisper. We stop in our tracks and I turn around to check who she is speaking of, only to find Sebastian himself coming towards us from just a few feet away. My jaw drops and my eyes widen at the sight of him. What on earth is he doing here?

"Sebastian," I manage to pull out in a barely audible voice, my eyes fixed on his tall and lean figure.

Gabi and I watch him strand in our direction, until he's finally close enough to speak to us. His eyes lock onto mine, yet his expression is unreadable.

"Julia." The way he says my name causes a flurry of emotions to settle into my belly. "I thought I might find you here. I'm glad my instincts were right."

I glance at Gabi, who seems to be enjoying the moment just as much as I am. There is a smirk on her face that lets me know she's already put the pieces together, and must know that Sebastian is my mystery dance partner. Since there's nowhere to hide, I start doing introductions in a failed attempt to appear unbothered.

"Well, um, Gabi… this is Sebastian. Sebastian, my best friend, Gabi."

They shake hands briefly, and before Gabi can slide a snarky remark, Sebastian speaks up first. "Nice to meet you, Gabi. Are you also studying Law?"

"Yep," she mumbles, just before trying to be nosy as usual. "So you and Ju—"

"Gabi wants to become a prosecutor like her dad," I interpose, preventing her from finishing her sentence.

"Oh, that's great." Sebastian plays along, his interest visibly piqued. "I'm also following in the footsteps of my dad."

Not wanting to make this moment anymore awkward, I say, "We were just on our way out. Do you, eh, want to walk with us?"

Sebastian nods, falling into step beside me. Gabi trails behind us, shooting me a sly grin every now and then. I can feel Sebastian's eyes on me, and it makes me feel like I'm walking on air. This is crazy, I barely know this man, and yet I feel like I'm under some sort of spell.

"So, are you enjoying your class?" he asks as we make our way through the campus.

"Yep, it's pretty good. It just started two weeks ago, actually, but it's been fascinating."

Sebastian continues asking me about my classes and my interests, and I find myself opening up to him in a way that I haven't with anyone else. I'm surprised by how easy it is to talk to him. We finally reach the entrance, and I turn to face him, feeling a sense of reluctance to say goodbye.

"Thanks for walking with us," I say, smiling up at him.

Sebastian returns my smile, his gaze intense. "It was my pleasure."

There is an awkward moment where the three of us stand in a loose circle, but Gabi eventually seems to give up on getting any more information out of the two of us, and she sighs. "I guess I'll get going and give you two some privacy."

I start to object, more on principle than from actually wanting her to stay, but Gabi leaves my side without another word, just a quick wave.

And now here I am, left alone with Sebastian van den Bosch. Gosh, it's hard to even think straight. I take a deep breath before approaching him, feeling somewhat nervous and unsure of what to say, especially with my mother's warnings still echoing in my ears even though I don't want them to.

Finally, I get my thoughts straight enough to speak before he can beat me to it. "What are you doing here? Not sure if you are aware, but Mom didn't really like the way you danced with me the other night." My tone is filled with amusement as I try to make light of it all, but Seb looks more serious now that Gabi is gone, as if he's let down the proper social mask he probably wears for the public.

"I do know, yes. And that's why I came here." I arch an eyebrow at his words, my interest piqued. "Looks like she made *my* mom aware of the situation rather quickly." He pauses, gauging my reaction. "That was an interesting conversation over breakfast, to say the least."

"What?!" Mortification sweeps over me and my mouth goes wide open as I ask, incredulous, "She called your mom?"

"She showed up yesterday afternoon to give her a word," Seb confirms.

"Oh my gosh, I'm so sorry." I press the heel of my hand against my forehead, frustration building into a genuine headache. "Mom is so overbearing. She went through a lot the past few years, and—"

"Julia," he interrupts, holding his hands up. "I don't want to cause you or your mom any trouble." I feel my heart freezing at his words, knowing exactly what he means by that. "So… I came here to apologize for that dance, and I hope I didn't make you feel too uncomfortable. Rest assured, I won't bother you again."

"No, Seb, that's not necessary," I insist, a lump forming in my throat. "I'm fine. More than fine, actually. And that's not what I want…." His eyes widen in surprise at my words, and before I lose what little courage I have left, I hold his gaze and finish my sentence. "I actually want you to bother me again." A sense of desperation creeps into my voice, but Sebastian holds my gaze in place, his expression as stoic as before. No one has ever had this kind of affect on me and

I'm about to lose him before I even really get to explore these feelings? Absolutely not!

"I didn't know your mom didn't like me. I'm sorry but I can't see you again." He delivers those words so mechanically that I wonder if the chemistry I felt between us was all in my head. Gosh, why does Mom have to ruin everything? It's just so typical of her. "I also didn't know your age until your mom told mine. For some reason, I thought you were older."

"But I'm an adult and that's all that matters, right? And it's not like I just turned eighteen, I'm actually turning twenty in a few months." In eleven months more precisely, but he doesn't need to know that.

He cringes. "Please don't make it any worse. I'll just… I'll leave you alone now," Sebastian replies, his tone resolute. "Have a good one, Julia."

While I fumble with my emotions, I watch him turn his back on me and walk away.

This can't be it!

My mind doesn't want to accept defeat. No, I can't let him go just like that, and in a second of impulsiveness, I rush in his direction, yelling, "Can't we just be friends?"

He stops at my question, shoving his hands in his pockets as he turns to face me. Sebastian chuckles, but continues walking toward his car once I make it to his side. "I don't think we can be friends, Miss Van Dieren."

"Why not?" I demand, still keeping pace beside him. "I will be a judge one day, I'm a good contact to keep around."

"Smart girl," he says, a hint of amusement in his voice. He continues walking, and I follow him, determined not to let him go.

He finally reaches his car, a vintage Aston Martin, and opens the door to slide into the driver's seat. Surprising even myself with my brashness, I slide into the passenger seat beside him, and Sebastian groans in annoyance. I can feel his eyes on me, and my heart races as I struggle to keep my emotions in check. With no idea of what I'm doing, I shut the passenger door and cross my arms. Now, it's just the two of us.

"What do you think you are doing?" he asks, clearly taken aback by my sudden intrusion.

"I'm hungry, aren't you taking me somewhere to eat?" I ask, trying to sound nonchalant, hoping my voice doesn't betray how nervous I am. I have no idea what I'm even doing at this point!

Sebastian huffs, head shaking, but a subtle smile escapes him. "I'm not taking you anywhere. I have no interest in being seen in public with you. I can only imagine how well that will look when it inevitably gets back to your mother."

"Too bad, I'm not moving," I insist, tilting my chin up stubbornly. "Honestly, what are you afraid of? I'm an adult so it's not like you're doing anything illegal." I try to read his expression, but he avoids my gaze.

"I know that—"

"So you are afraid of my mom? That's it?" I interrupt, trying to find a way to change his mind. I have the feeling that I've backed him into a corner, and the longer Sebastian lets me sit here in his car without forcing me to get out, the more sure I am that he actually *wants* me here, and is just trying to convince himself otherwise.

"I'm not afraid of anyone, Julia, but I just don't want trouble, that's all." He turns the engine on, signaling his intention to leave, but still he doesn't make any moves to pressure me into getting out of the vehicle.

Sebastian is obviously warring with himself over what to do. While he battles with himself, I take the time to admire how handsome he looks. His mid-length dark hair seems to be dancing with the wind of his open window, and his gaze is piercing, almost intimidating. I can feel my heart beating faster as he finally turns to me, his eyes locking onto mine.

"If we go to the middle of nowhere, no one will know," I suggest, trying to hide the way he makes my pulse race with a smirk. "There are plenty of pockets of nowhere around here, you know." He stares at me with a mix of amusement and exasperation before turning his attention back to the road, the car finally exiting the parking lot. "We could go to a park, a lake, a forest…" I suggest, my tone hopeful, and my eyes pinned on his face.

Seb lets out a sigh before finally saying, "Fine, but only on one condition."

I lean forward in my seat, intrigued. "Which is?"

"That you tell me what you were thinking about while dancing with Tom," he demands, looking at me expectantly, raising an eyebrow. "If I recall correctly, we were interrupted before you could tell me."

I feel a rush of heat to my cheeks as I recall the moment. Of course, he knows what I was thinking. How could I have been any less obvious? But I play along, trying to keep the flirtatious tone going.

"You know exactly what I was thinking about," I say coyly, recognizing he knows the truth.

Sebastian narrows his eyes now, challenging me. "No, I don't. Otherwise, I wouldn't be asking you."

I bite my lower lip as I look at him, taking in his strong jawline and the way his shirt fits him perfectly. "I was thinking about the man I had just met in the library," I confess, referring to him, of course. "I found him very handsome, and I was wondering when I'd meet him again."

I can see a hint of a smile forming on his lips as he glances at me quickly before turning back to the road. "Well, looks like it's your lucky day." His words cause me to mirror his smile, feeling a sense of triumph at the thought of spending more time with him. My lucky day, indeed.

***

To my greatest delight, Sebastian takes us to a secluded lake on the edge of a sprawling forest, remote enough that he can't recall the name of it off the top of his head, but public enough that there is a small parking lot where he slides his car into before powering it off and looking over at me.

"Alright, you've gotten your way. Want to take a walk?"

I smile at him softly. "Absolutely."

I'd have worn something different to walk around the lake at the slightly overgrown park had I known this is what I'd be getting up to this afternoon; the grass tickles my feet through my strappy sandals as we stroll, but it's far from the worst thing in the world to suffer in trade for spending this time with Sebastian. He walks with his hands shoved in his pockets, his face slightly turned upwards towards the sunshine, making him almost impossibly too handsome. I have the urge to run my fingers over his short beard to feel the stubble there, but file that idea away for later.

I look at the breathtaking scenery around us as I hear the gentle rustle of leaves in the surrounding trees. The air is fresh, and the sun is shining, casting a golden glow over everything. The lake is crystal clear, and I can see the ripples caused by the gentle breeze. It's a magical place, and I feel my heart flutter with the thought that this is pretty much a *real date* with Sebastian van den Bosch, even if he doesn't want to admit that it is. If he wanted nothing to do with me, there are plenty of uglier places he could have driven us, but instead, he chose somewhere picturesque like this.

His voice interrupts my thoughts, and I turn to face him. "You like it here? Seems like a place where no one can find us," he says, a playful twinkle in his eyes. "Just like you suggested."

"I do," I admit, my expression matching my excitement. "Sometimes I forget that there are places like this so close to the city."

I feel his hand brush against mine, not sure if he did it on purpose or not, but my heartbeat quickens in response. We sit down on the small dock that stretches out over the water, and I glance at him shyly. He looks so attractive, with his dark hair and sharp, intelligent features.

"I used to come here by myself when I was in college and wanted to be left alone," Seb says, breaking our comfortable silence. "No one else knew about this place. It was like my own little sanctuary away from the world." He then turns to me, his lips twisting into a side smile. "Until now."

I can't help but mirror his expression at the revelation. "What do you mean until now? You've never brought anyone else here before?"

He breaks eye contact, drifting his attention back to the lake ahead, before exhaling loudly through the mouth. "I'm embarrassed to admit it, but yeah, you are the first."

He sounds so honest and raw that his revelation leaves my mind reeling, but it also causes my heartbeat to quicken.

"I knew you didn't really want to stop seeing me," I say in a teasing voice, breaking the silence once more. "Otherwise you wouldn't have traveled all the way to my campus just to tell me." I can see him smirking at me, causing warmth to spread through my chest.

"Don't be so sure of yourself," he teases right back. "I have delivered tons of bad news in person."

I tilt my head, my curiosity piqued. "Yes, but I'm sure none of that bad news was directly connected to you. Your personal life, I mean, not work."

Sebastian searches my face for a moment, long enough that I've got to avert my gaze. I try to focus on the view ahead of me instead, but the impact his presence has on me makes it harder than I thought.

"I had already made up my mind to visit you this week, whether your mom had come to speak to mine or not. It only turned into a bad news delivery once our mothers had their chat, otherwise…" he stops mid-sentence, causing my eyes to look at his again. "Well, it'd have just been a visit."

My heart swells with happiness, and I feel a rush of affection for him, knowing he had truly planned to see me again so soon. "So you were already missing me?"

He chuckles at my question, his eyes twinkling before he gives me a warm smile. "Something like that."

"I knew it!" I clutch my hands in front of me, keeping the giddiness I'm feeling inside and resisting the urge to wrap my arms around his neck and kiss his stubbled cheek. "So that means you want us to be friends, right? Since you were missing me and all."

His sigh is resigned. "Friends, yes. But that's it."

"Friends are fantastic," I lie, knowing good and well I'm going to seek out more than just friendship with him. "We should bring a picnic next time we come here... as friends, of course," I add hastily, not wanting to seem too eager.

The look he gives me makes me think that Sebastian is onto me, but he doesn't press, changing the subject instead while he leans backward with his hands behind him on the dock.

"How is it living with Margaret Van Dieren? According to rumors, she ate her ex-husband alive." He might be joking, but the truth isn't too far from it. "But I suppose if your Mom had eaten your dad you'd be a little more traumatized than you appear right now."

I don't want to make fun of my mother too much, but a giggle does slip out. "Something like that. She isn't fun to be around, honestly. She's very stiff and cold, and, um, you know... overbearing."

"Do you know why they went through a divorce?"

I shift uncomfortably. "Yeah, it was everywhere in the news, so it's not a big secret. Dad had an affair with his secretary or something and had a son with her."

"Hmm," Sebastian is paying close attention to me again, as if he's trying to see if I'm bothered by his questions. "And how did you cope with it?"

I shrug. "I kept myself busy and avoided reading or watching anything in the media about them. It'd have driven me crazy if not..." I trail off, but when Sebastian continues to listen, I finish the thought. "The court system was a joke, if Mom hadn't taken care of everything herself, she'd have never had a fair case."

"Ah, things are starting to make sense. So that's why you want to be a judge?"

I nod. "If I can specialize in family law, I will. I definitely won't be nice towards cheating husbands, that I know. Or wives, but from everything I've seen, it's the men that seem to come out on top in those sorts of cases no matter what."

"I'd better be careful, then." His tone is teasing again, but this subject is a sore spot for me, and it's going to take more than a joke to make me feel better.

"Do you intend to cheat on your wife?" I ask, turning to look at him fully, and Sebastian stills.

"I don't even have a wife to begin with," he answers with a chuckle, as if I didn't already know that. I wouldn't be here on this dock if he were married.

"Well, if you intend to cheat, don't bother having one." My tone comes off harsher and nastier than I wanted to, but the divorce of my parents was a traumatic event, and as much as I try to play it cool, it did leave its mark on me. Sebastian is quiet now, watching me intently as if he's still processing what I just said. "What is it? Why do you keep looking at me like that?"

"I don't intend to get married, anyway," he confesses, sounding quite sure of himself before breaking eye contact and looking ahead to the lake. "Sounds like a lot of work." Despite his even tone, I think he's lying. Maybe lying to himself or just trying to convince himself that he really doesn't want marriage when his heart is telling him differently. There are the soft sounds of ducks on the water, and water lapping against the wooden dock, but otherwise, there is nothing but the two of us breathing together.

"If you choose the right partner, it can be very rewarding." This time, I keep my voice gentle and empty of any sort of judgment.

But Sebastian shakes his head in disagreement, a small smile playing at the corner of his lips. "You sound like my mom. She'd totally say that." The amusement in his voice makes me smile too and I keep observing him as he proceeds. "Truthfully, though, I think marriage's a lot of stress, and I already have a company to take care of that is stressful enough."

"I might sound like your mom, but she's right. Having someone by your side isn't supposed to be stressful. If it is, then you are with the wrong person. I guess when my father finally figured that out, it was too little too late." I turn my eyes back to the horizon, heaving a sigh as I consider my next set of words. "Just don't give up on your partner so easily, and they should always be there to make your life easier."

Sebastian nods, and we both sit there in silence, enjoying each other's company and the stunning view before us. It's a perfect moment, despite the serious nature of our talk, and I never want it to end. A fresh breeze starts playing with my hair and it's cold enough to give me goosebumps. I should have brought a jacket with me but I'm only wearing a sleeveless dress. Suddenly, Seb sits back up straight and without saying a word, wraps an arm around me, pulling me closer to him. The heat of his body soothes and warms me up. Our legs touching, I let my head rest on his shoulder, and we remain quiet, enjoying each other's presence while both of us are lost in our own thoughts. The sun is starting to set, casting a warm, orange glow over the lake, but every bit of my attention is locked on how close he is to me, and how all I have to do to be touching his lips is move my head up and over just an inch or two more.

"If only life was always so pleasant and simple," I hear him saying, his voice barely above a whisper, but loud enough for me to hear it.

"What do you mean?" I ask, lifting my head up so I can look at him as we speak. "You seem to have a great life. Aren't you happy with it?"

My question gives him pause, his gaze shifts to the lake ahead of him, and he exhales loudly as he thinks it through. "I don't know. All I do is work. I barely have time to do anything else. Dad's quite tough on me."

"I don't think we've ever talked about your dad's company. What do you do there exactly?"

Sebastian's face lights up as he starts to explain the ins and outs of his family's business. "I'm basically second-in-command, just behind my dad. We're currently working on expanding the company, finding the right partners and investors, and that's what we have been focused on this year."

As he speaks, I'm utterly impressed by his intelligence and drive. It's no wonder he's so successful, but I can also feel myself becoming more and more distracted by his presence. The way his lips move as he speaks, the way his eyes light up when he talks about something he's passionate about... it's all so intoxicating.

I feel a warm rush of attraction toward him, and for a moment I forget where we are and what we're doing. All I can think about is how much I want to get closer to him, to feel his arms around me, to kiss him....

But just as quickly as the thought comes, I push it away. I know I shouldn't be thinking about these things, not when we've just agreed to be friends. I can't push him too hard, or friends are all we'll ever be. But it's so hard to resist when he's sitting beside me, his presence like a magnet drawing me closer and closer.

Once Sebastian finishes telling me about his job in the family company, we sit in silence once again, the only sound the gentle lapping of the water against the shore. The sun has almost set completely now, and the sky is painted with shades of pink and purple. It's a beautiful sight, but all I can focus on is the man beside me.

Then he speaks again. "What you said about marriage and your dad figuring it all out too late… you are terribly wise for your age, you know that?"

I raise an eyebrow at him playfully. "When you witness a marriage ending in a nasty divorce, trust me, you get wise."

"And despite it all, do you still believe in it?" Sebastian's voice lowers slightly, and he gazes at me intently.

"Why wouldn't I?" I keep staring back at him, feeling a sudden heat spreading through my body. "It's the people in the marriage that make or break it, isn't it?"

"I—" He seems to be lost for words, and I hold back a smile, knowing how much talking about the subject of marriage with me affects him. "I like that you still believe in the institution. It's good to have hopes." But it's obvious he wanted to say something else, something more private. Why did he stop mid-way? That I have no idea.

For a moment, as we keep looking at each other, it seems as though he's going to lean in and kiss me. I can feel my heart pounding in my chest as his gaze flickers down to my lips. But just as quickly, he breaks the tension.

"I like being with you, Julia." His words are delivered with so much sincerity and warmth that I can't help but feel my heartbeat quicken.

"I like being with you too, Seb." I try to sound polite and keep how good he makes me feel under wraps, but the way his eyes pierce into mine makes it hard to concentrate on anything else. I feel like he's right on the edge of giving up this whole friendship charade and kissing me before we leave. Or am I just reading too much into it?

I've meant everything I said to him. Even though my parents' marriage ended in a messy divorce, I know that not all marriages are like that.

"You might barely know me," I pause for a beat, assessing whether I should say the rest of my thought out loud. "But I want you to know I'm here for you, if you need someone to confide in, no matter the subject, I'm here."

His mouth spreads in a wide smile that makes my face fall a little. "That's very kind of you."

"Well, that's what friends do, after all."

We share a quick chuckle, but then he remains quiet for a moment, as if thinking something through. "Do you like flowers?"

His question is so random and unexpected that my eyes widen in surprise. "Eh, of course. Why?"

"Just curious."

Once the sun has finally set, it'd be the perfect occasion for us to kiss, but instead, Sebastian abruptly stands up. "It's getting late. You must have homework to do, right?" he asks, extending a hand to help me up. I take his hand in mine, causing a jolt of electricity to rush through my body.

"I guess so." I sigh inwardly, disappointed at the lost opportunity, but I push the feeling away and grin at him. "Will I see you again soon?"

Seb smiles at me, his eyes twinkling in the twilight. "As much as I want to say no, I know I'd be lying."

All of a sudden, he leans down and kisses me on the forehead, his lips warm against my skin. I shut my eyes instinctively, reveling in the moment. His kiss, slow and gentle, spurs a trail of excitement through me. As he pulls away, I catch a hint of his cologne, reminding me of our dance.

"Let's get you home," he rumbles, and I take his offered arm and let him lead me back to where we parked.

As we walk back to his car, I find myself thinking about where this all might possibly lead. Will we just be friends as he said, or something more? Only time will tell… but I know what I really want from him. And it isn't friendship.

CHAPTER 5

Sebastian

Driving Julia back to her flat in the heart of Amsterdam, I'm both smitten and lost in my thoughts. Spending hours with her and being so friendly after hyping myself up all day to tell her we can't see each other anymore is overwhelming, but I know I need to get real. The last thing I need is to have her mother or even mine on my back, reminding me I'm not a good fit for her.

The drive is quiet, Julia fiddling with the radio to show me some of her favorite songs, and I'm shaken about how easy it is to be with her. I can't help stealing glances at her every once in a while. It still feels surreal that the young woman I first saw in the library, hiding from everyone, is now sitting beside me in my car. Fate is a funny thing.

As we stop at the curb, she turns to me with a suggestion, her voice full of hope and excitement. "We should have a picnic in that park next Saturday. It'd be fun."

My heart rate stutters as I hesitate, unsure of how to respond. I know that I want to spend more time with her, but I'm not sure if I'm ready to give up on my mission of separating myself from her slowly. "I've got to spend the weekend with my family."

Julia's eyes light up with anticipation as she responds, as if she knows she has me in her grasp, "We can do it on Thursday evening, then."

I consider my options, knowing if I decline she will be hurt. It'd be the right thing to do since that would ensure I'll never see her again, but I can't seem to find the will to go through with it. Damn it. I have seen her just twice and yet here I'm already caring about her. A gush of air rolls off my lips as I consider what to do next. "I have a better idea," I tell her instead. "I'll pick you up Thursday at 6 PM."

Julia nods, her expression filled with visible excitement. "Sounds perfect."

Before she exits the car, though, she leans in and kisses my cheek impulsively. I feel a rush of adrenaline shoot through me at the touch of her lips to my skin, like a stupid teenager, flustered over a simple cheek kiss from a pretty girl.

"Goodbye, Sebastian," she purrs, her lashes low.

"Bye, Julia."

Watching her walk away, her long legs and delicate figure disappearing into the ornate entrance of her building, a sense of longing starts taking over me, of wanting to be with her no matter the cost. I even consider what would happen if I just parked and followed her inside. Would she open the door for me, let me in? Would we spend our time on the couch just talking, or would she want to show me back to her bedroom…?

Gosh, why did she have to be Margaret's daughter?! Age gaps like the one between Julia and I are not uncommon, and on paper, we would be a fantastic, if unlikely, match. The unification of our families would be beneficial all around, given how affluent the Van Dierens are, and there is no doubt that I want her, that I feel for her. I'd never let her be unhappy. It just doesn't make sense why Margaret is going as far as talking to my mom to keep us apart.

Thinking about Julia's mother just pisses me off, so I let my mind wander to thoughts of our upcoming date. A picnic would be nice… a decadent spread of food, fine wine, and the two of us nestled together on a soft blanket in the park… but I have other things in mind, not to mention the fact that I wouldn't trust myself not to throw all the food aside and lay her down on the blanket to have her for dinner instead. Fuck, I can't wait to see her again, to feel her close to me, to show her how much I care. My cock jumps at the idea, and I have to adjust it in my pants or risk a rather uncomfortable drive home.

I know that our newly-lit romance may be socially inadequate, but I'm willing to do whatever it takes to make it work. It's been such a short time, but I can already see a future with Julia, and I'm determined to make sure we have a chance to give it a shot together.

My daydreaming is interrupted by the ringing of my phone. Unsurprisingly, it's Dad, reminding me of the dinner we apparently have planned with his associates this evening. I feel a pang of guilt for forgetting about it, but then I pause, frowning.

"Wait…didn't you tell Mom you'd be home tonight?" I ask, trying to buy myself a way out of this. "I don't think you told either of us about this dinner."

"Did I?" Dad responds absentmindedly. I can hear the chatter of the people in the restaurant in the background, and curse internally, knowing that if he's already there it will be impossible for me to avoid attending. "Well, we're all already at de Silveren Spiegel waiting for you. Hurry up."

I end the call with an eye roll and start the car. As I drive towards the restaurant, I almost instinctively try to stave off the annoyance I have concerning this dinner by retreading some of the moments with Julia today. The image of her lingers in my mind, the soft curve of her lips as she leaned towards me, the way her hair fell across her face....

No matter how she makes me feel, I can't let thoughts of her interfere with my responsibilities. I've got to focus on this dinner, on my father's expectations, and on my own place within the company. Yet, I still wonder if Julia feels the same way I do. It's pretty obvious the attraction is mutual, but does she think about me when we're apart?

I shake my head, trying to push away these thoughts. The future is uncertain, and I must be careful not to let my emotions cloud my judgment. I take a deep breath and steel myself for the dinner ahead. These events are more like verbal boxing matches at times and not peaceful meals, so I can't exactly let my guard down.

I arrive at the historic restaurant, and make my way to my dad's reserved table. Located in a heritage building on Kattengat Street, it's the oldest establishment in town, and one of my dad's favorites. And, according to him, it's where he took Mom on their first date.

The restaurant's interior is stylish and sophisticated, with a modern design that surprisingly complements the historic building's classic architecture. The dining room is dimly lit, with soft lighting creating a warm and intimate atmosphere. The walls are decorated with beautiful portraits of the founders, and the tables are covered with crisp white tablecloths, surrounded by comfortable chairs. The one meant for me is obvious. Dad's reserved spot is nestled in the corner, with about eight men seated around the circumference of the circular table, and a bottle of cognac already opened and being poured around the table by an unobtrusive server.

As I approach, I notice that my dad is sitting with his new protégé, Karl—a young man in his late twenties who has been making waves in the sales department. He's been bringing in new business left and right, and his success has not gone unnoticed. There is something about him that I didn't exactly warm up to in the beginning, but Dad seems to be convinced that he is an asset that we don't want to lose, and so far the younger man hasn't done anything to throw up any red flags. Plus, it can't be denied that he has been a boon for our business.

"There he is!" Dad booms as I stroll over, standing to shake my hand and pat me on the arm enthusiastically. I shake hands with all the other business associates, albeit with less affection than I had with my father, and take the seat that has been saved for me on the other side of him.

"What kept you?" Dad asks once I get seated.

"Just some personal matters," I say easily. It's not exactly a lie, but I'm definitely not going into detail regarding my park trip with Julia.

"Well, we're glad you made it, at least," he says with a sense of finality, clapping his hands together. "Alright gentlemen, while we wait for the food to arrive, should we talk about the proposal that Karl sent you earlier this week? What are your first impressions of it?"

When the server comes back around, I limit myself to ordering a single whiskey on the rocks and a medium-rare steak with asparagus. There isn't a specific reason for this meal, I came to learn soon enough. It irks me knowing that Mom expects him to be home tonight, but the family business has always been at the forefront of my father's mind and his primary interest in life. Conversation is light, nothing too serious, and I stay on the fringe, so I'm not forced to remain here any longer than necessary.

As the dinner progresses, I feel a growing sense of unease. My father is undoubtedly the head of the table, leading most of the talks, but Karl isn't far behind him. The younger man clearly wants to take a leading role, and isn't shy about letting everyone know it. Karl is an impressive salesman, sure, but his arrogance and lack of empathy towards others leaves me feeling uneasy. He seems to view everything as a competition, a game to be won at any cost. I can't help but wonder if this is the kind of person my dad admires and promotes.

As I glance over at my dad, I see a proud smile on his face. It's clear that Karl's success has made an impression on him, and he sees him as a valuable asset to the company. I try to put my reservations aside, reminding myself that this is just business. Plus, it isn't like Karl is cruel or unkind in any way, it's just how he approaches his job isn't familiar to me. Maybe I just need to catch up.

However, the more Karl talks, the more I find myself becoming disillusioned with the corporate world, and it really has nothing to do with Karl himself, but the entire mess of it all. It seems like success is measured only in terms of money and power, and the human cost is often ignored. I think of Julia and her mother's disapproval of our relationship, and I wonder if it's because she sees me as someone like my father who will dedicate his entire life to his career and be a distant and inattentive husband. It makes me lose my appetite briefly, and I sip my whiskey to try to settle my nervous stomach.

As the plates of food arrive, the conversation continues without me. My father leads the next discussion, asking the client about their current needs and goals. Karl chimes in with his own thoughts and suggestions, and I can see my father nodding in agreement.

I take a bite of my steak and listen to the conversation, trying to pick up on any useful information. The client seems pleased with the ideas being presented, and my father starts to discuss potential timelines and budgets.

Suddenly, Karl inserts a joke as the chatter begins to lull, and everyone at the table laughs. It's a welcome break from the business talk, especially considering the fact that it's getting late and the workday has been over for hours now. I'm well and tired of company talk.

As we continue to eat, the mood becomes more relaxed and light-hearted. The cognac is polished off and a deep red, dessert wine is brought to the table to round out the meal. We talk about sports, travel, and even a bit of our lives and interests. Karl's particularly good at keeping the conversation flowing, and I can tell Dad is pleased. I join in on the banter, sharing a few stories of my own. The clients seem to enjoy the more personal conversation, and I can see them starting to warm up to us as a team.

The meal winds down, and the staff clears the plates. My father and the client continue their discussion as Karl and I sit back, enjoying our last sips of wine.

"Good job tonight," I tell the younger man, surprising myself at how impressed I am. "I can see why my dad keeps you so close at hand all the time."

"Thanks," Karl grins. "I hope to be around a long time."

"I don't doubt it," I agree. "You keep up the pace you're at right now and you'll have no problem carving out a permanent spot for yourself."

After dinner, Karl, the rest of the associates, and the client say their goodbyes, leaving Dad and I as the only ones remaining at the large table. My father sighs, leaning back in his chair and folding his arms behind his head. "That went well, don't you think?"

I resist the urge to check my watch for the time. "Yes, I think so."

As we finish the last of our drinks, my father turns to me with a serious look on his face. "Seb, I need you to do something for me," he says, his tone lower than usual. "Karl is a valuable asset to our company, but he needs some guidance. Keep him under your wing, show him the ropes. You're both young, and I think you'll get along just fine."

I nod, but inside I feel a sense of frustration. I know that my father sees me as a tool for the family business, but sometimes it feels like he doesn't understand my own desires and ambitions. Julia floats across my mind, and thinking about her makes me want to worry about mentoring Karl even less. All of my spare time will be spent with her, if I can have any say in it.

"I understand, Dad," I respond tiredly. "But I have my own responsibilities, too. I can't be babysitting someone else all the time."

My father raises an eyebrow. "I'm not asking you to babysit him. Karl is one of our best salesmen, and I want him to learn from the best. You have a lot to offer him, and he has a lot to offer you."

I sigh, but I know that my father is right. We need to expand the business, and putting some work into those that can help us further the company is a priority I should take seriously, even if I have little interest in getting cozy with Karl. "Okay, I'll keep an eye on him," I say reluctantly.

My father smiles, patting me on the shoulder. "Good. Karl is dedicated and knows his craft, but there's always room for improvement. Together, you can take the company to the next level."

I nod, feeling a sense of responsibility and duty for my family's business. But deep down, I know that I also need to find a balance between my obligations and my own desires. It won't be easy, but I'm determined to make it work.

I just need to get to Thursday, I tell myself, closing my eyes briefly and thinking of sweet, vanilla-scented, honey-colored hair. Then I can actually enjoy myself for once.

Dad and I walk out together to where one of the family drivers is waiting for him. I hand the valet my ticket, and my father waits with me, his hands shoved in the pockets of his suit jacket. We aren't speaking, but now that I have him alone, there are a few things I want to ask him. The more I think about it, the more I'm sure that Margaret's objection has to lie in the fact that I could very well turn out to be a distant, absent husband like my father, and surely she doesn't want that for her daughter. From the outside, it would be easy to think that my parents have a good, comfortable marriage, but on the inside I can tell that they have never been further apart from each other, even when they sleep in the same room.

It might be out of line, but I have to ask Dad about it. I don't want them to both end up lonely as they age, too stubborn to both find their way back to one another. The idea of that makes my stomach sink. I turn to my father, my voice hesitant as I try to find the right words. "How are you and Mom?" I manage to pull off, hoping to get a glimpse of the relationship that's always felt formal and lacking in warmth.

My father's eyebrows furrow at my question. "Fine. Why do you ask?"

I stumble for a moment, not quite sure how to phrase my concern. "I, um, I never see you together except for official events or things that the two of you are expected to attend together…" I offer, my voice trailing off.

"Don't worry about any of that, Seb. We're all good," he reassures me. I'm still not convinced, but I can see the valet driving in our direction from just a few cars away and if I press any further with my father, he will know I'm trying to pry.

"Well… if you're sure."

Dad claps me on the shoulder as my car pulls up. "I am sure. Now, go home and get some rest, son. I'll see you bright and early tomorrow."

Driving home, my thoughts race, torn between my duty to the family business and my desire for something more. I don't want what my parents have. I want a genuine love match. I want fire and passion and someone that will challenge me every day. Someone like Julia. No. I want Julia.

But our respective mothers are against us even seeing each other, so I've got no idea how to even make it work.

I need some advice, just someone who understands what I'm going through, but I don't even know where to start. Who would I even bring this up to? My father is so business-minded that personal talks with him always feel stilted and uncomfortable. And now, with Karl in the picture, it feels like there's even more pressure on me. I can't let myself be overwhelmed. I need to find a way to balance everything.

Unlocking the door to my apartment, my mind is still consumed with thoughts of everything that has happened today, but especially Julia. The words she spoke about marriage and divorce are still ringing in my ears. I can't believe how easy it was for her to talk about something so personal with me. It's like we've always known each other.

As I walk into my living room, I think about how special she is. If it wasn't for her damned mother and that damned age gap, I'd have loved pursuing her.

I collapse onto my couch and close my eyes, letting out a deep sigh. The emotional rollercoaster of the day has left me feeling drained. I never expected to see Julia again, and now all I can think about is her, and I've made plans for a fucking date with her, too! Gosh! What was I even thinking?

I try to push the thoughts out of my head and focus on something else, but they keep coming back like a boomerang. It's like I'm under her spell, unable to think about anything else. Showering, brushing my teeth, and going through some nighttime stretches don't do anything to clear my head, and with how early I have to get up, drinking her out of my mind isn't an option, either.

Finally, I give in and allow myself to drift off to sleep once I crawl into bed, my mind still consumed with thoughts of Julia. The future is uncertain, but for now, all I can do is surrender to the overwhelming feelings that she stirs within me.

CHAPTER 6

Julia

I have no idea what time it is when something on the bedside table begins to squawk, but it scares me out of my sleep easily. I jump, blindly feeling around for whatever could be making the noise before I wake up enough to realize that I'm getting a phone call. Groggily, I reach for my phone, squinting as the screen lights up with notifications. After a moment, I realize that it's Gabi calling me, and I let out a sigh before answering.

"I need to know everything!" I hear Gabi saying as soon as I answer, her excitement dripping from her voice.

Trying to rub the sleep from my eyes, it takes me a moment to form a proper answer. "Gabi, it's eight am."

"In my defense, I'm in front of your door with a hot latte."

My interest is piqued and I ask reluctantly, "What flavor?"

"Hazelnut. And a fresh croissant." Her cheeky tone makes me smile. Well, I know that she's won this round. Those two items combined are irresistible to me this early in the day.

I quickly throw on a robe and make my way to the front door, the smell of freshly brewed espresso wafting through the air. Gabi is practically bouncing with excitement as I open the door, holding a drink carrier with our two lattes in one hand and a bag of croissants in the other.

"Good morning!" Gabi exclaims, thrusting the coffee and a pastry into my hands. "How come you were still sleeping? We have class in thirty minutes."

"It should be illegal to have class so early," I grumble, but inwardly I'm thankful that Gabi showed up. I had forgotten to set my alarm and surely would have been late without her. Not to mention without any sort of breakfast.

The first sip of the hazelnut latte warms me all the way to my soul, and it's so wonderful that I almost hug Gabi in appreciation, but there's clearly something more she wants from me way more than a hug—gossip.

As we make our way back to my bedroom, Gabi chatters excitedly about the latest vapid drama in school and her own life. I try to focus on what my friend is saying, but my mind keeps drifting to Sebastian. I consider lying to Gabi, but there really isn't any point. Seb might not be immediately recognizable, but anyone with any knowledge of the old money families around here would be able to quickly pinpoint who he is exactly, so I'd be caught in any lie sooner rather than later.

As I sip my coffee and slip into a pair of beige chinos, I wonder if he is thinking about me too. Does he miss me the way I miss him? Or is he busy with his own life and work, leaving me as nothing more than a pleasant afterthought?

The idea sends a shiver down my spine, and I try to push it to the back of my mind. There's no way he doesn't feel the same sort of connection that I do. I refuse to believe that. I know that my mother disapproves of Sebastian and his age, but I can't help how I feel. There's something about him that draws me in, a magnetism that I can't resist.

As I slip on a pale blue blouse and grab my black messenger bag, I take a deep breath, trying to steel myself for whatever the day might bring. Class is going to be difficult for me today… I don't know how I'm supposed to be able to concentrate with everything going on in my mind.

Gabi practically bounces on her feet as she waits for me to finish getting dressed. "So, tell me, who was that broody man who we saw yesterday?" she asks, a grin spreading across her face. "Holy shit, girl, that man looked like he'd kill for you."

I feel myself blushing at Gabi's words. I'm not one for flattery, but something about the way Gabi talks makes me feel warm inside. "Is that a compliment?" I tease, trying to sound nonchalant.

Gabi rolls her eyes. "Of course, it's a compliment, dummy. You have to tell me everything about him. What's his last name? What does he do? Why does he look like he wants to kill anyone who comes near you?"

I laugh, feeling grateful for Gabi's lightheartedness. "His name is Sebastian van den Bosch," I begin as I step into the ensuite bathroom, Gabi trailing closely behind me. "And I don't know why he looks like that. Maybe he just has a resting murder face."

With visible amusement in her gaze, Gabi leans against the wall of the bathroom, beside the sink where I'm splashing fresh water over my face. "Girl, you are too much. But seriously, you should ask him out or something. You two have some serious chemistry."

I feel my stomach clench as I recall doing just that yesterday. I grab a towel and dry my face as I gather my thoughts. Getting him to agree to the 'friendly' picnic was difficult, but oh so worth it. I hesitate whether or not to disclose I have already another meetup with Sebastian in a few days to Gabi, but I'd rather keep it to myself until it really happens. "I don't know if he's interested," I tell her instead, trying to keep my voice steady. "Well, I'm pretty sure than he is, but he insists that we can only be friends."

Gabi rolls her eyes, huffing at my words. "Yeah, right. You were practically glowing when he showed up, and he was looking just as intense! Stop overthinking and go for it, Julia. What do you have to lose?"

"He's just a guy I met at that ball Mom wanted me to go to." I look at my face in the mirror, shrugging my shoulders. "It's nothing serious. You're looking too much into it." Then I take my moisturizer and put some on my face.

"Well, looks like Mommy knows best," Gabi teases, winking at me. "If she dragged you to a ball and you met that gorgeous man there, then tell her to extend me an invite next time, too."

"She might have made me go to the ball, but it backfired on her, actually. Mom doesn't want me around Sebastian," I fess out, my voice lowering. "She didn't set me up with him. I just sort of met him there."

"So your mom knows him then?" Gabi asks, leaning in closer.

"Yeah, and she isn't happy about whatever connection he and I formed." A note of frustration creeps into my voice as I recall the way she intervened. "She actually caught us dancing and asked someone to split us up. It was pathetic."

"Ouch, why?" Her eyebrows furrow in concern and it's actually cute to see.

"Well, guess how old he is?" My voice's barely above a whisper as I wait for Gabi's reaction.

"Oh gosh, who cares?" Throwing her hands up in exasperation, she doesn't seem much bothered and gives another sip of her latte. "He likes you, you like him, it's all that matters."

"Yeah, right, go tell her that yourself," I say, rolling my eyes as I wash my hands. "But trust me, she cares. *A lot.*"

"Alright, but she can't forbid you to see him just because he's older." Her tone is insistent and her eyes even glint with determination. "How old are we talking about, anyway? Twenty-seven, Twenty-eight?"

"Try early thirties." My heart sinks as I say the words out loud.

"Oh boy!" A whistle escaping her lips, Gabi can't hide her astonishment. "Yeah, understandable that Margaret is losing her mind. Oh well, from my end, I can help if you need a cover-up excuse to be with him."

"I appreciate it." After drying my hands, I pat her arm softly, grateful for Gabi's unwavering support. "Now let's go, we're running late."

When we reach the bedroom door, I take a bite out of the still-warm croissant, careful not to get the butter on my blouse, and sigh in pleasure. "I don't know what I would do without you," I tell my friend as we make it out into the hallway. "Not just because of the food. Everything."

Gabi grins, grabbing her bag and following me out the door and through the hallway. "You don't have to worry about that, babe. I'll always be here for you."

We make our way to campus, the morning air crisp and cool against our skin. As we walk, Gabi chatters on about her latest conquests and drama with her roommates. I nod and laugh in all the right places, but my mind keeps drifting. It makes me feel like a less-than-stellar friend, but I promise myself that I'll be more attentive once everything with Sebastian settles.

There is this pang of anxiety in my chest, even though the morning is beautiful and I have the company of my friend. I know that my mother will do everything in her power to keep me away from him, and it's stressing me out to no end. Our connection is special… it has something that I can't quite put my finger on, but I can't exactly say that to my mother and expect her to suddenly accept whatever's going on between us.

As Gabi and I enter the bustling halls of the Law School building, I take a deep breath, trying to steady my nerves. I know that today is going to be a long day, but with Gabi by my side and caffeine buzzing through my veins, I feel more confident that I can handle whatever comes my way.

Just as we settle into our seats in the lecture, a delivery guy walks in, causing my heart to race and a knot to form in my stomach. It's like the second I lay eyes on him, I know that he's here for me, and embarrassment is already starting to brew inside me as every single student and even the professor turns to the door to look at him. The delivery guy clears his throat and speaks up. "Excuse me, is Julia van Dieren here?" he asks, holding up a massive bouquet of red roses.

I can feel my face turning red as everyone starts to chatter, their eyes wide, while some students point their fingers at me. The delivery man makes a beeline for my seat, and I can feel the eyes of everyone in the room shift from him to me. Oh gosh, I wish I could disappear.

Beside me, Gabi has her knuckles pressed against her mouth, her eyes shining with everything that she wants to say but is holding in. I know I'm never going to hear the end of this from her. My mind races as I try to come up with an excuse for why I'm receiving flowers in the middle of class, of all places, but I'm drawing a total blank.

As he approaches, I try to make myself as small as possible, hiding behind my textbook. A high-pitched giggle escapes Gabi at my attempt, but it's no use, and I find myself holding the bouquet with shaking hands.

I sign for the delivery, trying to balance the enormous flower arrangement with one arm and the pen in my free hand, and then take the small card from the middle. My eyes scan the message written on it: *Thank you for yesterday. I look forward to seeing you again on Thursday. S.*

My heart skips a beat as I read the note. I can't believe this is happening! How the hell did Sebastian figure out my class schedule, and what in the world is he thinking, interrupting my school time like this? In front of dozens of my classmates too! Surely he has to know that it's mortifying. I wonder if that was his intention.

Others in the class snicker as I carefully sit the bouquet of roses on the floor next to me, the scent of the flowers floating around me as a constant reminder that they are there even when I'm not looking at them.

"Looks like someone has a secret admirer," my professor teases, crossing his arms and raising an eyebrow at me. His words break the obvious tension in the class, and everyone laughs, including me, at how bizarre the situation is.

"Would you like me to put those on my desk? As beautiful as they are, I don't want yet another distraction if you accidentally knock them over," he offers, and I gratefully accept. Once the roses are away from me for the moment, I try to focus on the lecture, but my mind keeps drifting back to the audacity of Sebastian. Maybe this delivery was some sort of revenge for me forcing myself into the car with him yesterday. If so, then he has definitely one-upped me, and I'll have to stay on my toes if I want to regain the upper hand in our burgeoning relationship.

As the lecture comes to an end, I gather my roses from the teacher, blushing and averting my eyes as I do so. Gabi waits for me while I grab the rest of my things and make my way out of the auditorium. I briefly consider distracting her and leaving on my own so she can't immediately bombard me with questions and comments about the roses, but I know she would catch up with me before I could escape.

As soon as Gabi has me alone, she elbows me to get my full attention. "Alright, you have my blessing, you can marry him."

I roll my eyes and shush my friend. "Don't be stupid, Gabi," I whisper back, trying to ignore the amused glances from the students around us in the hall. It's not like I can hide what she's talking about, considering my arms are literally full of roses.

I can't deny that the gesture is sweet, but getting the flowers right when class was about to start is borderline inappropriate. Luckily, the professor was a good sport, but if he had been one of my more stoic teachers, it could have gone much worse for me.

Gabi continues just as giddy, though. "So how does it feel to be the most popular girl in school?"

I sigh heavily and laugh at her indirect question. "You know they're from Sebastian," I say, unable to keep the grin off my face.

Gabi feigns surprise. "What a shocker. I never would have guessed that your broody friend from yesterday would also be the flower sender!"

I give her a playful shove, and we both giggle as we continue walking down the concourse.

"I have to admit," Gabi continues as we walk beside each other. "I didn't think any man that you met at a high society ball would have had it in him to be so romantic."

I shrug, feeling a little defensive. "He's not just some wealthy stick in the mud, you know. He's got a sensitive side, it seems."

Gabi laughs. "I know, I know. I'm just teasing. I think it's sweet that he's making an effort."

I feel a sense of warmth spread through me as Gabi talks about Sebastian in a positive light. It's not often that I open up to people about my private life, but with Gabi, it feels natural. With Mom being so ridiculously negative about anything to do with Sebastian, it's nice to have someone on my side encouraging me to follow my heart, even if he is still a bit of a mystery to Gabi and I both.

Afterward, I hurry home to put the bouquet in my apartment while Gabi goes to her next class. I'm thankful for the gap in my schedule because there is a lot on my mind that I need to settle. Alone in my living room, I can't resist the urge to call Van den Bosch Industries, knowing that Sebastian will be there. We haven't exchanged numbers yet, so I have no other way to reach him. Normally, I would never dream of calling a potential suitor at work, but considering that he already crossed the line of politeness by embarrassing me in front of my entire class and professor, I figure that a phone call is perfectly acceptable.

The secretary picks up on the first ring, and I ask to speak to Sebastian. She asks who is calling, but once I tell her my name, she connects me immediately. This gives me pause... has Sebastian added me to a list of people that he will always be available for? If so, he's thinking way further ahead than I am. It means that he already considers me someone special enough in his life to always have access to him, and the thought of it leaves my mind swimming.

Once he picks up, he wastes no time in speaking first. "Julia, what a surprise!"

The corners of my mouth twitch into a grin at his warm voice. It's good to hear from him again. But I take a deep breath and keep myself focused on my next set of words. "Well, not as big of a surprise as you sending me flowers during one of my lectures, I suppose."

"Ah, yes, I'm glad you received my gift." He sounds quite proud of himself and I wonder if he knows how wrong the timing was. "Did you like them?"

I consider telling him that no, his timing of delivery ruined them for me, but as I glance at the ruby-red bouquet on my table, I know it's not the right move to tell him such a blatant lie. "I did, even though there was no need for such a big public display."

"Well, there was no need for you to follow me when I was going back to my car and yet here we are." I drag my hand over my face, hearing the confirmation that his little flower stunt was a direct reaction from me forcing him to take me to the park. "You made quite an impression on me yesterday, and I wanted you to know that," he continues.

How can he be so casual when saying such things?! Hearing him say that makes my cheeks flush immediately, but I try to play it cool. "Well, that's, um, very kind of you. I guess that I will see you Thursday, then?"

"Wait," he asks, stopping me. "Can I ask you for your mobile number so that I can call you once I arrive?"

I sputter to a stop, sucking in a breath. If we exchange numbers, Sebastian will have access to me at all times. The thought is thrilling and maybe a little frightening, but in the best way. "Oh, eh, yes, of course. Can you tell me yours, and I will text you mine?"

Sebastian chuckles from the other side before agreeing and giving me his number. As I hang up the phone, I can't help but feel a mixture of excitement and nervousness. I barely know this man, but there is something about him that draws me to him. Maybe it's his unwavering confidence, or maybe it's just the way he carries himself. Either way, I'm looking forward to seeing him again in a few days.

After the call, I text him, *Here we go. Now we are connected.*

Just a few seconds later, his answer pops up.

Seb: *Looks like it. X*

I smile as I read Sebastian's response, feeling a flutter of excitement in my chest as I clutch the phone to my heart. It's only been a few days since I met him for the first time, but I already look forward to each and every one of our interactions.

I can't believe I actually called his workplace to talk to him! It's so unlike me to take such a bold step, but I couldn't resist the urge to hear his voice again and thank him for the lovely flowers. Or… confront him about the flowers is more accurate, I guess. But I love them anyway.

And now, we're able to contact each other any time of the day or night, whenever we want. Just like that. It's amazing how technology makes everything so much easier.

But what does this mean? Does he really want to get to know me better, or is he just playing along in this game that we've started? I shake my head, trying to clear away my doubts. I won't know until after tomorrow, when we're supposed to meet again. Until then, I'll just have to keep my expectations in check.

But for now, I allow myself the chance to feel a little giddy as I look down at my phone and see Sebastian's name, and that flirty little 'X' that he ended his text with. Who knows what the future holds?

CHAPTER 7

Sebastian

I check my watch as I step out of the sleek office building, feeling the weight of the day on my shoulders. I'm only leaving about twenty minutes early, but I want to escape the office with enough time to spare. The sun will begin to dip below the horizon in an hour and, until now, not a cloud to be seen in the sky. I give a silent prayer of relief that the weather has held. I've caught up on everything I need to finish for the day, and shouldn't run into any problems meeting Julia at 6 PM. Even now I'm cutting it closer than I wanted, but I figure that I should be fine. I don't know what it is about this woman, but I'm desperate to make the perfect impression every time we're around one another.

Just as I'm about to turn the corner, my phone rings. It's my dad, of course, and his timing is terrible as usual. I close my eyes and curse under my breath, tempted to just ignore the call and continue on my way, but I know my father will be relentless about calling me if I don't answer. So, reluctantly, I do.

"Seb, where are you? Your PA told me you left your office?" he asks without wasting any time.

His inquiry is enough to make me stop walking, and a sense of uneasiness washes over me. "Yes, um, I've got something to do."

"Schedule it for another time, then, I need you here for a meeting."

I feel like throwing my mobile against the brick facade of the building. Of fucking course he would want to have a meeting right now!

I let out a frustrated sigh, feeling the pressure of the situation. "I have plans, Dad. Can't someone else attend in my place?"

"No, it has to be you. It's important," he insists firmly. "Plus, the workday isn't even over! You usually leave at six. Don't tell me that you're already done?"

I open my mouth to tell him a few much-needed truth bombs but stop myself, clenching my teeth instead. I exhale harshly through the nose, resigned at my fate. "Of course not, Dad. I'll be right in."

Annoyance pounding in my skull, I turn around and head back into the office building. As I make my way through the busy lobby, I spot Karl leaning on the front desk and chatting with the secretary. He's already got his own briefcase with him, ready to be done with the day, but I have an idea that just might get me out of this stupid meeting a little sooner. I lengthen my strides, walking down the hallway and pulling him aside.

"Karl, my dad needs us now," I say urgently, trying to keep my frustration in check. "We've got a meeting that I need you to attend with me."

Karl looks surprised but nods and starts trailing behind me. "Sure thing, Seb. I'm happy to help."

He tries to ask me what the meeting is about, but honestly, I have no idea either and just shrug his questions off. We enter the conference room where my dad and several other executives are already seated. The room is almost silent, filled with the weight of important decisions and high stakes, which only serves to make me more pissed off. How urgent can this damn meeting be if I knew nothing about it beforehand?

My dad begins to speak, discussing strategies and PR tactics, and I quickly catch on to what this is all about. Expansion. We've been discussing it as sort of a nebulous concept lately, but it will take a lot of effort and even more money from our clients and partners if we're going to make it happen. Even then, we won't know for a few years whether the change will be profitable or not.

As serious as this all is, I can't help but glance at my watch every few minutes, my mind racing with thoughts of Julia and the date that I have planned down to the very last detail. Each second that I'm stuck in this conference room with all these old men is a moment I could be spending making her laugh, touching her, or even just learning more about the fascinating young woman that has started to occupy so much of my mind. I can almost hear her voice in my head, urging me to leave this meeting and come to her, teasing me for being so stuffy and serious about work on such a lovely evening.

"Is everything okay, Sebastian?" Dad asks, noticing my fidgeting. He sounds annoyed but keeps it in check in front of all the other board members that are present.

I clear my throat, sitting straighter in my chair. "Yes, sorry. I just have… other arrangements tonight that I don't want to be late for."

My dad raises an eyebrow, and from the look in his eyes, I know that there will be a lot more questions once we are in private later. "Well, this won't take too long. We just need your input on a few things. I hope that the future of the business you're set to inherit isn't intruding on your personal plans too much, hm?"

I feel my neck get hot with embarrassment as some of the other men at the meeting chuckle.

"No, it's fine. Continue."

I keep my hands at my sides now, trying to focus on the meeting. But as the minutes tick by, I can feel the tension building inside of me. Finally, my dad wraps up the meeting and I stand up, eager to leave.

"I really have to go, but Karl is here and will report everything to me tomorrow morning," I say quickly, already moving toward the door.

My dad nods, but I know him well enough that I will get an earful about my behavior later.

I rush out of the conference room, practically sprinting down the hallway. I can feel the adrenaline coursing through my veins as I race toward the exit. Stepping outside, I take a deep breath of the cool evening air, digging my keys out of my pocket as I make my way to my car. It's time to make up for lost time.

As soon as I shut the driver's side door, I pull my phone out of my pocket and call Julia. She answers quickly, and hearing her cheerful voice reassures me that the night is still likely to go just the way I've planned it.

"Julia," I begin, my heart nearly racing in my throat. "I'm on my way, but I'm running late. Something came up at work, but I'll be there as soon as I can."

She makes an amused noise. "And here I was so sure that you canceled on me."

"Canceling plans with you? Never in a million years," I assure her, and she giggles again. Just hearing her joy gives me a rush of endorphins like nothing else in my life does.

Maneuvering through the evening traffic, my mind is filled with thoughts of the young woman that has bewitched me. I went from being determined to end any sort of contact between us to agreeing to attend and planning this extravagant date. There's something special about her, I can't pinpoint what it is exactly, but all I know is that I want more of her every minute of every day. Her mother might not approve, but as long as Julia is still willing to see me, I won't deny her. Plus, compared to all the cutthroats I deal with at work, how scary can Margaret Van Dieren really be?

Julia is waiting for me outside of her building when I pull up, and seeing her makes my heart flip-flop in my chest. I step out of my car and make my way toward her, watching a warm, welcoming smile spread across her sweet face. My eyes are immediately drawn to her stunning figure; she is wearing a beautiful white blouse and a long flowing skirt that sways with every step she takes toward me. Her hair is tied back in a neat bun, a few strands fluttering loose around her face, and her makeup is subtle but elegant. I feel a surge of desire rush through me as I take her in, but tamp it down. It's much too early for anything like that to be occupying my thoughts.

"Glad to see that you made it," she says with a teasing voice. I can't help but admire her smile. It's the kind of smile that can make a man forget all of his problems for a little while, and that's exactly what it does for me.

I take her hand and lead her to my car, opening the door for her. "Yep, it wasn't easy but I managed to carve out some time for you this evening."

She chuckles in return, head shaking, her expression bright. "I suppose I should feel honored that the all-important Sebastian Van den Bosch cleared his schedule for someone like me, then."

I'm about to be just as sarcastic, but when our eyes lock, only the truth seems to come out. "You're one of the few people I will make time for, Julia." She smiles back at me but doesn't say a word, and I wait until she tucks her skirt into the car to shut the door so I can slide into the driver's seat.

Julia peppers me with questions about where we are going and what I have planned for the night, but I keep my responses vague, wanting to see the look of surprise on her face when we finally arrive. All the while, the scent of her perfume, florals and vanilla, drifts around us and makes it difficult for me to concentrate on anything else except for wondering how much sweeter she would smell if I could bury my face in the crook of her neck. I swallow hard, the thought much too tempting to humor for long. The last thing I want is for Julia to see me get hard just driving her to a date.

We drive for what feels like forever until we finally arrive at a picturesque canal, the water reflecting the buildings and the sky rapidly going orange with the sunset. A boat is waiting for us, slim and modern, with a canopy covering the dining table I had specifically added for tonight. The boat has been made cozy and intimate, with a spread of picnic foods like a variety of cheeses, fresh and dried fruit, a selection of cured meat, and sparkling champagne in tall flutes. Julia had wanted to have a picnic, so I made sure to turn it up a notch. This will be a picnic that she will never forget, I've made sure of it.

Our waiter and captain greet us at the ramp, and I take Julia's hand to help her walk down onto the deck.

"This is so incredible," she gushes, looking up at me with the most brilliant smile. "I can't believe you planned all this on such short notice!"

Once we are both inside, the boat moves gracefully away from the dock, and we sit down at the picnic table. The sun is beginning to set, casting a warm golden glow over the surroundings and sparkling on the water like a million little diamonds. I can see the admiration in Julia's eyes as she takes in the view, and the gentle sound of the water lapping on the side of the boat as we slowly cruise through the water as soothing as the gentle breeze.

Julia is obviously excited, looking in every direction as she slowly drinks her champagne, nibbling on a strawberry between drinks. I didn't think it was possible for her to be more beautiful, but the warm sunset colors suit her so well.

"So, was it worth it to switch from a picnic in the park to one here?" I ask, gesturing around us at the boat.

She turns to me, a huge grin on her face. "Absolutely. This is amazing. I've never had a picnic on a boat before."

I feel a sense of relief wash over me. I had been nervous about whether she would like this better or not, concerned that I had possibly gone a little overboard, but her reaction makes me feel like I've made the right choice.

Why does this woman make me second guess every single little decision I make? Funny how I can't think of this as anything but a date, considering that we both agreed to just be friends.

"How did you come up with this idea?" Julia asks, interrupting my thoughts. "I mean, I know we already talked about a picnic, but this is so much more unique."

"I just wanted to do something special for you," I reply with a smile. "And judging from how unenthused you were at the ball, I figured that you would prefer an outing away from the general public. Just you…" I reach across the table and take her hand, "and me."

"Well, you definitely succeeded," she says, giving my hand a playful squeeze. "You're going to have a hard time topping this when we go on our next date."

I raise my eyebrows at her statement. "Oh, you're so sure I want to take you on another date?"

She wrinkles her nose at me. "You'd better! I'm not a one date kind of girl."

"I thought we were just friends, though."

She snorts delicately, chewing another bite of fruit before responding. "I think we're both done kidding ourselves about that, Seb."

"Well… you're not wrong."

As we enjoy the champagne, peace settles over me. For once, I am not thinking about work or the stress that comes with it. All I can focus on is Julia, and how lucky I am to have her in my life. Friends…or more… I'll take whatever I can get from her, but if I'm being honest with myself, I know

I'll never be satisfied to sit back and let her walk out of my life. She's got me all tangled up inside, for better or for worse.

It's funny—we've had only a few meetups: the almost-kiss in the library, the chemistry-charged dance where we again almost kissed, and then the park outing, but I connect with Julia in a more genuine way than I ever have with anyone else. This is a woman with deep thoughts, desires, and an appreciation for love and marriage despite the ugliness of her parents' divorce. She's truly a diamond in the rough.

Julia looks at me with a soft expression, loose strands of hair dancing around her lovely face, and says, "I can't get over all of this. Wait until I tell Gabi what we did tonight, she's never going to shut up about it." She makes an amused sound, squeezing my hand again. "I didn't know you were such a romantic, Mr. Van den Bosch...."

I feel my body heat up at her words, and cough to try and cover up my flush, feeling once again like a teenager so far out of his league. I'm thirty-three for fucks sake, how can I be blushing like this in front of this girl!

The night progresses, and we talk about everything and nothing at the same time. The food is rich, sweet, and salty, and we empty one bottle of champagne and have the waiter bring out another rather quickly. We share stories, laugh, and enjoy the simple pleasure that comes with each other's company. For a brief moment in time, it feels like we are the only two people in the world, watching the sun disappear below the horizon and the sky go soft shades of purple and pink in the twilight.

We finish the meal and move to the cushioned bench seat at the back of the boat. I snag a throw blanket from one of the other seats and spread it across our laps to fend off any nighttime chill that might make Julia want to end the date early, and she gifts me with another cheek kiss when I do so, making my heart feel like it's stuttering in my chest.

"Like I said," she murmurs, snuggling into the seat next to me. "Such a romantic."

Feeling the warmth of her body and smelling the scent of her skin should make this one of the best moments of my adult life, but something about the things she's saying are making other, less comforting thoughts take flight in my mind. I can't shake the knowledge that she is only nineteen, but that pales in comparison to the largest problem that I can't seem to brush away—Julia thinks I'm such a romantic, but my mother used to say the same thing about my father. Am I just following in his footsteps, making this incredible woman fall in love with me knowing that my life will be consumed with the family business as I age? That is not the future I want, at all, but I'm also not sure how to avoid it, either. It almost feels like a family curse of sorts.

Julia looks up at me with a curious expression when I've been silent for a stretch of time. "Seb? You seem lost in thought. What's on your mind?"

I take a deep breath and decide to open up to her. It's not fair for us to continue this… well, whatever is happening between us, without her having full knowledge of what she's getting herself into. "It's just… well, you keep telling me how romantic this all is… and, um, my dad used to be a big romantic with my mom, too. They were so affectionate when I was a kid, even up until a few years ago, and it was beautiful to see. But now… I'm not sure. It seems like he's only in love with his work, and my mom has completely disconnected from him too."

Julia reaches for my hand once more and gives it a gentle stroke. "It must be tough to see your parents like that, growing apart. I can relate, trust me."

I nod my head, feeling a lump form in my throat. "It's just… they used to be so happy together. I don't know what went wrong."

Julia looks out at the water, contemplating her response. "Sometimes life can get in the way. Work can be consuming, and people change. It's important to make time for the people you love and nurture those relationships."

I take in her words, feeling grateful for her understanding. "You're right. Maybe I should talk to my dad and see if we can do something to bring them back together."

Julia smiles at me, her eyes sparkling in the moonlight. "I think that's a great idea. You have such a big heart."

I swallow past a suspicious tightness in my throat. "It really isn't fair for me to be saying all this to you when your parents went through such a nasty divorce. How can you be so open and wise about everything with all of that hanging over you?"

She shrugs one delicate shoulder. "I guess it gives me a different sort of perspective. I'm not sheltered from the truth by any sort of faked affection between my parents anymore… like I've had the blindfold pulled off fully. It's shown me exactly what I don't want from my marriage in the future."

"Maybe that's where you're better than I am, then, Julia," I tell her sincerely. "Because seeing my parents' marriage start to crumble has just made me feel jaded. So fucking jaded."

Julia leans in closer. "Is this why you've never been in a serious relationship before?" she asks, her voice barely above a whisper.

"How do you even know that?" I ask immediately, unable to hide my astonishment.

Julia gives me nothing but a side smile. "Just a hunch."

I hesitate for a moment, unsure if I should share my deepest thoughts with her. But then, looking into her eyes, I know that I can trust her. "Yes," I fess out, heaving a sigh. "I've never believed in 'forever love' given what I've seen at home and around me, which might explain my lack of interest in pursing a serious relationship with anyone."

"So you bring women on romantic dates just to sleep with them?"

Her blunt question makes me chuckle, and I can't help but smile in amusement as she stares intently at me. "I don't need to do any of this," I point out, glancing around the boat, "for anyone, really. If I want to have sex with someone, I just take them home and that's it."

Her lips twist into a smile I've never seen before and I know at this point she understands the meaning and depth of my confession. She reaches up to stroke my cheek, her touch soft and affectionate, leaving me yearning for more.

"When you find love, you have to nourish it, like a garden. Your parents might have had that forever love, but if they both let it die, then that's their fault. It's not a sign that you would do the same. The opposite, really, since you know better."

I smile at her, feeling grateful for her understanding. "God, are you sure you want to be a judge? I think you might have missed your calling as a relationship counselor."

She huffs a small laugh. “But honestly, I hope you’re right, because life seems pretty shallow if I have to go through the entire thing alone. Shallow, and boring.”

To my surprise, she lets out a quick giggle, her eyes twinkling at me. “Something tells me that life with you would be anything but boring, if a first date on a canal cruise is anything to go by.”

She leans her head on my shoulder, and her warmth and presence comfort me. Her words strike a chord, making me realize that I have been letting my father's actions dictate my beliefs about love and relationships. I’m not exactly ready to say that she’s changed my point of view irrecoverably, but it’s been a long time since I’ve heard someone speak of love and romance like she does. Not many other people around me still believe in it, I guess.

“You don't have to be like him, you know,” she says quietly. “And the woman you marry doesn't need to be like your mom. You get to choose your partner and the way your marriage plays out. Don’t make the mistake of repeating something that you’ve already watched fail, you know?”

I look down at her, wondering what I did to deserve such an angel spending her time with me, helping to fix the broken pieces of my belief in all things sweet and loving. “I know, but it’s hard not to be influenced by what you see growing up. It’s not like I never believed in love, but I find myself looking at all the other couples my parents’ age, and so many of them are in the same position as Mom and Dad. Still together but distant. Barely speaking, cordial instead of affectionate. You know the type. It feels like a fatality.”

Julia nods in understanding. “I get it. But you have to remember that your parents’ relationship is not a reflection of what's possible for you. My parents are divorced, and they had the worst relationship you can possibly imagine, but I don't let it define me. I know that if I get married, I will make it work."

I smile, heart swelling in my chest with affection for her. "You are very pure, Julia, but I'm afraid that life can screw even the purest people."

Julia raises herself up so we are face to face, her eyes searching mine. "Things can be different, Seb. And they will be, with the right person."

"You might be right," I say, pondering her words. "I don't want to be like him. I want more out of my life than to just be running a company and nothing else."

Julia scoots even closer to me. One more inch and she will basically be in my lap, and I have to take a few deep breaths to keep myself centered and not give into the urge to pull her against me. "I bet you're nothing like your father," she breathes. "You have a good heart and you know what you want. You just have to believe that love is worth fighting for."

I squeeze her hand, feeling a renewed determination to keep this woman with me. It might be foolish, but I don't mind feeling like a fool right now. "How can you say that? You barely know me."

"I don't know… it's hard to explain…." She pauses for a moment, her eyes locking onto mine. "And don't lie to me and say that you don't feel the same connection that I do. It feels like I've known you for years, Sebastian, not days."

She leaves me reeling with her words. I feel exactly the same, like I know Julia's heart, her mind, which is ridiculous if I look at it logically. I'm too old to be head over heels like this, too experienced in the real world, but being close to Julia makes all of my logic flee.

My body seeming to work on autopilot, I tuck a loose strand of hair behind her ear like I did the day we met in the library. Touching her feels like the most addictive thing in the universe. Julia's eyes go wide, her breath hitching, and I feel a sudden surge of emotions. Before I know it, our lips are touching, and she leans into me with a contented sound that has lightning flashing through my veins.

The kiss is soft at first, as if we're both unsure, but then it deepens. My head spins, pulse pounding in my ears, blood lighting on fire until I'm suffused with heat. With need.

Her lips are soft and warm against mine, my heart racing with excitement. I put my hand on her cheek, holding her face gently as we continue to kiss. Something inside me is screaming that I've been waiting for this moment my whole life, and I don't want it to end.

"*What are you doing?!*" my mind interrupts. "*You're going too fast!*"

Suddenly, a wave of guilt washes over me, and I pull away, apologizing profusely.

"God, Julia, I'm sorr–"

But to my surprise, she leans in for another kiss, and I can't resist her. We kiss again, and this time it's even more intense, like we're both trying to communicate something without words.

When we finally break apart, she looks at me with a sparkle in her eye, and I can tell that we're both thinking the same thing—this is just the beginning. Logic and overbearing parents be damned.

But the guilt is still there. She's so young. Was that her first kiss? Is she going to regret, someday, that her first kiss was with a thirty-three year old man? If it wasn't her first… who else was there in her life?

"Why did you apologize?" she asks, tilting her head to one side.

"I don't want to make your mom hate me." I pull the reasoning out of thin air. It's not exactly a lie, but I'm pretty sure that Margaret already hates me, and we both know it.

Julia waves my worries away dismissively. "Sebastian, you're worrying too much. My mom isn't here, and I'm not her. I'm my own person, and I'm allowed to make my own choices," she reassures me, placing a gentle hand on my arm.

"I know that, and I'm not trying to undermine your decisions, but if she hates me then things are just going to be messier between you and I."

She shakes her head, a wry smile on her lips. "Let it go. Better that she hates you than me, anyway, right?"

I groan, and she laughs. Pulling her in for one last, chaste peck on the mouth, I keep her in my arms while the captain of the boat brings us back to the dock.

"You're so special, Julia," I say, my voice barely above a whisper. "I feel so blessed to have met you. You're exactly the person I need to shake up my life."

Julia's cheeks flush a rosy pink, and I am certain a more beautiful creature has never walked this earth. God, she's so stunning.

"You're pretty special too, Seb," she says, her voice soft and gentle.

We sit there for a few moments, lost in thought. The sun is gone now, letting the stars twinkle in the sky amongst the sliver of the moon which hangs low. I take a deep breath of the cool, crisp air and feel a sudden need for the night to go on just a little bit longer. I want just a little bit more of Julia, before I release her back into her own life and reality sets in again.

Breaking the comfortable silence, I ask, "Hey, do you want to go for a walk?"

"Sure." Julia stands up and offers me her hand. "I think that would be lovely."

We carefully depart the boat and as we walk along the canal, we continue to talk, sharing stories about our childhoods and our dreams for the future. I can feel myself falling deeper and deeper for her with each passing moment, and I know that I want her in so many different ways. But Julia isn't a woman my age, experienced in life and the intricacies of dating and the odd social demands of doing so in our old money social circles. One slip up, and everyone around us will believe I'm taking advantage of the younger woman. So I'll have to be careful, treat this thing between us like it's made of glass, otherwise it'll shatter and I don't know if I will ever be able to pick up the pieces.

"What if I speak to your Mom?" I ask her as we continue strolling along the canal. "Maybe if she knew me, she wouldn't hate me so much."

Julia looks up at me, her eyes widening. "You'd go as far as meeting her for me?"

Her question makes me stop instantly in my tracks as if offended by it. I reach out for her hand, turning her around to face me. My eyes lock onto hers, and a wave of determination takes over me. "I'd go as far as meeting your whole family for you, Julia."

CHAPTER 8

Sebastian

Friday passes in a blur. I know in the moment that I'm doing all of my work and keeping up with my responsibilities at the office, but I feel like a machine, just getting everything sent out while I relive the night before over and over in my mind.

It'd be all too easy to call Julia and see if she wanted to get together again tonight, but I've promised myself that I will give our burgeoning relationship room to breathe. I've given up completely on the ruse of us just remaining friends, but I still have to be careful with her. It's a fine line that I'm walking with her, and the wrong move could have Margaret coming down on us both like a firestorm and then I might never see Julia again.

It's a stretch, sure, but everything that I've been told about Margaret Van Dieren makes me certain that she's not a woman to be messed with, and that she does nothing by half-measures. She probably considers hiding her daughter away from me a totally reasonable move.

Before leaving the building, though, I pass by my father's office. Given the glass wall, I can see him still working at this desk with his brow furrowed and a black coffee mug near his hand, steam rising out of it in curls as if it was just delivered to him. I frown, knowing that this all means that he'll be working late again, but what can I do? If I interrupt him, I might get dragged into his late night work session, and considering how I barely applied myself at all during the normal work day, I definitely don't want to be doing more.

On the other hand, I know that my mother will be waiting on him once more at home, spending her time alone with my younger siblings, probably wondering why she no longer is worth any of her husband's time. It makes my heart ache, but I've already asked Dad about his marriage, and he's blown me off effortlessly, so I think if I want to try and help my parents reconnect I'll have to speak to Mom about it instead.

Pushing away a wave of guilt, I turn around and walk away from Dad's office to the elevator, ready to head back to the family estate for the weekend and sort through the various problems that are plaguing me in the relative peace of my childhood home.

On the way out the door, I pass Karl, who has his arms still full of papers and is heading up into the building instead of out.

"Time to get going," I tell him, pointing to my watch, but Karl shakes his head.

"Your father asked me to stay and go over a few of my more recent sales with him. That's where I'm headed right now." He looks uncomfortable, as if I'm going to be annoyed that he's been tapped as the late-night partner for the evening. And maybe I am, a bit, but if he wants to talk sales then Karl is the obvious choice. I don't want to stay anyway, but the fact that I wasn't even asked….

"Make sure he doesn't stay too late, okay?" I tell Karl, clapping him on the shoulder in a friendly manner. "It's not good for his health. But don't tell him I said that."

Karl laughs nervously, but nods, eyes darting to the elevator. He's clearly in a hurry. "I'll do my best. Er… see you on Monday?"

"See you then, Karl."

Before I push the office door open to walk into the late evening air, I turn back and watch my father's new protégé hustling onto the elevator, and wonder if I feel bad for him, or guilty that I didn't make more of an effort to take his place. But then I let the door shut behind me and let the work day fall away from my shoulders.

I roll the windows down in my Aston Martin as I make the long drive back to my family's estate. I try my damndest not to think of my father still cooped up inside his office of his own volition, or the young man that he's roped into staying with him. It's none of my concern. Right now, I'm going home, and I'm going to talk to my mother to try and get to the bottom of the rift in my parents' marriage, before it's too late for them. Just like it was too late for Julia's parents.

***

I hand the keys to the car off to one of the house staff, unbuttoning the top few buttons of my shirt as I bound up the steps and into the estate home. I look up to the second floor and consider going to shower and change before speaking to my mother, but once she figures out that Dad isn't coming home on time, she may just retire to her quarters for the night, and I don't want to miss out on the opportunity.

"Where's Mom?" I ask a passing maid, who tells me that she's having a light evening meal out on the terrace. Both of my siblings are otherwise occupied, so this means that it's the perfect moment to speak to her in private.

So I skip the shower and outfit change, instead just rolling up my sleeves as I head out to the terrace. Decorated in a Mediterranean style with a number of plush seating areas and warm lighting from lit torches, the terrace is one of Mom's favorite places to get away from the world.

I find her right where I expect to, in the corner on a pillow-covered bench, under a canopy with a book in her hand. There's a half-empty charcuterie board next to her, and a glass of white sangria on the small end table. My heart swells seeing her here, doing the same things that she's always done, and for a second I'm transported back to my childhood. When I was small, she'd let me climb up next to her and snuggle into her side while she read, maybe covering us both with a soft blanket until I dozed off.

Now, though, I lean down to kiss her cheek in greeting, and she smiles warmly. "Good evening, darling. It's good to see you home."

I settle into a seat across from her, waving over one of the staff and having them bring me two fingers of whiskey. When Mom frowns, I add on a bottle of water, and she nods in approval. I roll my eyes as she immediately takes a drink of her own sangria, but I guess some things never change.

"I suppose you're alone," she states, her words spoken in a sigh. I know she's asking about Dad, in her own roundabout way.

"Yes, Mom. He's still at work." I pause, thinking before I continue. "I don't know when he'll be home either. I was afraid if I stopped to ask he'd drag me into staying late, too."

Mom takes a deep breath and her shoulders fall. She dog-ears the page of her book and sits it on the bench next to her, lifting the charcuterie board onto the table between us and waving at me to partake. I plan on ordering something more substantial once I'm done with our talk, but for the moment, I fold a sliver of fig into a piece of prosciutto and pop it into my mouth. My mother is like any other, and it makes her happy to watch me eat, and it also ascertains that she won't pinch my arm later and tell me that I need to eat more and work out less.

"That's alright, dear. I figured that he wouldn't be home on time. He never is." She waves her hand in the air in front of her, as if dismissing the subject. "I'm going to have a book club meeting in the morning over brunch, anyway, so I wouldn't want him to keep me up."

I know she's lying, but I don't mention it. "Sure." I help myself to another piece of meat and a slice of brie, chasing it with the whiskey when it arrives, to give myself some liquid courage before I start what I know is going to be an awkward conversation. "But in the same vein… Mom, can I ask you something?"

She looks up at me, giving me her full attention. "Of course. What is it?"

"Are you and Dad… God, I don't even know how to ask this. Are you and Dad like… okay? Things just seem so off between you two."

She blinks a few times, shocked, before gathering her thoughts and answering. "Yes, Seb. We're fine. Sure, I wish he didn't work so much, but—"

"I don't just mean that," I interrupt, causing her to squeeze her eyes in suspicion. "It's been like this for months, if not years. There seems to be no…romance, I guess, between the two of you. I know that him working so much overtime has a lot to do with it, but it just feels deeper than that, and it worries me."

Her gaze sharpens as she looks me over, pursing her lips. "Does this have anything to do with the parents of a certain lovely young woman you may have met at the ball? Because I assure you, there is nothing at all similar between myself and Margaret Van Dieren."

I groan, rubbing my face with my hands. "Mom, we both know that this oddness between you and Dad has been going on a lot longer than the amount of time that I've known Julia."

She waves her hands dismissively again. "Darling, don't worry about us. I'm sure there is quite enough on your plate without being forced to play relationship therapist for your parents."

I hate that she's trying to blow the entire subject off, but I know this must be a sensitive subject for her, so I try not to press too hard. But I do order a second drink upon finishing the first. "It's just… you guys don't seem to be in love at all anymore. I haven't seen you two kiss in years."

"Sebastian..." Mom reprimands slowly. "We're aging, and like all couples, those sorts of things begin to slow down." It's clear that she's lying to me, and maybe to herself, but I don't want to hurt my mother by calling her out on it. Especially if, like I suspect, she's trying to force herself to believe everything that she's telling me. "Just because you don't see us kissing doesn't mean that there is anything wrong. But enough about all that."

"Mom—"

"Hush, you. Since you got the chance to talk about uncomfortable things, now it's my turn, and I expect you to sit there and listen to me just like I did for you."

I can't help but roll my eyes, anticipating the worst. "Oh God...."

"I just think we should revisit the night of the ball, don't you? My son, the successful and handsome man that he is, has a single dance with the Van Dieren heiress and suddenly I have Margaret on my doorstep harping on how I should keep you away from her precious, innocent daughter." Mom laughs into her napkin, indicating to the server that she needs a fresh glass of sangria while plucking a blueberry from the empty glass and chewing on it. "You must have made quite the impression on the girl for all of that to happen. For someone who didn't want to go to that ball, you quickly changed your tune when you met Julia."

Another piece of brie and chutney goes into my mouth so I can stall, but my mother watches me expectantly with her hands folded in front of her, and I know I'm not getting out of this talk. Oh well, it had to be done anyway. "I took her out last night," I admit, gauging her reaction. "I swear that I tried to cut things off like you first suggested, but when I went to see her, she was pretty adamant that she didn't want us to stop speaking to each other. So, who am I to try and tell a woman what to do?"

Mom isn't amused by the joke. "Sebastian. I don't blame you for being attracted to the girl and taking her out, but Margaret isn't one to mess with. Julia is *quite* young for you, I have to agree with Margaret there, but the age difference doesn't strike me as being as much of a problem as the fact that Julia's mother clearly doesn't approve of the match."

I shake my head. "I'm not afraid of her. And after spending time with Julia last night… well, it's safe to say that things are going pretty well between us."

Mom blanches. "Please tell me you didn't sleep with that girl."

I choke on my drink. "Mom! No! Christ…." I down some water and catch my breath.

"Then how well, exactly, Sebastian? I was just poking fun at first. I had no idea that you were really dead set on pursuing Julia."

I inhale slowly before speaking, my throat still burning. "I'm thinking of setting up a meeting with Margaret myself and telling her that I'm serious about her daughter."

Mom blinks in confusion. "How serious?"

"Well, you know… serious enough to get engaged and all that."

Any color that had started to make its way back into my mother's cheeks flees once more, leaving her looking pale and shaken. "What! Darling, you barely know the girl. This is going to be the most troublesome partner that you could possibly have chosen. There are plenty of other—"

I shake my head once, quickly. "No, Mom. There is no other Julia. And I find it funny that you and Dad are always harping on me to find someone to settle with and when I do, there is suddenly an issue with it."

"Sebastian, love, I want nothing more than for you to be happy. But I just don't think you understand the depth of difficulty you're getting yourself into. Margaret is *very* protective of her children, and it's common knowledge that it is unlikely for there to ever be someone that she considers a good match for any of them unless she hand-picks them herself. Margaret is a fierce, dangerous woman, and I just don't want you to be caught up in her web if this thing you have with her daughter is just some sort of passing fancy."

I struggle to understand everything that she's saying. Thus far, Margaret has just been on the sidelines, disapproving but not interfering with the time I've been spending with her daughter. I guess there's the possibility that she doesn't know anything about it, but still.... Everyone keeps talking like getting past the woman will be impossible.

"This isn't a passing fancy, Mom. It's not a game, either. I'm going to propose because that will show Margaret that I'm utterly serious about her daughter. Even if she doesn't like me, our family reputation is almost flawless and a marriage uniting us all will be nothing but beneficial. And I will make her daughter happy, whether she believes that or not."

"Not even a proposal will help, Seb," Mom sighs, sounding oddly defeated. "Margaret didn't pick you, and she finds you too old. Once she makes up her mind then that is that."

Anger is beginning to spread in my chest, making it hard to breathe. The last thing I want to do is snap at my mom, but the fact that she keeps insisting that my situation is hopeless makes me want to scream. Surely Margaret can't deny her daughter forever, and I know that Julia wants to be with me just as badly as I want to be with her. Ultimately, Julia is an adult, so while I understand the importance of parental approval, I can't imagine that it would prevent us from getting engaged in the long run.

"I don't get it," I fume. "Doesn't she think our family is honorable enough? We come from nobility just like her family does."

Mom reaches across the table and pats my hands comfortingly. "No, Seb, I don't think it's that. Margaret went through a hell of a divorce, and it was *very* public despite her wishing otherwise, and it was incredibly messy and sad for her. I think it made her paranoid about any sort of match made because of love, and not just duty. She probably doesn't believe in love anymore, if I'm being honest."

Just like what I told Julia last night about how I don't believe in forever love. Huh. What a weird coincidence.

"I'll figure out a way to convince her," I insist, even when Mom shakes her head.

"Just be careful, darling," Mom says, standing to kiss me on both cheeks and hug me before I head back inside and leave her to her book. I'm tempted to just spend the rest of the evening out here with her, talking about easier things, knowing that she's lonely without my father, but I have a lot to think about. I make a promise to myself to take my mother out somewhere soon, just the two of us, since it's becoming obvious that my father isn't going to treat her correctly on his own.

I'm tossing around the idea of calling some friends over to play billiards and have some drinks so I can bounce ideas about Julia off some other men my age who may have gone through similar things, when I see Freddie bounding up to me out of the corner of my eye. I sigh internally, watching him run in my direction with all the energy of a golden retriever and an equal amount of excitement.

"Seb," he calls. "Hey, Seb!"

I turn reluctantly, crossing my arms as he reaches me, grinning from ear to ear. "What, Fred?"

"Hey, so, like, I was wondering...." He rakes a hand through his hair, showing his nerves, and I already know what he's about to ask. "I have a date tonight and—"

"No."

His face falls immediately. "You don't even know what I was going to ask...."

"Okay," I raise my eyebrows at him. "How about this... if you were going to ask me anything besides, 'Can I take the Aston?' then I will automatically say yes. So, what is it?"

Freddie scoffs. "Whatever, man. You never let me drive the DB5. All I want to do is impress this girl...."

"We have literally a garage full of cars, most of them you are fine to drive, and you just want to obsess over the single one that is mine alone that I don't want you to touch. It's vintage, and you drive like an asshole. Get over it."

"But—"

My brother isn't a kid anymore technically, but I still grab him and ruffle his hair until he yells and struggles for me to let him go. "That car is my baby, Fred, so just drop it. I'm sure this girl will love whatever you drive."

He leaves cursing my name, fixing his hair as he goes, and I can't help but laugh. My 1965 Aston Martin DB5 has become an obsession with my little brother, but as much as I love him, I still don't trust him. One day, though, I might.

It's just not going to be tonight.

CHAPTER 9

Julia

I hesitate in front of my apartment door, bag in hand, considering if I even want to go back home for the weekend or not. Normally, home is a welcome respite from the busy and sometimes chaotic city and University life, but today is different.

I have seen Sebastian two days this week, and yesterday was obviously a date. Knowing my mother, there is no way that she isn't aware of this. I don't want to have to explain myself or argue with her, but it's not like I can avoid it forever. Plus, I know I'm not seeing Sebastian this weekend anyway, because he told me himself that he was going back to his own family estate for the weekend, hopefully to talk to his parents about the gradual distance growing between the two of them.

I think about my parents' own divorce, and my stomach clenches. That is something I'd rather not revisit right now, if possible.

Blowing out a long breath, I flick the lights in my apartment off and make the decision to go ahead and face my mother. I can't avoid this confrontation, but I can attack it head on, and hopefully get an upper hand that way.

One of the family drivers is waiting for me outside, and blessedly has a bottle of Perrier chilled and in the cupholder for me when I get in. My mouth is dry from nervousness, and rolling the bottle over my heated forehead after drinking some is a relief.

I practice the conversation I'm going to have with Mom in my head multiple times on the drive home through the countryside, hoping to be able to have a mental script ready as soon as I get there. She's so sharp and intelligent that it's easy for her to talk over me and railroad me on any subject that I'm not totally prepared for, and I can't risk her being able to get a leg up on me when the subject of this talk is so very important to me.

Thinking back to last night, being hip to hip with Sebastian and the way he kissed me so gently, only makes me even more sure that I have to succeed in convincing Mom that our match is a good one. I have to make her believe that Sebastian and I getting together officially is inevitable.

On a whim, I message my brother Alex, who told me earlier in the week that he might be spending the weekend at home too: *Did you make it home, and if so, where is Mom?*

Alex: *Nice to talk to you too, J. Anyway, Mom was in her suite last time I saw her.*

I exhale slowly. Okay, so she is home. I guess this conversation really is going to happen today.

When we arrive, I waste no time with anything else, just go upstairs and walk the long hallways to the master suite that Mom has all to herself these days. The door is closed, and I bite my lip, considering whether to knock or just enter. Ultimately, I knock, since I know I would want her to do the same if it was the other way around.

"It's Julia," I call through the door preemptively.

"Come in, dear!" Mom responds, and I do just that, pushing open the heavy wood door that opens into the sitting area of her suite.

Mom is seated at her small marble breakfast table, which is covered now in a cloth to protect it as she receives a manicure from a nail technician I don't recognize. With her hands otherwise occupied, my mother greets me with a smile, nodding toward the empty chair next to her. My heart is pounding as I sit down, twisting the hem of my shirt in my hands as I do so.

"Did you have a good week at school?" she asks, her tone friendly. I can't tell if she knows about the time spent with Sebastian or not, so I don't know if she's trying to trick me into a lie. My mother always plays these ridiculous games, and it makes my anxiety spike.

"It was fine," I tell her as I sit on the edge of my chair. "Glad to be off for the weekend though."

"Indeed…" she drawls, taking a look at her nails, before her eyes flicker back to me. "Any plans for the weekend, dear?"

I shake my head. "Just relaxing…. Er, it looks like you're doing the same," I reply, nodding to her nails. The nail technician just raises her eyebrows, buffing my mother's fingernails silently.

"I didn't feel like going out, so I just decided to get my weekly manicure at home instead." She sighs, pausing for a moment to catch her breath. "It's nice, but I do miss the spa."

Why are we talking so much about nothing? I think but out loud just tell her, "Oh, I bet."

A few minutes stretch, filled just with vague questions about my class work and upcoming projects, before my Mom finally strikes. "So… when were you going to mention the beautiful flowers you received on Tuesday?"

I shrug one shoulder, trying to play nonchalant. "I didn't think much of it."

"You didn't think much of receiving roses *in class*?" she demands, vitriol creeping into her tone. The nail tech starts to work faster. "That is not what you are in school to be doing, Julia. All it is is a giant distraction."

"It's like I asked to get them in the middle of a lecture," I gripe, and Mom just sneers.

"And I assume they were from Sebastian Van den Bosch, hm?"

"They were," I confirm, squaring my shoulders for what is surely about to be a fight. "What of it?"

"Ha!" she barks, turning her eyes to the other side just for a brief moment. "Only that I've already told you that you're forbidden from messing around with that *grown man,* and here he is sending you roses. My girl, men don't send roses just because. What exactly have you been doing to have him so smitten?"

My mouth falls open in shock. "Mom, what exactly are you implying?"

The nail tech finishes, drying my mothers' hands and massaging lotion into them as quickly as she possibly can before she starts to clean up. Once my mother has her hands back, she points one long, freshly manicured finger in my direction. "I'm implying that you've been sneaking around with that pervert, because I know that you have."

I roll my eyes and cross my arms right as the manicurist disappears out of the bedroom door and Mom and I are truly alone. "Oh, come on, Mom. We went for a walk in the park and a boat ride. That's all. Nothing so nefarious as what you're trying to say I've been doing."

"So you have or haven't slept with Sebastian?" she demands.

"I *haven't*," I hiss, quite offended that she even had to ask in the first place. "But with the way you're taking this, it's unlikely I'd tell you the truth even if I did!"

She sucks in a breath, standing in a flash so she looms over me. "I know you think you're grown, Julia, but you are far from it. You're being naive and selfish, and this match is simply not going to happen, no matter how much you moan and complain. This is my home, and you are my daughter, and it's about time that you remember that."

I rear back as if slapped. "I'm my own person, Mom! Sebastian is a good man, and he's been nothing but a gentleman to me thus far, but you still insist on calling him a pervert and insinuation that I'm an idiot for believing that he's a good man."

Mom sinks back into her seat and folds her hands in front of her, trying to keep her composure after snapping. "I was like you once, Julia, and look at where it got me. Alone, and humiliated in front of my peers. Connecting with someone out of some misguided notion of love will only lead to pain and heartache later in life. I refuse to let that happen to you."

"You have to let me make my own mistakes," I insist, yet the memories of her painful divorce making headlines bring tears to my eyes. "I know if you wanted to, Sebastian would talk to you himself. Maybe that would make you—"

She slashes her hand in the air, cutting me off. "Absolutely not. All I have to do is look at his father, up in his ivory tower at Van den Bosch Industries at all hours of the day and night, to see your future if you are with Sebastian. You're foolish to think that it wouldn't be the same if you, God forbid, married him. He'd be shackled to his job first and foremost, and you would always come second."

"That's not true!" I lean across the table, wanting her to hear every word I'm saying. "We talked about exactly that, Mom, and the last thing Seb wants to be is anything like his father when he gets older. He'll be a loving, doting husband and will never put his job before—"

"Before who?" she snaps, her eyes fixed on mine. "Before *you,* Julia? Because you see yourself as his wife in the future? Ha!"

Furious at the way she keeps belittling what I have to say, I slam my hands on the marble table and stand, yelling my next words louder than I intended. "If he wanted me to be his wife, I would say yes! And there is nothing you can do about it!"

Cold as ice, my mother searches my face with her eyes. She's silent for long minutes, to the point where I fidget uncomfortably where I stand, my pulse starting to pick up with the slightest edge of fear.

"Nothing I can do about it, *hm*?" she says coolly. "Well, we will see about that, but for the moment, I am done hearing about your ridiculous love affairs and how you're ruining your future for some idiot. So, get out of my suite and don't bring this up to me again, do you hear me?"

"But Mom," frustration is building inside me to an unbearable level, "why can't you just talk to him? He wants to speak to you one on one, so he can show you who he really is. You don't even really know Sebastian, why can't you just give him a chance?"

She stands up from her seat and brushes past me, ignoring what I'm saying and dismissing me without saying another word. It's hard to not cry right here and now, but I won't give her the satisfaction of knowing that she's won. Because she hasn't. There is no way I'm going to stop seeing Sebastian just because she demands it. If that means I'm going to have this strained, terrible relationship with my mother from here on out, then so be it.

When I'm sure that she isn't coming back, I storm out of the room, all but running to my own suite while desperately blinking away tears. Mom has always been controlling and overbearing, but never like this! Never to the point that she would ruin my chance at happiness just so she can win and have her way. She'd rather that I be miserable than have to admit that she's wrong.

Maybe I'll just go back to Amsterdam for the weekend, call Gabi, and order takeout while I cry my heart out to my friend. It sounds better than staying here under the same roof as the woman who wants to ruin any chance of romance that I may have, but I'm on the verge of bawling my eyes out and shaking from the stress of it all, so I'm in no mood to leave right this second anyway.

I slam my bedroom door behind me and launch myself onto my freshly made bed, laying face down and letting the sobs wrack my body. I cry out of sadness, knowing that Mom will never approve of Sebastian, but also out of pure, unfiltered anger at her. For nearly a year now she has talked about two things only: me graduating university and me finding an appropriate *prospect*. The list of men that she finds appropriate for me has been told to me over and over, but not a single of them interests me at all. Mom isn't trying to find me a husband that will be compatible with me, but instead is trying to find the man that most benefits the family if I marry him. Her choices have also been full of meek, spineless, boring men. Not all of them, of course, but a majority of them have seemed so blasé that I'm exhausted just hearing their names.

It's clear why she chooses the way she does—my mom obviously doesn't believe in love anymore, after what my father did to her. She's always been a hard-edged, relentless woman, but Dad leaving her has also made her cruel. I feel like I don't even know the woman that I just argued with. If she wasn't my mom, I would be frightened of her. She's just that cold now.

A soft knock comes from the door, and for a single bright moment, I think it might actually be Mom coming to apologize. But then I hear a much deeper voice speaking from the hallway.

"Hey, Julia. Can I come in?"

I sit up, dragging my forearm over my face, thankful I didn't have mascara to smear all over my face today. I sniffle once before answering. "Alright Alex, come on."

My twenty-year-old brother looking like a grown man is still a surprise to me every time I see him, but when he sits on the side of the bed and gives me a playful nudge on the arm I know he's still the same annoying Alex. He's always been a good older brother, if a bit sarcastic at times, and I'm sure he's had his own issues with Mom before too, so I'm not embarrassed asking him for advice.

"Do you need like, a hug or something?" he asks, and I snort.

"I guess that means you heard us fighting, then."

"The entire household heard you fighting, J, and that includes the horses outside in the stables." He chuckles, while still giving me a comforting pat on the arm. "But that's okay. We've all had our rows with Mom. It's a rite of passage or something I'm sure."

"This isn't like getting in trouble for breaking curfew or something," I tell him, exasperated. "This is a decision that will affect my adult life forever, and Mom is refusing to even hear me out."

"Just to play the devil's advocate, nineteen is a little early to be making life-changing decisions, don't you think?"

"I firmly believe that when you know, you know," I tell him, trying to sound confident, "And I just *know* Sebastian is the right one for me."

"Even if Mom was totally normal, she'd still be apprehensive about this, Julia. He's so much older than you, and you aren't even twenty yet. You've never had a serious boyfriend, and now you're basically ready to run to the altar with him. Combine that with the fact that Mom is anything but chill about anything these days, and well…" he laughs sardonically, his eyes flicking up and down at me. "You get this whole mess."

"But she's been trying to set me up with guys all year," I insist, but Alex shakes his head.

"Guys, Julia. Not men in their thirties mere years from taking over a multi-million dollar company. It's different, and you know it."

"Ugh!" I flop back on the bed. "Why is Mom so fucking against him, though? Don't even pretend that she wouldn't be acting the same way if he was twenty or whatever. It's just insane. What did he ever do wrong to her?"

"Well, he was born male, and that's already an issue for Mom," Alex teases, but it doesn't lift my mood any. "Honestly, though, I wouldn't bother myself with Mom's opinion if I were you. The Van den Bosches are a good family, and Mom didn't seem to have any problem with them until Seb showed interest in you."

He seems pretty comfortable with the idea of me dating Sebastian, I think, pushing myself back up into the sitting position and considering my brother for a moment. "So... you'd be okay with me marrying Sebastian? You approve?"

Alex balks, his jaw dropping at my question and he takes a step back. "Jesus, Julia, *marriage*? It's been like a week since you met the guy." He rubs the back of his neck, looking at the ceiling. "I mean, if you guys had a normal courting period, then sure. Sebastian is a stand up guy as far as I'm concerned, and he hasn't done anything to raise any red flags for me."

Sensing that I have Alex right where I want him, I strike. If I can use my brother to my advantage, I just might have a chance to convince Mom. She'll have a much harder time telling him no, I think. "Okay, then I need a favor from you. I need you to talk to Mom and tell her just what you told me, that you approve of Sebastian, and make her understand that he's the man that I want and it's in everyone's best interest if she just accepts that we're going to be together."

Alex stands now, pacing the length of my room while raking his hand through his hair. "Julia, you barely know him. How can you possibly know he's the right man for you? That's crazy."

"Don't you believe in true love, Alex? I *know* he's the one. I know it in my heart and soul. Please help me," I beg, clasping my hands together. Alex stops, looks at me for a long moment, and curses under his breath.

"Fine. I still think you're going about this the wrong way, and that you should just stop worrying what Mom thinks, but if you're serious I will see what I can do. I'm not making any promises, though. Mom isn't exactly an easy person to convince about anything these days."

I leap from the bed and wrap my arms around my brother's neck. "Thank you, Alex!"

"I hope we're both right about Sebastian being a good man," he huffs. "Otherwise, we're both going to look like idiots."

CHAPTER 10

Sebastian

Hey, I've got a few hours free tomorrow. Shall we meet at the Amsterdamse Golf Club. Say, 9:30 AM?

Nothing else. No phone call, no follow-up message once I confirmed, nothing. Just that single text, and I'm expected to just show up and play nine fucking holes with Alexander Van Dieren, Margaret's oldest? Sure, Julia is nothing like her mother, but there is no way for me to say the same about the other siblings. The young man isn't totally foreign to me, of course, given how close he is to a common friend—Jan DeVries—but it's not like Alex and I are confidants either. He's an acquittance at best.

Now I have this cryptic message from him and I'm supposed to… what exactly? Just hang out?

I guess so. Which is why I'm here, despite my better judgment, at Amsterdamse Golf Club on a Thursday morning with my father's clubs on my back since I don't even own my own set. Inside, the teenager behind the counter tells me that someone has rented out the entire course for the morning, but once I give him my name he tells me that Mr. Van Dieren is waiting at the first hole for me.

The day is clear and crystal blue, not a single cloud in the sky, which is quite unusual for mid-October, and I pull my aviator sunglasses over my eyes before stalking out onto the garishly green grass to find Alex. It's not hard, since he's the only one out here, leaning against a rented golf cart and holding a metal water bottle, looking bored.

Alex is a hair taller than I am, with the same piercing sapphire eyes that his mother has, which are somehow muted to a sweet cornflower blue in Julia. He watches me approach, dressed in white golf shorts and a salmon polo, but somehow he still looks intimidating as hell. I know I'm much older than he is, but that doesn't make me any less uneasy. It isn't that Alex frightens me—far from it—but I've not exactly made a good impression with the rest of Julia's family thus far, and making a good impression with her oldest brother is becoming more important to me by the minute.

"Sebastian," he says in greeting, standing up straight and offering me his hand. I take it and we shake, Alex's grip firm. "Nice to see you again. It's been a while."

"Good to see you too," I respond when we drop hands and I lug my clubs to the golf cart and throw them inside. "Before we get started, I should warn you: I've only played a few times in my entire life."

"I'm not an expert either," Alex admits, giving me a comforting smile. "I just thought it'd be a crime not to go out and enjoy such a sunny morning."

I relax a little, knowing that this golf game isn't going to be a real competition. "Good to hear."

We both take drivers from our bag and Alex sets his ball, hitting it and making it fly. He shades his eyes with his hand and watches it go, stepping aside for me next.

"I assume you know why you're here," he states while I get my ball set up.

"Not just for a friendly game between men, I'd hope," I quip, and Alex snorts.

"Julia has dragged me into this thing the two of you have going on, and asked me to talk to Mom about the two of you and try to get her to change her mind," Alex tells me as I square up to hit the golf ball. "I know of you, but I don't *know* you, so I figured we should meet."

I hit the ball, and it flies far, if a bit crooked. "Trying to get an idea of who your sister is dating, maybe intimidate me a little bit?"

Alex shakes his head while he climbs into the golf cart. I take the other seat and he drives us to our balls. "Not exactly. Man to man, I think I need to give you some hard truths that my sister both won't accept and wouldn't tell you even if she did; our mother is never going to approve of this union. Ever. So you both either need to let it go or come to terms with the fact that if you want to continue, you're going to be doing so against Mom's wishes and then… well… may God help you."

I cringe, watching and following Alex's lead as we continue to play while we talk. "I know she doesn't like me, maybe because of the age thing, maybe because she doesn't know me, but I haven't let that stand in my way so far."

The other man levels me with a serious look. "Yes, but imagine how much harder it is for Julia to just brush whatever Mom says aside. She's her mother, and probably the closest person to Julia in the world. It's killing her inside that she doesn't approve. Is that what you want?"

I hit my ball once more and shake my head at Alex. "No, man, it's not, but I'm also not going to be the type of person to break up with Julia 'for her own good'. I respect your sister enough to let her make her own decisions, and so far she's decided to stick with me."

He asks me a few more surface level questions as we move across the course, and I can feel my blood pressure rising with each one. There's something he's not saying and I wish he'd just hurry up and drop whatever bomb he's holding so we can all move on with our day.

"Alex," I snap finally, "I'm going to continue to see your sister until she doesn't want to see me anymore or until we get married. That's it. Did you have anything to add, besides telling me that your mom hates me? Because I already know that."

He drags a frustrated hand through his hair, shoving his club back into his bag harder than necessary. "Fine, let's just get on with it, then. I assume, like everyone else, you know that my parents are divorced?"

It had been a scandal so large, when Lord Hendrik and Lady Margaret had split, that everyone in our social circles knew about it. It's not as if I keep up with gossip like that, but it was such prevalent information that I found out without even trying to.

"Yeah, I know of it," I admit, not sure why it's even relevant.

Alex crosses his arms, and I see that he's full to bursting with anxious energy. It gives me pause, because nothing that we've talked about thus far has given him any reason to feel this way. I watch his expression closely as he begins to speak, and I pay closer attention than I have all morning. Whatever he's about to tell me is important, and I think it's information that's going to be brand new to me.

"What you don't know is that I haven't heard from my father for a long time." Alex shoves his hands in his pockets and looks up at the sky while he speaks. "Mom found out he was having an affair, and they fought, and fought, and fought… then the divorce followed. After that, Dad was just gone." Alex laughs, but there is no humor in it, just pain. "Supposedly, according to the media and my mother, he left the Netherlands out of shame to live with his lover or whatever. But if that was the case, why has he never called? And why won't my mom tell me where he is?"

A cold finger drags itself down my spine. "What are you trying to say?"

He fixes me with that deep blue stare. "I'm not going to spell it out for you, man, because I think you know what I'm saying. I'm sure people have told you things like, 'Margaret is dangerous' or, 'Margaret isn't one to be messed with', right? I think you understand what I'm getting at. I haven't spoken to my father since he… left."

Goosebumps come over me and I shiver, a tiny seed of fear burying itself in my chest. Is he really insinuating that Margaret did something to permanently get rid of her ex-husband who humiliated her publicly and broke her heart?

"That's… that's heavy," I say finally, not sure how else to express how insane everything he's just told me is.

"There are rumors, of course, but no one knows that our father hasn't contacted… or been able to contact us… since the divorce. So I need you to know that everything I've just told you is a secret, and you need to pretend to know nothing about it from here on out. If I learn that you've been telling people what I just said, then I don't care if God himself comes out of the sky and tells me that you and my sister are soulmates, I'll still make sure you never see her again."

I nod once. "I understand. Clearly that's a family matter anyway and none of my business…" I struggle to find anything to say, wanting to laugh hysterically as Alex suggests we continue playing the game. After a few more hits, I can't help but blurt out. "What the fuck, man. I'm still trying to wrap my head around everything. You really think your mom…?"

Alex takes a deep breath, hiding whatever emotion he must be feeling. "All that I know is that I've underestimated my mother my whole life, and I can confidently say that I have no idea what she is really capable of. She scares me, and I hate that. My own mother scares me." He blows out a long breath. "So if you ever needed a reason to just walk away from Julia, this is it. I don't think anyone wants to get tangled up in our family after everything with Dad. Julia will understand."

I pause with the putter in my hands and stand up straight. "I never said I was done with her."

"Are you seriously saying that after everything I've just said, you're still interested in dating my sister? I mean, as of right now, you are my Mom's main antagonist in her life. It's not exactly a good place to be, Sebastian."

"I don't care about that, to be frank. I know you're going to say it's impossible, just like everyone else has, but I really have feelings for Julia, and rumors be damned, I still plan on meeting your mother and talking to her about it. I'm keen to ask Margaret for Julia's hand, and even if she refuses, I'm still going to propose down the road. But I have to try and do it the right way."

Alex looks like he can't believe the words I'm saying, shaking his head in disbelief. "You barely know her. You have met her, what, like three times?"

I smirk at him, but he frowns. I don't hold it against Alex that he doesn't believe me when I say I'm serious about his sister… hell, it still shocks me to admit it to myself… but it makes complete sense that he wouldn't understand right away. He's just trying to protect Julia, and I respect him for that immensely. But it still won't stop me from pursuing the woman that I know is the one for me.

"I knew the day that I met her that she was the one. I can't really explain it, but it just feels obvious to me. And I think it's that way for her, too." I smile, remembering the jolt that had gone through me seeing her for the first time in my family library. "You can be sure I will take good care of her for the rest of our lives if she'll have me. It's as simple as that."

He narrows his eyes, crossing his arms, and looks like he's deep in thought. Finally he mutters, "Fuck…okay, you know what? It still makes zero sense, but I believe you. Your heart is in the right place, at least."

"Thanks, Alex. You don't have to go to war for us or anything, but it's at least good to know that Julia's *entire* family doesn't hate me at least," I say with a chuckle. "Maybe I can win you all over one at a time."

"Ha. Well, good luck with Mom, anyway." He pats me on the back, looks around at the green field, and we both realize at the same time that we have no idea what hole we are on.

"You just want to call this game and be done with it? Because I do."

"Hell yes. This was some deep talking for a round of golf," I tell him, despite my laugh.

Alex and I gather our things, and he drives us in the cart back to the main building. My mind is swimming with thoughts about the crazy things Alex has just told me, but I'm comforted by his approval of Julia and I. At least I'm leaving on a positive note.

In the parking lot, Alex extends his hand and we shake once more. "We should go hunting some time," he suggests. "I've heard you're a good hunter."

"I'd like that." The invitation makes me smile and I realize how much in common we might actually have. "Thanks for this, Alex. I appreciate it. It certainly couldn't have been easy."

"It wasn't," he admits, his expression just as light. "You know, I sort of wish that I didn't actually like you as much as I do, because now I really do have to try and convince Mom to accept you and my sister. It's going to be a shit-show."

"And I appreciate that, too."

"You'd better," Alex scoffs and then chuckles. "See you around."

***

I drive back to my apartment to change for work, and make it just in time for the meeting my father has scheduled for us. Yet another damn meeting… they seem to never end. I'm just tightening my tie as I walk into Dad's office, but stop short when I see the chair across from his desk already occupied by Karl.

"Should I come back later?" I ask him, slightly taken aback. Karl turns quickly to look at me but my dad just shakes his head.

"No, son. We're about finished here, anyway."

So I stand in the hallway and wait for Karl to exit, about two minutes later. He greets me only briefly before leaving towards what I can only assume is his own office, ready to do whatever task Dad has given him.

Once I take the previously occupied seat, I relax. Dad seems to be in a decent mood—happy, even, so maybe I won't be here for all that long.

My father's office reflects his taste well, with heavy, hand crafted furniture and the walls painted a deep green with wood accents. His bookshelves are full to overflowing, but some of the shelves are dusty. He doesn't have much time to read these days.

"That kid, Karl…. he's going to go far," Dad starts whispering, a small smile creeping across his face. "I'm telling you right now, he's the real deal. He's bringing in more business than his entire department. Make sure to treat him well, alright?"

"*This again?*" I think, but repress the groan that tries to sneak out. "I've been doing that, Dad. Ever since you told me to last time."

"Ah, that's right." Dad flips through some papers on his desk, and then leans back in his chair, steepling his fingers. "Karl and I were just discussing something that I want to run by you, son. He has this great idea that we should take our best clients on a hunting trip in Hungary in search of red deer. Most of our clients are actually hunters, and those who don't hunt will still have a great time getting fresh air and fishing." He raises his eyebrows, and when I don't respond, he asks, "What do you think?"

"In Hungary? Why Hungary?"

"Your Uncle Leopold has a big estate there surrounded by forest and lakes. It's the perfect hunting ground, and, by extension, the trip would be the perfect opportunity to discuss expansion with them."

The idea sounds… fine, I guess. A little over the top, but not a horrible option all things considered. "And I suppose, since it was Karl's idea, he'll be coming, too?"

"Of course," Dad huffs, before leaning forward, his elbows resting on the desk. "The man is the one who suggested it, after all."

I frown. It's very convenient for Karl to suggest this extravagant trip and then also get to go on it with all of us, even though the sales department has very little to do with the prospect of expansion. Dad seems to read my thoughts on my face, and exhales slowly.

"Seb, I know what you're thinking, but the kid comes from nothing. He didn't have a silver spoon in his mouth growing up like you and your siblings. He was raised by a single mother… he didn't have an easy childhood by any means. I want you to treat him right." I open my mouth to explain, yet again, that I've been doing just that, but Dad isn't finished. "I already gave him a big bonus, and do you know what he did with it? He bought a home for his mom. Completely selfless… that's the type of person you want to surround yourself with, trust me on this."

"I do trust you, Dad. It's just that we've never done anything like this, and all of a sudden it's just happening? I'm just a bit thrown off… but fine. Who all is coming? Are Mom, Adelina, and Fred coming too? It'd be great to have them with us."

His brow furrows and his lips flatten. "What, on a business trip? No. Plus," he laughs sardonically, "your mother will be more than happy to get rid of me for a few days."

Reminded once more of the tension between my parents, I jump on the opportunity to ask Dad the same things I did Mom. "Speaking of that… are you and Mom doing okay? You guys seem so distant from each other. Maybe you should consider bringing her with you on the trip, business or not…."

"Ah, Seb, don't worry about any of that. After thirty-six years together it's more than normal that things aren't as cute and romantic as they once were," he says dismissively, but if I'm not mistaken, I sense a thread of vulnerability in his words.

"*Is that really normal?*" I think to myself. "*I hope that it's never like that for me. I always want there to be romance.*"

"If you say so… but you know you can talk to me, Dad. I won't tell Mom if you want to keep things between us." He doesn't answer, just fidgets with things on his desk, and I sigh. "Fine, though. When is the trip happening?"

"We leave next Thursday."

I temper the quick hit of shock I'm feeling. "Damn, Dad, that's no time. Surely we can take some more time to prepare and what not."

"Next Thursday is what works for Leopold, so that's what we're doing," he tells me, a sense of finality in his words. "I'll email you all the details so you can prepare."

Reeling, I leave my Dad's office. *Seven damn days! What the hell!* I can't believe that my Dad would not only be okay with leaving so quickly, but that he will actually tear himself away from the office long enough to go hunting. Maybe he justifies it in his mind because it's technically a trip for work.

Mom is going to be devastated. I bet he didn't even run it by her, which means I'll have to be the one to break the news.

On the way back to my office, I pass Karl's and pause. On a whim, I knock on the open door frame, and he looks up quickly.

"Can I come in?" I ask upon seeing him.

"Sebastian." Karl rises at once from his chair and nods politely. "Of course. Sit anywhere you'd like."

After closing the door behind me, I go and take the seat across from him, while looking quickly around the room to get a better idea about the man who is rocketing upwards in the family company at record speed. The office is sparse, but there are a few things that give me a hint about Karl's personality—pictures of who I can only assume are his mother and maybe grandmother, books like *Think and Grow Rich* and other business-oriented literature, and a few black and white paintings by an artist I don't recognize.

"How did your meeting go?" he asks me, and I notice he's jittery. It's immediately apparent why, from what he says next. "I assume your father told you about the trip. I certainly didn't expect us to leave so soon, and I hope I'm not inconveniencing you."

"It's… a surprise, that's for sure, but I didn't have anything on my calendar, so it's fine. Next time, though, it's fine to push back if my dad suggests such a wild timeline." Karl nods, but something tells me that it's highly unlikely he'd push back about anything with his boss. "Anyway, it's a great idea, if a little different than anything we've ever done before. Good thinking."

"Thanks," he says, beaming. "I have a lot of ideas about how to make this trip really worthwhile for us. Would you like to hear them?"

I nod, and he launches into an explanation about how we can use this trip to not only get everyone onboard with expansion, but how to convince them to put more money in to make the expansion happen faster. I expect to find some flaw in his plans, but as he speaks, I'm surprised to realize that everything makes perfect sense. By the time he's finished, I'm quite impressed.

Once he's done, I ask, "My dad told me that you just got a home for your mom. I suppose she's quite happy about that?"

"Yes, she is." Karl's expression, full of love for his mother, is genuine, and it warms up my heart. "The place she was living in was terrible and very humid. I'm really grateful for the opportunity your father has given me. I didn't grow up with any father around so I really appreciate all the mentorship he's given me."

"*Just temper your expectations,*" I think, but don't say out loud. He's not the best role model, for marriage at least.

"I'm happy to hear that, Karl," I say out loud, measuring my words. "You can count on us for anything you need. Consider us your second family."

Karl stands as I leave the office, shaking my hand, his eyes suspiciously bright as he thanks me again. I'm still not completely sold on the hunting trip, but it looks like I'm going no matter what, so I might as well get used to the idea.

Once I'm alone in my own office, I pick up the phone and dial Julia. I hate the fact that I'm going to be gone for any amount of time just as she and I are exploring the connection we have, but there's nothing to be done about it.

She answers at the second ring, her voice soft and melodic. "Hey, stranger. I was wondering when you were going to call."

"Sorry," I respond apologetically, feeling even worse. "I've had a lot going on."

"Mmhm, like golfing with my brother?"

I pause. "Oh. I didn't think he told you about that."

"Alex is not a very good liar, at least when he's lying to me. But I think it's cute… my brother and the guy I'm dating meeting up to hang out."

I roll my eyes at her sarcasm. "It wasn't a hangout, Julia. Not exactly."

"Well, whatever," she huffs. "Did you need something?"

"Yes, actually," I lean back in my chair, dreading what I'm about to tell her. "When can I see you again? I'm going on a hunting trip to Hungary next week, and I really want to see you before I leave."

She's quiet for a moment, long enough for me to feel my heartbeat steadily rising in anticipation. "This is awfully sudden."

"You're telling me. My dad just told me, and I was as thrown off as you are. I wish I didn't have to go, but… work, you know?"

"I get it," she sighs, pausing for a moment as she considers my question. "I'm home now, if you want to stop by after work. I've got a lot of classwork for the next few days, so I can't say how much spare time I will have after this evening."

I hesitate. Being alone with her in her apartment is a temptation that I'm not sure I should test myself with. We haven't spent too much time together, but I want her an insane amount, in every sense of the word, and I don't exactly want to test my restraint having her all to myself in private. Plus, I wanted to talk to Margaret before anything goes any further between Julia and I, and she's just nineteen....

I shake my head hard, dispelling any doubts. Julia is a damned adult, living in her own flat, and she invited me over. Just because Margaret is crazy...and potentially dangerous, doesn't mean that I can't see Julia. She wants me there, so I will go.

"Okay," I agree, and Julia makes a happy noise on the other end of the line. "I'll see you in a few hours."

"I can't wait!" she chirps, and her joy is a balm on my stressed soul.

"Me neither."

CHAPTER 11

Sebastian

Julia buzzes me in right away, but I'm already starting to feel a sense of trepidation about being here. It's a sort of sinking feeling in my stomach, the kind that someone feels when something they want desperately is right at their fingertips, but the act of taking it would only end in ruin.

That's how I feel about being alone with Julia. I want her, God do I want her, and I honestly think she wants me just as much. Therein lies the problem, though. If she shows me even an ounce of resistance or insecurity, then I know I will be able to stop easily, but if she gives in to me, lets me touch her and kiss her… I know I will be lost.

I'm not even going to be gone all that long, so why are all these feelings shooting through me like this? Why does this feel so much like goodbye?

Beautiful Julia is dressed in a soft, comfortable dress, and her hair piled on top of her head in a messy bun. When she smiles at me she rivals any silver screen starlet. Casual or dressed up, Julia gets my heart pumping, there's no denying it.

"It's so nice to see you," she tells me, leaning in for an embrace, allowing me to take in the sweet smell of her hair before she pulls back. "I can't believe you're leaving so suddenly. Are you excited, at least?"

I shut the door behind me as I walk into her apartment. "I guess. I feel like it's just been sprung on me out of nowhere, and technically, that's the truth, but I think it will be good for Dad to get out of the office, even if it is still related to work."

She shoots me a flat look. "I asked about *you*, Seb, not your Dad."

I rub the back of my head, chuckling. "Sorry. I just worry about him, you know? It takes up a lot of my mind. But yeah, I enjoy hunting, so as long as we don't have anyone with us that is completely hopeless, it should be an enjoyable excursion."

Once fully inside, I'm greeted by a cozy and young atmosphere. The space is small, but every inch of it reflects Julia. The apartment door opens directly into the living room, and the first thing that catches my eye is the floral-patterned couch and matching loveseat. The living space is completed by a small coffee table and a fluffy rug underneath.

Julia's walls are painted a soft shade of lavender, which gives the room a calming vibe, and she's decorated the space with vintage-inspired trinkets, an antique vase and a set of ornate candle holders. The curtains are made of delicate lace, and they filter in just the right amount of natural light.

"Would you like a full tour?" she asks playfully, taking my hand in hers. "It's not a huge place, but I don't need much."

"I'm surprised your mother didn't insist on the biggest and the best," I tease, following her. "Margaret doesn't seem like someone who would be content with anything lesser."

"She didn't have much say in picking the location, honestly. It made her so angry, but I spend enough time at the family estate that she's eased up on the subject somewhat."

Julia is proud of her apartment, I soon come to learn, and it's easy to understand why. With a mother as controlling as Margaret, having control over her own living space must be one of the most liberating things in Julia's life. The kitchen is crowded but functional, with a few potted herbs on the windowsill, and there's a small table that's perfect for a cozy dinner for two. The appliances are all retro-inspired, and she's added a few floral accents to add a pop of color.

Just like its occupant, the home is full of charm and personality. Every corner is filled with something that makes Julia light up as she describes it to me, and that endears the little space to me more than anything else.

The sweet affection I'm feeling morphs into something sharper, more dangerous, when I notice an open door that leads to what can only be the bedroom. While Julia puts the kettle on to make us some tea, I walk slowly to the door, and push it open more so I can get a better look inside, my pulse pounding in my ears.

Julia's room is painted pastel pink and green, which contrasts beautifully with her snowy bedding. White and pure, just like Julia herself. The thought makes my mouth go dry. Her headboard is upholstered with a silky fabric, and there are a few throw pillows with different shades of pink on them. The bed is perfectly made, completely tidy and put together, and nothing about it should make me feel the things I'm experiencing right now.

Lust, thick and cloying, fills me as I envision what Julia would look like spread out for me on that virginal white bedspread. I think about what she wears to bed, or if she sleeps nude on the hottest nights of the year, sweat making her fair skin glow….

Fuck. Fuck. I've got to get out of here before I do something that I regret.

"Seb?" Julia says softly from right behind me, and I whip around to face her, feeling like a kid caught with his hand in the cookie jar. "Are you alright? The tea is ready."

"It's way too dangerous for me to be here alone with you," I blurt out, dragging my hand through my hair restlessly. Having her this close to me, right on the threshold of her bedroom, is going to undo me, I'm sure of it.

She blinks, tilting her head to the side, totally oblivious. "Dangerous? Why?"

I touch her. I have to, or I'm going to go up in flames with want. Gently placing my hands on her shoulders, sliding them down her arms, I say, "You have no idea the impact you have on me, do you?"

Julia's expression changes, from confusion to flirtation, in an instant, her lids lowering as she looks at me from beneath her lashes, stepping closer. "Maybe I do, actually…." She licks her lips, her tongue bubblegum pink. "And maybe that's why I invited you here."

I act on pure instinct, pulling her into my arms and slanting my mouth over hers in one smooth motion. Julia makes a surprised noise at first, but her body softens almost immediately and her arms wind around my neck sinuously, letting me know that she's giving me her full approval to continue. I don't know that I can stop for anything, now, being able to taste her sweet mouth and hearing the content noises she makes as my lips move over hers. Julia's mouth opens, and then our tongues are tangling over one another, hot and wet. She may be young, but she kisses me like a woman who knows exactly what she wants.

Kissing Julia puts me in a fog of bliss, and the things that I do don't even feel like conscious decisions. When she arches her spine to press into me harder, I grab one of her legs, coaxing her to wrap it around my waist, and when she complies wordlessly I do the same for her other leg, pressing her against the wall and kissing her until we're both breathless.

The damned bed is right behind us, and before I know it, I'm carrying her to it, lying her on top of the comforter where Julia stretches out, keeping her legs locked loosely around me while I drop down to claim her mouth again. This time I'm also bracketing her head with my arms on either side of her, closing out the rest of the world so it's just her and I.

When she begins to squirm against me restlessly, I drag my mouth from her and to her jaw, kissing a trail from there down to the long column of her neck, exploring with my teeth, lips, and tongue until I find the places that drive her the wildest. Julia sucks in a quick breath when I dip my tongue into the hollow of her throat, and her sounds take on a desperate whine when I start to drag her dress up her body, wanting to feel her bare skin so much that's making my palms itch for it. Julia has her legs around me so tightly that I barely get a glance at her pink panties, but even through my pants I can feel how hot she is for me, and my hips work against her core as if on autopilot.

The moan she lets out at that movement is unlike anything else so far, deep and needy, so I continue to thrust against her while I slant my mouth over hers again. I move my tongue against her in time with the pistoning of my hips, Julia digging her hands into my hair and holding me to her.

Soon, my name is falling from her lips while I nip at her throat, and it makes me harder than I've ever been in my entire life. My whole body and soul is on fire for her, but when I pull back just enough to gaze down at her beautiful face and kiss-swollen lips, something makes me pause. I want her so fucking badly, but Julia is a siren song I know I shouldn't answer. Alex warned me about how serious their mother is about keeping me away from Julia, and if she ever finds out what's going on between her daughter and I right now, Julia will undoubtedly be snatched back to her mother's home before she can blink.

I don't want to give Margaret any credit, but she is right about one thing. I might be too old for Julia, and it's that thought that allows me to still the movements of my hips and rest my forehead against hers, trying to lower the heat between us.

"God, Julia, I'm sorry," I mutter, shutting my eyes as I let the gravity of the situation settle in. "I shouldn't have—"

"Of course you should," she purrs, trying to pull my mouth back down to hers and tightening the grip of her legs, but I just can't. Not with the reality of what is happening becoming crystal clear now.

I stand, pressing the heels of my hands to my forehead and breathing deeply, hoping that she isn't just staring at my erection. "No, this isn't right. You're so damn young. Maybe your mom is right… maybe we really should stop seeing each other."

She raises herself to her elbows, expression shocked. "What in the world are you talking about? We aren't going to stop seeing each other because of Mom. That's ridiculous."

I sit down on the bed next to her, but don't move close enough to touch her. "Your mom has a reputation. I've got no idea what she did to Lord Hendrik, but the man disappeared from the Netherlands and never came back."

Julia looks abashed, but doesn't back down. "She's not as evil as you think…."

"Julia–"

"Sebastian, look. I know I'm young, but all of this feels more than right to me. Isn't it the same for you?"

"Well, of course it is. But again, I'm so much older, and…" I close my eyes and sigh, forcing the question out, "have you even ever…you know…?"

Not at all shy with me, Julia finishes the thought. "Had sex with someone?"

"…Yeah. That."

She pivots to face me fully, tucking her legs underneath her and leaning forward until she's once again in my personal space. Despite knowing better, I welcome the intrusion. "No, I never have. Most of the guys at school were just as boring and plain as Tom, the guy I met at the ball."

"Oh God, that guy…." I roll my eyes, and Julia giggles, taking away so much of the tension in the room as she does so.

Julia grabs the front of my shirt, fingers working the top two buttons as she pulls me forward. Feeling both foolish and totally smitten, I let her. "Whatever happens here stays between us," she promises, voice soft. "No one needs to know but us."

Then she's on her back again and I'm hovering over her. Julia lifts up enough to nip at my bottom lip, and my blood ignites in my veins once more at the feeling of her teeth, undeniable. Her hands keep at the buttons of my shirt while I drag the straps of her sundress over her shoulders, peppering kisses over the smattering of freckles I find, and then across to her collarbone, my tongue tracing the hollow of it.

Julia gets my shirt open and her hands roam my chest anxiously, her touch cool on my heated skin. She's wearing a lacy, strapless bralette, which I pull down to join her dress, my heart pounding so hard that I can feel my pulse against my eardrums. Her taut, pink nipples make my mouth water, but I resist, wanting to take things as slow as possible for sweet Julia. I stand, gripping her garments where they are now bunched at her waist, and without even a word of direction, Julia arches her back to help me. I undress her almost completely, sliding the dress and bra down her long, toned legs and depositing them on the bed beside us, leaving her in only her petal-pink panties and nothing more.

God, she is radiant. Almost unearthly in her beauty. I know I'm not worthy, but she wants me and I'm too far gone to deny her anything now.

Her eyes are hooded with lust, and she reaches her hands out to me as I descend on her once more, but she's only able to card her fingers through my hair as I stop short, rasping the soft skin of her stomach with my beard and placing a slow kiss above her belly button that has her gasping. I can smell her desire, begging me to taste her in her most intimate areas. I'm more than ready to give into that temptation, making it only a few inches lower with my mouth, right at the waistband of her panties, when I feel the most ill-timed thing on the entire planet.

My cell phone ringing in my pants.

It's loud enough that Julia hears it, and she raises up on her elbows with a questioning look on her face. I place a hand on her sternum and push her back down on the mattress, gliding my fingers over her nipples and rasping, "Ignore it," before laying my mouth on her once more.

The call ends. And then whoever is calling does so again, and the ringing begins anew.

"Fuck." I pull the damned device out of my pocket, and of course it's my father, one of the only people who might call me that I can never ignore. I shoot Julia an apologetic look holding my finger to my lips to indicate she should be quiet, before I stand and answer.

"Dad, I–"

"Where the hell are you?" he exclaims, cutting me off.

"What's going on?"

"We were supposed to be at the studio to record the interview!" my father rants. "The reporter is here, my assistant is here, your assistant is here, I'm here, but where the hell are you?"

Flabbergasted, I sit on the mattress beside Julia, who has now risen and is covering her body somewhat with a blanket. "I, uh, didn't get notified."

Dad's voice is muffled as he covers the mouthpiece with his hand. "Amelia! Did you place the interview in Seb's calendar?" I hear my assistant give the affirmative in the background, and I can't help but wince. "She is telling me that she did, and that she reminded you of it this morning!"

I close my eyes and lower my head into my free hand. "I'm sorry. I had a lot on my mind. Someone dumped the news of an impromptu hunting trip in my lap, if you'll recall."

Dad ignores any excuses. "Just get your ass here right now."

I suppress the litany of curse words that want to spill out of my mouth, and instead mutter a short, "Will be there soon."

I hang up, tucking the phone into my pocket and heaving a sigh. "I can't believe I forgot about that interview with my dad...." I turn to try to explain myself to Julia, and she has the sheet held up just enough to cover her breasts and nothing more, her long legs folded to the side and every bare inch of her skin calling to me. And of course, I have to go. I can't believe this is happening. "Fuck, you are so damn beautiful."

She chews at her bottom lip, looking up at me. "When will I see you again?"

Tonight! I want to scream, but these few minutes of separation have cleared my head some, and I know that would be a terrible idea. She just tempts me too much, making it almost impossible to resist her and tell her no. I'm not even sure that I want to cross Margaret, but the idea of giving Julia up is too much the bear, so I'm going to have to figure it out in no uncertain terms before I continue things with this incredible girl.

"After the hunting trip, most likely," I sigh. "I'm leaving next Thursday, but I will be back soon, I promise."

Julia doesn't look thrilled. "It's going to feel like an eternity here without you."

I can't help myself, I have to kiss her again, leaning towards her and cupping the back of her head to pull her face into mine. It's a gentle press of lips, meant to keep things easy between us, but the residual heat from before comes roaring back, and in seconds my tongue is in her mouth and I'm wrapping my arms around her body. Realizing what I'm doing, I snap out of it and stumble back to my feet, leaving her even more flustered on the bed than before, alone. I have to go, even if it feels like it might kill me to leave her like this.

"You have no idea how much I hate to leave. I feel like I just want to skip that damn interview and stay here with you."

"That's fine by me," she responds huskily.

"Julia… Julia…" I can't help but laugh sardonically, head shaking. "You are such a terrible temptation, you know that? I used to have my life in order before meeting you."

"As if." She rolls her eyes, pulling her sheet tighter against herself. "By having your life together do you mean spending every waking minute working? You know, even your dad had time to get married and have children."

I didn't think anything could take me off guard, but when Julia mentions marriage and children I feel a flush coming up my neck and into my face, making me feel hot as I button my shirt and tuck it back into my slacks. I have a vision of Julia, sitting in our own bed, somewhere completely new, sun streaming in and illuminating her rocking our new infant, and an unnamed emotion swells in my heart like a river after a monsoon. God, how simple and wonderful everything would be if she was my wife. No bothersome parents, no overbearing job…just Julia, and I.

I don't balk at the idea, but instead look her directly in the eye. "That's true. We should talk about it when I get back."

Julia's mouth falls open, not expecting such a serious response from her quip I'm sure, but I take the opportunity to kiss her once more in the following silence, breathing her in and savoring this moment before pulling back and telling her goodbye. She replies in kind, weakly, and I finally tear myself away and out of the apartment.

In my car and on the road, away from the spell that surrounds Julia, I know one thing for sure: I have to speak to Margaret about my intentions when I get back. Not only is Julia too special, too precious to me, to ever be something as casual as a fling, but the last thing in the world I want is for Margaret to enact some sort of awful revenge for me having an affair and tainting her daughter. I need her to know that my intentions are honorable—I want to make Julia Van Dieren my wife.

CHAPTER 12

Julia

Sitting in the university library, surrounded by the musty smell of old books, my mind is constantly drifting back to the conversation I had with Sebastian just a few days ago in my apartment. It quickly got out of hand; what was supposed to just be a quick visit turned into Sebastian stripping me nearly naked as we were making out in my bed. I can't lie to myself and say that I didn't half expect that outcome, expected it, even, but it was still so much, so fast. The thought of him fills me with a sense of anticipation and excitement, but also a hint of fear.

It's as if Sebastian is a wild animal that I'm trying to tame, and the act of doing so could lead to either joy or sorrow. I'm very, very rapidly starting to feel incredibly strong things for him, and now I'm even fantasizing about the way our life might look if things get more serious. Our connection is so real and powerful that there is no way I can deny what he makes me feel. Heck, I was ready to let him take my virginity right there in my bed before he got the phone call that tore him away, and I've never even gotten close with anyone else! The thought of his touch, his kiss, sends shivers down my spine.

My heart races with the possibility of a future together. I can see us building a life filled with love, passion, and adventure. But at the same time, I feel a sense of trepidation, as if this dream is too good to be true. How well do I really know Sebastian? We've been on a few dates, talked constantly over the phone, and texted when we couldn't be together in person, and then had one incredibly heated encounter in my apartment–but that's it. Sebastian also met Alex, who apparently approves of him for the most part, but that still doesn't mean that we've had a traditional courtship that would naturally lead to marriage. Instead, we've been doing almost everything in secret, falling for one another while completely shutting the world out.

I look around the library, thinking about how I should be studying, not getting myself all tangled up in tenuous ideas of the future. It's so hard, though, because I realize that nothing in life is certain, and I don't want to waste my chance at happiness, even if it is with a man my mom isn't thrilled about and who is significantly older than I am. When I am with Sebastian, I feel like we are invincible. It's only when I'm alone that these doubts begin to worm themselves into my thoughts.

I close my eyes and imagine a future with him, I can't help but feel a sense of euphoria wash over me. I know that whatever challenges we may face, we'll face them together, as a team. And that's all I could ever ask for.

Just like the words he spoke before he left, promising that we would talk about marriage when he returned, I know that he and I are on the same page. We share a bond that goes beyond mere attraction, but said attraction is burning so hotly between us now that not much else can get through my brain. It's like two single thoughts bouncing in my skull constantly: marriage with Sebastian, and sex with Sebastian.

Feeling my cheeks warm, I pull the book I'm trying to read about criminal law up to cover my face, and groan internally. "*Get yourself together, Julia!*"

My musings are interrupted when I hear someone speed walking through the silent library towards me, and look up from my book to see Gabi rushing over, a magazine clutched in her hand. She sits down, clearly buzzing with energy, and brandishes the gossip rag she's carrying with a high-pitched squeal. A few of the other library goers whip their heads around or narrow their eyes, annoyed, but Gabi pays them no mind, waving the damn thing in my face.

"Look what I found," Gabi says, pointing to a page in the society events section. "It's you and the broody man, dancing at the ball!"

I take the magazine from her and study the picture, feeling a slight blush creeping up my neck as I look at Sebastian's face. He looks so handsome in his tuxedo, his arm wrapped tightly around my waist as we sway to the music.

"Where did you find this?" I ask Gabi, trying to hide my embarrassment.

"I was at a beauty salon during my lunch break, and they had this magazine lying around," she tells me, grinning. "I was just flicking through it when I stumbled across this picture of you and your man." Gabi puts a heavy emphasis on the last word, lowering her voice and raising her eyebrows.

"His name is Sebastian," I correct her, feeling protective of him as I quietly close my book and set it aside so I can give all my attention to the picture of us.

Gabi leans in, her eyes sparkling with curiosity. "Well, then. How is *Sebastian* doing?"

I begin to lower my gaze, lost in thought about our intimate moments together, which only causes Gabi to start giggling and teasing me to spill all the juicy details.

"Oh, I know that look! You need to tell me right now what the two of you have been up to!"

I playfully shove her shoulder, laughing. "I'm not telling you anything, Gabi. A lady never kisses and tells."

But in truth, I'm tempted to tell her everything about my feelings for him, my fears about him leaving for his hunting trip, and my hopes for our future together. After all, Gabi is my closest friend here at school, and she'd understand my heart's deepest desires. Even better, I know she won't judge the more steamy activities that Sebastian and I got into the other night, other than some light teasing. Yet, when I look inward, I find that I don't actually want to share those sorts of details with anyone yet. I want to keep them for myself, my own little private memories that are only shared between Sebastian and I. They're… special to me, I guess. So, I give her the next best thing to sate her curiosity.

"I'm in love with him. Like seriously," I confide in her, feeling my heart race with excitement and nervousness all at once. "Sebastian is leaving for Hungary in two days, but we plan to take our relationship to the next level once he gets back."

"By next level you mean… having sex with him?" Gabi asks, her eyebrows raised even further up her forehead.

I chuckle, shrugging. "Maybe, maybe not. But I think so." Gabi sucks in a shocked breath, her eyes going wide, and I hold my hands up to stop any loud exclamations she might be about to utter. "You cannot tell anyone about this, Gabi. We shouldn't even be talking about it publicly, honestly."

She wrinkles her nose, sitting back in her chair. "I think you might be overreacting about all the secretiveness. No one is concerned around here about who you're dating, unless you mean—" A look of comprehension comes over her face. "Oohhh…you're worried about word getting back to your mom, aren't you?"

My thoughts immediately shift to my mother, and I feel a wave of anxiety wash over me. "I have to talk to Mom," I say, my voice tinged with worry. "I've got no idea how to change her mind and persuade her that Sebastian is the perfect man for me. She is so ridiculously against the idea of it that I don't think anyone on the planet could convince her otherwise. Mother doesn't like to be proved wrong, that's for sure."

"Hmm…." Gabi pulls the tabloid back over to the other side of the table and stares down at the picture of Sebastian and I thoughtfully. "I mean, she can't do much, can she? You are an adult living in Amsterdam and studying law, like what can your mom do?" Gabi questions, her voice reassuring.

I pause, considering her words. "That's true, but you don't know her, Gabi." My mind starts racing with memories of past arguments with my mother over all kinds of topics and almost shiver. Lately, the biggest point of contention has been my reluctance to make appearances in society. Now, though, nothing can eclipse how angry she is about Sebastian. "God knows she's crazy, I'm telling you."

As much as I try to push away my concerns about my mother, I know that I'll need to find a way to convince her that Sebastian is the right choice for me. I can't bear the thought of losing him because of my mother's disapproval. But with Gabi by my side, I feel a glimmer of hope from her lightheartedness that maybe I can turn the tides of my mother's ire. It's unlikely, and it's not often that I win an argument with her, but Sebastian is reason enough for me to try.

CHAPTER 13

Julia

We're supposed to be having lunch, but I've never been less hungry in my entire life. I had called one of the family drivers to bring me to the restaurant this afternoon, not wanting to risk the possibility of arriving late and annoying my mother from the start, but the black sedan with the dark tinted windows just feels so stifling right now, almost like a cage. A cage I can't wait to escape.

The car pulls up to the curb, so I take a deep breath and force myself to step out. The sun is shining, and the air is crisp, but my stomach is in knots. Today is the day I've invited my mother to lunch in Amsterdam proper, and I'm terrified of how it's going to go. I suggested the restaurant De Plantage since it has a beautiful ambiance with high ceilings, along with natural light pouring in from the windows, and greenery all around, hoping that the lovely setting will be enough to have Mom in a good mood for this conversation that I know she doesn't want to have. To be fair, I don't want to either, but she's given me little choice with her stubbornness. I've been trying to get her to accept my relationship with Sebastian for some time now, but she's so unmovable and set in her ways.

I smooth down my dress and check my reflection in the car window before making my way toward the restaurant's entrance. The day is so beautiful, and the restaurant looks bright and inviting, but I can't focus on any of it. All I can think about is how desperate I am for my mother's approval, and how much I fear she won't give it.

Inhaling slowly and holding my head high, I push open the door and step inside, trying to ignore the pounding of my heart in my chest.

As I walk into the restaurant, all I can think is how most women would be feeling excited having this chat with their mothers, but for me, it's only dread. Of course, I'm looking forward to spending time with my mom, but the entire point of the lunch is to discuss Sebastian, and I just can't anticipate how exactly she's going to take it. A tiny piece of me still hopes that she will be open to the possibility once she sees how serious I am about him, but it's admittedly a long shot. Mom doesn't offer me very many pleasant surprises when it comes to my personal life and decisions, especially when I go off script from what she thinks is appropriate for me. And Sebastian Van den Bosch isn't anyone that Mom ever had in mind for me.

It's bizarre. He's from a wealthy, old money family, and even Alex approves of him. Certainly it can't just be our age difference freaking Mom out so much.

Speak of the devil, I notice Mom waiting for me at the bar, her honey-colored hair pulled up in an elegant bun.

She's at least drinking a glass of champagne, and I hope the alcohol will make her a bit more agreeable.

I walk over to where she is and put on my most welcoming tone, "Hey Mom, thanks for coming."

"Julia, dear, finally." She greets me with a lukewarm smile, standing and kissing each of my cheeks without much enthusiasm, and I can already tell she's not thrilled about being here. I take a calming breath and remind myself that I need to stay calm and composed, no matter what she says.

We are escorted to our reserved table, and I can't help but notice the beautiful interior of the restaurant as we take our seats. The walls are adorned with paintings, and the ceiling is painted with intricate designs. The tables are set with white linens, and it's just busy enough to have a warm and inviting feel. "It's nice here, isn't it, Mom?"

"Fine," she sighs, unimpressed. "But I have a feeling that you aren't wanting to talk about interior design, correct?"

I wince. God, I was hoping that she would at least give me a few minutes to just talk and enjoy each other's company before we had to get into the more difficult subjects! Mom is giving me zero time to prepare, and it leaves me reeling.

The server approaches us, and we both order our drinks. I opt for a refreshing iced tea while Mom asks for another glass of champagne. I can even feel her eyes on me as I take a sip of my drink, ice clinking cheerily in the glass, and I try to ignore the tension that's building between us.

"So you were right," I confess, putting the glass back down on the table. "I did want to talk to you, but we don't have to get right into it. I'm pretty hungry anyway, so—"

"Let me guess," Mom begins, looking both entertained and Machiavellian at the same time. "Sebastian again?" Her voice is laced with disapproval. "I thought the subject was closed."

I shut my eyes and take a second, trying to steady myself while her words ring in my ears. "This is going to be hard to hear, and I understand that, but I love him, Mom. I truly do, and I wish you could see how happy I've been since I met him."

Her expression remains unchanged, and I can see the skepticism in her eyes, followed by something much more dark and sinister. It scares me, and as much as my mom drives me crazy sometimes, I've never had reason to fear her, and it makes me shiver.

I know I need to tread carefully if I want to convince her. As we wait for our food to arrive, I try to think of ways to persuade her, but my mind draws a blank. All I can do is hope that she will eventually come around and see how much Sebastian means to me. Or if all else fails, just that she trusts me enough to let me make my own decisions without trying to interfere.

"Why are you telling me all this?" my mother demands after a beat, her eyes narrowing.

I take another sip of my iced tea, wishing now that it were wine, trying to steady my nerves. Other patrons of the restaurant go on with their meals all around us, and their laughter and happiness start to grate on my nerves. Why can't it be like that for us? Why can't I be happy? Giving in to my uncomfortableness, I wave the server down and order a glass of white sangria, wanting to settle myself without getting too foggy to continue the conversation. I need my wits about me when Margaret Van Dieren is involved, just like anyone else would. She doesn't have a reputation of being an easy woman to deal with, after all.

It takes an immense amount of willpower to not crumble under my mom's scrutiny and say the rest of my piece, but I have no other choice. Not if I want to get my way for once. "Well, we're thinking of… you know," I have to pause, my pulse racing, "Taking our relationship to the next level," I say, choosing my words carefully.

"And what does that mean? What exactly are you referring to?" My mother's voice is sharp and she leans closer, her forearms resting on the table.

I can see the disapproval in her eyes, and it makes me feel small and vulnerable. I know I shouldn't let her opinions affect me so much, but it's hard not to care what your own mother thinks of the man you love. I take another sip of my drink, hoping that it will give me the courage to speak my mind.

"The next step meaning connecting our families, but I think you knew that already," I deadpan, and Mom's expression goes taut.

"You mean getting *engaged*?" At this point, Mom has no care for her volume, and it's not only me who jumps at her words. Everyone around us does, too. "Julia, for fuck's sake!" she exclaims, her face turning red with anger.

My heart sinks. I had hoped that this lunch would be a chance for my mother and me to reconnect, to find some common ground, but instead, it seems to have only made things worse. I can feel the weight of her disappointment crushing down on me, threatening to drown me in a sea of regret.

"Mom! I won't hear it again," I insist, feeling a surge of frustration. "Whether you like him or not, this is the man I want to be with. So get over it!"

As I finish speaking, our meals arrive, and the waiter places them carefully on the table, looking frightened and ready to be far away from us. I clench my fists in my lap, trying to calm the storm of emotions inside me. This is it. I've said my piece. Now it's up to my mother to decide what to do next.

Any hope inside me dies and is replaced by fearful adrenaline as my mother stands up abruptly, her voice rising with each word.

"What a brainless idiot you can be sometimes," she spits out, her words like venom. "The divorce with your father didn't teach you anything, hm?" I can feel my face getting hot with anger and shame as she rants. Why does she always have to bring up the past like that? Can't she see that I'm trying to move forward with my life?

I feel like I've been slapped in the face. How could she say something like that? My father's infidelity has nothing to do with me or my relationships. But before I can even open my mouth to respond, my mother has already dropped her napkin on the table and stormed out of the restaurant, grabbing her bag and stomping out, her heels clicking on the tile floor and echoing in the quiet that her words have wrought.

I sit there for a moment, stunned and hurt, as the other diners look on with curiosity. I watch her go, silence pressing on my ears, miserable and so incredibly embarrassed that it's hard to breathe. At first I can't move, staring blankly at my untouched plate of food. My appetite is gone, replaced with a gnawing feeling of sadness and frustration. Why can't my mother see how happy Sebastian makes me? Why is she so stubborn and unwilling to accept my choices?

Then, in a flash, shame fades enough for me to gain control of my body again. I gather my things and leave as well after settling our bill, the taste of anger and sadness lingering in my mouth. Another failed attempt to connect with my mother, another reminder of how little she understands me.

Once I'm outside it feels like I can breathe again, and I sink down onto a wooden bench, a hand pressed against my chest as I try not to cry. I can feel hot tears welling up behind my eyes, threatening to fall and embarrass me more, and I breathe in and out as slowly as possible to keep them from doing so.

On a whim, I reach into my bag and pull out the tabloid I had brought with me, flipping to the page with the photo of Sebastian and I. Gabi had let me take it without complaint, and I'm grateful, because the photo of Seb and I twirling under the ballroom lights brings me a sense of peace that makes it possible to get control of myself after my mother's outburst. I trace my finger over the glossy image, feeling a sense of longing and nostalgia. What I would give to go back to that night....

Just then, my phone rings, and I see that it's Sebastian calling. Tears rise in me again, but this time, in relief. Oh, even just seeing this man's name on my phone screen reminds me how worth it he is. My heart lifts at the sound of his voice as I answer, and I can't help but smile. "Hey, how's everything going?" I ask, trying my best not to let any of my sorrow bleed through.

"I'm about to board my plane," he informs me, his voice so comforting, "and I already miss you like crazy."

My smile widens, and I feel a warmth spread through my chest. "Have a safe flight, and, um, I miss you just as much." My voice is filled with affection, but a little sniffle escapes me as I can't help but still be affected by the fight I just had with Mom.

"Are you okay, Julia?"

Pushing back my tears, I nod, and take a few deep breaths to steady myself and make me sound less overwhelmed. "Yes, just Mom being Mom, but don't let me keep you. We can talk about it later."

He lets out an exasperated sigh. "Gosh, I'm so sorry. I—"

"It's not your fault, really," I interpose immediately, cutting him off. "Please, enjoy your flight and send my regards to your dad."

There's a short silence before Sebastian finally decides to move on and drop the subject. "Alright, I'll text you as soon as I land." I can hear the sincerity in his tone causing my lips to twitch into a smile.

I hang up the call and hold the phone in my hand as I contemplate what to do now. Part of me wants to call my mother and force her to finish this talk, making the both of us face the demons that are haunting our mother-daughter relationship. Another bit of me wants to just go home and order takeout to replace the food that I left cooling on the table back inside the restaurant, but I'm restless, the unsettled feeling making me want to walk, so I call the driver to tell him that I will ring when I'm ready and make my way down the sidewalk.

It's a gorgeous part of town, shops lining the streets, and the activity helps me burn off all the bad feelings swirling inside of me. As I walk down the streets of Amsterdam, I allow myself to get lost in the memories of the short amount of time Sebastian and I have spent together, savoring them bit by bit like the sweetest, richest chocolate.

It's not fair. I love Sebastian, and I thought maybe, just maybe, my mother would be able to see that and support me. But instead, she just proved once again that she's incapable of putting her own biases and judgments aside.

I don't know what to do next. All I know is that I need to get away from here, away from the hurt and disappointment. Maybe a long walk by the canals will be exactly what I need to help clear my head.

CHAPTER 14

Sebastian

Our flight was short and uncomplicated, which was a boon, since everything else in my life seems to be as complicated as humanly possible. Now, as we pull up to Uncle Leopold's estate where we will be staying for the next few days, I try to shut off the thoughts of everything back home and get myself focused on the hunt as well as doing my best to make sure that our business associates have a good time.

We've taken a number of private cars from the airport to the estate, and it's just Dad, Karl, and I in the one I'm currently in. The driver takes us around the circular driveway, stopping at the front steps of the estate and joining the row of cars that have already arrived. I step out of the vehicle, taking in the grandeur of my uncle's expansive property. The sweeping lawns and thick forest on the property's edge are a far cry from the busy city life I'm used to, and the air is crisp and fresh. Out here it smells like evergreen and the underlying, deeper scent of the woods, which tells me it should be a satisfying hunt. We are suitably far away from civilization, my uncle's estate the only home for miles.

Leopold comes out of the home and down the stairs, his arms open wide to greet his brother with an enthusiastic embrace and hearty laugh. He slaps my father on the back a few times before letting him go and moving to me, where I receive the same treatment.

"Johannes! Sebastian! So good to see you. It's about time that you come and visit," he booms.

I have to admit, it's good to see my dad laugh and some of the ever present stress fall away from his face as he talks to his brother. He reminds me of a younger version of himself; the man who taught me how to shoot a gun, how to drive a car, and how to treat a woman just by watching him treat my mother with so much love and kindness over the years. Now… he's different. Distant and strung out. But it's a bit of a relief to see that the better version of himself is still somewhere inside, deep down, showing through now as he reconnects with family.

Karl exits the car and stands next to me with his hands in his pockets and aviators covering his eyes, watching the two older men as well. Leaning closer toward me, he lowers his voice and comments quietly, "He seems happy."

"I don't believe for a second that this hunting trip was anything but a way to further the business to him, so this is definitely a positive addition that I didn't expect," I agree, crossing my arms and turning my head to look at Karl. "I guess we should go make sure all of our group is alright and can find their rooms okay while the senior citizens catch up, huh?"

Karl snorts, but follows along. "Yeah, you're probably right. Let's get to it."

Leopold's staff unloads everyone's things and does a decent job of escorting all of the businessmen to their rooms while Karl and I go with them, shake hands, and answer any lingering questions they may have about the upcoming hunting trip in the morning. Most of them hunt on a regular basis, while others have never held a gun in their lives, but there are a few that land somewhere in between and express interest in having a lesson to reacquaint themselves with shooting a rifle and all the little details that come with such a hunt. Happy to have something to keep myself occupied, I agree to gather with them on the edge of the property right before the forest begins where Uncle Leopold has a few targets set up and go over the basics so that everyone who is interested in hunting is able to do so. It wouldn't hurt to get some practice in myself, and Karl seems agreeable to helping me. It's shaping up to be an enjoyable evening, all things considered.

But, on the edge of my mind, like always, there is something haunting me. Or someone, I should say. Julia, her laugh like the ringing of angelic bells, her skin like the softest silk, her hair that smells like vanilla and juicy oranges exploding on my tongue. It's fair to say that I'm obsessed with the woman, and as much as I want to drown in that obsession and turn myself over to it fully, I know this trip is a blessing because it will give me the time to clear my head and approach the relationship with her in a proper way. I want to marry her, make her an honest woman, and then indulge myself in all the wonderful things Julia has to offer.

That such a smart, clever, and gorgeous girl would knock me off my feet out of nowhere wasn't something I ever anticipated, but it's certainly been a pleasant, if undeniably frustrating experience. There is just one barrier that is forever in my way: her mother.

I look over again at my father and uncle. Two powerful, influential men, my father especially. He should be more than a match for Margaret Van Dieren, but everyone I meet, Mom and Dad included, seem to handle the woman like she's a burning hot coal in their hands. When we get home, I'm going to have to put my foot down with Dad and have him help me with the Margaret situation, leaning his importance in society in my favor to help turn the tides. I've given him so much of myself for the family business, and will continue to do so, albeit to a lesser degree if I marry Julia, for the foreseeable future. He might not approve of the match fully, but I'm confident he will help me.

I think of my sweet mother reading on the terrace, her beloved face in the light of the sunset, loneliness radiating from her even if she will never speak of it, and decide to leave her out of the situation if at all possible. She's going through and has been through enough already.

***

The sun is beating down on us as we make our way to the back of my uncle's property where the shooting range is. Everyone has their rifles slung over their shoulders and the energy is relaxed. The range hasn't been used in quite some time according to Leopold, but we don't need any bells and whistles to accomplish our task. Just a safe place to shoot and some targets.

Karl and I are joined by five businessmen who will be joining us on the hunt tomorrow. They're the part of the group that has all shot rifles before, but it's been a while for these five, so we're giving them a refresher course so the hunt tomorrow can go as smoothly as possible.

I can't help but feel a bit nervous as we approach the range. Shooting is serious business, and safety is always a top priority. But I remind myself that I've been handling firearms since I was a kid and that I know what I'm doing, and from what Karl says, he is a pretty accomplished hunter, too. Surely the two of us can handle five grown men that are at least passingly familiar with a gun.

Karl is leading the group, walking them through the basics of safety and handling. He's a natural teacher, patient and encouraging. I'm impressed by his expertise and his ability to make the experience fun and accessible for everyone.

"Alright gentlemen, let's get started." I speak up once Karl has finished going over the very basics. "Grab your rifles and take aim at those targets over there."

Karl then speaks up again. "Remember, steady hand and deep breaths. Don't want to miss and have a buck charging at us."

There is chatter of agreement from the men.

"Yeah, we wouldn't want that now, would we?" I chuckle, loading my own gun and entering one of the separated shooting booths and pulling my ear protection on.

"I haven't shot a rifle in years. I hope I haven't lost my touch," I hear one of the clients, named Ralph, say.

"Same here. I used to be a pretty good shot though," another one answers, and I frown, not liking the uncertainty in their tone.

Walking closer to them, I give them each a pat on the back in reassurance. "Don't worry, it's like riding a bike. You never forget. Just take your time and aim carefully."

"And don't forget to exhale before pulling the trigger," Karl adds from the booth next to mine.

"Good point. Alright, let's get started. Ralph, you're up first. Take your time and don't rush."

As they take turns shooting and giving each other pointers, the atmosphere becomes more relaxed and playful—even the businessmen who were initially nervous start to enjoy themselves.

"Hey, I think I hit the bullseye!" I hear Ralph say, and I smirk. So far, so good. They're all having a good time already, and we haven't even had our first official hunt.

Karl whistles in appreciation. "Nice shot! Looks like you haven't lost your touch after all."

I line up and take a few shots myself, the bullets sinking into the wooden targets covered with paper bullseyes and emerging to thunk into the dirt berm. Each shot of mine rings the center of the bullseye, with two of them hitting directly. "See? I told you guys, it's like riding a bike."

"This is actually pretty fun. I might have to take up shooting again." I hear someone say, and mutters of agreement from around the range.

"I agree. And thanks for the refresher course, Sebastian and Karl," Ralph says, his expression lighthearted. "I'm very impressed by the care you have taken to make this an accessible opportunity for all of your clients, not just the experienced hunters. I will definitely be talking about this for weeks when we get home, much to my wife's chagrin, I'm sure."

His praise makes my chest swell with pride, and I'm sure it does the same for Karl, too. This is exactly what my father wanted from this trip. "No problem at all. Just glad to help out. And who knows, maybe we'll have some fresh venison for dinner tomorrow."

As we continue shooting, I feel my nerves about the trip overall melt away. There's something about the concentration required for shooting that always manages to calm me down. I watch as the other men take aim, and I can tell that they're all enjoying themselves equally. These men are probably similar to Dad; always cooped up at work, forgetting to have moments like these that make life worth living. We might have to make this hunting excursion a yearly thing.

Karl and I exchange some banter as we move from one station to the next, giving individual pointers where they are needed, and I can't help but feel grateful for his company. He's the perfect hunting partner, skilled and knowledgeable, but also easy to get along with. I can see why Dad likes him.

As the afternoon wears on, the sun begins to dip lower in the sky. We finish up our session and make our way back to the house, feeling confident and ready for the hunt tomorrow.

***

Dinner is served in the grand dining room at a long, mahogany table surrounded by plush chairs. Uncle Leopold tells us the table is made from wood harvested from the forest on his property, and regales us with stories about how the woods are simply brimming with red deer ripe for the hunting. Everyone's good moods cast a warm glow over the room, and the scent of roasted beef fills the air as the dishes come out. My father is in his element, laughing and joking with our guests, all of which are eager to start the hunt tomorrow.

Karl is a little starry-eyed now that we're back from the range, and I think the grandeur of the whole ordeal must be getting to him. From what my father has said, Karl comes from a modest upbringing, so something like this must be a lot for him to swallow. I take pity on him and pull him into my conversation with my father, for which he seems grateful. We discuss the plans for tomorrow's hunt, the excitement palpable in the room.

It's an easy, affable gathering… but as I sip my wine, my thoughts keep returning to Julia. I wonder what she's doing right now, if she's missing me like I'm missing her.

As the meal wears on, my father and Uncle Leopold are in deep conversation, discussing the best hunting grounds on the estate. Karl is practically bouncing in his seat with anticipation, and I can't help but grin at his enthusiasm.

While the first course is served, I can't help but feel a pang of longing for Julia. The tender beef melts in my mouth, but my mind is elsewhere. I wish she were here, and imagine her as my lovely dinner companion. Even better is the fantasy I indulge in of her greeting me with a sultry smile as I return from the hunt tomorrow, leading me by the hand to the showers to wash off the sweat of the day….

"So, Sebastian," Uncle Leopold says, turning to me with a twinkle in his eye and snapping me out of my reverie. "Are you ready for tomorrow?"

I nod eagerly. "Absolutely. It's been too long since I've been able to take some time off and enjoy the great outdoors."

My father chuckles. "Yes, it's been all work and no play for us lately. I'm looking forward to this trip as well."

Karl chimes in, his eyes shining, "I can't thank you enough for including me in this, Mr. Van den Bosch. It's truly an honor to be here."

My father smiles warmly at him. "Nonsense, Karl. You're practically part of the family. Besides, this hunting trip wouldn't have even come to fruition if it wouldn't have been for you. It was your idea, after all."

As the meal goes on, the conversation flows easily between us. Uncle Leopold regales us with tales of past hunting trips, and Karl shares stories of his time moving up as a salesman in our company. My mind keeps wandering back to Julia, but I force myself to stay present and enjoy the company of those around me.

After dessert is cleared away and coffee is served, my father and his brother excuse themselves to discuss final preparations for the hunt as everyone else filters back to their rooms. I'm craving some fresh air and peace before bed, so I pull a server aside and ask for a cigar and port to be delivered out to the terrace, and make my way there to enjoy the evening air.

I thought Karl had gone with my father and uncle, but as I clip the cigar and light it, taking a few puffs and blowing them into the air above me, I hear the terrace door opening and the younger man walks out to join me. There is a second of annoyance at not being able to even have a short moment alone, but Karl has been a good companion today. I can cut him some slack. He pauses in the doorway, seeing me, unsure whether he should go back inside or come all the way out.

"Hey, Karl," I say, gesturing for him to stay a moment longer.

He nods and takes a seat across from me on one of the padded outdoor chairs, sighing and folding his hands behind his head. "What a day, huh? I can't believe it's gone so well thus far."

"Agreed. Things have a way of spiraling out of control when there are this many moving parts, but we've done well." I slide a glance over at him. "Thanks to you, in no small part."

He grins appreciatively. "I just wanted to thank you again for not only listening to my idea, but inviting me along. This is the opportunity of a lifetime for me. I never thought I'd be hunting on a private estate like this."

I nod, taking a sip of my port. "Well, I'm glad you're enjoying it. And if you need anything, don't hesitate to ask."

Karl nods, his expression serious. "I mean it, Sebastian. Your family has been so good to me over my time at the company. I owe you all quite a bit."

I wave off his gratitude. "Don't be silly. You're a valued member of our team, Karl. We're lucky to have you."

He bows his head slightly, humbled. "Thanks. That means a lot to me."

I notice a glimmering golden ring on Karl's finger, the first time I've seen it. "Are you married, Karl?" I ask him, my curiosity piqued.

Karl grins, looking down at the ring. "Oh, yes. She works in the modeling industry and is getting more famous by the day. Not sure how I managed to get so lucky, but here we are."

I offer him a congratulatory nod. "Fantastic! That sounds great for you both."

Deep down, though, I feel a pang of jealousy. Karl, five years my junior, is already married and settled down. I want what he has so badly that it makes it hard to breathe. Imagining marriage with Julia is too much, too tempting, and if I let myself linger on the thought too long then I will never be able to resurface from it. Just like when I think of what she and I had been up to in her bed the last time we saw each other....

"How are your in-laws? Do they treat you right?" I ask him, attempting to sound cordial, but really hoping that he might be someone I can commiserate about Margaret with. Although, I doubt anyone has a potential mother-in-law quite as intimidating as she is.

"They're great. My wife grew up with just her mom, and we all connected very well. No complaints there," he responds, a smile playing on his lips. I nod pensively, and then the conversation takes a turn toward my own love life. "And you? Do you have someone in your life?" Karl asks, and I can't help but feel a knot form in my stomach.

"Well, let's say the woman I'm in love with has got the most overbearing mother I have ever met," I confess, feeling a weight lift off my chest just from being able to share that small tidbit of information. Karl might not be familiar with my situation, but he's proven to be a good person to bounce things off of thus far.

Karl listens intently as I continue, my frustrations pouring out of me like water from a faucet. "I just don't know how to make it work if her mom hates me so much. Her dad is out of the country, and I have no idea where he is. He and her mom got divorced two years ago."

"If she really loves you, I think she will choose you over her mom," Karl offers sagely. "Sometimes our parents might not approve of our choices, but they are ours to make and no one else's. If she loves her daughter and wants the best for her, she'll come around eventually. After all, your family would be a wonderful one to marry into I would think."

His words ring true, and I thank him for the wise advice. "I'm happy to have met you," I blurt out with a genuine smile, feeling a sense of camaraderie with Karl that I hadn't expected. I guess Dad was right about keeping Karl close and forging a friendship with him. It has been worthwhile so far.

My gaze drifts away from Karl as my mind makes its way once again back to Julia. The thought of her overbearing mother and the complications that come with our relationship makes my chest tighten. How much longer can we continue like this? Despite all the challenges, I know I can't help how I feel about her, but I'm not made of iron. I can't wait forever.

I remember the way her eyes light up when she talks about her dreams, and the way her laughter sounds like music to my ears. It's these little moments that keep me hooked, even when it seems like everything is against us.

As I bring my attention back to Karl, I'm grateful for the kind words of wisdom that the young man has shared. It dawns on me that I need to take a page out of Karl's book and have more faith in my own choices, even if they go against the expectations of others.

CHAPTER 15

Julia

I'm still in a deep slumber, dreaming of Sebastian, when I'm suddenly jolted awake by the insistent ringtone of my cell phone. I glance at my clock angrily; it reads 10 AM. I don't have class today until noon, so I could just ignore the caller and go back to sleep, but I know it's not going to happen. Taking the phone from my nightstand, I unplug it and feel a pang of disappointment when I see it's Gabi's name flashing on the screen. I decide to ignore her for now, turning the sound off. I try to sleep again, turning right and left in bed, but it feels pointless. Getting up reluctantly, I head to the kitchen to make myself some coffee, trying to shake off the sense of dread that is weighing me down.

Just as the coffee starts to brew, I hear the doorbell ring. Once. Twice. Three times. Whoever it is, they're not giving up. I groan, knowing that I won't be able to ignore it like I did with my phone, shuffle over to the door and open it, still in my pajamas.

Groggily, I check the peephole to confirm my suspicion that it's Gabi on the other side, feeling disoriented and sluggish. I haven't been sleeping as well as usual, and last night my dreams had been plagued by Sebastian in both pleasurable and miserable ways. In one dream, we would be back in my bed, but there would be no interrupting phone call this time around, and in others I watched him walk away from me while my mother tells me that she told me so.

It is indeed Gabi ringing my bell, but even in the fish eye lens of the peephole, I can see that something is off about her. She has her thumbnail in her mouth, and she looks pale. Before she can reach for the doorbell again, I pull the door open to let her inside, my worry burning away some of the tiredness plaguing me.

"Julia, have you heard the news?" she blurts out as soon as I open the door. Her hands fly up to my shoulders, her eyes locked on mine, wide and concerned.

"What news?" I ask, my confusion deepening.

Without another word, Gabi rushes past me and reaches for the remote to turn on the TV in my living room. I follow her as if in a daze, feeling apprehensive. Coffee percolates in the background merrily, the antithesis of whatever is bothering Gabi. It's freaking me out.

As soon as the news channel comes on, my heart drops to my feet. A reporter is announcing that a bomb has exploded in a 1965 Aston Martin DB5 at the Van den Bosch estate, killing three people. My mind goes white with panic, only abating the smallest amount when they list the deceased, and Sebastian isn't among them.

But nearly his entire family is: his mother, sister, and younger brother have all perished.

I sink onto the couch, feeling boneless, and my thoughts go blank as I watch the footage on the screen taken from the street camera, eyes wide with shock. The scene is chaotic, with flames consuming the car and debris scattered everywhere. It's like a scene straight out of a horror movie, so violent and all-consuming that it feels surreal.

I feel a hand on my shoulder and jump, turning around to see Gabi staring at me with a look of concern etched on her face. In truth, I forgot that she was even here.

"Julia, are you okay?" she whispers, her voice laced with worry.

I try to answer her, but my voice catches in my throat. How can I be okay when Sebastian has just lost his entire family in a matter of seconds? His entire world is literally burning to the ground, and there is no way for me to help.

Shakily, I make my way back to my bedroom to get my phone and dial Sebastian's number, praying that he will answer. The agony he must be in is inconceivable, and I don't even know what I'm going to say to him. All I know is that I need to hear his voice and know that he is safe. The news is still playing, and I can't fathom what I am hearing; his entire family is gone in an instant.

My heart races as I hear the click of the call connecting, but no speech. I can hear in the background of the call wails of sorrow, and closer, the rabbit-quick breathing of whoever has answered. The weight of the tragedy hits me like a ton of bricks, and tears begin to stream down my face.

"Sebastian?" I ask, my voice trembling with panic.

"Julia," he replies, his voice monotone and lifeless. I can sense the pain and grief in his tone, and it breaks my heart even more.

"I'm so glad you're okay," I gush, relieved that he's at least physically unharmed. "But, oh God, Sebastian… your mom! Your siblings! I just heard. Are you…?"

"I'm not okay, no," he tells me, cutting me off before I can finish my question. "Physically, sure."

He sounds like a total stranger, all the joy and vigor gone from his deep voice, and it makes me want to reach through the phone and hug him tightly, to take away some of his pain. But I know that's not possible, not right now.

"I don't even know what to say… Sebastian…" I choke out a sob, unable to hold back my emotions any longer. It hurts to imagine him in so much pain, and I can't help but feel his loss as my own.

"You don't need to say anything. I'm hanging up," he says, his tone final and cold.

"Wait!" I call out, desperation creeping into my voice as I try to stop him from hanging up. "I-I'm here for you, Seb. No matter what you need, no matter what time, I'm here for you."

For a moment, I think he might open up to me, let me be there for him in this time of need. His breath hitches on a sob, but then more silence. He has clearly shut down, and I can tell that he's not ready to talk about it yet.

"Stay home," he finally says. "Stay near your mother and don't go out in public alone for a few days, okay? Listen to me, Julia, because I can't lose you, too. I just—" he stammers, his voice breaking. "Just keep yourself safe."

I nod, even though he can't see me. "I will," I promise. "But Seb—"

"We'll talk when I'm back," he interrupts, his tone growing stern. "For now just… fuck, Julia, all I need from you right now is to stay safe."

The call clicks again as the connection is severed, and I hold the phone woodenly in my hands as I try to process everything that is happening right now. The majority of the Van den Bosch family is now dead…murdered… and the crime occurred in Sebastian's car. I recognized the burnt shell of it on the news, have ridden in the passenger seat with the wind in my hair and my mind carefree. Never again, though. My mind is in chaos as I struggle to comprehend the magnitude of the tragedy.

"Who would do such a thing?" I ask, my voice trembling with shock and disbelief. "Oh my gosh, they tried to kill him! It was his car, it was aimed at him!"

Gabi places a comforting hand on my shoulder. "Look, right now you have to calm down, Sebastian is coming back soon, okay? He's going to need you more than ever now. There is barely anyone left that even can be there for him."

But I can't calm down. I feel so powerless and helpless right now. Sebastian is my everything, and the thought of losing him because someone wants to kill him badly enough to rig his car to explode is unbearable. I can't imagine what he must be going through, losing his entire family in one fell swoop.

I shoot to my feet, full of nervous energy, and pace back and forth. The TV continues to play in the background, showing footage of the family, the estate, the car, and telling the story over and over again. It looks, and feels, like a nightmare. I want to turn it off, but I can't stop watching, hoping beyond hope that something in the headline will change as it will become even a little less tragic.

It doesn't change. Things like this never do.

Tears stream down my face as I try to make sense of it all. Why did this happen? Who could be capable of such a heinous act? My mind races with a million questions, but there are no answers to be found.

I feel a sudden urge to hold onto something, someone. So I turn back to the sofa, sitting slowly, where my best friend watches me with tears in her own eyes. I reach for Gabi and hug her tightly, as if trying to hold onto the only anchor I have left in this storm. Gabi hugs me back, her arms a shelter from everything, understanding the depth of my pain the best she is able. It doesn't ease the ache inside of me, not really, but her grip, firm and sure, keeps me in one piece, at least.

***

The minutes drag on as we wait for more news from Sebastian. Gabi pours out the now cold coffee and makes me some fresh, pouring it and bringing me the mug, already doctored with cream and sugar, carefully sitting it in my outstretched hands. It's hot, close to burning, but I don't mind at this point. The heat centers me.

My thoughts are in turmoil, jumping from one idea to the next. I think about the time I've spent with Sebastian, and the things he's told me about the family that he obviously loves very much. He would pretend to sound annoyed about his responsibilities as the oldest sibling, but I never doubted that he cared for his brother and sister with his entire heart. Now all that happiness has been snuffed out. How can someone experience something like that and possibly go on?

Gabi stays for a while, emailing my professors for me and forcing me to shower once I've finished my coffee and the nearly-burnt toast that she made me. I go through the motions in the shower as if on autopilot, barely towel-drying my hair before emerging, changing into a sweatshirt and leggings, and going back to the couch where I have been holding my somber, silent vigil. When I check my phone, Sebastian still hasn't called.

She eventually has to leave, but tucks a blanket around me before she does so, kissing my cheek and squeezing both of my hands in hers to let me know that she's here for me if I need her. It's almost a relief when the door shuts behind her, because now I can let the tears fall and the sobs come without disturbing her.

I never turn the news off, and it never stops covering the Van den Bosch tragedy. As the sun begins to set outside of my window, the news reports that the rest of the family—Sebastian and his dad, Johannes—is safe and on their way back to the Netherlands. There are no further details about it, but it's good to know Sebastian will be home soon.

Startling me, my phone rings, and I scramble to answer it, my heart in my throat. To my surprise, and disappointment, it's my mom on the other end of the line.

"Julia, darling," Mom breathes, doing her best to sound sad. It isn't convincing, though. "I've only just heard the news, my love. I know how hard this whole situation must be on you, but why don't you come home for a few days? I'm sure it'll do you some good to be away from everything and it will give me some peace of mind to know that you are safe."

I consider the offer. Being back at the family home and in the comfort of the place I grew up does sound nice, but I need to be available for when Sebastian returns. I will never be able to see him if I'm under the same roof as my mother, and I know deep in my heart that he's going to need me, even if he denies it. So, for Sebastian, I decline.

"I appreciate your offer, Mom, but I think I should stay here. I've still got class over the next few days," It isn't an outright lie, but definitely not the entire truth, either.

"I don't think it's prudent for you to stay alone in Amsterdam, Julia. You need to be with your family right now," my mom insists.

I can feel the tears welling up in my eyes, but I blink them back. "I will be fine, Mom. I promise. I'll keep in touch and let you know if anything changes," I say, trying to sound more confident than I feel.

We say our goodbyes, and I'm left alone with my thoughts once again. As much as I love my family, I can't bear the thought of having Sebastian showing up at my door and not being home for him in his most vulnerable moments. He needs me now more than ever, and I need him too. The thought of not being able to see him or hold him when he returns is almost too much to bear. I feel so alone and helpless in this moment, and I'm not sure how I'm going to get through it, but immediately feel selfish for having such thoughts. I am not the victim right now, not even close.

I take a deep breath and try to gather myself, knowing that I need to be strong for him when he comes back. But as the minutes tick by, my anxiety grows, and I can feel my resolve slipping away. I just hope he comes back soon, before I completely fall apart.

I reach for my phone and scroll through our messages, reading through our old conversations. The memories flood back, and I'm overcome with longing for him. All his happiness, all his humor, and the things that make him shine so brightly to me have most certainly been destroyed. Will he even be the same man?

I know I need to be strong for Sebastian, but right now, all I can think about is how much I need him to be here with me. Easier said than done, I suppose.

With a deep sigh, I put down my phone and try to focus on the present moment. Sebastian will be back soon, and we'll get through this together. For now, I just need to take things one hour at a time and stay strong.

Sleep comes for me as I still lay on the couch, wrapped in the blanket Gabi gave me, my stomach rumbling but having no desire to eat. It's an uncomfortable night, with the ghostly blue of the television screen filling the room, but I can't make myself get up to find my bed, either, so I accept the restless sleep and wait for dawn.

***

I wake up the next day to a world that feels different from the one I knew just a few days ago. Everything seems to have lost its color, its joy. I drag myself out of the couch and try to make my way through the day, but every little thing reminds me of Sebastian and his family.

And still, he hasn't contacted me.

My stomach lets me know, in no uncertain terms, that we are not skipping out on breakfast, so I decide to walk down to the cafe near my apartment building and get something small just to hold me over, and maybe a few pastries to go in case I get hungry later. As I'm getting dressed, my phone starts buzzing with notifications, but as I've come to expect by now, it's still not Sebastian. It's not just my friends, either, but also the media, who have somehow found out about my connection to Sebastian, probably because of the picture of the two of us dancing that had been published recently. God, it seems like another life, that night that we danced in his ballroom.

The media is relentless, though, and I can't block the numbers fast enough. They're all asking for exclusive information, wanting to know every little detail about what happened. Even if I knew it all, I wouldn't give them a single crumb of info. Seeing them circling this tragedy like vultures makes me feel ill.

I try to ignore the calls and texts as I head out the door, but they keep coming in, one after the other. It's like a constant barrage, and it's starting to drain me both physically and emotionally.

When I arrive at the cafe, I'm relieved to see that it's empty except for a few regulars. I take a seat at my usual table and order an iced coffee, sweet and strong, hoping that the caffeine will help me focus. But as soon as I take a sip, my phone starts buzzing again. This time it's a call from a prominent news reporter, and I can feel my anxiety rising as I answer. Maybe if I take just one single call, the news that I have no information will spread enough that they will leave me alone.

"Can you confirm that Sebastian was on a business trip in Hungary with his dad at the time of the bombing?" the reporter asks the very second the call connects.

"I'm sorry, I can't comment on that," I say, trying to keep my voice steady.

"Are you sure? We just want to get the facts straight," the reporter presses.

"I can't say anything. Please respect the family's privacy during this difficult time. And mine," I add before hanging up. I hope my voice was firm enough, but now, I'm not so sure it was.

I try to drink the coffee, picking at my pain au chocolat, leaving my phone turned upside down so I can't see the screen, but the constant buzzing keeps me on edge. What if it's Sebastian trying to get a hold of me? What if something else terrible happens and I'm just here, ignoring my calls and eating pastries?

Resigned, I look at the phone again. Besides the unknown numbers, there are my friends trying to contact me, most asking if I'm okay since I skipped class yesterday, but some also asking uncomfortable questions. Had that tabloid not published the picture of Sebastian and I at the ball, no one would even know that I'm seeing him. Now, it feels like everyone is privy to my personal life. I love the picture and felt butterflies when it first came out, thinking about how everyone would now know that Sebastian is interested in me, but the memory of it only leaves a sour taste in my mouth now. I try to tell myself that my friends mean well, but it's hard not to feel like they're just using me for information. It's like I'm living in a fishbowl, with everyone watching my every move and waiting for me to slip up.

I try calling Sebastian again, but there's no answer, of course. The silence on the other end of the line feels like a heavy weight in my chest, and I wonder if he's even gotten my messages. All I want to know… all I need to know, is that he's okay.

The day drags on, and my anxiety grows too. I can't shake the feeling that something is terribly wrong. I reason with myself that he's probably just busy with the funeral arrangements or that he's somewhere he can't answer, but the worry in my heart won't go away.

Now, just before dinner as I'm doing some school work on my laptop, watching the always-on television, the news anchors announce the funeral time and location. I feel a rush of relief, knowing that Sebastian is still okay if the funeral is happening, but it's quickly followed by a hollowness inside of me. I desperately want to be there for him, but I might need an invitation to get inside the cathedral. I can't stand the idea of him being there, with only his father, and no one to comfort him at this horrible time. But how can I get an invitation if he won't even contact me at all?

The day comes to a close, and I realize that I've spent the entire day waiting for a call or a message from him. Yet, he hasn't said a word, and my entire being is heavy with worry.

I crawl into bed, my thoughts consumed by the horror of the past few days. I try to picture Sebastian's family in my mind, but all I can see are the images of destruction and chaos from the news…all of it meant for Sebastian. I feel like I'm on the precipice of losing him for good, and it's killing me. All I want to do is hold him.

CHAPTER 16

Julia

I wake up to a dreary morning, my eyes still heavy with sleep. I glance at my phone, hoping for a message from Sebastian, but just like the past few days, there's nothing. Our last call feels like a distant memory. And I can't help but wonder if he has decided to just move on from me to just focus on the grief. I'm sure we're on the same page as far as our relationship, but the last few awful days have made me sick with doubt. I try calling him again, but it goes straight to voicemail.

Today is actually the day of the funeral, and I'm torn up inside thinking about what I should do. I want to go, simply to see Sebastian and be there for him if he needs me, but I feel like I'll be a pariah if I do. No one will know me there, and if Sebastian ignores me, I will be all alone at a terribly tragic, untimely funeral.

But I have to go. There really isn't a choice if I want him to know how seriously I care for him. I know I need to get ready, but my mind is consumed with worry for Sebastian. Where could he be? Is he okay? The worry that whoever killed his family has managed to hurt him too weighs on me every minute of every day, and the fact that he is radio silent isn't helping me at all. I force myself out of bed, trying to push the thoughts out of my head.

My heart is heavy as I try to go about my morning, showering and then eating some yogurt for breakfast. It tastes like sawdust. I try to distract myself by checking the news, but every headline and post only reminds me of the pain and loss that Sebastian's family has suffered.

As the morning drags on, my anxiety grows. I can't shake the feeling that something is wrong, causing Sebastian to ignore me. I pace around my apartment, my mind racing with worry and fear. Finally, I decide that I can't just sit around waiting for Sebastian to call or message me. I need to take action.

The thought of facing the funeral alone, without Sebastian or anyone that I know, makes me feel like a ship adrift in a tempestuous sea. I take a deep breath, trying to steady myself, and begin the process of getting prepared.

I stretch my aching limbs, and my gaze falls upon my wardrobe. What the hell is someone supposed to wear to the funeral of their future husband? I rummage through the hangers, searching for something suitable for the occasion. The dress code for a funeral is somber, but I don't want to look too dreary. After much deliberation, I finally decide on a black dress with an understated floral pattern, also in black, but matted so it only shows in the light. It fits well, which is about all I can ask at the moment.

My reflection in the mirror reveals dark circles under my eyes from lack of sleep. I know I can't afford to look too tired, not when I'm supposed to be a steadying presence to

Sebastian, so I try to cover them with makeup. I apply a few strokes of concealer, dabbing lightly with my fingers until the circles fade away. I don't want anyone, especially Sebastian, to worry about me.

I slip on a pair of black pumps and grab my purse. As I leave my apartment, even the fresh morning air doesn't do anything to erase the dread and sorrow hanging over me. In fact, it seems to hang over the whole world. The wind howls as I hail a taxi, adding to the overall sense of unease.

In the distance, the sky is blue, but directly overhead, heavy gray clouds linger. Rain starts to fall, a light drizzle that seems to match my mood. I give the driver the address of the cathedral in Utrecht. I don't want to call my family's estate to get my own driver; it will tip my mother off to what I'm doing because at this point, I'm pretty sure the entire country knows about the Van den Bosch funeral today. I can't remember there ever being such a big news story since the divorce of my parents—the tragedy is unmatched, and things like this make for great news, at the expense of a family's peace, of course.

The drive is quiet, the only sound is the gentle hum of the engine and the tapping of the rain on the windows. I stare out at the passing buildings, my thoughts drifting back to Sebastian. I can't shake the pit of my stomach. What if something's happened to him? What if I never see him again?

During the long ride to Utrecht, my phone rings and I see my mother's name flashing on the screen. My heart drops, anticipating a scolding for attending the funeral of Sebastian's family. But to my surprise, her voice is gentle and concerned.

"Julia, dear, are you going to the funeral?" she asks immediately. I feel cold, and then hot, but there is no escaping the truth. I might as well be honest with her and hope for the best.

I swallow hard, caught off guard by her knowledge of my plans. "Y-yes, Mom," I reply, after some hesitation. "I need to be there for him."

She pauses for a moment before responding. "I understand, darling." Her voice is softer than usual, and I can't help but find it strange. "If you feel like coming home afterward, I will have a great supper ready for us and we can talk about this tragic event. I hope Sebastian is doing okay?"

My mother's empathy catches me off guard, and tears prick at the corners of my eyes. "I'm not sure, honestly, but I would assume not. But thank you for calling, Mom," I tell her, my voice choked with emotion. "I appreciate it."

As I hang up the phone, I realize that despite the miles between us, my mother's unexpected support is a comfort in this difficult time, even if it is a complete shock. I guess that even if she hates Sebastian, my mother can still look past that to feel kindness toward his family during such a horrible time. I take a deep breath and steel myself for the emotional toll of the day ahead.

I fiddle nervously with the hem of my dress, lost in thought. What will Sebastian say when he sees me? Will he be surprised or upset that I came without him inviting me directly? My thoughts spiral out of control until we arrive at the sad destination.

The taxi pulls up to the cathedral, and I pay the driver before stepping out. The building looms above me, its tall spires disappearing into the low-hanging clouds. I can see the crowds gathering outside; media vans line the street a distance away from the church itself, held back by orange barriers, and reporters are milling about, trying to get exclusive information about the tragedy that has unfolded.

"Wait for me, here," I instruct the driver, before giving him some more cash for him to do so.

Apprehension rolls over me. I know that they will recognize me as someone close to Sebastian if I get within eyesight, and they will want to talk to me, but I can't deal with that right now. I just want to see him and make sure he's okay.

The ominous sight of the church sends chills down my spine. Making my way toward the entrance, my eyes scan the crowd for a familiar face. I expected it, but my chest still feels tight and sweat breaks out on my forehead when I realize there really is no one I know, at least in the crowd outside. Only family and close acquaintances are in the cathedral itself, so maybe I will have better luck there.

I push my way through with my head down, trying to avoid eye contact with anyone. My anxiety is barely held at bay as I approach the entrance to the cathedral. Inside, it's almost silent, except for one voice that carries above all the others. As I step inside, my eyes land on Sebastian standing at the podium, giving his eulogy. Pride cuts through my sadness as I watch him speak. Despite the tragedy that has struck his family, he remains composed and articulate, a true leader.

Looking around, I am struck by the somber atmosphere. People are dressed in black and there are flowers everywhere, which is to be expected, but the air is so thick with grief, and the three caskets at the front of the church pull my eyes to them, no matter how much I want to look away. A knot forms in my stomach as I give a few more steps ahead, wanting to be unobtrusive and not interrupt Sebastian, but still wanting him to know that I'm here.

Then he looks at me—our eyes meet, and the chasm of agony inside of him is evident even from this far away. Sebastian's gaze locks me in place, standing in the middle of the cathedral aisle between the rows of pews, unable to move. He only stops speaking for a moment after seeing me, and I am struck by how composed he sounds. But I know him well enough to see through the facade. I can hear the sadness in his voice, the pain he is trying so hard to hide.

As carefully as I can, I sink down onto the edge of one of the empty pews in the back and continue to watch him give his eulogy for his loved ones. Sebastian keeps it together for longer than I would ever expect, but it doesn't last forever, and I watch as he struggles to speak, his words choked with emotion. My heart breaks for him, and I want to rush to his side and hold him. But this is something he has to do alone if he's ever going to find closure. With a tragedy of this magnitude, a part of me doubts that he ever really will.

"...but their deaths will not be in vain," he says, his voice rising in volume and bouncing off the stone walls and stained glass windows. "Whoever did this doesn't know what we're capable of. The Van den Bosch family will not sit silently by while the ones we love are killed in cold blood. No matter how long it takes, we will find the murderers responsible. I give you all my word."

There is vitriol and cold rage in his tone, and it makes even me, the woman that he's spoken about marriage with, shiver in fear. Listening to Seb talk like this, I believe every word he says. God help whoever did this to him.

Tears stream down my face as I watch him, and I know that I will do whatever it takes to support him, to help him find justice for his family. Together, we will get through this.

***

After Sebastian's eulogy, he goes to sit with his father, and the weight of his words hang heavy over the entire church. I stand as everyone else does, but the press of bodies and the way they all flow towards the doors is unavoidable, and even though I try to turn and see where Sebastian is in the crush, it's impossible. I ache at the thought of coming all this way and not seeing him, especially after the emotional catharsis of his speech, but there's nothing to be done about it. So I go outdoors with everyone else, where the clouds are clearing and the sun is making a slow appearance.

I paid the cab driver extra to wait on me just in case I can't ride with Sebastian to the cemetery, and seeing how many people are still here milling around, I'm glad that I did. Plus, I guess I didn't really understand how dark and personal this would all feel. It's like I'm a foreigner here, and of course Sebastian will want to ride with his father, not his almost-fiancé that he hasn't spoken to for a week now.

Cars are starting to depart and the media is slowly pushing past the barriers as it becomes clear the event is over, so I slide back into the cab and inform him to follow the procession once it gets going. I hope Seb doesn't think that I left without speaking to him, but I will see him soon enough, anyway.

The drive to the cemetery is short, and by the time we arrive, the clouds have fully departed and the warm sun gives the place an oddly cheerful appearance. The funeral procession has already arrived, and as the cab pulls up and out of the way, I can see Sebastian helping his father out of the lead car. The older man looks so unfamiliar that I do a double take. He looks to have aged decades in just days.

There are far fewer people here for the burial, for which I'm thankful. The taxi driver seems annoyed, so I send him off, figuring that if the worst happens, I can just call another one, but I'm determined not to leave without at least having a minute alone with Sebastian. He can't avoid me forever, even if I feel silly and unwelcome here.

Despite the soft yellow sunshine that feels pleasant on my bare arms, the crowd huddled around the empty graves is surrounded by a pocket of coldness, as if their grief is bleeding off of them and into the air. I stand barely behind Sebastian and his father, and up close, leaning heavily on a cane, I can barely contain my shock. He looks so frail, like he could collapse at any moment.

Sebastian and his father move to the edge of the open graves, their faces etched with pain and grief. I know I should stay back, but I can't stop myself from moving forward with them, unseen, wanting to be close, and also feeling heartbroken myself.

The priest speaks the final part of the sermon, his droning voice carrying over the soft sobs and sniffles from the shell-shocked group around me. When Sebastian embraces his father, who breaks down and cries in his arms, my own tears flow freely, and I hate that I have to witness this pain. Then, I hate myself for being so weak that I can't even hold it together for Sebastian like I know I need to. I dash the tears away, feeling Sebastian's eyes on me as he finally notices my presence.

Anguish reaches a fever pitch as the caskets are lowered into the ground, so inescapable that it's hard to breathe. In front of the graves, a few other men joins them. I feel like an intruder, but I can't bring myself to leave. The scene is heart-wrenching, and it seems to drag on forever, like we're in purgatory. Finally, Sebastian turns away from the graves and excuses himself. I realize this might be my only chance to speak to him… he might not want to talk to me right now, but I can't just leave him alone in his misery.

Without hesitation, I walk towards him, my heart heavy with the weight of everything that has happened. We embrace wordlessly, holding onto each other as if our lives depend on it. Sebastian takes a shuddering breath, his face buried in my neck, before pulling back so slowly that I think he won't be able to let me go at all.

Now, Sebastian takes me by the arm and leads me behind one of the small gray stone mausoleums. We are the only two back here, everyone else either departing or lingering around the graves as they are filled. When Sebastian turns to me, cupping my face in his hands and looking down at me, I can see the pain in his eyes, and I want to take it all away, to make him smile and laugh like he used to.

"Julia," he starts, his voice gravelly and strained. "You shouldn't be here. I told you to stay safe."

"Of course I should be here!" I reply, affronted, while keeping my voice low enough so as not to draw attention. "I want to be here for you. You don't have to cut me out of your life just because you're going through hell, you know. We can go through this together."

"Together?" he laughs darkly, head shaking. "For what, exactly? Whoever did this," he motions with both hands back towards the graves, "isn't going to stop until I'm dead. Julia, I really like you. You're a sweet girl, but—"

"But you think you are too dangerous for me? Is that what you think?" I narrow my eyes at him, annoyance cutting through the thick negativity of the moment. I can't believe he's trying to brush me off like this after all the waiting around I've been doing for him! I could slap him, except… I want to kiss him, instead.

Sebastian pinches the bridge of his nose, frustration rolling off him in waves. "I will only bring you pain and suffering, and you don't deserve that. Plus, my dad needs me more than ever. Willem has already been dropping hints that I might need to take over the company sooner rather than later. I'm… fuck, Julia. I'm just not the right guy for you."

"I don't agree with that—" I try to insist, flustered, but he holds a hand up before talking over me.

"My mom and siblings just got killed for fuck's sake," Sebastian's words seem to explode out of him, like he doesn't want to speak them out loud, but can't hold them in any longer. The volume and vehemence in his voice makes me flinch. "God knows what else is going to happen, and staying with me will only put you in harm's way. I refuse to let that happen."

I start shaking my head before he's even finished, stubbornness rising up in me. Who does he think he is, to try and tell me what to do? If he doesn't want me as a lover, or as a wife even, that doesn't mean I'm going to just disappear. I'm remaining in his life one way or another…he needs me. "What if I just stay around as a friend? I can't just go home when you're here in this state. Let me be here for you, Sebastian, please."

He opens his mouth to speak, and his expression tells me that he plans to argue, but before he can, a tall, thin young man walks around the mausoleum into our view. He's dressed for the funeral, but his shoulders are hunched, and he looks sheepish, probably at having to interrupt what is obviously a very personal moment between Sebastian and I. Behind him there are two much larger men, clearly security guards, and it's a stark reminder that Sebastian is in danger every minute of every day now until the killer is caught.

"Seb," the thinner man says. "I'm sorry to interrupt, but we have to make that meeting with your dad, remember?"

I can see Sebastian flush with annoyance, but he doesn't look back at me as he responds. "Of course. I'm coming now. Can you, ah… give us a second?"

The man nods before he leaves, but both security guards remain, lingering close by but with their heads turned away to give us an illusion of privacy. It puts my hackles up in an instant, but I can't tell Sebastian to dismiss them when there are assassins after him.

He turns to me now, and his expression softens. The wind kicks up gently, and brings me the scent of his cologne and skin, and I want nothing more than to take him home with me, pull the curtains shut, and hold him in the darkness so he can spill out all the horrible things that he's holding deep inside. My Sebastian… how do we recover from this?

With a heavy sigh, he pulls me into another embrace, this one lacking the urgency of before but instead full of unsaid things. Sebastian is trying to tell me, without speaking, how much he wants and needs me, how much he doesn't want to leave right now, and I hope I'm conveying the exact same things. Our time here is too short, too steeped in agony. I want more. I want to spend my time running my fingers over the new lines in his face and see if I can put this man that I love back into one piece.

I'll work forever, if that's what it's going to take.

Finally, after a small eternity that still isn't long enough, he pulls back and speaks. "I'll get you a car and you'll go home, alright? Tell your mom I send her my regards."

Looking up at him, I frown. "I'm not going home. I will wait for you at your place, but I don't want to go home."

I can see him waver as his eyes travel up and down my body, lingering on my lips before he meets my eyes once more. For a few brilliant seconds, I think that he's going to agree and take me with him, but then we hear his father speaking to someone on the other side of the mausoleum, and his face shutters once more. I've lost him. "Home, Julia. I will come to see you there, I promise."

"When?" I demand.

He tucks a strand of hair behind my ear, the same soft gesture he did the first time we met. "When the time is right."

Not good enough. I need something more concrete than that. "And when exactly is—"

"I'm so sorry to disturb you but can I get a photo of the two of you? It's for the family album," I hear someone ask, turning to see a photographer with a camera looped around his neck. Annoyance surges in me at being interrupted again, but Sebastian nods. I want to scream, knowing that he's going to use this break in the tension between us to try and get his way, making me leave.

Sebastian wraps his arm around my waist and pulls me against him, side to side, his body warm but his stance stiff and unyielding. I have no idea what to do in a photo at a funeral of all places, so after sneaking a look at Sebastian's face, I allow a small smile to form on my lips until the camera flashes and I can let it fall away once more.

Once the picture is taken, Sebastian grabs my hand before I can continue my argument, weaving our fingers together and leading me back to where all the cars are parked, waiting. He opens the door to an empty one, motioning for me to get inside. I bite my lip, trying to keep my complaints inside, before giving in and bending down to get into the back seat. His eyes flash as he looks inside the car at me, and I'm sure that he's about to kiss me goodbye at least, but then his gaze hardens and he pulls back, shutting the door on me before walking to the driver's window and telling him where to take me. The entire thing only lasts about two minutes, but Sebastian managed to get rid of me before I was even close to being finished talking to him. Defeated, I slump down in the leather car seat as the driver pulls out onto the main road, and cradle my head in my hands.

***

My family home is usually a welcome sight after tough days, but not so much now. I walk through the door, and my heart feels like it's been shattered into a million pieces. I can barely keep my composure as I try to put on a brave face for my mother and fend off the bone-deep exhaustion that I'm suffering from.

It's not that I think Mom will be upset if she can tell how awful I'm feeling, but more so that I'm afraid she will sense how vulnerable I am and pick me apart for information, or to try and get me to agree with her about giving up on dating Sebastian once and for all. She was sweet to me on the phone earlier, sure, but my mother has a very limited well for empathy.

Stuart, our butler, lets me know that she's already in the dining room and that dinner is ready and waiting for me. For some odd reason, we're having dinner in the formal dining room instead of the breakfast nook or in one of our private suites, so the room looks startlingly empty when I open the door and join her. The scent of the food is suffocating, as if it's mocking me for not being able to enjoy it.

Mom rises out of her chair and comes to hug me immediately, smoothing my hair down and holding me for a moment longer than usual. I hug her back, closing my eyes and accepting the comfort that she's offering.

"My poor girl," Mom murmurs, pinning a soft kiss on top of my head. "What a hard day for you."

I sit down at the table, in the seat right next to my mom, and begin picking at my food. I'm barely touching it, my mind elsewhere, lost in a sea of thoughts and emotions. Mom starts talking about the funeral and asking how sad Sebastian seemed to be, but I keep my answers short and succinct, which seems to annoy her. Sebastian's tragedy isn't an appropriate dinner conversation, anyway, and I wish we could talk about anything else.

Still, though, I do feel rejected by him. I know he is hurting, but I can't help but feel like he's pushing me away, even when I came simply to support him if he needed it.

She continues to try and ask questions about the funeral, but I'm lost in thought, trying to process everything that has happened. The family estate, this dinner, Sebastian's coldness—it all feels like a distant dream. I can feel the weight of her words, and how her tone gets more insistent, but they don't seem to penetrate my heart. It's as if I'm numb to everything around me.

The only thing that brings me back to reality is when my mother's voice changes from frustrated to genuine worry. "Julia, please eat something, dear," she says, her voice laced with concern. But I can't bring myself to take a bite.

I give up the charade, and let the fork fall to the plate with a clang. "I just can't. I feel sick about all this."

Mom carefully sits her silverware down and folds her hands on the table, regarding me. "I understand that this is an awful thing, Julia, but you seem more traumatized by it than I anticipated. Why?"

I sigh deeply, still pondering whether to tell her the truth or not. "Sebastian is understandably depressed, but at the funeral, he barely acknowledged me. When he did, he was distant…."

"He might need time," my mother reasons, before taking another sip of her wine. "And his dad will definitely need him more now that the rest of his family is gone. It's much too early to expect him to act like his normal self."

I nod silently, not wanting to engage in conversation. I feel like I'm losing everything. My family, my relationship, my sense of security.

"Maybe this is a sign you shouldn't be around that family," she ventures when I don't say anything. The effect on me is instantaneous, though, and I can feel my blood boil.

How dare she suggest something like that? I know the family has its issues, and now an added layer of danger, but how is this the right time to bring this up? I glare at her but she continues, "I'm just saying…."

I can feel the anger rising inside me, but I know it's not fair to take it out on her. "I'm gonna go upstairs and get some rest," I say, pushing away from the table and heading for the stairs. She calls after me, at first she's kind, then cajoling, and finally, angry, but none of her emotions manage to move me. Not when I'm so busy drowning in my own.

As I climb the stairs, I can feel the weight of the day bearing down on me. The thought of going to bed alone, without any sort of hope or reassurance from Sebastian, is almost unbearable. But I know I have to keep going, keep pushing through the pain. If I have to pretend to be his friend to get close to him, then so be it.

I collapse onto my bed, grabbing a pillow and covering my face with it. I don't know how I'm going to get through this, but I know I have to try. It's just so damn hard….

***

A few hours later, I'm still lying in my bed, a book open but unread on the blanket beside me. Now, I'm staring at the ceiling and trying to push away the thoughts that threaten to pull me down even further than I already am, when my phone rings. It's Sebastian. A vast array of emotions hit me at once: joy, anger, annoyance, and concern. I can't answer fast enough, hands scrambling for the device, my voice barely audible when the call connects. "Hey."

"Hey," he replies back, the sound of his voice a balm to my soul. "Um, I'm outside. Can I come up?"

In a jump, I sit up straight on my bed, barely believing what he is saying. "What? Seb, it's late. Is everything okay? I expected to hear from you during the day."

I want to see him, of course, to be comforted by his presence, but I also don't want to burden him with my pain

"I just need to talk to you. Are you available?"

The concern in his voice makes me worry even more. "What's going on?"

Seb lets out a sigh, taking a moment before answering. "I'm, uh… I'm in front of your gates. Can you let me in?

I frown in confusion. "Like… now?" The thought of knowing he's here, right in front of the gates makes me both thrilled and deeply anxious. Oh gosh, if Mom knows he is here, I can't even imagine what she'd do! Things can turn ugly pretty fast with her around.

"Yeah."

I ponder for a few instants, knowing perfectly well he can't come inside, no. It's too dangerous with Mom around. "I think it's best I come out. Wait for me there."

After hanging up, I get dressed quickly, shutting my door as quietly as possible behind me, and make my way down the stairs. To my annoyance, as I'm about to cross the foyer, the butler intercepts me. "Miss Julia, may I ask where you're going?"

"I'm just stepping outside for a bit," I reply, trying to sound nonchalant, as if he isn't going to repeat to my mother what I'm doing at the first chance anyway.

"Shall I accompany you, Miss?"

"No need," I reply immediately, making my way to the front door. "I will be right back."

Once outside the gates, I see Sebastian standing next to his car, leaning on the vehicle with his hands shoved in his pockets. He gives me a small smile, and I can't help but feel a flicker of warmth in my chest. Despite everything, he still has the power to give me butterflies and lift the veil of sadness, if only for a little while. Instinctively as I approach him, he pulls me into a deep hug, wrapping his arms around me. The warmth of his body comforts me and soothes my racing heart.

I notice how deep and sincere this hug feels, and after a few more instants, I lean back, trying to search for his gaze as I ask him, "What's going on?"

Without answering, he grabs my hand and invites me into his car. I climb into the passenger seat when he opens the door for me, and as soon as he's in and we're completely in private, I take his hand on mine forcing his attention back on me and repeat the question. "Seb, what's going on?"

He inhales slowly before responding, while I keep his hand in mine. His skin is warm, but there is the slightest tremor in his grip, and it breaks my heart. "Nothing. Everything."

My heart sinks at his words, knowing how deeply troubled he must be. I give his hand a gentle squeeze, letting him know I'm here for him. "What happened?" I press softly.

A gasp of air expels from his lungs, his eyes flicking back to mine. "I can't tell you everything yet, Julia, but having you here is helping."

Giving me a reassuring smile, he strokes my knuckles softly, leaving me to wish we could spend the whole night here. Yet, at any moment, Mom is going to find out what's going on and it's going to be a mess. "I'm here for you, Seb, but I only have a few minutes. I wish you'd have called earlier…."

Sebastian looks crestfallen, and I can tell that he's been struggling with something for a while. Something different than the family deaths. I wish we were anywhere else, somewhere that I could hold him like I really want to.

"Do you like me, Julia?" he asks suddenly, his voice hesitant.

I feel my cheeks flush as I process his question. "Hm? What do you mean?"

Sebastian clears his throat, looking embarrassed, and repeats his question, "Like do you enjoy my company despite our age gap?"

After a moment of hesitation, I answer honestly. "I do, yes. Very much so… and you?"

Sebastian's expression softens at my response, but then his tone turns serious. "I... I do too, but my dad isn't too happy about it."

I roll my eyes and chuckle. The cliché is the woman's dad being overprotective, but here we are with the tables turned. Sebastian's dad might be hesitant, but at least he's present. Mine isn't even around. "Well, if that makes you feel any better, my dad has no idea that you exist, so we're zero for two on the dad front."

Sebastian hums. "Don't you ever call him?"

I haven't made the effort to call my father in a long time, mostly because he has never made the effort to call me, either. It hurts, but we weren't close, even when he and Mom were together. "Sometimes, but Mom would be quite furious if she knew I was talking to him. Better to not complicate things by bringing you into the conversation, as well."

He seems to think things over before speaking again, and if I didn't know better, I would think that he's having a difficult time saying the words. "Speaking of your mother, does she know about us? I mean, does she know we're more than friends?"

It's a difficult question. Does she know? Yes. Does she approve even the tiniest bit? Hell no. "To a certain extent..." I say, my voice trailing off. I reach for the controls for the heated seats, trying to distract myself from the conversation.

But then he presses me for more information, and I find myself opening up to him. I tell him about how my mother knows about us, but she's not exactly thrilled. The surprise on his face is evident, and I feel a mix of relief and anxiety at his reaction.

"I assume she already hates me, then," he jokes, but I know that there's a part of him that's serious.

"You assume correctly," I say with a sad smile, but then I lean in closer to him, wanting to end these pointless, frustrating, negative conversations about our parents. Sebastian inhales sharply as I move into his personal space, his pupils widening. "But that doesn't mean I give a damn about it."

As our eyes meet, I can feel a spark of desire flicker between us. His touch on my cheek sends shivers down my spine. I want nothing more than to feel his lips on mine, but he pulls back and speaks.

"I want to meet your parents before going any further," he demands, and I can't help but be surprised.

My eyes widen at his words and I find myself struggling to form a proper sentence. "Are you serious?"

He nods firmly, his voice deep with emotion. "Why not? I don't want to hide this. I don't want to treat whatever we have as some sort of dark secret that we have to be ashamed of. You deserve to be in the light, Julia."

Sebastian's words hit me right in the heart, and if I've ever had any doubt that he's the right man for me, it's all gone now. I search his face for any signs of hesitation but find none. "Fine," I say, still not sure that it's the right choice. "But Dad isn't going to fly to Amsterdam, let me tell you right away. He's gone and can't come back."

Sebastian hesitates. "Why can't he travel?"

Not wanting to get into a deep conversation about this, I simply shrug. "It's got to do with Mom. That's all I know. It's not like either of them would ever talk to me about it."

He blinks a few times, processing what I've told him, before he speaks up again. "I will speak with your mom, then," he says confidently. "I want her to know that my feelings for you are serious and true."

I can't believe what I'm hearing. "You want to meet Mom?" I gasp. "Oh gosh, I don't know about that."

"She can't be as scary as my dad," Sebastian jokes, but I can't bring myself to laugh. The reality of the situation looms large, and I can't shake the feeling of trepidation that washes over me. When I don't respond to the jest, his grin slowly starts to fall. "Can she…?"

Lost in thought, I'm caught off guard by the sound of my phone ringing. Checking the caller ID, I let out a sigh upon seeing that it's Mom. I've been busted, and our rendezvous has to end now if we don't want my mother pounding on his car's windows any second.

"I have to go," I tell him, my anxiety already steadily rising. "I'll try to set up the meeting, but you can't rush me. It's not going to be easy."

Sebastian exits the car and opens the door for me, a small act of chivalry that I'm grateful for. I wrap my arms around him, not nearly satisfied by the hug but taking what joy and closeness I can from it. Despite my reservations, and all of the terrible things that have happened, I can't help but fall for him hard.

CHAPTER 17

Sebastian

This morning caught me off guard. When I woke up, it didn't hit me until I was brushing my teeth after my shower: today is my first day as the CEO of Van den Bosch Industries. It took me by such a surprise that I almost dropped my toothbrush, but managed to keep a hold of it and coax my galloping pulse down to a normal rhythm.

Now, I'm here—at the high rise that holds my family's business, which I'm now at the helm of. I've seen these two doors a million times it feels like, but today they look completely foreign to me. This reality still doesn't seem real… with the death of my mother and siblings, and my ascension in the company, my world has changed so drastically in just a mere few days that I wonder if I'm even the same man as I was before.

I step closer to the doors, taking a deep breath before pushing them open. The office is just as I remember it, with its sleek, modern design and polished wooden floors, and employees bustling around to get the day started. At first, I start to go to my normal office, but pause. Instead, I change course and head to the office that still belongs to my father, but will soon be mine. I might as well get used to the new routine, I guess.

Inside the huge room, the scent of leather from my dad's favorite armchair fills the air, and for a moment, I'm transported back to my childhood. I walk over to his—well, now my—desk and take a seat in his chair. It feels strange to be sitting here without him, but I remind myself that I have a job to do. I have to keep this company running, no matter how out of place I may feel. I've been preparing for this my entire professional life, but I'd give it all up to have my family back. But, as it is, I just have to make do.

A knock sounds from the door, and I look up to see Karl, dressed in the finest suit I've ever seen him wear, with his hair slicked back. He must be nervous for today, too, and I can't really blame him. As the son of Johannes Van den Bosch, the reins were always going to be passed to me, but Karl is undeniably Dad's protégé in the sales portion of the company. He's expected to become my right hand man now, so the first day jitters are affecting him as well.

I take a deep breath, feeling a sense of gratitude wash over me. Dad might have stepped down, but I still have Karl. And for that, I'm thankful.

"Good morning," he greets softly, giving me a reassuring smile. "How are you holding up?"

I shrug, not sure how to answer. "I don't know, Karl. It still doesn't feel real."

"I know." His voice's gentle and he takes a few steps in my direction. "But we have to keep moving forward. Your dad wouldn't want us to stop."

I nod, feeling a lump form in my throat. He's right, of course. My dad was never one to dwell on the past. He was always looking to the future, to the next big idea… but the way he's talking about my father makes me feel ill. Dad isn't dead yet, like everyone else, so why is everyone acting like he is?

"He's not gone," I force out between my teeth, pushing my anger at the world down. It isn't Karl's fault I feel like this, though. "He's still going to be a part of the company, serving as the new chairman."

"I know," he responds quickly. "I think we both know that he isn't functioning at his full capacity right now, and most of this is going to fall on you for the time being. But you're not alone. We're all here to help you. We're a team." Karl joins me in the room, taking a seat in one of the chairs across from me. "So, what's the plan?" he asks, his eyes meeting mine.

I take a deep breath, trying to steady myself. "First, we need to review the financials. I want to make sure we're on track for the next quarter."

Karl nods in agreement. "Okay, I'll pull up the reports."

As I start typing away at the computer, I can't help but feel a sense of harsh apprehension wash over me. My dad made it look so easy, running this company and managing the finances. But now it's my turn, and I'm not sure if I'm ready for it.

We spend the next hour going over the reports, discussing sales numbers and projections. Karl is a wealth of sales knowledge, and I'm grateful for his assistance. But as we dig deeper into the financials, I start to feel a sense of panic. What if I can't do this? What if I'm not good enough?

Karl notices my unease and puts a hand on my shoulder. “Hey, don’t worry. You’ll get the hang of it. It takes time, but you’ll get there.”

I nod, grateful for his words of encouragement. “Thanks. I just wish my dad was here to at least ease me into everything. There’s just no way I can possibly ask that of him right now, but I feel like I’ve just been thrown in the deep end, you know?”

“I get it. Go easy on yourself, though. You lost your family, too.” He raises his wrist to look at his watch, and inhales sharply. “Hey, it’s almost time for the press conference. Are you ready?”

No, I’m far from ready, but what choice do I have?

I stand, straighten my suit, and square my shoulders. “As ready as I’ll ever be. Let’s go.”

***

Karl and I arrive at the auditorium, where the press conference is already in full swing. All of the company’s employees are gathered here, and as I scan the crowd, I feel a jolt of nerves as I realize just how many people are watching.

But I can't let that show. I take a deep breath and step up to the podium where there is a microphone pinned on, the bright flashes of the cameras momentarily blinding me as I address the crowd.

“I want to thank you all for being here today,” I say, my voice steady despite the churning in my stomach. “As you all know, my father was the heart and soul of this company. My family built it from the ground up, and I'm honored to be taking over as CEO."

The audience responds with a murmur of agreement, and I feel a small surge of pride at their positive reception. This is what my dad would have wanted. For the company he loved to continue to thrive, no matter what.

"My dad will be stepping down as CEO, but he'll still be here as the chairman," I continue. "And I promise you all that we'll continue to innovate, to grow, and to make him proud."

As I speak, I can feel my family's presence all around me. Memories of them flood my mind, and I take a moment to steady myself before continuing.

The crowd listens intently as I field a few questions from the audience, doing my best to answer them, even as my mind is filled with thoughts of my loss, especially my mother. How proud she would have been of me, how hard it will be to care for my father without her, how much I miss her already.

Despite my nerves, I feel a sense of purpose growing within me as I speak. I know that I have a lot to live up to, but I'm determined to honor my father's legacy by leading this company to even greater heights.

I look around constantly throughout the conference, searching for my dad, hoping that as the new chairman, he would at least be in attendance. But he is nowhere to be found, and it gives me a shiver of nervousness. I hope he's okay.

As the press conference comes to a close, the employees file out of the auditorium, leaving Karl and me alone in the room. The sense of responsibility weighs heavily on me, and I know that the real work is just beginning. I have big shoes to fill, but if everything goes to plan, Dad will be at my side for a long time yet to guide and support me.

We make our way to my old office, where I intend to work until the changeover is complete. Hell, if Dad wants to keep his office even as chairman, I don't care. As long as he's here with me. While we walk, Karl puts a hand on my shoulder, and I turn to him.

"Sebastian, if you ever need anything, anything at all, you know where to find me," he says, a look of genuine concern on his face.

I nod, feeling grateful for his support. "Thanks, Karl. That was a lot, wasn't it?"

He chuckles. "Yeah, it really was, but you handled it way better than anyone else I know could have. Do you need anything else from me right now before we finally get started on our actual jobs?"

"I don't think so. Just… can you let me know if…erm, when Dad gets here? I expected him at the press conference, but he wasn't there."

"Absolutely. Hey, and good luck on your first day, boss."

Despite how miserable I feel, I laugh. "I'll try."

***

I take my lunch with some of the company directors, and while I'm not the only one that notices my dad's continued absence, I do well enough that I think they are all impressed and relieved to find me nearly as capable as my father. We're walking through the office building, just chatting, when suddenly, my assistant catches up to me, her heels clicking sharply on the polished marble floor.

"Sebastian, there's a woman named Margaret who would like to speak with you," she says, her voice low and sympathetic, eyes darting around to the other men that are with me as if she isn't sure if she's interrupting or not.

My head immediately begins to pound at the thought of Margaret. She's never been fond of me, but over the last few days, I've put some pieces together that cast in her the darkest light possible. There's evil, and then there is Margaret. And I want to marry her daughter, so it isn't like I can avoid her.

"Of course. Please show her to my office," I tell my assistant steadily, watching as she departs.

I take the time to shake hands with the directors and wish them well, but my mind is elsewhere. I knew this meeting with Margaret was coming sooner rather than later, but I thought I would have more time to formulate my plan of attack. Convincing her to let me marry Julia is going to be a nearly-impossible uphill battle, and I need all the advantages I can get. She's clever, catching me off guard at my weakest like this, but I make a promise to myself not to let her get the best of me.

When I reach my office, I see Margaret waiting for me there, standing with her hands clasped behind her back and examining one of the pieces of art with a critical eye. She turns as I approach, and I immediately notice the sharp expression on her face. I greet her with a polite smile, but her response is dripping with sarcasm.

"I figured since you wanted to meet me, that I would make your life a bit easier and show up at your office. I hope you don't mind." Her smile is saccharine and completely fake.

"Of course not," I respond, waving a hand to one of the plush chairs across from my desk. "Please, have a seat."

At my invitation, she sits gracefully, crossing one long leg over the other while I take my seat across from her. She watches me with eyes like a cat, narrowed and missing nothing. The tension in the air is palpable, and I can't help but feel on edge. I wait for her to speak, unsure of what to expect. But instead of offering condolences like everyone else, Margaret gets straight to the point.

"Sebastian, I want to talk to you about my daughter."

My stomach twists even more. I knew this was coming, but I had hoped to have a bit of time to grieve before dealing with Margaret's drama. I steel myself for what's to come and try to remain calm.

"I know why you came here, Ms. Van Dieren," I start, my tone neutral. "I can assure you—"

"Oh, please, call me Margaret," she interrupts, waving a perfectly manicured hand.

I take a deep breath and prepare myself for the inevitable rejection. "Well, Margaret, I know why you came all the way here, and the answer to your request is *no*."

Margaret's response is swift and cutting. "Oh, that's going to make our conversation much more difficult, then."

I can feel the weight of her disapproval bearing down on me. I love Julia with all my heart, but Margaret doesn't seem to understand the depth of my feelings. I need to make her understand, and if that doesn't work, I need to make her see that I'm not going to back down so easily.

"I love Julia. And despite what I feel for her, I've never done a single inappropriate thing with her."

"And what do you expect in return? An award?" Margaret sneers. "I'm sure you know that I'm not your biggest fan, Sebastian…" her voice is laced with barely-concealed disdain, causing me to grit my teeth.

I know I'm not the most reputable person, but I've never felt this way about anyone before. "I want to propose," I say firmly. "The death of my mother and siblings made me realize how short and precious life is. I don't want to waste any more time."

Margaret's response is nothing but disgust. "But of course. A new trophy to add to your collection."

I can feel my blood boiling, but I try to stay composed. "She feels the same about me, you know."

Margaret scoffs. "She's nineteen, she's got no idea what her feelings really are. She's conflating lust and love. And you seem to be making the same mistake, which is honestly laughable for a man of your age." She turns her nose up at me with a curl of her lip. "I expected more from the Van den Bosch heir, honestly."

My resolve falters. I know Margaret has never approved of our relationship, but her words still sting. I take a deep breath and try to respond as calmly as possible. "I assure you, Margaret, if I only wanted her for her body, I wouldn't be sitting here discussing this with you," I state, my voice unwavering.

Margaret raises a skeptical eyebrow. "You've only known her for a matter of weeks. How can you be so sure?"

My body fills with determination. "I knew from the moment I met her that she was the one I have been waiting for all my life."

The older woman rolls her eyes and cackles. "Ah yes, love at first sight. How charmingly naive."

I take a deep breath, fighting to keep my composure. "I'm certain that she feels the same way, and yet you have dismissed her feelings just as you are dismissing mine."

She lets out a long, exaggerated sigh. "I understand that you believe this is something more, but it's time to face reality. This little fling of yours ends now."

Blood pounds in my head like the beat of a thousand drums. God, this woman makes me angrier than I ever imagined being. "I'm afraid I cannot do that," I say as calmly as I can, staring directly into her eyes. Her gaze is as sharp as a knife, but I am stone, and she can't cut through me.

The tension in the room is so thick that it is almost palpable. Margaret is fidgeting impatiently, and her eyes dart around the room before settling on the photograph of my family on the desk. She stands, folding her hands behind her back again as she bends at the waist to see the picture better. I feel a chill run down my spine as I watch her inspect it.

"What a beautiful family," she says, feigning sympathy. "I'm so sorry for your loss. So terrible for someone to have done such a thing to them."

I can feel my muscles tense up as I respond through gritted teeth, shooting to my feet with nervous energy and resisting the urge to pace. "Thanks, but they were not the target. I was."

I pick up the frame and examine it closely, studying every detail of my family's smiling faces. My heart aches for them, and I can't shake off the feeling that Margaret had something to do with their deaths. But I keep my suspicions to myself, knowing that any accusation will only make things worse.

"It's just a matter of time before we find out who did it," I add, placing the frame back on the desk.

Margaret's sly smile tells me that she knows something I don't. "Let's hope you catch them before they take down their actual target." There's a flash of something sinister in her eyes. "You."

I clench my fists and stare her down, my resolve hardening with each passing moment. I won't let her get away with this. "I will catch them," I say, my voice low and steady. "And when I do, they will pay for what they did."

Margaret van Dieren is a bitch, but as the minutes pass, I'm more and more sure that she's a monster, too. She shrugs one thin shoulder, replying flippantly, "Maybe so."

"Margaret," I growl, and she whips her head around to look at me, the change in my voice startling her. Good. "If you let me marry Julia, I won't put you in jail, and your daughter will never know it was you."

She looks shocked for only a portion of a second, but then her face becomes stoic. She's clearly an experienced negotiator and not easily rattled.

"As much as I'd love to remove you from this planet, it wasn't me." There's a hint of disdain in her voice, and she checks her nails nonchalantly. But I'm more observant than that, and I can see her pulse fluttering as fast as a hummingbird's wings through the thin skin of her neck.

I won't let her off the hook that easily. "I'm afraid whether it's true or not, you had a strong motive, which makes you the number one suspect," I continue, watching as she begins to consider my proposal. "Margaret, I know you hate me, there's no denying it. And I can easily take this story to the media and the police," I add, hoping to sway her.

"You have no evidence," she counters, still not looking up from her fingernails. But her spine is ramrod straight, and her chest rises and falls more swiftly with each passing moment.

"The media don't need evidence to publish a story," I point out, circling her where she stands like a shark. "And once public opinion starts railing against you, a prosecution will follow. You know well how those things work." I grin cruelly, feeling a sense of satisfaction as I watch her finally start to crack.

Now she looks at me, eyes narrowed like a snake and hisses. "Whether you marry her or not, I will never like you."

"I've never, and will never, ask you to like me. Just don't ruin your daughter's happiness. That's all I'll ever ask," I cajole, hoping to strike a deal. She's on the ropes now, and I know it.

Margaret seems to consider my words for a moment before snipping, "Well, that was a very enlightening discussion." She begins to leave, grabbing her bag and walking quickly towards the door of my office, but I stop her with a firm grip on one of her shoulders. I can feel her bones under my hand, and it disturbs me. Hate has worn this woman so thin, burning everything but misery out of her.

"Do we have an agreement?" I demand, feeling a sense of anticipation.

"I will let you know soon enough," she snaps, looking directly forward. As soon as I release her, knowing this is the best that I will get today, she adds a short, "Goodbye," and exits the room. I don't watch to make sure she leaves, but I do page security on the desk phone to make sure someone has eyes on her leaving the building.

I'm left standing here now, alone, wondering if I've just made a deal with the devil.

Fuck it. Devil or not, Julia is worth it. I'd walk through hell for her, and if her mother has her way, I might have to do just that—and I will. I swear I will.

Sinking into my leather computer chair, I rest my elbows on my desk and my head in my hands, setting out a shuddering breath as I sit alone in my office. I inhale deeply, trying to settle myself somewhat, and pick up the phone to call Julia. My heartbeat is still pounding in my ears, made even louder as it echoes off the phone as I wait for her to answer.

Julia's voice, in total opposition to the icy sound of her mother just minutes ago, is like the signing of angels. "She came to your office, didn't she?"

I laugh darkly. "Yeah, she sure as hell did. God, Julia, you couldn't have at least given me a heads up?"

I can hear her suck in an empathetic breath. "I meant to, really I did, but I wasn't sure if she'd actually go through with it, and if she didn't, I didn't want to bother you on your first day as CEO."

"Well, for one, you're never a bother. Second, if it involves your mother, I don't care what I'm doing, please, *please* warn me."

"How'd it go?" Her voice is small, but I can hear the anticipation in it. Julia has no idea what I suspect her mother of doing, and if I can help it, she never will, so I'm counting on the hope that she'll believe that I was able to crack her mother just from my own willpower alone.

"As well as I expected," I reply, trying to keep my tone confident.

"I think Mom will come around eventually. She just doesn't like to lose," Julia reassures me, and I can hear the hope in her voice.

"I understand. Our family is—" I stop, feeling like someone is choking me, before I push the words past my throat. "Our family *was* like that, too. We played to win." I hope Julia can't tell that I'm trying to mask my growing anxiety. "She might not lose often, but she definitely underestimated me."

She giggles. "Oh, is that so? I'll have to remember never to do the same. But, Sebastian… when will I see you again?" There is a clear note of hope in her tone, and I can feel the pressure mounting. As much as I want her in my arms right now, there are other obligations I can't escape. Not yet, at least.

"Soon enough. I've got a lot of work to do with all these new changes in management, and my dad needs me," I say, praying she won't push me further.

"I see…" Julia trails off, and I can sense her disappointment.

"Julia?" I ask, trying to sound reassuring. "Give me some time, okay?"

She lets out a downtrodden sigh. "Okay, bye."

"Julia," I say again, but she's already ended the call. I curse, hating this less than stellar ending to my confrontation with Margaret, but I know there is no help for it. I just need to get through these next few days, and then I will have so much more time for Julia.

I lean back in my chair, and I can feel the weight of the situation bearing down on me. The stakes are high, and I know I need to tread carefully if I want to win. Margaret is a formidable opponent, and I can't afford to underestimate her. But I have a plan, and I'm confident that with time, I can make it a reality. I just need to stay focused and keep pushing forward. This whole situation is like a high-stakes game of chess, and I'm determined to win. But I can't get too cocky.

I take a quick glance at the photo of my family on my desk. They were taken from me too soon, but I won't let their deaths be in vain. I'll use everything I have to make sure Julia is happy and safe.

I check my watch and realize I need to get back to work. I have meetings to attend, emails to send, and plans to make. This is just the beginning, but I'm ready for whatever comes my way.

***

Once I end the call with the last client of the evening, I take a moment to collect myself. My mind is racing with thoughts of what I need to do next to secure my plan. I know that I need to make sure that Margaret doesn't try to cross me, but I also need to find a way to get Julia fully on my side.

I walk over to the window and look out at the city below. The lights twinkle in the distance, and I feel a sense of power. I know that I have the ability to make things happen, to bend the world to my will, but I don't want that. Not even a little bit. All I want is *her*.

My mind begins to wander, and I can feel the heat rising in my chest as I think about her soft skin and her beautiful smile.... The sudden knock at the door pulls me back to reality with a jump. I turn to see my assistant, Amelia, standing there with a stack of papers in her hand.

"Sorry to interrupt, Mr. Van den Bosch," she says quickly, "but I have the new financial reports for you to sign."

I take the papers and quickly scan them. I sign off on them without really looking at the details and hand them back. It's all just a distraction, but the paperwork is a necessary evil.

As Amelia leaves, I have to stomp down a wave of frustration. I know that I'm wasting my time on these mundane tasks, but I also know that I can't ignore them. I take a deep breath and try to clear my mind.

I return to my desk and begin to go over my notes. I have a list of people that I need to talk to, and I know that I need to be strategic about how I approach them. I spend the next hour going over the details of my next few days, regarding both Julia and Margaret, but also Dad and the company, making sure that every aspect is covered.

Despite how awful I have felt recently, there is excitement building. I know that I'm on the cusp of something big, and I can't wait to see it all come together.

CHAPTER 18

Sebastian

I'm just about to pack up for the evening when my office phone begins to ring. I consider not picking it up at all, completely done with the day, but something makes me turn around and pick the receiver up.

"Sebastian, it's Karl. Your dad came in about thirty minutes ago to see how the day went and he's in his office. I was going to come tell you in person but my secretary just told me that she buzzed a nurse in to go see him, so I figured you'd want to know as soon as possible."

My blood runs cold at his words. "Thanks, on my way," I tell him shortly, hanging up and not even bothering to say goodbye. Of course my stubborn, ridiculous father would arrive without telling me and then have some sort of medical emergency!

Only the fact that it's a nurse attending to him and not a gaggle of paramedics keeps me from sprinting all the way up the stairs to his office. Everything is still relatively peaceful once I'm in the hallway leading there, so I slow down and catch my breath, not wanting to alarm him by busting in wheezing.

The lights are down low, and I see my dad sitting on the couch with a nurse taking his vitals. There is an IV stand next to him giving him fluids, while the machine on the top of it keeps track of his pulse. I feel a twinge of worry in my chest. He's always been so strong, and to see him like this is jarring.

"My boy," Dad says softly, and I come to him, bending over to give him a quick embrace before jerking my head to the nurse, indicating I want to talk to her off to the side.

The nurse quietly tells me that his pulse is very low, and she recommends that he be admitted to a hospital. I nod, feeling the weight of the situation settle on my shoulders. I know that I need to be strong for him, but it's hard when everything feels like it's falling apart.

"Does he need to go tonight?" I ask, and the nurse shakes her head.

"He's stable, and I'll stay with him once he gets home, as well. I just worry that one nurse isn't enough care for him."

"How…" I swallow past the lump in my throat, "how long do you think he will need to stay? He loves his job…."

"The stress and grief are very, very hard on his heart. I think your father would also benefit from seeing a therapist. When he begins to process his grief, his physical health will improve, too."

After thanking the nurse and dismissing her, I go to sit next to my father, who looks glad to see me. Dad is normally never on the couch. He's always behind his desk, looking like he's in control of the entire universe, and it's so painful to see such small but clear indications of his decline.

"Everyone tells me that you handled the press conference perfectly," Dad says, patting me on the shoulder as I sit down next to him. "Good job, son. I knew I was leaving the company in the best possible hands."

"Thanks." I take a deep breath and try to steady my nerves. "Dad, look, I know firsthand that there's nothing like losing those we love." My voice is barely above a whisper. "And I want you to know that grieving takes time and it's okay. It's all okay. We'll get through it together. But you can't neglect your health."

He turns his head away, shaking it. "I don't want to talk about this right now. I didn't come to the office to talk about my damn health."

I refuse to hear it. He can't continue to avoid things just because it hurts to face them. "There's nothing we can do but move forward, Dad," I insist, leaning in so he can't avoid looking at me. "We can't go back in time no matter how much we want to."

My dad lowers his gaze and then, to my horror, begins to cry in earnest, his tears falling freely down his face. It's the first time he's cried since the funeral, and it breaks my heart to see him in such pain. As if on instinct, my arms go around his shoulders, and I pull him into me so I support him as he exercises his demons, tear by tear.

"I should've spent more time with them," he gasps between sobs. "But I didn't, and now they're gone. I—fuck, I don't even recall the last time I told Dina I loved her. I'd give anything to hold your mother one more time."

It takes every ounce of my willpower not to succumb and cry too, and I have to suck in air through my teeth to remain in control. "Dad, you need to take care of yourself," I say firmly. "You can't keep pushing yourself like this."

As I sit there with him, I can't help but think back to all the missed opportunities we had as a family. The time we could have spent together but chose to prioritize work or other commitments instead. It's a painful realization, but one that I need to confront in order to move forward. Julia's face passes through my consciousness, and I make a silent vow to never let her fall by the wayside. Seeing my dad fall to pieces reminds me all over again how much she means to me, and how I plan to treat her as best as I possibly can for the rest of our lives.

"I know it's hard, Dad," I say softly, breaking the silence. "But we can't change the past. All we can do is learn from it and make the most of what we have now."

My dad looks up at me, his eyes filled with gratitude and soul-deep grief. "You're right, son," he says, his voice barely above a whisper. "I just wish I could have done things differently."

"I know," I say, squeezing his hand. "But we can't dwell on the past. We have to focus on the present and the future."

We sit there in the quiet for a few minutes, lost in our own thoughts. I can feel the weight of the situation bearing down on me, but I try to remain strong for my dad. It's not easy, but I know that I have to be there for him, just like he was there for me when I needed him.

Eventually, my dad speaks again, and now his voice is steady. "Sebastian, I'm sorry for everything. I'm sorry for not being there for you like I should have been."

I shake my head. “No, Dad. You did the best you could with what you had. And you’ve always been there for me, even when things were tough.”

He nods weakly, and I can see the fear in his eyes. I know he’s scared of what’s happening to him, and I feel a sense of helplessness that is completely foreign to me. I wish I could fix everything, but I know that’s not possible. I want to tell him how much I love him and how grateful I am for everything he’s done for me, and how much I still need him in my life, especially now, but the words get caught in my throat.

If I can’t broach the subject about everything between us right now, at least I can tell him about everything happening in my relationship with the Van Dieren heiress. Sucking in a breath, I quickly go over the words in my head. It’s time to tell my dad the truth. About Julia. About us.

Gathering my thoughts, I clear my throat. This conversation with my dad has been a long time coming, and I can feel the weight of it pressing down on me. Margaret and her disapproval is a shadow hanging over our lives, and the quicker we can get past her, the better.

“Dad,” I begin, my voice as calm as I can possibly make it. “There’s something I need to talk to you about. It’s important.”

My dad looks at me curiously, sensing the gravity of the situation. “What is it, son?”

“It’s about Julia,” I reply, my heart pounding in my chest. "Margaret Van Dieren’s daughter. I’ve been keeping something from you… something that I need to tell you.”

My dad’s expression becomes more serious, and he leans forward slightly in his chair. “Go on,” he says, his eyes fixed on mine. "I think I have an idea of what you're about to tell me, but maybe I will be surprised."

I chuckle. "No, you're probably right on the money. I spoke to Margaret about Julia earlier today," I continue, my words coming out in a rush. "And I think she'll eventually come around and accept us. Begrudgingly, of course."

There's a moment of silence as my dad takes this in, his brow furrowed in thought. Then he asks the question that I've been dreading.

"So she's not just a friend, is she?" It's clearly a rhetorical question. He already knows the answer.

I shake my head, both uncomfortable admitting all of this to him and relieved to have it all out on the table. "No, Dad," I admit, feeling a sense of uneasiness at what I'm about to say. "She's not just a friend. She's a very special woman and I'd like to propose to her so she knows I'm not wasting her time."

For a moment, my dad just stares at me, his face unreadable. I can feel the tension in the room, the air thick with anticipation. Then he speaks, his voice surprisingly gentle. "You don't have to rush, son. Take your time. Make sure she's the one you want to spend the rest of your life with."

"I'm not rushing, Dad," I interpose immediately. "I know we're meant to be together. And I want her by my side, always."

My dad nods, seeming to understand the depth of my feelings. "Well, if you're so sure, then you should bring her over. I'm not the one who's going to forbid you to be with the woman you love."

Just like that, everything falls away from me, and I feel a freedom that is as pure as snow. There. It's done. He knows my intentions. My dad may not be completely on board with my relationship with Julia, but he's not actively trying to stop me either. It's a start, and certainly, a better one than I've had with Julia's mother.

We continue talking, delving deeper into the intricacies of my relationship with Julia. I tell my dad about all the things that I love about her, about the way she makes me feel alive and whole. And as I speak, I can feel the love that I have for her pouring out of me, filling the room with its warmth and intensity.

My dad listens patiently, nodding along as I speak. He asks questions, wanting to know more about this woman who has captured my heart. And I answer, eager to share everything that I know about the woman that I love.

As the conversation comes to an end, my dad reaches out and takes my hand. "Just remember, son," he says, his voice reassuring. "No matter what happens, treat her with all the reverence and love in the world, every day of your life. Things can change in an instant, and living with regrets is by far the hardest thing I've ever done."

I grip his hand firmly in a gesture of affection, while the hollow of what we've lost lies between us. "I know, Dad. I know."

CHAPTER 19

Sebastian

My confrontation with Margaret had flooded me with adrenaline in the moment, but I didn't expect it to linger so long on my mind. When it was the first thing that I thought about the following morning, and I couldn't shake it, I came to terms with the idea that I'll need some time to process the fight.

I think, all things considered, that I won the argument and came out on top, but when I pick all the words said apart in my brain, I feel less and less confident of this fact. Plus, the fact that Julia is the only thought that I have when I'm not analyzing the argument with her mom isn't helping, either.

I decided to reach out to her so we can see each other again. Emotions are almost painfully high between us after meeting up at the funeral, but I can't let them spin out of control, or everything we've gone through so far will be pointless. So, even though when I see her next, I want to sweep her into my arms and kiss her senseless, or tell her how far I'm willing to go to make her mine, I don't. I keep her at arm's length just enough that we both are able to keep our wits about us, and some of the horrible tension I've been holding since the funeral starts to slowly bleed away.

We decide to meet each other a few times through the week and explore places around the city where we are least likely to be interrupted by people who may know us, or even the media. I cherish every moment I spend with her. The hours I spend at work and taking care of my father are gray and dull, but the hours I manage to carve out for Julia and I are brilliant and full of color and life. Despite not wanting to raise her expectations too much about a potential proposal, considering that I don't think that things are completely settled with her mother just yet, it's impossible not to drop little hints here and there about it. We talk about our future together like it's something that's expected, inevitable, even, and it feels so natural that it boggles my mind when I look back on it.

During an afternoon when I extended my lunch break to be with her, we find ourselves strolling together in a park more crowded than usual. It's a warm, sunny day, and the park is bustling with people, the edges of the paths lined with perfectly manicured flowers and fat, fuzzy bees buzzing from one to the other. We stroll along the winding paths, taking in the sights and sounds of nature around us. The leaves rustle gently in the breeze, and the birds chirp merrily in the trees.

She talks to me about classes, the things that she struggles with, and the things at which she excels, and her sweet voice lulls me into a statement of blissful comfort. She has a way of making everything feel right in the world.

We find a quiet spot near a small pond, and we sit down on a bench. I lean back, close my eyes, and breathe in the fresh air.

I open my eyes to see Julia staring at me, a small smile on her face. "What are you thinking about? You look so pensive today."

I shrug, feeling a grin spread across my lips. "Nothing, really. I'm just happy to be here with you."

She leans in, placing a gentle kiss on my cheek. "I'm happy to be here with you too."

Even a simple, platonic-seeming kiss on the cheek makes my blood thrum in my veins at the memory of her lips, and mine, on other inches of our bodies. Every ounce of physical affection that she gives me makes me feel like this, and I have to breathe through my nose slowly to regain complete control and not embarrass myself by crashing my mouth against hers here in this family-friendly park.

Needing to move so I can shake off the sinful things on my mind, I coax her up so we can continue our walk. As we stroll through, I take her hand, and we stop to admire the scenery. But while Julia is enjoying the view, I can't help but turn my attention towards her.

She turns to me, a curious expression on her face. "What?"

I sigh, pondering the best way to tell her what I have in mind. "You know, after I lost my mom and siblings, I thought I'd never smile again. But just being here with you...." I reach for her hand, squeezing it in mine. "Gosh, you make life so worth it. I can't thank you enough for being here for me." Then I take a deep breath, feeling an unfamiliar tightness in my chest as doubts start to creep in. "I know we've talked about similar things before, but… is this something you want for the rest of your life?" I motion to the park around us. "Time like this with me, I mean, even knowing that your mom hates every atom of my being."

Julia chuckles, giving me a coy look. "Only if you make an honest woman out of me someday."

Her words make my heart soar, knowing we are exactly on the same page about our future. "That is something I have definitely planned on, if things play out in my favor."

Her face lights up, and a smile spreads across her lips, her curiosity visibly piqued. "Sebastian, are you asking me to marry you?"

I shake my head, feeling a flush of heat crawl up my neck at how flippant my words just were. Damn, I really need to keep my tongue on a leash! "No, no. I'm not asking you to marry me." Her face falls, and I quickly add, "Not yet, at least. I just wanted to know how you felt about it."

She squeezes my hand, her eyes sparkling with joy. "Well, then yes, Sebastian, I want more of this with you, no matter what my mother thinks."

***

Julia and I venture out to a new coffee shop in town one evening. It's an unconventional time for coffee, but we don't mind. The shop is cozy and welcoming, with a pleasant atmosphere. We order our drinks and settle at a small table by the window.

As we chat about our day, I feel an indescribable sense of comfort and familiarity with her. It's as if we've known each other for years. Outside, the sun sets, casting an orange glow over the city. People bustle past, going about their daily lives. But for that moment, Julia and I are in our own little world, enjoying each other's company.

While our conversation flows, the world outside fades into the background. Our voices fill the space between us, and the warm aroma of coffee envelops us. I can't help but smile at the way Julia's eyes light up as she talks about her dreams and aspirations. She has such a passion for life, and it's infectious.

Once we finish our drinks, I feel a twinge of sadness—I don't want the date to end. I know there will be more to come, more memories to be made, and more time to spend with her, but each time I have to leave her, a heavy sense of sadness plagues my thoughts.

Outside on the sidewalk, the night air is cool and crisp. Julia takes my hand, and we walk through the city streets, lost in our thoughts. Neither of us wants the night to end. It's a beautiful one, and I can't imagine spending it with anyone else. We laugh and joke, and time seems to fly by.

As we reach the end of our walk, I can hear the sound of faint, lively music floating in the night air. Julia turns to me with a mischievous grin, an idea forming in her head. "Wanna do something crazy?"

I grin back at her, wondering how this girl can make me act so completely out of character. Had anyone else asked me that question the answer would be a resounding no, but for Julia, I say, "Always."

Julia leads me to a small park, where a group of people have gathered around a gazebo stage where the source of faint music is originating from. A band is playing, and people are dancing and swaying to the music. She grabs my hand and pulls me into the crowd, a much more casual and free version of the first dance we had. Then, it was formal wear and sparkling chandeliers, but now Julia's sundress spins like it's weightless and her laugh is equally as buoyant. Among the crowd, we are no different than anyone else, and it's freeing. We dance there under the stars and street lights, and for a moment, nothing else matters. It's just us, the music, and the moment.

Even though I don't want it to, the night eventually comes to a close, and we make our way back to my car. I turn to Julia, my heart filled with gratitude. "Thank you for tonight. It was amazing."

Julia smiles, and I know she feels the same. There are a million things left unsaid between us, serious and deep, life-changing things, but just like me, she doesn't want to ruin the fun, light, carefree feeling the evening has left us with. So instead of delving into those serious things, she just gives me a wink and another kiss on the cheek, telling me, "Anytime, Seb. You're the best, you know that?"

"You might be the only one that thinks that," I reply in a chuckle. "But you're the only opinion I care about these days, so it all works out."

***

Logically, I know that there is no way that this blissful bubble that Julia and I are in will last forever. We've been pretending that tragedy and devastation aren't lingering there for us when we return from our little dates and reenter our real lives, and so far it's been working, but it's also a sort of limbo. I can't pursue a serious relationship with her like I want to if we don't acknowledge the elephant in the room that is Margaret Van Dieren. Julia, of course, has no idea what horrible things I believe her mother to be guilty of, but even if she were completely innocent, she'd still be a huge roadblock for the two of us spending our lives together.

Which is why I don't know why I am surprised that something unfortunate is waiting for me when I come back to the family home early from work one day, suffering from a migraine brought on by a lack of quality sleep and the stress of taking over as CEO. Actually, the unsavory guest isn't here for me, and I don't think I'm supposed to even know that she's in the building at all, but thankfully some of the staff in the house still have loyalty to my mother even with her being gone. It's led to a lot of them treating me like a child these past weeks, checking on me and making sure that I'm eating and drinking water and not just whiskey all day long. These are tasks that would usually be left to my mother, of her own accord of course, but now have fallen to those who miss her, and know how much she would worry about me if she was still here.

Ingrid, my mother's maid who had become more of a personal friend to her over the years as Dad pulled away and my siblings and I grew up, is the worst of the bunch. I've been spending most nights at the family estate, wanting to keep a close eye on my father and his health, and it's a little unsettling to exit the shower and see a folded robe and prewarmed towel alongside a glass of ice water and two aspirin waiting for me that wasn't there when I started. Or all the alcohol slowly being taken from my wet bar in my quarters and ending up back in the main bar near the kitchen instead, but I know that she means well. I've been meaning to speak to her about boundaries, but when she greets me at the door to the estate, Excedrin migraine pills and yet another damned glass of water in her hand, I'm glad that I haven't had that discussion yet. In fact, I might never have it, seeing how useful she is.

"How did you know I had a headache?" I ask, tossing the pills back and chasing them with a drink.

Ingrid looks around, making sure that no one else is nearby, and speaks quickly and quietly. "I could tell from the way your face looked when you got out of the car. That little pinched expression between your eyebrows... but that's neither here nor there. Look...." She leans in so she can whisper. "You didn't hear this from me, sir, but there is someone with your father in his study that I think you would want to be aware of."

I still, growing cold. "Who, Ingrid?"

Her gaze darts around again before she answers. "Lady Van Dieren. Not the younger Lady, mind you."

Handing the water back to the maid without a word, I quickly make my way through the hallways of our family estate, heading towards my father's study. Something in my gut tells me that whatever Margaret is here for, it can't be good, and I need to find out why.

As I approach the door, I can hear muffled voices coming from inside. It sounds like Margaret and my dad are having a conversation, but both of them sound strained and quietly angry.

My heart sinks as I push the door open and see Margaret standing over my dad as she speaks to him as if she is flaunting her good health in his face. Dad looks exhausted and pale, his hands shaking where he has them clasped over the ornate head of his walking cane even as he sits, the pointed end of it digging into the Persian carpet. I can feel my blood starting to boil as I step into the room, wondering what on earth she could be saying to him. Margaret quickly turns to look at me as I enter, a look of shock and panic flashing across her face.

Before I can say anything, Margaret quickly makes her exit, leaving me alone with my father, sweeping past me without even a greeting or goodbye. I turn to follow her, enraged, but I'm stopped by my father's quiet request. "Wait, Seb."

Turning, I can feel his gaze piercing into me as he stares me down. I know he's not happy about whatever it is he's just heard from Margaret, and I'm spiraling thinking about what awful things she could have told him. Lies, no doubt, but she's enough of a snake in the grass to make them believable.

"Close the door and sit down, son," he rasps, and despite my better judgment, and how much I don't want to hear what he has to say, I shut the door and take a seat. "Sebastian, we need to talk." His voice is stern and unyielding. He pauses for a moment, looking at the void in front of him as he seems to mentally prepare himself for his next set of words. Finally, he turns to me, his expression restrained. "This relationship has gone too far. I can't allow you to continue seeing Margaret's daughter."

I can feel my anger rising at his demand. How dare he tell me what I can and cannot do? But I know I need to keep my cool if I want to salvage this situation. I need my father firmly on my side, but I also need him to keep calm for his health's sake. Maybe I should have been more transparent about my intentions with Julia from the beginning, but it's too little too late now.

"I understand your concerns, Dad," I reply, trying to keep my tone even. "But I care for her. I'm not going to just give up on something that I know will be good in the long run just because Margaret is being as difficult as possible about the whole thing. I won't apologize for spending time with someone whose company I enjoy."

My father's expression softens slightly, but I can still see the disappointment in his eyes.

"I'm not just concerned about your relationship with Margaret's daughter, Sebastian." His voice's low and there's a sadness dripping from everything he says. "I'm disappointed in the son I raised. The threats you were making against Margaret without any evidence… that's not who we are as a family."

My heart sinks at his words. He knows. Margaret must have told him everything. My intentions to marry Julia and the threats I made to Margaret in my office days before. Up until this second, there has been a part of me that has hoped that my father would have changed after losing Mom, and that he'd be on my side when it comes to asking for Julia's hand, but now I know that was a false hope.

"I won't apologize," I grit out. "Especially not for that—"

He holds up a hand, and I snap my jaw shut before the words can escape. My dad looks at me with a mixture of fury and sadness in his eyes. "How could you do this to us, Sebastian?" he asks, his voice shaking with emotion. "After everything we've done for you, after all the sacrifices we've made, this is how you repay us? By throwing away everything we stand for, by throwing away our family's legacy?"

I take a deep breath, trying to control my own rising fury at the whole situation. "Dad, I truly hope you are being facetious right now. Nothing that I have done thus far has ruined our legacy, and there is zero threat of it doing so. I'm not throwing anything away," I say, my voice firm and resolute. "I love Julia, and I want to be with her. Our union would benefit both families, no matter what Margaret says. We both want to get engaged, and nothing you or anyone else says can change that."

My dad's face contorts at my pushback, his fists clenching on the head of his cane until his knuckles go white. "You don't know what you're talking about, son," he spits, his jaw flexing. "You're young, naive, and foolish. You don't understand the real world and the consequences of your actions."

I feel my own emotions starting to boil over, my inability to keep them under wraps making me even more annoyed. I'm so sick of everyone acting like they know what is best for Julia and I. We are both adults, and I am no fool to mistake what we have as anything but love. In a world like mine, true love is a rare and precious thing. "I know exactly what I'm talking about," I manage to say, my voice rising. "I'm a grown man, and I can make my own decisions."

My dad shakes his head in disgust. "You're not thinking clearly, Sebastian." I can see that the pain on his face is genuine, but how much of it is affected by the loss of his wife and children, I will never know. "This girl has bewitched you, clouded your judgment. You can't see the forest for the trees."

"I know exactly what I'm doing," I press, growing tired of his opposition as I rise from my seat. Then pointing a finger at my dad, I proceed. "And I won't let you, Margaret fucking Van Dieren, or anyone else tell me otherwise. I love Julia, and I want to be with her. She feels the same. I'm going to propose, Dad, and if that means going against your wishes, then so be it."

The tension in the room is palpable, the air thick with heavy negativity and frustration. I can feel my heart racing, my hands trembling with adrenaline. My dad looks like he's about to say something else, but before he can, he clutches his chest and collapses to the floor.

Time seems to stop, and in an instant, I want to take back every word I've said in the last five minutes and cram them back down my throat, never speaking them again. I have a million thoughts, swearing to some higher power that I will marry Julia in secret and never tell Dad if only this moment will stop and rewire, but nothing changes. He still slumps to the floor in a heavy, muted thump.

"Dad!" I shout, rushing over to him and supporting him so his head doesn't hit the ground. "What's wrong?"

He's gasping for breath, his face bone white and contorted in pain. "Heart… my heart…." He raises a hand to touch my cheek. "Seb, my son…."

Balancing him on my lap with one hand, I dig my phone out of my pocket with the other, the migraine that had been fading in my skull roaring back to life as I'm dialing for help as quickly as I can. Sick, horrible dread settles over me, even as the nurse that we have on staff rushes in after I scream for help, helping me lay Dad on the ground so she can check his vitals.

It all happens in a blur, but I can't take my eyes off his face, and the fear that I can read there. More frightening by far is that, under the fear, I see two emotions that scare me to my very soul—relief and acceptance.

"You're going to be okay, Dad," I choke out as the paramedics roll the gurney out of the room. "You're going to be okay."

I wish I believed it.

***

I wait with bated breath in the cold, sterile waiting room, the ticking of the clock on the wall seeming to reverberate in my ears with each passing second, tormenting me. Every moment feels like an interminable stretch of time as I sit here, consumed by my thoughts of worry and guilt.

Finally, the door creaks open, and the doctor steps out, her expression unreadable as she approaches me. I clench and unclench my fists as I wait for the diagnosis, my anxiety reaching new heights. How the fuck did I let this happen after losing almost all of my family in one fell swoop? How could I be so damned careless?

"Your father is stable," the doctor begins, sparking a flicker of hope within me. But the glimmer of relief is fleeting, as the doctor continues, "but unfortunately, he is suffering from heart failure."

My world, and even my breathing, stops as I hear the words, and I can't shake the feeling of culpability for my father's condition. "*No, no, no!*" I think frantically, swallowing hard.

I know our argument was the cause of his heart attack, and I'm seized with regret for not maintaining my composure and letting my emotions get the best of me. A wave of guilt crashes over me, threatening to submerge me. The doctor continues to speak, but her words fade into the background as I struggle to come to terms with the gravity of the situation. My father's health and, possibly, his life are at risk, and I am the cause of it all.

"It's not a death sentence by any means," the doctor assures me. "But only if he is very careful with his health from here on out. Your father has lived a high stress life, and the recent loss of your family has made him very fragile. You must be careful with him from now on, and make sure he is following the care plan we give up word for word."

As the doctor lists off the precautions my father needs to take, my mind is consumed with thoughts of what I could have done differently. I replay the argument in my head, scrutinizing every detail for any signs that could have alerted me to the impending danger. But as the minutes tick by, my thoughts shift from guilt to determination. The past cannot be altered, but I can control the future. I make a vow to do everything within my power to help Dad recover and live a healthy, stress-free life. He might hate me for it, but I refuse to give up on him. He's all I have left, and I know I will be haunted by the relief I saw on his face when we thought he may actually die. I don't care if Dad is ready to go—I'm still here, and he's not going to leave me if I have anything to do with it.

When the doctor finishes speaking, I take a deep breath and straighten my posture. The weight of my remorse still lingers, but it is now accompanied by a sense of purpose as I take the thick stack of papers explaining my father's diagnosis and lifestyle changes I will have to assist with. I'll read this damned packet a million times over if I have to.

Once the doctor leaves, I make my way to my dad's room, and there he lies, still asleep. The color has returned to his face, and his breathing is even, not labored, and seeing him alive brings me so much relief that it's dizzying. I get another chance to do this right, thank God.

I pull up a chair and sit next to his bed, taking his hand in mine, feeling the weight of the situation, the reality of how serious it is.

"I'm sorry, Dad," I say in a whisper, tears welling up in my eyes before I blink them swiftly away. He'd probably be horrified to see me near to crying. "I didn't mean to cause you this much stress. I should have been more understanding of your concerns and not let my emotions get the best of me."

I can feel my father's hand twitch in mine, and I hold it tighter, hoping that he can hear me and understand the depth of my regret. Everything is like a hurricane inside me– I still don't want to give Julia up, but if my love for her and the repercussions of it does this to my father…? How can I possibly still pursue it?

I sit here for a long time—with the way everything seems to flow together, it may have been minutes or hours, I can't be sure—watching over my father and making sure he's comfortable. The reality of what's happened weighs heavily on me, pressing down my shoulders and spine, and I feel like I've let him down. In fact, I *know* that I have. He told me in no uncertain terms how much I've disappointed him. I vow to make things right and be a better son from this point forward, but figuring out how to do that without giving up the woman I am sure is the one true love of my life seems impossible….

Sometime later, the hospital room remains silent except for the rhythmic beeps of the machines monitoring my father's vitals. My neck aches from the hard hospital chair, and my eyes are heavy from lack of sleep. I feel a sense of unease settle deep within me, knowing that my dad's health hangs in the balance. I just wish he would wake up so I could tell him what I'm feeling in person.

Suddenly, I hear footsteps approaching, and in turning my attention towards the door, I see Karl waking in the room. His usual bright smile fades when he sees the tense atmosphere. His eyes widen with concern as he takes in the scene before him.

"Gosh, what happened?" he asks, his voice low and serious. "All I heard was that your father was in the hospital, but I just thought it was for something minor…."

I huff a sad laugh. "No, Karl, the complete opposite of minor actually." I recount the events of the past few hours, telling him how I argued with Dad and how it led to his heart attack. Karl listens attentively, his expression softening as I speak.

"That's terrible," he says, his tone sympathetic. "How is he doing now?"

I shake my head, unsure. "I don't know. The doctors can't tell me anything until they run more tests." My stomach rolls at the thought of more bad news, and I press a fist against it to stop the ache.

Karl walks across the white room and places a comforting hand on my shoulder. "It's okay, Seb. We'll figure this out together." His words offer me some solace, but I know that the situation is far from okay. Some might consider it odd that Karl is here, offering me support, but it seems that Dad's constant reminders to treat Karl like family have paid off. Having him here is a relief, and a small comfort, as well. At least I'm not here alone, and Karl, more than most, knows the struggles and heartache Dad and I have been facing.

He asks me a few questions, and despite wanting to keep quiet about it, all roads lead back to Julia. I hesitate before telling him everything—all about our whirlwind romance, meeting at the ball, and her mother's staunch, cruel disapproval. I explain Margaret's presence in my dad's study today and how it was the catalyst for our argument. I'm not sure how he'll react, but I need someone to confide in. Karl listens patiently as I explain my relationship with Julia and how it's the root cause of my conflict with my dad.

"I understand why your dad would be concerned about your career, but he can't control who you love." Karl takes a seat in the chair next to me, his voice filled with empathy.

I nod. "I know. But it's not just about Julia. It's about the fact that he's always trying to control me and make decisions for me without considering my feelings. I've felt for years now that his primary concern is work, but after losing my mother and siblings, I was sure that he'd be able to see how important love and family is. For whatever reason, he simply doesn't want me to see Julia—though I'm sure a lot of that has to do with Margaret. During our argument, I pushed him towards accepting the situation, and—" Emotion closes my throat, and all I can do is wave at my dad laying there on the hospital bed.

Karl hums in thought, giving me a blessed moment to swallow past the lump in my throat and regain my ability to speak. "I can see why you're feeling conflicted," Karl muses after a minute or so. "It's not an easy situation, but you have to stand up for what you believe in and fight for your happiness. There has to be some sort of middle ground that you both can agree on without causing another incident like this."

"Dad told me, multiple times today, that he was disappointed in me," I manage to choke out, feeling like there is ice where my heart should be. "He's never said that to me before, Karl. Never."

For the first time, I see a flush of annoyance come over Karl's face as he looks at my still-unconscious father. "That's… fuck, Seb, that's harsh. I can't believe he would say that to his only remaining child. After all you've done, taking up the leadership at the company and everything…."

"It's like I said… work always comes first. Even now, it seems."

"No, I don't think that's true." Karl turns to me in his chair, his expression even. "Old habits die hard, it seems, but I think that he will come around. Just…maybe you're going to have to find a different way to approach it. This Julia… she's worth all this, though?"

Thinking about Julia brings me the first flush of happiness I've felt all day, and it eases the pounding in my head. "She's… she's worth everything. I just don't know if there is room for her in my life, no matter how much I want her."

"It sounds like you really care about her, though." A small smile flickers on the younger man's face as he speaks.

When I laugh softly this time, it isn't quite as bitter, "I do. More than it makes sense to after so short a time, but… yeah, I really do."

Karl stands up and stretches. I do the same, rolling my neck to try and loosen up some of the soreness within. He looks down at Dad again, an unreadable expression on his face, before shaking his head just slightly. "Your father needs to be careful, or he's going to stress and work himself into the grave."

His words strike a chord in me, and I wince. "I'm more than aware," I grumble.

"Well, at least you will know what to do going forward. And..." Karl reaches out his hand for me to shake, and I do, letting him pull me in for a quick hug and shoulder slap before he releases me. "I'm here for you, Sebastian. Your family has treated me better than I could have ever really imagined, so if you need anything, just let me know. And if you need a best man, I'm here for that too." His seriousness morphs into a teasing grin on the last sentence, and I feel a flutter of amusement.

I chuckle despite the seriousness of the situation. "Thanks, Karl. I really appreciate your support. My father was right to trust you."

Karl's lips tighten, as if what I just said really affects him greatly. "He raised a good son, and I know you'll make things right with him."

As Karl leaves the room, I can't help but feel grateful for his friendship and support. It's moments like these that remind me of the good in people, and I'm determined to make things right with my father. Julia's lovely face flashes in front of my mind's eye, and I have to push down the wave of feeling that rushes over me when it does. Dad first, then Julia. That's just the way it has to be right now.

But why does it feel so wrong to think that way?

***

Try as I might, it's impossible for me to quickly process everything that just happened. My dad, the one person who has always been there for me, is lying in a hospital bed because of our argument. One petty, stupid argument. And it's not just any argument. It's about the woman I love, the woman I want to spend the rest of my life with.

I try to sleep, just to make the hours pass faster, sitting in one chair and propping my feet up on another, but rest just will not come. I can't say I'm surprised, but being awake is getting old, fast. I start to think, over and over again, about how I've already lost every member of my family besides the man laying on the hospital bed in front of me. My mom, brother, and sister all perished in an attack meant for me, and now, yet again, I'm the reason for harm coming to one of my family members. All I can do is hope that Dad pulls through… Mom and my siblings weren't given that chance.

Fuck… the only person I have left really is my dad, and now I've pushed him away too—maybe even killed him just by opening my stupid mouth. In this second, I feel like I'm all alone in the world.

It isn't like Dad and I haven't had disagreements in the past. We've had our fair share of arguments, but this one felt different, even before the heart attack. The way his face contorted, the clear rage in his tone… this one feels like it's the end of the line for us. How can we come back from this?

I try to think of a solution, a way to make things right with my dad. But the more I think about it, the more I realize that I don't know how to solve this issue. How can I make him see that Julia is the one for me, that she makes me happy in a way that no one else ever has? How can I make him understand that I can't just let her go, even if it means losing a part of myself? Margaret shouldn't matter, and she certainly shouldn't be someone that can convince my father to tell me what to do, but here we are....

Why did he listen to her? What could Margaret have said to shake my father up so badly?

I feel lost and helpless like I've been backed into a corner with no way out. I don't know what to do, and it's eating me up inside. I'm so attached to my dad, and the thought of losing him forever is too much to bear. I can't be alone in this world. Not yet... please, not yet.

I can't let this argument be the end of our relationship. I just don't know how to do it yet. First, he needs to wake up. As long as Dad is okay, I'll make everything else work, I swear it.

With a jolt, I'm shaken out of my spiraling thoughts by my phone ringing. I see Julia's name flashing on the screen, and hesitate for a moment, unsure if I should answer it. I don't know if I'm ready to face her after everything that's happened. Everything before the heart attack—her mother being at my estate, her talking to my father, me telling Dad how I felt about her...all of that is Julia's business, though, and she deserves to know the truth if she asks. So I take a deep breath and pick up the phone.

"Hey," I rasp trying to keep my voice steady and failing miserably.

"Sebastian, is everything okay?" Julia asks, concern laced in her voice.

I take a moment to compose myself before telling her what happened with my dad. I can feel the lump forming in my throat as I explain how he had a heart attack and is currently in the hospital. Julia gasps, and I can feel her worry even through the phone. When I get to the part about her mother being in my father's study, speaking to him in private, I pause, trying to decide on the fly if I should tell her about it or not. I can already hear the tears in her voice, though… she's so sweet and full of empathy that it makes my chest feel tight. Despite feeling that she should know everything, I skip that piece of information for now. This is something that needs to be said face-to-face, not over the phone.

"Where are you? I'll come to the hospital," she says, her voice urgent.

I hesitate, not sure if I want her to come. But before I can say anything, she insists.

"Please, Sebastian. I want to be there for you and your family." Julia's voice, sweet and full of care for me, tugs at my heartstrings, but something that she says brings me up short.

"The only family here is my father. He's all I have left, and you don't even really know him at all."

She sputters, and I can feel her embarrassment bleed through over the phone. "Oh God, Seb, I'm so sorry, I—"

"Julia… it's fine." I take a deep breath, feeling torn. On one hand, I don't want to involve Julia in all the drama and tragedy that seems to happen when her family and mine are brought together. On the other hand, I don't know if I can handle all of this alone. What choice do I really have, though? "Listen, maybe it's not a good idea for you to come. I don't want to put you in an uncomfortable situation."

But Julia isn't having it. "I want to be there for you." Some of the sweetness fades from her voice and is replaced with a chilly cold. "I feel like this is just another chance for you to shut me out."

I feel a pang of guilt as she says that. I know she's right, but I also know that the last thing I need is for my father to wake up and see the woman that started our argument. I'd never say that she had anything to do with his heart attack, but I also can't risk something like that happening again by having her here before Dad is even awake.

"That's not what this is, Julia…" I pinch the bridge of my nose between my fingers. "We'll talk later, okay?" I hope she can't tell that I'm trying to end the conversation before I say something I regret.

"Fine," Julia says, her voice strained. "But we're going to talk about this, Seb. You can't keep shutting me out of your life like this, especially when you're obviously suffering. Anyone would be, in your situation." She lowers her voice. "And we've gotten so close over the past few weeks… I thought things were going differently. Better."

I don't know what to say to that, but it hurts me to my core to hear her words. "I'll call you when I have time to see you. I…" I exhale slowly, not knowing how to end this conversation without hurting her. All I do is hurt everyone I care for lately. "Thank you for calling, Julia. I've got to go now. Bye."

"...Bye."

I hang up the phone, feeling conflicted and overwhelmed. I don't know how to make everyone happy. All I know is that I don't want to lose anyone else. Looking over at my father, how pallid he is, and all the wires and tubes coming from him, makes my stomach turn and acid crawl up my throat. God, I don't want to be here. I just want to be home, knowing that Dad is healthy and in his study catching up on the news of the day. Maybe Mom would be reading on the terrace, my brother in the garage tinkering with a car that he would be too young to drive, and my sister painting a scene she had been building in her head all day. But I can't have that anymore, not ever. Just loneliness, misery, and maybe if I'm lucky, my father for a few more years.

Whether I can have Julia, no matter how much I want her, no matter how much she makes me burn, is yet to be seen.

I adjust myself in the uncomfortable chair, the bars of it digging into my back and side, and close my eyes. Maybe I can sleep, even for a few minutes, and have a respite from the terrible things hanging over me. All I know right now is that I'm not leaving my dad's side. I will be here when he wakes up.

***

"Seb, what happened? Why am I here?"

My father's voice sounds like he's speaking past a throat full of razor blades, as if the few words he manages to get out are the most painful he's ever uttered. I snap out of my restless, borderline painful sleep and jump to my feet.

"Dad," I breathe, voice shaking with emotion. "You're awake."

The hospital room is dimly lit, the only sound coming from the beeping machines and the occasional shuffle of footsteps outside. He doesn't speak at first, waving his hand for a drink from the cup with a straw next to his bed, and I bring it down so he can take what he needs. After a few mouthfuls of water, quenching his thirst and appeasing his dry mouth, Dad relaxes against his pillow and looks at me. He looks frail and weak, his skin pale and his breaths shallow, but he's alert and still here with me. It's a start, at least.

I reach over and take his rough hand in mine, and his skin is cold to the touch. "Dad, you suffered a heart attack," I tell him softly, breaking the silence. "You've been at the hospital for a day now."

He blinks slowly, trying to process what I'm telling him. "What happened?" he whispers hoarsely. "The last thing I remember was the two of us in my study, talking…" He frowns. "We were arguing, weren't we?"

I take a deep breath, steeling myself for what I have to say. "I confronted you," I admit, feeling guilty. "I caused you to get stressed, and it led to a heart attack. This is all my fault, and I'm sorry. So, so sorry, Dad."

My father's eyes widen in surprise, and I can see the confusion etched on his face. "Why did we do that? What in the world could cause us to argue that angrily, considering everything we've lost as of late?"

I hesitate, unsure if I should tell him the truth. But I know I can't keep it from him any longer. He will remember soon enough on his own, anyway. "I was angry," I admit, my voice trembling slightly. "Angry about Julia, and how you didn't approve of her. Angry because you had been talking to Margaret before I arrived and because I knew she was plotting against me. I couldn't hold it in anymore." I close my eyes and take a deep breath. "I acted like a child… like a little boy, and look what happened…."

My father's expression softens, and he reaches out to take my hand. "Son, stop. I'm sorry." His voice was filled with regret, and underneath it, love. It kills me inside to hear how weak his voice is. "I didn't mean to cause you pain. I just want what's best for you, and what's best for our legacy."

I sigh. "Dad—"

"Seb, stop, let me speak." He coughs, and when he finds his words again, Dad's voice is weak, but it's clear he has something important to say. "Sebastian," he proceeds, turning his head to look at me fully. "If something happens to me, promise me you'll take good care of the family estate, of the company, and of Karl."

I feel my heart sink. I don't want to think about losing my dad, but I can see the seriousness in his eyes. "Of course, Dad," I reply, trying to keep my voice steady. "You know I'll always be there for him."

Dad nods, his expression softening. "Good. Karl's been with us for a while now, and he's always been loyal to the family. He deserves to be taken care of."

For what feels like the hundredth time today, there is a lump in my throat that makes it hard for me to force words out. I swallow once, and then twice, before speaking past all the hurt inside of my chest. "Dad, you don't have to worry about that. You're going to live for many years to come." I try to lighten my tone, and hopefully, the mood along with it. Even if any positive feelings will be entirely false on my part. "You're going to see me get married and have kids, and we're going to take all the hunting trips around the world that we've always talked about."

My dad looks at me with a mixture of love and sadness in his eyes. "I appreciate your optimism, but you don't have to make promises you can't keep. I know my time is limited, and I just want to make sure that both you and Karl are taken care of."

I find myself nodding, even though I find his insistence on a point I've already agreed upon odd. "Like I said, Dad. I'll take good care of him—"

"Like family," he insists.

I sigh, pinching the bridge of my nose again. "Yes, Dad, I swear. Like family." Then, remembering earlier in the day, I chuckle softly. "You know, he was actually the first one to come and visit you today."

Dad relaxes on his bed once more, head heavy on his pillow and a small smile on his dry lips. "Ah, good. I'm not surprised. He's a good man. Like you, my son." My dad gives me a pat on my hand and I feel tears welling up in my eyes. Just like before, I tilt my head towards the ceiling and blink them away before they can be noticed. "Seb, I want you to know that I love you. You may not always make the right decisions, but I know you have a good heart. Promise me you'll make things right if things go south here with me."

I swallow hard and try to hold back the tears. They burn my eyes, and the grief of everything all at once is pounding in the back of my skull. "I will, Dad. I promise, I will."

As I sit by my dad's side, I realize how much he means to me. He's the only family member I have left, and I can't bear the thought of losing him. I apologize for all the stress I've caused him and tell him how much I care about him. The words just spill out of me like water, so quickly that I can't even hear myself over the ringing in my ears and the blood rushing through my head from my elevated pulse. He listens, quietly, and never interrupts, not even speaking until I've said my piece. I'm grateful for that—I don't know that I could have finished if he had stopped me.

Now, he looks at me, exhausted but otherwise steady and says, "I know, son. And I love you too. Thank you for being here with me. Just remember to make things right. I know you will, won't you?"

His words feel like a set of heavy steel chains settling over my shoulders. I can hear the subtext in them, and the way he expects me to fix the Julia and Margaret situation before it spins out of control even more and taints the name of our family. The thing is, what he considers to be the right thing, and what I do, have two vastly different outcomes.

But tonight he's here, in this hospital bed, fighting for his life, and there is no way in hell I will be arguing with him, or even denying him the promise that he seems to need to be able to rest. So I just take his hand in mine once more, letting him pat the top of my knuckles absentmindedly.

"I'll make everything right again, Dad." My father grips my hand with surprising strength, and I add, "I promise I will."

CHAPTER 20

Julia

Standing in front of my apartment door, adjusting my backpack on my shoulder, I try to call Sebastian one more time before going to class. My fingers tremble as I grip my phone tightly, waiting for him to answer. I don't really expect him to, not after the hours of radio silence, but there is still a little seed of hope in me that makes me call him over and over again. I really thought we had something beyond special, and with it, a future together….

Each passing second feels like an eternity, and with each ring, that little hopeful piece of me starts to fade away. When his voicemail greeting plays, a wave of sadness rolls over me. What if something terrible happened? What if he's hurt or in trouble? I try calling him again, but the same result, straight to voicemail. Just like I knew it would.

Gabi and a few other girls are waiting for me on campus, but when she gets a good look at my face, she waves the other girls away so we can have some privacy, for which I am grateful. As Gabi and I walk towards our first lecture of the day, it's impossible not to feel the unending stress of everything that's been happening in my life recently. Even as I have that thought, another one follows right on its heels–how selfish does that make me, when the things going on in Sebastian's life are so much worse than my problems?

I glance over at Gabi, and she gives me a knowing look. "You look terrible. Gorgeous, of course, but terrible. Do you want to talk?"

I inhale slowly. It's been a few days since Sebastian's dad had a heart attack, and even though he's out of the hospital now, I haven't heard from Sebastian since the day it happened.

"Gabi, I'm worried about Sebastian," I finally fess out, breaking down and telling my friend the truth. I'm sure she would have guessed it eventually, anyway. "I haven't heard from him since his dad got out of the hospital, and I don't know what's going on with him."

Gabi looks at me sympathetically. "What do you think is going on?"

"I don't know…." There is so much I could tell her, that I want to tell her, but I can't just spill all my secrets and most private thoughts all at once. "Last time we spoke, he was in the hospital with his dad. But now, he won't return my calls or texts. I'm starting to think that maybe something's wrong."

Gabi nods thoughtfully. It's a gorgeous day, and the morning sunshine makes her look so young and beautiful… but most of all, she looks carefree. I miss feeling like that.

"Maybe he's just dealing with a lot right now," she suggests. "I'm sure he'll get back to you soon."

"I hope so." I bite my bottom lip, trying to keep the worry out of my voice. "I just feel like something's not right.

Sebastian hasn't exactly been the best about communicating, but over the past few weeks, before his dad had the emergency, things have been different. He's been sweet and available. Easy to talk to. But now it feels like right after the explosion when he was shutting me out and refusing any sort of comfort."

As we continue walking, I explain to Gabi what happened with Sebastian's dad and how he was in the hospital for a few days. I tell her how Sebastian was really stressed out and worried about his dad, and how he seemed to be distant when we spoke on the phone.

"I just don't know what to do," I say, sighing. "I feel like I should be there for him, but he's not letting me in."

Gabi puts a comforting hand on my arm. "Men are a mystery at the best of times, and it sounds like Sebastian is going through some stuff that you and I can't even imagine. Just give him all the time and space he needs right now, and when he comes back around you two can have a talk about how pulling away like this isn't something you want from your long term partner."

Her words bring me a modicum of comfort. It's nice to hear her speak like the idea of Sebastian and I staying together long term is a given, and not something that is still up in the air.

"Thanks, Gabi," I tell her honestly as we arrive at the lecture hall. "I guess all I can do is wait it out."

Once inside the vast classroom, I find myself trying to push my worries to the back of my mind. I know that Gabi is right, but it's hard not to let my anxiety get the best of me. I just want to be there for Sebastian and support him through whatever he's going through. Who in the world can go through losing their family and then a health crisis with the last remaining member of said family, all so close together? He might look okay on the outside, but I'm almost sure he's falling apart on the inside.

And then, there are also the things he and I have been dancing around for weeks now. Our relationship. A future and a life together. Where does all of that fit into the chaos of his life? It might be me thinking a little too highly of myself, but I'm almost positive that if I was his wife, that I could make things easier to bear for Sebastian. He just has to let me in.

As Gabi and I settle into our seats, it's impossible not to feel distracted, my mind racing with all the different possibilities of what could be happening with Sebastian. I try to focus on the lecture, but my attention keeps wandering, and I find myself checking my phone every few minutes. The uncertainty gnaws at me, making it impossible to concentrate. Maybe I should have just taken another sick day.

Hours drag by, and my phone remains stubbornly silent as I move through the campus, attending class after class. Really, there are two scenarios that could be playing out right now. Either he's so swamped with all the things going on with his business and his father that he has no time or mental space for me, or he's deliberately ignoring me because he doesn't want me in his life anymore. That thought sends a shiver down my spine.

Then there is the other instinct that I have, which keeps popping up again and again, telling me that my mother must have something to do with this. A split between Sebastian and I is all she wants right now.

Just as I am about to give up hope, my phone vibrates in my hand where I'm holding it inside my backpack, not wanting to miss a single alert. I hastily excuse myself from class to answer it, almost tearing up in relief when it's Sebastian's voice that comes over the line. He's finally called! He didn't simply answer my attempts at contact, he reached out to me first.

Sebastian's voice is low and steady, and he sounds different than usual. "Hey, Julia. Can you meet me at the first park we went to after five? I really need to talk to you face-to-face."

No sweet hello, no apology for his disappearance, just a curt invitation. Still, my heart leaps into my throat, and I can barely contain my excitement. The park where we had our first unofficial date is somewhere special to both of us, and in my mind, there is only one real reason he'd want to meet up there instead of one of our apartments.

Is this it? Is he finally going to propose? The thought of spending the rest of my life with him fills me with joy and anticipation. Despite my worries and fears, everything might finally be falling into place.

But a part of me can't help but wonder what has changed. I nibble at my bottom lip, thinking. It'd be so easy to just accept. I want to see him so badly. Something is off, though, I just know it. But I don't think that I can resist, even though I know that logically it might not be the best choice. The last time we spoke, he was in the hospital with his father, and his voice was distant and cold. I don't know what has happened in the intervening days, but I'm not about to question it when he's finally giving me what I want.

"I can do that," I tell him quietly. "At what time exactly?"

Seb tells me to be there by 6 PM, just in time to watch the sunset, and where in the park to meet, still not giving me any small talk or other polite conversation. Just instructions. Then he's getting off the phone, and I'm left holding the device while my emotions twist and turn inside me like a cyclone. I'm so torn… what exactly is going on?

I hear the creak of the lecture hall door, and Gabi slips out into the hallway to join me. She must have seen me leave to take the phone call. Without hesitation, I grab Gabi by the hand and spill the news. She screams with excitement before slapping her hands over her mouth to hush herself in the empty, echoing hallway, and a smile creeps onto my lips despite how stressed Seb is making me feel.

"You really think he's going to propose?" she asks, taking both my hands in hers.

"I… I think so. But there is something about the invitation that doesn't make sense. Don't you think it's weird that he just, out of the blue, called and wants to immediately meet up somewhere to propose? It's the only thing that I could imagine him doing at this park, but I really thought we would have some time to unravel the last few days and what it means for us first."

"Girl," Gabi laughs. "If this is some spur-of-the-moment idea that Sebastian is having, you need to strike while the iron is hot. Seeing how he tends to pull away when things get rough, who knows when you will have another chance like this one? Go to the damn park."

She finishes the lecture by telling me to wear my best dress and do my hair and makeup perfectly. I take her advice, leaving class a few minutes earlier and all but running back to my apartment to change. I pick out a beautiful dress that accentuates my curves and flatters my skin tone. I clearly don't have hours to get ready like I'd prefer for something like this, but I'm confident that Sebastian will find me beautiful no matter what. Still, I can't help wanting to look my absolute best for him in case he does propose.

Sebastian sends a car for me, which does nothing to settle my nerves. I would feel better in my own family's car, but I'm still trying to keep my meetups with Seb as secret as possible from Mom. I'm sure she knows that we are seeing each other, but the less I rub it in her face, the better. What she doesn't know won't hurt her, I guess.

I keep playing scenarios in my head, trying to predict what he might say or do. Will he really get down on one knee? Will he recite a heartfelt speech? I'm sure that if a proposal is really in my future, only minutes or hours away, it will be perfect no matter what. I'm more than ready for whatever surprises await me.

The logical part of me keeps trying to rear its ugly head and scream this isn't right! Something isn't right! But I tamp it down the best that I can. I want to go into this hopeful, happy, and be the beacon of light and positivity that Sebastian will need in the upcoming weeks and months as he works his way through his new life and reality.

"*Sebastian would never propose off the cuff like this,*" my treacherous brain hisses. "*You're reading this entire situation wrong and you're going to look like a total fool!*"

At the park, Sebastian is waiting to open the door for me. I suck in a breath, affection, and desire rolling over me as soon as I see his large hand in my vision as he reaches down to help me out of the car. Just touching his skin and smelling his woodsy cologne has butterflies taking off in my stomach like mad. I want so much right now! I want to hug him, kiss him, bury my face in his neck and never let go. I've missed him so damned much, and despite all the words I've been practicing in my head on the drive over, that's all I can say when I open my mouth.

"I missed you," I breathe, hovering on the edge of initiating an embrace myself and waiting for him to reach out. "I've really, really missed you, Seb."

He doesn't reach out, much to my disappointment, but he gives me a lukewarm, "Missed you too," as he laces our fingers together and leads me towards an empty bench on the lakeside. He glances over at me, and then down my body at the way the wind is pulling my dress against me, displaying my curves to full advantage, before he meets my eyes again.

"You're quite dressed up for just having come from class," he points out, settling on the bench and waiting for me to do the same.

I do, smoothing my dress down as I sit. "I left class a little early to change. I wanted to look my best for you."

His eyes soften and his body sways towards mine, and for one hopeful second, I'm sure that Sebastian is going to try and kiss me. But then… he doesn't, squaring his shoulders and sitting back against the bench once more.

The sun is shining down on us as we sit together, staring out at the crystal-clear lake with a million words unsaid between us, and still none of them being spoken. My heart is racing with excitement and nervousness, but as the seconds tick by, the nervousness starts to take control of anything positive. I exhale slowly and close my eyes. "*Calm down, Julia,*" I tell myself, willing my pulse to slow, "*Just talk to him. It's what you've wanted to do for days, isn't it?*"

"How is your dad? I heard through the grapevine that he is home now," I ask, hoping to break the tension that has been building up between us.

Sebastian sighs. "Well, yes, he is home, but his quarters are basically a miniature hospital room now. We've got medical staff at the estate twenty-four hours a day, but I can see as he gets his strength back how he's trying to brush them off and be his stubborn, independent self." He launches into an explanation of what exactly happened with his father's heart medically, getting into the minute details of potential procedures that can be done and how his father's life will change from here on out. I try to listen attentively, but my mind is elsewhere. All I can think about is the anticipation of what might happen next.

"That sounds like a lot, Seb," I tell him truthfully when he trails off. I might not have absorbed everything he just told me about his father's incident, but I'm positive that he was just getting it all off his chest, anyway. Maybe grateful for someone to listen to.

"It is," he admits, his words filling me with sympathy for how vulnerable he sounds.

I consider dropping any questions or concerns about how he's treated me the last few days, but Gabi was right. I need to tell him how I expect to be treated in the future, and how cutting me off when things get hard isn't acceptable. So I gather my courage and ask, "Seb, listen… why have you been so distant lately? I feel like the moment bad things happen you close the door on me and I'm left standing out in the cold."

Sebastian looks at me with a pained expression, and I can feel my heart sink. "Calling what I've been going through 'bad things' is sort of trivial, don't you think?"

I wince. "You know that's not what I'm trying to convey...."

I can feel the breeze tugging at my hair and the sun hot on the back of my neck as we sit in a now uncomfortable silence, the only sound the soft lapping of waves against the shore. I feel my heart heavy in my chest as Sebastian still doesn't say anything, or even look at me. A proposal seems less and less likely by the second. He looks so exhausted, his pain is etched onto his face, and it breaks my heart to see him suffer.

"I'm so sorry," he says finally, his voice barely above a whisper. It's so soft that I whip my head around to look at him and confirm that it really is Sebastian speaking. "I didn't mean to shut you out, Julia. In fact, it's the last thing I actually wanted, but... it's just been so hard."

I want to comfort him, to let him know that he's not alone, but there's something holding me back. A nagging feeling in the pit of my stomach tells me that there's more to this story, that Sebastian isn't telling me everything.

Finally, I gather my courage and ask him, "Is there something else going on? Something you're not telling me?"

Sebastian hesitates for a moment, his eyes searching mine before he finally speaks. "My dad keeps talking about the end of his life and dying. I'm consumed by the thought of it. I can't lose him... he even asked me to take care of Karl if anything happened to him. I didn't want to burden you with all of that. Julia, you're so bright and wonderful.... I hate even thinking about you surrounded by all the death that has become such an overbearing part of my reality."

I feel a confusing swirl of love and annoyance as he explains himself. Does he not think I can handle this? I'm a future judge, I thrive under pressure!

I know how close Sebastian and his dad are, and the thought of losing him must be unbearable. But the weight of taking care of someone else, on top of everything else going on, is almost too much to bear. "Karl, your employee? You've mentioned him a few times, but why would he be someone that your dad would be so worried about?"

Sebastian shrugs. "He sees something in the guy, and I have to admit, Karl and I have hit it off, but… I think Dad is reaching out for the few connections he has left in the world now that my mom and siblings are gone, and Karl has this sad history that he's managed to pull himself out of, and Dad likes that." He furrows his brow, and for the first time today, I feel his hand absentmindedly squeeze my knee as he thinks. "He asked me to treat him like family. That's strange, isn't it? I didn't think so in the moment, but I was so damned tired."

I hum as I mull his words over. Sure, it's a little weird to want your son to treat a coworker like family, but sometimes family can be the people that you chose, not just the people related to you by blood. So I guess Karl must be someone like that for the senior Van den Bosch. "I mean, it's somewhat odd, but it's also sweet in a way. Does it bother you?"

He shakes his head. "No, not really. Karl deserves the best in life after all he's been through, and like I said, I enjoy the guy's company too. He even came to see Dad first thing after the heart attack."

We've gotten off topic from anything that I really want to talk about, but I don't really mind. Sebastian clearly needed to speak to someone about this, and him casually touching me is a good sign. Maybe slowly, but surely, he's letting go of some of the pressure inside of him, and when he's finally done, he'll be more like himself.

Gosh, I've missed him so much. I hate everything that has come between us… how difficult my mother has made this, not even mentioning the tragedies in Seb's life. I feel the weight of our shared pain, so I reach out and take his hand where it rests on my leg, giving it a gentle squeeze. "I'm here for you," I say softly, meaning every single word. "Whatever you need."

Sebastian's eyes meet mine, and I can see the gratitude in them. "Thank you, sweetheart."

His affectionate name warms me from the inside out like a mug of hot cocoa on a cold day. We sit here for a while longer, lost in our own thoughts.

Then, Sebastian turns to me once more. He flips my hand over, tracing the lines of my palms with his fingers like he's in a trance, causing me to shiver from pleasure. "Julia," he begins, his eyes lock on mine once more and he's got my full attention. "Since the day I met you, I've felt such a strong connection with you. It's unlike anything I've ever experienced before, so strong and magnetic. I truly, honestly felt like I had met my future wife."

My heart does a little somersault at the word "wife" causing my lips to part open. Gosh, I can't believe what I'm hearing, and even tears start to well up in my eyes. "Seb…."

His hands move from my palm to cup my face, his thumbs ghosting over my cheekbones as emotion swells in me so large that it's hard to breathe. He observes me attentively, his dark brown eyes, soft and tender, as he utters four little words.

"I love you, Julia."

This is it! It's happening!

My heart pounds with excitement, blood rushing through my body and flushing my cheeks and chest, turning them a rosy pink. I'm sure he's about to propose any second, and the urge to press my lips to his, to taste the words on his tongue before he says them, is overwhelming. Yet, just as I'm about to kiss him, he lays a hand right above my heart and holds me back.

"Let me finish."

Hope is still hovering like a moth above my head, but it's hanging on by only a single thread. Just like before, my brain is fighting with my heart, chanting, "S*omething is wrong, something is wrong.*"

"I had to say it to you, because it's what I really feel, and you deserve to know the depths of my feelings for you." Sebastian licks his lips nervously and fixes his eyes out on the blue water, away from me. "Having said that, I can't forget the fact that my dad is so against our union. Our argument…" he stops mid-sentence, and I can see how much he's struggling to proceed with what he's got in mind. "God, this is so hard to talk about." He then pauses for a moment, heaving a long sigh as he gathers the courage to finish. "Our argument before he had the heart attack was about you and I. My father knows about us now, and it nearly killed him."

Time stops, holding still for one long moment as I forget to breathe, and then it all hits me like a ton of bricks.

Lurching away from him, I stand on shaky legs, not wanting him to touch me at all in this moment. Knowing about us nearly killed his father? How can I possibly live with that knowledge? Why is he telling me this?

I'm beyond stunned by his words, holding my hands over my chest to try and contain the aching inside of it. "What does that mean?" I ask, feeling a knot form in my stomach.

Sebastian looks down at his feet, and I can see the pain in his eyes. "It means that I can't just ignore my dad's wishes," every word is a struggle, his voice low. "I love you, Julia, but I can't go against my family. It's tearing me apart, but I have to do what's right for my father."

My heart shatters as I realize that he's not going to propose after all. I take a deep breath, trying to hold back my tears. "I don't understand. Why…why in the world would you bring me here to tell me that you want me, but at the same time, don't want to be with me?"

He closes his eyes as if he can't bear to look at me. "Because this is how things are and you deserve to know the truth. I can focus on my father and our company, and you can focus on getting your law degree. You already mentioned leaving class early today to see me and I never wanted to get in the way of your education–"

"Five minutes!" I interrupt, clenching my hands into fists. "I left class five minutes early, Seb. Stop making excuses or trying to shirk off any responsibility for what you are doing right now. Either you want me, or you don't."

"Julia… of course I want you. But I can't have you. Not now, maybe not ever. My life… the longer it goes on, the more that I'm sure I'm meant to spend it alone. But you need—" he quickly stops, and I see a quick flash of anger on his features, which gives me pause. He can't say that I deserve someone else! He doesn't want to consider me being with another man, which means he still doesn't want to give me up. There is still hope.

"Say it," I demand, my annoyance burning bright. "Say that I need a man that can give me everything I want. Another man. Not you."

"I…" the words stick in his throat like peanut butter, so much so that I see him unconsciously rub his neck. "Fuck. You know I think you deserve the world Julia, but it's not right to sit here and make me imagine you with someone else. Not when I just told you that I love you!"

I laugh in disbelief, throwing my hands up. "Do you really hear yourself right now? You want to break up, but you love me, and although I deserve all the love in the world you can't accept that it will be with someone else. You don't want me!"

Now Sebastian is on his feet, stepping close enough to me that I can feel the heat rolling off his body. "I do want you!" he roars, chest heaving. "Just because my father doesn't want us together doesn't mean that I don't want you. *Need* you, Julia. But he asked me to make it right, so I am."

My eyes widen in disbelief. "You're being ridiculous. I can't believe you're just going to accept his request like that. I'm ignoring my mother's wishes to see you, you know. We can't let the last generation control ours."

Sebastian folds his hands behind his head, blowing out a breath. He moves away from me and paces the length of the bench a few times, coiling his strong emotions back inside of himself until his breaths come slowly once more and the volume of his voice is level once more. "I know, but he nearly died, like I've told you. You might feel comfortable ignoring your mother's wishes, but she isn't taking this lying down, you know that, right?" I blink a few times, unsure of what he's saying. "Your mom came to talk to my father and told him about us," he fesses out. "It was her insistence, and the shock of knowing that you and I were together, that made us argue…that made him have a heart attack."

Now all I can feel is rage at my mother. I've always known that she was going to make this difficult for Sebastian and I, but how could I be so oblivious that I had no idea she went to talk to Sebastian's father? It's unbelievably cruel, knowing what the poor man has lost… I'm shocked at the coldness of my mother. There have always been rumors about her… surely she can't be the witch everyone makes her out to be? My own mother?

It feels like I'm short circuiting as I realize the severity of the situation. It's too much for me to handle. "I had no idea," I say softly, feeling a sense of guilt wash over me. "But that doesn't mean we have to give up on each other. Maybe… maybe you can let me talk to him?"

Sebastian shakes his head sadly. "Dad needs a stress-free life," he tells me, his voice heavy with emotion. "He's the only person I have left, Julia. Please try to understand."

There is a pause in our conversation, the setting sun glimmering off the ripples in the water and the hushed sound of duck's wings overhead as they come in to land on the water. Sebastian and I are both reeling, both struggling with the impossible difficulty of what lay between us.

There is love, but there is also pain, and disapproval, and responsibility to do right by the other people we care about in our lives. Sebastian is right here in front of me, but there might as well be oceans in between us.

"We can be together," I insist, fixing him with a stare. "I'm sure if your father sees you standing up for what you believe in, he will understand and respect that."

Sebastian hesitates for a moment, considering my words. "Or he will die of a heart attack for good. Surely you can see how that isn't a foundation for a marriage, or a life together. There is no way forward for us."

I laugh bitterly, feeling a sense of frustration and anger building up inside of me. "Very well. One shall not offend daddy dearest, huh?" My tone is dripping with sarcasm, but it's all to cover up the shockingly sharp hurt within me. "I'd have gone against my entire family for you, Sebastian. But I guess the feeling isn't mutual."

Sebastian reaches out to touch my arm, but I pull away from him. "I'm sorry, Julia," he says, his voice full of regret. "I never meant to hurt you."

I turn to face him, my eyes filled with tears. "That doesn't make it hurt any less."

He takes a step closer to me, but I back away, feeling hurt and the ghost of what could have been washing over me. "I need some time to think."

Sebastian nods, his eyes filled with sadness. I see his fingers moving at his side, as if he's fighting off the need to touch me. I want him to, so much, but if he's dead set on doing things this way, I can't let myself give into an embrace like that, knowing how it will just make the coming days harder.

"I understand." His words are so quiet I barely hear them, but when I do, I pivot on my foot and leave. One hollow blessing is that both his car and the driver who brought me here are still waiting in the parking lot, so I won't have to have the embarrassment of waiting for a cab while Sebastian watches me from the lake.

As I walk away, I can feel the weight of my heartache with every step. I had thought that Sebastian was the one, that we were meant to be together. But now, I'm not so sure. I can't help but wonder if love is worth sacrificing everything for, or if there's a point where you have to let go and move on. I can't believe that he's willing to let go of us so easily, just because his dad is against our union. It all feels so unfair.

Inside the car, with tears streaming down my face, I know I need to talk to someone. I pull out my phone and dial Gabi's number. I need to tell her what just happened, and I need her support now more than ever. She answers on the first ring.

Gabi picks up, her voice brimming with excitement. "Julia! Oh my god, did he propose?!" she practically shrieks into the phone.

My stomach drops at the mention of a proposal. I can't even imagine what it'd have been like if that had happened. I had the scenario so built up in my head, all these thoughts of joy and what it would be like for us to finally start our lives together… how could I have believed something so stupid? But I know I need to tell her what really went down.

"No, Gabi," I confess, my voice cracking. The brightness and happiness in her tone is breaking my heart into even more pieces. Not only did I not get a proposal, I got broken up with, instead. "It didn't go well."

There's a moment of silence on the other end of the line before Gabi speaks again, her voice now filled with concern. "What happened? Are you okay?"

I take a deep breath before launching into the story of how it all fell apart. I tell her about how I had thought everything was perfect, and how I had imagined a future with him. But then he told me that he couldn't commit with all the other things going on in his life, and how he's so worried about the opinion of his father that he's willing to let me go for good.

As I speak, I can feel the tears streaming down my face. But Gabi is there for me, just like always. She listens to everything I have to say, never once interrupting or judging me. She lets me cry and vent, and I know that I'm not alone in this.

When I finish, there's a moment of silence on the other end of the line before Gabi speaks again. "I'm so sorry, Ju. That's awful. But you know what? You deserve someone who wants the same things as you do. Someone who's willing to commit and build a future with you. And Sebastian obviously wasn't that person."

Her words should be comforting, a balm to my broken heart, but something deep inside me refuses to believe that he isn't the one for me. "I think he is that person, Gabi. My person. He's just too stubborn and set in his ways to see and accept that fact."

I hear her humming in thought before she offers. "Come to my place. Let's talk about this face-to-face. I don't want you to be alone, not tonight, anyway."

***

It's fully dark when I arrive at Gabi's apartment, and Sebastian's driver seems reluctant to let me out at the random address I insisted he bring me to. He's supposed to deliver me either to my apartment or family estate upon Sebastian's orders, but after a hushed conversation with Seb on the phone, the driver sighs and drops me off.

Getting out of the car, my eyes are puffy and red from all the crying I've been doing. I feel numb and broken, but at least I know Gabi will be there for me. She's always been the best friend anyone could ask for.

After dragging my hands over my eyes, I knock on the door, and Gabi answers almost immediately, a soft smile on her heart-shaped, freckled face. I can't help but feel a pang of guilt as I see her, knowing that I'm about to ruin her night by venting and sobbing all over her and her apartment, and I open my mouth to tell her that I won't be long.

But before I can even say anything, she pulls me into a tight hug, wrapping her arms around me and holding me close. Gabi is shorter than I am, and I can rest my chin on the top of her head, her steadiness soothing me already. I can feel the warmth of her embrace, and for a moment, I feel like everything will be okay.

"Come on, girl." She leads me to her bedroom and gestures for me to sit on the bed. As I sink into the soft mattress, she disappears into the kitchen. I can hear the sound of the freezer opening and the clink of spoons as she returns with two big bowls of vanilla ice cream.

Gabi hands me a blue ceramic bowl, and I take a spoonful, savoring the cool sweetness on my tongue. It's a welcome distraction from the pain I'm feeling, and I can't help but feel grateful for Gabi's presence.

"You had this all planned out, huh?" I ask, swallowing the sweet treat. "What was the protocol if it had been a proposal and not a dumping?"

"There's champagne chilling, but I figured that you wouldn't be coming here or home if it had been a—" she stops herself when pain makes me scrunch my face up, clicking her jaw shut before she can say any more about the proposal that never was. "Actually, who cares? You're here now, and that alone is a reason to enjoy ourselves, right?"

Gabi holds her spoon up like a champagne toast, and we clink the silverware together instead of glasses. As we sit there in silence, spoonful after spoonful, Gabi finally breaks the quiet. "What happened at the lake?" she asks softly. "I want to hear it all, not the short version you gave me on the phone. Hit me with all of it."

And then the floodgates open. I tell her everything, from the awkward silence to the painful words. I can feel the tears welling up again, but Gabi is here, offering me tissues and a shoulder to cry on.

She listens patiently, never interrupting or judging, taking my empty bowl and sitting it on her bedside table, letting me lean my head on her shoulder when I need to. And as I finish my story, she wraps me in another tight hug, holding me close and promising to be here for me no matter what.

In that moment, I know that I'm not alone. I have Gabi, and that's enough.

"Sometimes I wish I never met him," I grump, wiping my eyes with a clean tissue and balling it up in my hands.

"Don't say that." Gabi rubs a hand on my arm in a comfortable gesture. "I'm sure it's not over. Some men are just stupid and hard-headed, especially the old money ones. But you should know that better than anyone."

"But what if it is?" I sniffle, feeling a sense of hopelessness creeping in. "What if this is just how it's supposed to be?"

Gabi sighs. "Maybe things are tough right now, but that doesn't mean they'll always be that way. You and Sebastian have something special. Don't throw it away without a fight."

I take a deep breath and try to absorb Gabi's words. Maybe she's right. Maybe I shouldn't give up so easily. But how can I fight for something that feels so out of reach?

"I don't know if I have it in me to fight," I admit, feeling defeated.

"You do." Gabi gives my arm a little squeeze, her lips twisting into a smile. "And I'll be here every step of the way. We'll figure it out together."

***

It was late when Gabi tucked me into a cab and sent me back to my apartment, but no matter how much I want it to, life isn't letting me sleep in today. As the morning sun streams through the windows, casting a warm glow over the room, I lay under my sheets battling with a sense of emptiness. The buzzer for the door sounds, and I shrug on a soft cashmere robe and sulk to the door to let the guest in. I expect Gabi to be the first one to come over, to comfort me with her endless supply of hugs and ice cream. But instead, it's my brother Alex who shows up at my door, looking at me with a mix of sympathy and concern. He is perfectly dressed even this early, one hand holding a drink carrier with two short cups of something that smells divine, and the other a brown paper bag. I narrow my eyes at him, wondering if the food and caffeine is worth having to explain what is going on with me and Sebastian all over again, but Alex isn't taking no for an answer.

"Morning, kid," he chirps, pushing past me. I sigh and let him in, trailing after Alex as we make our way to the living room and sit down on the couch. "Heard you had a rough night, huh?"

I groan. "Gabi told you, huh?"

"Mmhm," he confirms, teeth coming down around a croissant that he's pulled out of the bag. "Which is why there is a double shot of espresso in that latte. Extra sugar, too."

Looking between the latte and Alex, I give in with a resentful, "Fine!" The coffee tastes like the perfect blend of bitterness and sweet, and the caffeine zings along my nerve endings, bringing me to life. Okay. I can do this. I can get through this day.

"I'd still like to hear it from you, though." Alex muses, leaning back on the sofa. I take a deep breath and start to explain everything to him. I tell him how Sebastian ended things, how he couldn't handle the pressure of his dad's health scare and our mother's disapproval. He winces when I bring up Mom, his face pulled in an expression of understanding and sympathy. I guess if anyone knows how that goes, it's him.

As I speak, I can feel the weight of everything hitting me all over again. The pain, the confusion, the hurt. It's all still there, raw and unyielding. But having Alex here with me, listening and understanding, makes it a little more bearable.

"Should I talk to him for you?" Alex offers, his voice gentle and soft.

I shake my head, the thought of begging for Sebastian's love makes my stomach churn. "No, I don't want to do that. If he's meant to be in my life, he'll find his way back to me."

Alex nods in agreement, his hand reaching out to give mine a reassuring squeeze. We sit in silence for a few moments, the only sound the ticking of the clock on the wall, and then the sound of my brother digging through the paper bag for another pastry, but some things never change.

Finally, Alex breaks the silence. "You're strong, Julia. Stronger than you give yourself credit for. You'll get through this."

His words are healing my wounded heart, and I feel a glimmer of hope start to spark within me. I've got Gabi and Alex by my side, and I start to think that I can face this misery and come out the other side better for it. Wiser.

And maybe, just maybe, with Sebastian, if he pulls his head out of his ass and realizes my worth. Despite my prickly exterior when he first arrived earlier, it's nice having my brother here, and I hug him tightly, grateful for his unwavering support. "Thanks, Alex. For everything… but especially for not siding with Mom. I know it'd be easier."

"Nah," he says, patting my back before letting me go. "I guess we're both just the problem child."

After a while, we both get ready to head to campus. Alex is studying business, and we both have classes today. On the way out the door he offers to walk me to my classes, and I accept. I know that my brother's classes are on the other side of the campus, but I like having company right now. Maybe it will help keep the bad thoughts at bay.

It's useless, though, and once we're outside and out of the comfort of my apartment, I can't help but feel a deep sense of heartbreak. Sebastian's face seems to be everywhere—in the faces of strangers on the street, in the familiar buildings we used to walk by together. I check my phone obsessively, hoping for a message from him, but there's nothing. Not even a simple, "Good morning."

With each passing minute, I feel more and more stupid and naive for believing that Sebastian would go to the ends of the earth for us. I trusted him, believed in him, and he let me down. It's hard not to feel betrayed, as though our entire relationship was just a lie.

Alex notices the sadness etched on my face and puts his arm around me, offering a comforting embrace. "I know it hurts, Julia. But things will get better. You'll see."

I give him a small, false smile, but can't muster up any small talk as we enter the campus grounds. Alex fills the silence with anecdotes and chatter about his own classes, but I think he and I both know that I'm not really giving it my full attention.

We turn the corner, and suddenly, Gabi appears, as if she's been waiting for me. Knowing my steadfast, sweet friend, she probably was, but she tries to make our meeting look natural. "Hey, girl. How are you holding up?" Gabi asks, concern evident in her voice even as she tries to sound chipper.

"Not great," I admit, fighting as hard as I can to keep my voice from breaking. Alex is on one side of me, and Gabi on the other, but there are still other students all around and I don't want them to see me breaking down.

"No word yet, huh? He's probably just scared," Gabi reassures me. "Give him some time."

"But what if he never comes back?" I ask, my voice trembling.

"Then he's not the one for you." She links her arm around mine as we walk, and lowering her voice, she adds, "But I don't believe that's the case. He loves you too much to just let you go. He just hasn't realized it yet."

I wish I could believe that. But right now, I can't see past the pain and betrayal I feel.

"I don't know, Gabi. I feel stupid and naive for believing he'd go as far as I would for us," I fess out, my voice barely above a whisper.

"You're not stupid or naive. You believed in something beautiful, and that's something to be proud of."

I take a deep breath and try to calm down. Gabi is right. I shouldn't blame myself for believing in love. Still, he's haunting me--every couple holding hands, every guy with dark hair and deep, soulful eyes, reminds me of him…how am I supposed to get through the day like this? I keep checking my phone obsessively, hoping for a message or a call, but there's nothing.

Gabi notices my distress and takes my hand. "He'll come around, Julia. I know it. For right now, though, let's get to class, okay?"

"Okay," I breathe, and Gabi squeezes my hand before letting me go to bid my brother goodbye. I whisper another thanks to him, and follow Gabi to our lecture, keeping my eyes on the ground so I don't have to see all the little things that make it impossible to get him out of my head. One day at a time… I guess that's all I can do.

CHAPTER 21

Julia

A week has passed since that awful day when Sebastian broke my heart, but the pain continues to linger like a stubborn stain that won't wash away. He's everywhere, in every corner of my mind, and I can't seem to escape his memory.

I throw myself into school work, pulling my already stellar grades up until they can't go any higher. Here on campus, it's acceptable to shut out the world if it's for the sake of studying and schoolwork, so no one bothers me when I hole up in the corner of the library, reading law book after law book until I feel like my eyes are crossing. Then, when I'm finally exhausted beyond measure, I can sleep.

This routine, with quick delivery dinners and grab and go breakfasts weaved in, works well for the school week, but at the end of the day on Friday, I find myself outside of the closed library with nothing else to do and nowhere to go but home.

In my apartment, I make myself some tea while the TV is on, playing an episode of *Friends* for me to catch up on. Gabi calls a few times, but I ignore the ringing. When the door buzzer goes off, I assume it's her, wondering why in the heck I'm not responding to her repeated attempts to talk, but once again I'm surprised to see my brother waiting there instead. I'm about to ask him why he's bothering me on a Friday evening when Gabi's short form pops out from behind my brother's much taller frame with a Cheshire grin on her face.

"Ready to go out?" she warbles, flowing around Alex and into the apartment. "You should probably change."

"I'm absolutely not going anywhere," I declare, waiting until Alex is inside to close the door behind the two of them. Annoyance bubbles inside of me at their easy assumption that I'm up for a night on the town. It's the last thing I want to do.

"Come on," Alex gripes, crossing his arms. "We're just going to take you out to eat. There's live music, too. You'll like it."

"No means no." I don't feel like going out, I just want to stay in my apartment, drink my tea, and wallow in my misery. But Gabi is a whirlwind of energy, and she insists that I need to get out of my own head and do something fun.

Alex watches the episode playing on my television as Gabi searches through my closet, picks out my outfit, and fluffs my hair while I apply a quick coat of makeup to cover the ever-present dark circles I seem to wear constantly these days. I shimmy into the dress Gabi has picked, hating every second of this, while my friend gets more and more excited for the night ahead.

"You'll see, this is exactly what you need," she promises, holding my hand as we exit my apartment, following my brother to his car. "Nothing heals a broken heart better than food, booze, and maybe some hot guys."

"Gross," Alex adds, and this time I agree with him wholeheartedly.

We arrive at our destination, a restaurant, and the colorful exterior and live music is drawing the crowds in. Normally, I'd feel alive among the bustling crowd and the intoxicating scent of food, but not tonight. Still, the upbeat music creates an inviting atmosphere, and Gabi is vibrating with excitement for the night ahead.

The interior is trendy, with modern art adorning the walls, and dim lighting creating a cozy vibe. The tables are set elegantly with white tablecloths, and the plush chairs look inviting. The atmosphere is electric, with people moving energetically on the dance floor at the end of the restaurant.

"This is nice," I admit reluctantly, placing my clutch on the table and picking up the drink menu to flip through. "I'm a little hungry."

"Yeah, well, hurry up and eat, because we're here to dance!" Gabi declares, shifting excitedly in her seat.

Alex nods in agreement. "Yeah, I don't think a meal is going to do much to shake you out of the boring routine you've picked up this week. I'm going to order some of the good stuff. You both like champagne, right?"

"Yes," I answer for both of us, before letting out a sigh, feeling grateful for their support. "Thanks, guys. I still don't want to be here, but you might be right about needing a change of scenery. I don't know what I'd do without you."

Gabi gives me a warm smile. "That's what friends are for."

Alex then adds, "And family too."

I grin weakly, feeling a sense of comfort in their words. But the pain still lingers, and I know it will take time to heal. A lot of time, if the depth of my emotions are any indication.

Gabi waves a server over, and while he and Alex talk drinks, my friend leans in and whispers, "You don't have to force yourself to be okay, Julia. It's okay to not be okay. Just try and enjoy the night a little, alright?"

"I will." Hearing the worry for me in her voice makes me even more determined to at least try and make tonight work. "Promise."

The band on stage is playing a mix of popular hits, and the lead singer's voice is captivating, making me want to get up and dance despite the misery swirling in my head. The music seems to flow through my veins, and I can't help but tap my feet to the beat. The waitstaff is dressed in sleek black outfits, making them look effortlessly stylish. They move gracefully between the tables, taking orders and serving drinks with a smile.

I order a few small bites as the place starts to fill up with more and more people, ordering an espresso martini, and then a second one, while I wait for my food. After it arrives, Alex orders a bottle of champagne, and I finish off my martini so I can enjoy the glass he pours me. I chew on a bite of bacon wrapped asparagus that does nothing to soak up any of the alcohol in my stomach that has already started to make my head spin.

A few more friends and acquaintances join us, but I can barely muster the strength to socialize. I keep drinking, trying to numb the pain, but it only makes things worse. I can see my brother frowning as I clumsily pour myself another glass of champagne, but he's pulled into a conversation with one of his friends, and he fails to stop me from continuing to imbibe.

Wow… the alcohol is making me feel better, but it's also unleashing all of my most private thoughts, too. Sure, I'm not feeling nearly as depressed, laughing and joking with the people around me, but thoughts of Sebastian have nothing to do with our breakup. Flashes of our heated moments in my bedroom start haunting me, so I press my hands to my face to try and stop myself from blushing. It doesn't work, though, and it's like I can feel his lips drifting down my neck, ghosting over my collarbone… ugh! I can't take it anymore!

I excuse myself and head to the bathroom to splash water on my face and try to compose myself, holding onto the ceramic sink until the room stops spinning and throwing on the tap until I can cup handful after handful of cold water in my palms. It's like ice on my cheeks, but it chases away those lewd memories, at least for a few seconds, and steadies my shaking legs.

As I look at my reflection in the mirror, I don't even recognize myself anymore. I feel broken, shattered into a million pieces that I don't know how to put back together, and at the same time, blushing from fantasies of when I almost gave the man that broke my heart my virginity! I can't help but wonder if I'll ever be able to love again, or if this pain will haunt me for the rest of my life. Then I think about what Sebastian might be doing right this second. Could he be thinking of me? How can one man make me feel so many highs, and then such terrible, inescapable lows? I went from thinking he is my future husband, to knowing without a doubt that he is my ex.

Looking around the bathroom, I realize that no one is in here but me. In the hidden pocket of my dress, the weight of my phone suddenly feels like a million pounds, and it's begging me to take it out and make a horrible, irresistible decision: Call Sebastian.

Alcohol is coursing through my veins, liquid bravery, and it makes dialing his number all too easy. I don't even know what I want from him when he answers, but I need some sort of closure.

Or hope. A little hope might be nice, too.

I suppress a hiccup when he picks up, confusion in his voice, "Julia?"

"Tell me one thing, Seb," I slur into the phone as I pace around the empty bathroom. "How do I go from the love of your life to a nobody in the blink of an eye just because your dad said so? One little chit-chat at the park and that's it? Our plans for the future are meaningless to you? As I come to think of it, are you such a heartless monster that it doesn't bother you to move on so swiftly?"

I can hear his hesitation on the other end of the line before he finally responds. "Julia, gosh, I thought it was an emergency—"

"Oh, it *is*," I interrupt, my anger rising at his words. "I need closure. I need to know if I should keep hope or should I just… I don't know… go to one of Mom's balls and find some companionship there. It worked the first time, maybe it will work again."

There's a moment of silence before he finally responds. "Julia, my dad just left the hospital and is under twenty-four seven care here at home. He needs my full attention. He has depression and—"

"I need your attention too, Seb," I say louder, cutting him off. "Did you ever consider that? We had plans for fuck's sake! Life plans. And excluding me from your life wasn't part of it." I can feel my bottom lip wobbling, and I'm infinitely glad he isn't here to see it. "We were supposed to build a future together. A family, even."

I hear him let out a heavy sigh, but he doesn't answer immediately. "I can't gamble with my dad's health, Julia. He needs time—"

"Very well." I try to mask the pain in my voice, but I'm sure it's all too evident. "Have a good one."

"Ju—" is all I hear before I'm cramming my phone back into my pocket, grasping the sink with both hands and breathing slowly, in through my nose and out of my mouth, to keep from crying. Damn Sebastian! Damn him and his stubbornness… his lack of care for me!

I need him, and I hate him for it. The worst part is, though, that I hate myself, too.

I want another drink, right now, but I don't know if my legs will work anymore if I have one. Was I being too harsh on him? Was it really fair to expect him to choose between me and his father? But then again, wasn't love supposed to conquer all?

I've still got my eyes closed, head bent over the sink as Gabi enters the bathroom. She finds me there, all but slumped over, hot tears streaming down my face. My phone is vibrating in my pocket, but I don't give a damn if Sebastian is calling me or not.

I look up at Gabi when she comes up next to me, and she immediately understands. "Are you okay?" she asks, placing a hand on my shoulder.

Looking into my friend's face, I know for a fact that she heard me talking on the phone with Seb. Any other time it would make me feel stupid, embarrassed, even, but not tonight. She and my brother went through all this work to get me here, and they don't deserve for Sebastian to ruin their nights, too. So, I put on a brave face, and lie. "Always. Let's go have some fun, shall we?"

We make our way back to the table, and I can feel eyes on me. I know my friends are worried, but I don't want to talk about it. Once we arrive, Gabi whispers to Alex, who gives me a sympathetic look. I try to shake it off and act normal, but my mind is still reeling. I sit down and take a deep breath, determined now more than ever to enjoy the night despite everything.

My brother, who is sitting next to me, asks me as quietly as he can while still being heard over the music, if I'm okay, and I give him a forced smile. "Never been better." I order a round of shots, hoping to numb the pain just a little bit more, but it only seems to make things blurrier and harder to focus on. Oh well, I guess that also means I can't focus on Sebastian, either.

As I listen to the music, it courses through me, the drumbeat in my bones. I feel a sudden urge to dance. This song is familiar, and one of my favorites. A little reminder of the things in the world that bring me joy, Sebastian or no Sebastian. Without thinking twice, I grab Gabi's hand and pull her to the middle of the dance floor.

The two of us dance, and I feel a rush of emotions. Anger, sadness, and confusion all swirl around inside me. But for the moment, I'm able to forget everything and just enjoy the music and the moment.

I don't know if it's the drinks, the music, or just how inebriated I really am, but as I dance with Gabi I can feel the weight of the world lift off my shoulders. It's like all my problems disappear and I'm able to just be in the moment, swaying to the music and feeling the beat pulse through my body. I don't know how long it will last, so I'm determined to soak it all in.

Gabi is not only the perfect friend, but also the perfect dance partner, matching my movements effortlessly and encouraging me to let loose and have fun. I feel so grateful to have her in my life, and I can't help but smile as we twirl and spin around the dance floor. The music is loud and the lights are flashing, but at this moment, everything is just right. I feel like I can be myself with Gabi, and that she understands me in a way that no one else can.

As the song ends, Gabi pulls me in for a tight hug, and I feel a surge of affection for her. "Who needs a man when one has a Gabi in their life?" I joke, but there's a hint of truth to my words.

"I'm sure things will come around," Gabi says, and I know she means it. She's always been here for me, through the ups and downs of my life, and I know that I can count on her to be here for me now.

I take a deep breath and let it out slowly, feeling a sense of calm wash over me. Maybe everything will be okay after all. Maybe I don't need closure from Seb to be happy. Maybe all I need is my friends, some good music, and a little bit of fun.

CHAPTER 22

Sebastian

Mondays look different now that I am the head of the company and no longer just second in command. I can't say that I'm enjoying the change, but I understand the need for all the extra work. The day ahead of me is packed with back-to-back meetings, and my secretary has just informed me that a few new projects have come in. Taking a seat at my desk, I close my eyes, take a deep breath, and mentally prepare myself for the busy day ahead. I'm running on caffeine and adrenaline, trying to stay on top of everything while also trying not to think of how much I miss Julia.

My phone pings—I check and see it's Amelia reminding me that I have a meeting in ten minutes. So much for having any time to mentally prepare for another crushing shift. I quickly glance over the notes and try to prepare myself for what's to come. After a while, it all seems to run together, and it takes a series of blinking and head shakes to even get through the summary of what is on the first meeting agenda. Luckily, I wear the mask of a competent CEO well, no one will ever know how disconnected I really feel.

Meanwhile, the actual issues floating around in my mind are haunting me: breaking Julia's heart—and my own in the process—and my father's failing health.

A million memories of working with my father hover over me as I walk the long hallway to the conference room, like my first day working here, watching and learning from my father, noticing as work began to take precedence over his personal life, and then watching him work his last few days as CEO as a shadow of his former self. None of those memories can be good anymore, it seems. Even the ones that seemed positive at the time.

As I step into the conference room, I'm immediately bombarded with questions and concerns. A lot of the investors and board members, while supportive and caring at first, have started pushing my boundaries, no doubt to test me and see if I really am worthy of my father's previous position. I meet their challenges head on, but it exhausts me after some time. The meeting lasts longer than expected, and by the time I leave, I'm already behind schedule for the rest of my daily responsibilities.

It's when I'm rushing back to my office that my cell phone rings, and I see that it's my secretary being forwarded from my desk phone. I answer, half-expecting her to tell me about yet another task that needs to be done, and my instincts prove to be correct. She informs me of a last-minute interview that needs to be scheduled, causing a wave of frustration to wash over me. I'm already stretched thin, and I'm not sure how I'll manage to fit it in, but what choice do I have?

Moving from one task to another, my mind drifts to Julia, as it always seems to. The phone call from her still echoes in my mind, brought to the forefront of my thoughts each time my cell rings. The hope that it's her flashes in me every single time. I can't seem to shake off the thoughts of what went wrong between us, how I only gave her up to help keep my father well… but it doesn't mean that I don't miss her terribly. I try to focus on my work, but my mind keeps drifting back to her.

I take a quick break to grab a cup of coffee while I flip through the pile of resumes from candidates I'll need to interview, hoping that the coffee will help me stay focused. I'd rather be picking out possible additions to the team at home, reading each resume at my leisure, but that just isn't in the cards for me. As I sit down at my desk, I realize that the day is far from over. I have several more meetings and tasks to complete before I can even think about going home.

Despite my best efforts, I can't shake the feeling that's been nagging at me all day—the feeling that I'm bearing a burden that is too heavy for any single man to bear. I take a deep breath and remind myself that I can do this. I can handle the workload, no matter how stressful it may seem. But as the day wears on, I find myself feeling more and more drained. The weight of my responsibilities seems to be crushing me, and I feel like I'm drowning in the sea of work. By the end of the day, I'm exhausted, both mentally and physically. Gathering my things to leave the office, I wonder how I'll manage to get through the rest of the week.

The evening air is heavy with the humidity of impending rain, the streets busy with everyone else heading out from their own jobs for the evening, laughing and talking.

Probably because they aren't stuck with so much responsibility that it seems unfair, like I am, and frankly I'm jealous of all of them. It's been such a short time since I've taken over but I can't even remember what it's like to clock out and leave work behind me to focus on my personal life.

I'm spiraling, and considering walking down the road to the nearest bar instead of going home to get the rest I so desperately need. Then, as if on cue, my phone rings. My heart skips a beat, once more thinking that it might be Julia, but then I see her brother's name flashing on the screen. I hesitate for a moment, unsure of whether to answer, but eventually pick up.

"Hey, Alex," I say, trying to keep myself steady. I have to think of him as just a man, not the brother of the woman I love and have lost because of my own decisions.

"Seb, man, how's it going?" His voice's casual and aloof, which is a relief. It means that he isn't calling to talk about Julia.

I relax a little, grateful for the friendly tone. "It's going… well, as good as things can be in my situation, I guess. How about you?"

"I'm good, thanks. Listen, I was wondering if you're coming to the hunting game this weekend at DeVries estate? They have a ton of land. Jan's hosting it, and we thought it would be great to have you there."

A pang of longing and heartache hits me at the mention of the hunting game. The last time I went hunting it went from enjoyable to the worst moment of my life in an instant. I wonder if I can even separate the sport from the tragedy of that phone call, and it makes me hesitate. Plus, this is Alex Van Dieren inviting me, and the unavoidable connection of him being Julia's brother doesn't sit well with me. What if this is just some ploy on her end to get me alone, and Alex is just a willing pawn?

Before I can even reply, Alex speaks again. "And no, my sister isn't going to show up, if that's what you're afraid of."

I feel a twinge of guilt at the mention of Julia, and how he must have known exactly what I was thinking. I hurt her deeply, and I know that I'm the one to blame for our breakup. But I also know that I can't let my own feelings hold me back from spending time with my friends, and while I barely know Alex, he hasn't done anything to make me think that he would be so shady as to set me up for an ambush by his sister. I shouldn't have jumped to that conclusion…and it'd be nice to get out with young guys and not the senior citizens that seem to make up most of my professional circles at work.

Feeling steadier, I take a deep breath and reply, "Sure, I'll be there." Then, surprising myself, I laugh. "Man, you really read my mind about Julia."

"Yeah, well, the women in my family can be intimidating, but I'm not anyone's errand boy or some tool used to manipulate people, so you don't need to worry about that with me. The hunt will be good for you, Sebastian. I'm looking forward to seeing you there."

We finish the call, and I hang up, pocketing the phone and considering everything that was just said. I hope Alex is right, and that this hunt does provide some stress relief. It cannot be overstated how much I truly need it.

It's funny to think that I'm becoming friends with Margaret's son, considering how much I dislike her. But I do feel a fondness for at least two of her children, Alex and Julia.

Despite our past romantic relationship and subsequent breakup, I still care about Julia deeply. And now, as I consider getting to know her brother better, excited about the prospect of building a new friendship.

There's also the chance that knowing Alex better gives me more chances to encounter Julia naturally, but I can't focus on that too much. I shouldn't want to run into her in any capacity, but the temptation swirls darkly in my thoughts. I would give so much just to see her, even if we didn't speak. It would be so painful, but worth every second.

***

With the sun sinking in the sky and turning things a burnt orange, I head home to find my father tending to the garden. It isn't easy to locate him at first—he isn't in his suite resting, or in his office doing the work that he really should be leaving up to me, which is where I can usually find him now that his health is declining and he can't come into the office as often. I get the feeling that he is feeling lost without work to occupy all of his time, and without my mother or siblings to turn to, and me running the corporation, he spends a lot of his day with his home nurses, trying to heal. There are times, though, that I doubt that he even wants to. The hole left behind from losing my mom, sister, and brother is achingly hollow, barely scabbed over, and I simply cannot lose my Dad right now too. Surely the universe can't be that cruel.

I'm just starting to get worried about not finding Dad when I spot the bright blue of his nurse's scrubs sitting in a chair on the edge of the flower beds that my mother used to love. Just a few feet in front of the nurse is my father, looking so odd to me in his casual clothing and gardening gloves; he has a small pair of shears in his hands as he deadheads one of the rose bushes.

For anyone else, this scene might be reassuring. He's outside, staying active, and engaged in a hobby. That has to be good for an older man who is still actively grieving and dealing with a health scare, right? But to me, it just looks like Dad is going through the motions, nothing more. I know he has never given a damn about this garden before, but without my mother here to tend to it, no one else will.

"Hey, Dad," I say softly, and he lifts a hand in greeting as I move to join him, rolling up my sleeves as I do so.

He looks tired and frail, the simple act of bending at the waist to make a cutting leaving him winded. There is a pang of guilt in me for not spending more time with him.

"Your mom adored these roses," he begins, his eyes scanning through the flowers. "She used to take good care of them. They were her pride and joy."

I can tell that the memory of Mom still haunts him, and I can't help but wonder if his new interest in the roses is a way to keep her memory alive.

"Every morning, she would come out here and enjoy her morning coffee when they were blooming."

I watch as he gently touches the velvety petals of a deep crimson rose, his eyes distant yet filled with bittersweet longing. The scent of the flowers fills the air, mingling with the heaviness of our shared grief.

"It feels like just yesterday. Her presence still lingers in this garden," I reply softly, my voice barely audible above the breeze.

He nods, a wistful smile playing on his lips. "Yes, it does. Sometimes, I find solace in tending to these roses, or at least something like it. She'd probably get a laugh out of seeing me do it."

I can see the weight of his loss in his eyes even as he tries to inject some humor. It's in the way he delicately handles each rosebud, as if they were delicate pieces of her soul. It's as if the roses themselves carry the essence of my mother's spirit.

"I wonder," I venture cautiously, "If you being out here is too much, too fast. You just got out of the hospital, you know."

He pauses for a moment, his gaze fixed on the blooming flowers. The silence hangs heavy between us, filled with unspoken emotions and shared sorrow.

"You might be right," he finally responds, but there is a note of stubbornness to him that is all too familiar. "But I'm fine, Sebastian. Try not to worry so much."

I reach out, placing my hand on his arm, offering him a small measure of comfort in our shared understanding. "That's not possible. I'm always going to worry about you. Until you start taking better care of yourself, that is."

"Hmm. I appreciate it, son, but I don't need a babysitter, either." He cups a wilted bloom in his hands, positioning the shears and clipping it off in a flash.

His response annoys me somewhat. Does he not understand how hard it was for me to sit there with him after his heart attack, wondering if he was going to make it or not? "Dad—"

"Did you take care of the relationship?" my father asks, his attention focused on the flowers.

My mouth snaps shut on whatever I'm about to say, his question immediately putting me on edge. "I did. It's over," I reply, feeling a twinge of regret in my heart.

My father nods, a small smile appearing on his face. "Good," he utters nonchalantly, turning to me. "You will find someone, don't worry, son."

His words are meant to comfort me, but they only serve to remind me of the pain I feel. I wonder if I'll ever find someone who truly understands me, someone who will love me for who I am and not for my family's wealth. Someone who can possibly compare to Julia… makes me feel like only she ever has.

Without responding, I shove my hands into my pockets and I watch my father tend to the roses. In a strange way, they are like a symbol of the life that I'm expected to lead. A life of duty and tradition. Growing only in the way my father finds appropriate, never free to flourish as I wish. But as I look closer, I notice that the roses are not as beautiful as they once were. Maybe they aren't so much like me, but more like the man clipping them. They are withered and weak, just like my father.

I wonder if my father is tending to them out of love, or out of guilt for not being able to keep my mother alive and not loving her the right way when she was here. And I wonder if my own obligations will lead me down the same path, a life of emptiness and regret.

But for now, I push those thoughts aside and help my father tend to the garden. It's a small gesture, but it's a way to connect with him, to show him that I care, even if it breaks my heart to see what he's become these days. Losing my mom did this to him, and it makes me question if love and marriage are even worth it, if losing your partner can turn someone into a walking zombie.

CHAPTER 23

Julia

It's Friday afternoon and I'm in the car with Alex, heading back to the family estate for the weekend. My heart feels heavy as I think about Sebastian, and I'm still having issues accepting that things are really over. Deep inside, I'm positive even now that he's my soulmate, but how is someone supposed to just get over something like that? It's impossible. Maybe I'll be grieving him forever.

I try to hide my sadness from Alex, responding when he talks to me and trying to joke around, but he can tell that something is off. Damn sibling connection.

"Still thinking about Seb, huh?" he asks, his voice teasing.

I sigh, unable to deny the truth. "Yeah, I guess I am. It's just hard, you know? I really thought we had something special."

My brother keeps his eyes on the road, but I can see him raise an eyebrow. "Just special? Or something more?"

I hate how well he can read me, and my stomach sinks at his words. "Does it matter? Even if it was something more, he doesn't want it, so it doesn't matter."

Alex chuckles, refusing to be brought down to my melancholic level. "He must have done some serious witchcraft to have you so smitten."

I roll my eyes, but a smile tugs at my lips. Alex has always had a way of lightening the mood. But in truth, I know that Sebastian is more than just a passing crush. He is the one who has captured my heart and made me believe in love. Real love, not just something quick and fleeting or some match made to benefit two families.

Looking out the window, watching the beautiful countryside go by, I can feel the emotions welling up in me again. Alex has done all he can, and more, to make me feel better, but it just isn't working. And I'm really regretting coming home for the weekend. Seeing my mother and knowing that this is the conclusion that she wanted for my relationship with Sebastian is just going to rub salt in the wound.

As we drive through the winding roads which lead to the estate, memories of Sebastian flood my mind. I remember the way he used to make me laugh, the way he would hold my hand, and the way he would look at me with such intensity, like he saw who I really was. But all those moments are gone now. Sebastian is no longer mine, and I'm left with a heart full of longing and regret. I feel a lump forming in my throat.

"Alex, do you think I'm a naive idiot?" I blurt out, and my brother frowns at how unexpected my outburst is. "I know that everyone feels terrible after a breakup, and that this sounds cheesy, but… it's like it was written in the stars that Seb and I are meant to be together. I feel such a pull towards him that it's impossible to explain."

He stares at me for a moment, considering my words. "I've never been in love like that, Julia, so I can't tell you whether it's crazy or not. But you've always had a good head on your shoulders and been mature for your age. I've never known you to be overly dramatic about anything, so if you say that you're in real, true love, I believe you."

"Really?" A little spark of hope comes to life inside me. If Alex trusts me, then maybe I'm right, and Sebastian won't be lost to me forever. Not if it's fate bringing us together.

"Yeah, really." Alex sounds stoic, but it doesn't take but a few seconds for his joking smirk to start pulling at the corner of his mouth. "Listen, Ju, if you ever want to elope, let me know and I will help you out."

I snort. "You're joking."

Still watching the road, Alex reaches over and grabs my shoulder affectionately. "I'm not. Plus, how often do I get to be involved in something that causes so much chaos without revolving around me?"

Joy threatens to overtake the sorrow in me, but I can't let it. Not yet, when all of this is just words between my brother and I. "It's a nice thought, but Seb cares more about his dad's approval than he does me, so why even bother?"

Alex's grin widens, and I narrow my eyes at him. He's acting strange.

"He might change his mind. Who knows?"

Pivoting in my seat to see him better, I examine his face for any trace of dishonesty, but find none. "Are you up to something, Alex?"

"Me?" he asks innocently.

"Yes, *you*." All of this is making me think that something is going on right under my nose with me still being blissfully unaware. “I don’t need you or anyone else out here trying to convince him that he’s making a mistake. The only thing worse than not having Sebastian in my life would be having him with me reluctantly.”

Alex waves his hand at me dismissively. “No, Julia, nothing like that. I’m not going to try and convince him of anything, don’t worry. I wouldn’t want you with someone that wasn’t going to fight for you, anyway.”

“Hm.” I cross my arms and lean back in the seat, feeling a strange combination of worried and amused. “I don’t know that I trust you, Alex, but I’ll give you the benefit of the doubt.”

“Good.” Alex’s face grows serious once more. “I’ll always be your ally, Ju, and something tells me that you might need one sooner than you think. You can always turn to me, okay?”

Warmth glows in my chest. “Okay, Alex. I will. I love you.”

“Love you too, kid.”

***

As we pull up to the estate, my mind is still lost in thoughts of Sebastian and whatever weird things that Alex has cooking up regarding my recent breakup. I try to focus on school, but while I’ve been participating in my classes like always, none of the information seems to be sticking. Making a mental note to email Gabi to get some of her notes, it’s a relief that I can at least keep myself busy with college work instead of socializing with my mother.

"*Oh, Seb, do you have any idea how much I miss you?*" I think with an internal sigh. It's impossible not to wonder if he ever thinks of me, if he still remembers the moments we shared.

If, by some terrible chance, he's moved on already.

I try to shake off the sadness as we step out of the car, but it lingers like a heavy cloud over my head. The weekend stretches out ahead of me, feeling endless even though it's just a few days. How am I going to get through it with my mind and heart full of the man that has left me heartbroken?

I miss his laugh, his smile, the way he would make me feel like I was the only person in the world that mattered. I miss the way he would hold me when I was upset, and how he always knew just what to say to make me feel better. And now he's gone. I still can't believe it. We were supposed to have a future together, and now that future is gone. We had *plans*!

I wonder if Alex can see the sadness in my eyes, if he knows how much I'm hurting. But I don't want to burden him with my pain any more than I already have. Talking to him in the car actually helped me somewhat, and just because of that he's done more to help than anything else has so far. My younger siblings are home, too, and I don't want to bring anyone else down into this pit of depression with me.

As soon as Alex mentioned eloping, I knew that he was more involved in this entire thing that I originally thought. Elopement… I guess I never really considered it as an option. Weddings in my world are huge, preplanned affairs that have been organized down to the very minute. Could it really be that easy? Could Sebastian and I run away and get married without either of our parents being aware, without them having any say at all?

But then I remember Seb's unwavering dedication to his father's approval and my hopes are dashed once again. Still, Alex's earnest offer to help me elope feels strangely reassuring. Is he really serious about this? Or is he just trying to cheer me up? I know my brother loves me, but he's also known for his mischievous streak. What could he be up to this time? I eye him warily as we get out of the car, wondering if there's more to his offer than meets the eye. But when I asked him if he's up to something, he just dismissed me and looked innocent. For a moment, I wonder if I'm being paranoid. Maybe I'm just looking for hidden meanings where there aren't any. Or maybe… just maybe… Alex really does have a plan. Either way, I can't shake the feeling that my life is about to take a dramatic turn.

As soon as we get inside the house, I can hear my mom greeting Alex, but I don't even give her a chance to say hi to me. I rush up the stairs to lock myself in my bedroom, desperate for some time alone, and for the hours I have to spend here at the estate to pass quickly. I hear Mom calling after me, but it's easy to ignore her, like she has ignored all of my feelings thus far.

I breathe a sigh of relief as I shut the bedroom door behind me and turn the lock. Logically, I know that my mother probably has a key, but at least I have a modicum of privacy for the time being.

I try to distract myself by reading a book or listening to music, but I can't stop thinking about Sebastian and how things have gone to hell so fast. Without anything else to pass the time, I go to my bag and pull something special out of it—the picture of Sebastian and I dancing at the ball that I just framed a few days ago. My little secret. I could have never imagined that things would spin out of control the way they have.

Touching the picture with a gentle finger, my heart aches at the sight of it. We were so happy then, so carefree, and now everything feels so heavy and complicated. The high of meeting Seb and the spark that ignited between us wasn't even that long ago, but it feels like it was in another lifetime. I'd do anything to go back to that moment, when his mother and siblings were still alive and when there was still a chance for us. Maybe if we had eloped soon after that ball, we would be happily married and at peace right now, without our parents being able to do a single thing about it.

I think that Sebastian's mother wouldn't have minded our love match so much, though. I wish I had time to get to know her, to see if she would have approved of me as a wife for her oldest son. Closing my eyes, I hold the picture to my chest and exhale slowly. Everything has changed so much, but my feelings for Seb are stronger than ever. This can't really be the end, can it?

My mom knocks on my door after about an hour, saying my name softly, but I don't answer. I don't want to talk to her right now. I need some time alone with my thoughts.

A few hours later, there is another visitor trying to get my attention with a few hesitant knocks.

"Go away. I don't want to talk," I yell.

"Julia…it's me." I hear the quiet voice of my younger sister Maud and frown. She's either here because she's worried, or because Mom has put her up to it. The only person who I'd open the door for without suspicion would be Alex.

Still annoyed, I say, "What, Maud?"

"Uh, well, dinner is ready. Everyone is already in the dining room, and Mom is asking for you."

In my mind I can see my sister standing outside the door with her head down and her hands clasped in front of her. I don't really want to go down and eat, but I know my mom will force me to do so if I don't comply. "Maud, I'm not in the mood. If Mom needs me she can come and get me herself."

Maud makes an uncomfortable noise. "She said she already tried earlier and that you weren't having it, so...."

I let out a sigh, knowing that I can't avoid dinner any longer. As much as I want to stay locked up in my room, I can already tell that my mother is going to win this battle. It's her house, and therefore her rules, no matter what. I know she will keep nagging me until I show up. I take a deep breath and make my way to the door, opening it to find my younger sister standing there with a sympathetic look on her face.

"If it was up to me I would have left you alone, but you know how she is," she says as she observes me attentively. "Are you okay?"

I shake my head and let out a small laugh. "Not really, but I guess I have to face the music sooner or later."

Maud nods, understandingly. "Yeah, Mom's not going to let you hide away forever. She's already got her attention focused on you, so it's better to just get it over with I would think."

I roll my eyes. "Of course. No peace for me, I guess."

Maud takes my hand and gives it a squeeze. "Come on, Ju, let's go downstairs. Maybe some food will make you feel better."

Affection stirs for my young sister. At least I know she isn't unaware about how mom is manipulating her, and feels some remorse for it. "I doubt it, but there's no reason to have her getting on your case just because I'm not complying. Let's go."

I let her lead me down the stairs, my mind still lost in thoughts of what Alex said. *Elopement.* Will I ever be able to let that impossible idea go? Even if it was an option at one point, I think that it's passed by now.

Approaching the dining room, I can hear the chatter and laughter of my family. The closer we get, the more anxious I become. What will they say when they see me? Will they try to talk to me about Sebastian? I don't think I can handle that right now, especially from Mom.

Maud gives my hand another squeeze before letting go and heading over to the table. I take a deep breath and force myself to follow her. As soon as I step into the room, all eyes turn to me, and I can feel the weight of their stares. Everyone falls silent as I try to ignore the awkwardness and take my seat.

Dinner is the last place I want to be. There's a pork roast with an orange glaze being carved and served, along with a fresh salad and roasted potatoes, but to me it all looks terrible. The evening hangs over me like a dark cloud.

My mother is trying to be cheerful, but it only makes me feel more uneasy. She gives me a motherly hug as I circle the table, which I find incredibly odd. Mom is not an overly affectionate person.

"So glad you could join us," she tells me, squeezing me close. "I was afraid you were going to shun us all night."

"You didn't give me much of a choice, but I'm here," I grumble, but hug her back so I don't cause a scene with the rest of the family here.

Maud has gone to sit next to my youngest sister Yara, who is already seated and chatting away. Usually I would want to catch up with both of them, but I can't bring myself to join in.

Alex's making small talk with Mom and the girls, but I can tell he's doing it out of obligation rather than genuine interest. Anything to keep the peace, I guess. I'm a bit off, lost in my thoughts and still mourning the loss of Sebastian. But then my mother drags me reluctantly back into the conversation before I can find a way to avoid it.

"You know Julia, tomorrow I'm going for tea at the Van Lawicks. Tom will be there with his younger brother Elliot. Would you like to join?"

Tom, the boring guy that she all but forced me to interact with at the ball. I try to contain a laugh at the mention of his name, but it comes out as a bitter scoff instead. My mother's obliviousness astounds me. She knows I don't want to see him, let alone spend an afternoon with him. I can't imagine a worse fate.

"No, thanks, Mom." I reply, trying to keep myself steady and even.

She's relentless, though. Like always. "It's Elliot's birthday and a lot of young people will be there. Maud and Yara are coming. Are you sure you don't want to join?"

I shake my head. The thought of having tea time with Tom and his family is unbearable. But then, a new thought occurs to me. If I don't go, I'll be stuck here with nothing to do but study—which normally would be equally as boring, but as of right now it feels like the perfect excuse to stay home. Surely my mother wouldn't want me to neglect my education.

While fumbling for a response that will end the conversation as quickly as possible, my eyes light upon my brother, and I realize that she didn't mention him going, either. Maybe this is a way out. If Alex doesn't have to go, why should I?

"What about you Alex, aren't you going?" I ask, suddenly curious.

"I've got a hunt with Jan and a few of his pals," he replies between bites of roast.

Of course Alex has plans, he always does. I turn back to my plate, my appetite gone. The thought of spending the day alone in my room studying seems like the only option, but there is also a sense of dread at the thought. Studying is one thing… but it also means being alone with my thoughts. And all of my thoughts lately are of Sebastian.

I shake my head, pushing food around my plate. "I'm good, Mom. I've got some schoolwork that I was planning on using the weekend to catch up on. I have a few big projects due, so…."

She thins her lips, all but glaring at me, but I see her square her shoulder and let the subject go, turning to Maud to talk. It's unlike her to give up so easily, but if Mom has decided to respect my decisions finally, I'm not going to second guess it. I shift my attention back to my dinner and eat, even though it's tasteless to me. If I'm occupied with chewing, maybe Mom won't address me again.

Dinner finishes with relatively little drama, and I pat my mouth with the cloth napkin before standing and pivoting to go back to my bedroom. I've got a lavender essential oil bath on my mind, hoping that it will help me relax, and I'm so lost in thought about it that I don't hear Mom the first time she addresses me.

"—in the library?" I catch, and turn, seeing that she's looking at me.

"Uh, sorry Mom, I didn't catch that. What did you say?"

She looks slightly miffed, but repeats herself. "Will you join me for tea in the library, Julia?"

The word 'no' is right there on my lips, but I've already shut her down about brunch at the Van Lawicks tomorrow, so I guess the least I can do is have some tea with her before bed. Part of me is screaming that it's a trap, but on the other hand, this is my mother. I can't avoid her for the rest of my life, and maybe if I give her this little tea time she will leave me be for the rest of the weekend. And if that's true, it's totally worth it.

I nod, agreeing to it. I settle into one of the high-backed chairs once we make it to the library, watching as one of the house staff pours the steaming water into our individual cups and adds just the right amount of cream and sugar for me before departing and leaving us alone. Mom, as usual, takes no sweetener.

There is a long few minutes of quiet between us, only the sound of the silver spoon on the ceramic cups filling the high-ceilinged room. Eventually, Mom sighs airily. "Listen, my dear, I'm sure you know that I'm aware of the little breakup between you and Sebastian. I won't disrespect you by lying and saying that it doesn't make me happy to know it, but I know you're feeling down about it, and that I am sorry for."

I can feel my hands starting to shake a bit, clutching my tea cup tighter and feeling the heat bleeding through to my palms. Why does this have to be the first thing we talk about? Why do we have to talk about it at all?

"Mom… I'm not an idiot. I'm sure that you had some hand in this. But I still don't want to get into it. Can we not?"

She exhales through her nose, amused. "What choice do we have with you moping around? Your sisters don't need to see you so beaten down by the rejection of some man."

"He's not just some man," I snap, setting the cup down on the side table before it splashes over the rim and burns my lap. "He meant something to me, Mom. He still means something to me."

"Well, regardless of whatever feelings you're still hanging on to, I appreciate Sebastian coming to terms with this nonsense," she says, before gracefully taking a sip of her tea. "It might be the first smart thing that man has done in his entire life. And while I'm saddened to see you like this, I think you'll understand one day that I did it to protect you."

I scoff, annoyance making my head pound. "*Protect* me? From what?"

She takes a long drink, the orange light coming from the flames in the fireplace casting her face in sharp angles. "Julia, if he's anything like his father, you're better off without him."

I feel a jolt of anger surge through me. "What are you talking about?"

She chuckles, like she's enjoying a private joke. "Do you think that only your father has had affairs? Let me tell you a secret, my love... his best buddy did too."

I'm stunned. I don't know what to say. So she's confirming, here and now, that his father had an affair? I feel like everything I thought I knew about the Van den Bosch family is a lie... and then there is the fact that my father's best friend just so happened to be... Sebastian's own damn father.

The world feels like it's tilting around me. "Does Sebastian know?" I ask, feeling a knot form in my stomach.

"I don't think so," Mom says, shrugging one thin shoulder as she finishes her tea. "But if he's like his dad, then he's not a man you should ever consider being serious with."

Closing my eyes to try and find my equilibrium, I speak slowly, not wanting to say the wrong thing when she's giving me such groundbreaking information. "Does Sebastian also have a... well, you know..." I trail off, not wanting to say the word.

"A *bastard* in the family?" Mom asks, with a raised eyebrow and zero hesitation. "I'm afraid I can't disclose that."

She's being absolutely ridiculous. Mom can tell me about everyone's affairs and hint at a love child out there somewhere, but she won't take this final step and tell me whether that potential child exists or not? "Mom! Please! Seb needs to know!" I practically plead with her.

"Julia, enough!" my mother bites out the words. "It's none of your business. It is up to his dad to disclose such a private matter. If his father decides to do it, then that's their business."

I stare at my mother, incredulous. How could she keep such a big secret from Sebastian? And from me, for that matter? I can't believe what I'm hearing. How can she live with herself, knowing something like this but keeping it quiet? She knows how close Sebastian and I have been, breakup or not, and it's utterly unfair to tease me with truths like this.

But even if she does tell me… do I tell Sebastian? I know that if I were in his position, I would want to know. But it's clear that my mother is not going to budge on this. Picking up my now-lukewarm drink, I finish my tea in silence, feeling frustrated and powerless. Once we are done, I stand up, pondering what other secrets my mother might be keeping from me.

"Well, this was certainly enlightening," Mom says after a moment, standing and straightening her pants. She walks gracefully over to me and leans down, kissing me on the top of the head and making me stiffen from surprise. "Truly, daughter, all things I do is for the love of my children. You may find me and my actions distasteful right now, but when you have children of your own—with an appropriate husband, that is—you'll understand. And maybe then you can forgive me."

My mouth is hanging open as she leaves the library, and I'm left alone with my thoughts. Instead of leaving back to my room, the silence and coziness this study offers makes me sit back and tuck my legs underneath me, curling up in the chair as I take in the comfort of the firelight while I try to put everything together in my mind. The pieces of the puzzle are finally falling into place, and it's like a wave of realization has hit me. All this time, I had been so angry and confused about Sebastian's sudden change of heart, but now it all makes sense. Mom must have threatened Sebastian's dad with this secret, and he had no choice but to convince Sebastian to end things with me!

I can't keep this to myself. I need to talk to someone, and there's only one person in this house right now that I trust.

My heart is pounding as I burst into Alex's room, finding him getting ready to go out. He looks shocked, his hands frozen on the buttons of his shirt, and had I been less hysterical I might have been embarrassed for interrupting him in his own room like this. But I can't hold all of this new information inside.

While he is still looking at me with wide eyes, I waste no time in asking him the question burning on my lips, "Did you know Sebastian's father has a bastard?" The words tumble out of me in a rush, and I can hardly believe what I'm saying.

Alex blinks a few times in shock, mirroring my own feelings. "What? How do you even know that?" he asks me, eyes wide with disbelief.

"Mom just said it. Although she didn't say yes directly," I reply, my mind already working through the possibilities. "She danced around confirming it the entire time, like she was doing her damndest to make me believe it without outright saying so."

"Huh." Alex walks over to his loveseat and sits down, having abandoned his effort to button his shirt. "Well, I have no idea whether that's true or not. But Julia… it's none of our business. You have to know that."

Despite his rational and well-intended reaction, I'm not willing to let it go. "Aren't you going hunting tomorrow?" I ask him, knowing full well that Sebastian might be there. After all, he and Alex run in the same social circles.

My brother's eyes narrow in suspicion. "So what if I am? How does that have anything to do with all of this?"

There's this feeling of anxiousness in me that has my heart pounding, but I try to keep my cool. I've already shown Alex how worked up I am by barging in without knocking, so I don't want him to think I've lost all common sense. Slowly, I join him on the loveseat, keeping my tone casual as I say, "I'm sure Seb will be there, is all."

"How can you be so sure?" Alex demands, clearly still unsure of what I'm getting at. "Julia, I'm not going to harass this poor man while he's trying to relax on a hunting trip. He's been through enough."

"I know that!" With my heart in my throat, I turn to look my brother full in the face. "It's not Sebastian I want to talk to. It's his dad."

Alex huffs. "Julia...."

I hold up a hand to stop him. "I know you think it's a bad idea, but please just make sure he is on the hunting trip. I need to speak to his dad without Sebastian finding out."

"Why exactly? What are you up to?" Alex asks, his eyebrows furrowing.

Frustration threatens to make me snippy, but I keep it under control. Alex has every right to be suspicious of me. "I'll tell you after, but I need you to promise me that Sebastian will be with you, and if he doesn't show up, that you will let me know. Okay?"

After some insistence, Alex finally agrees, but he reminds me to be careful. I know there's no turning back now. I'm going to confront Sebastian's Dad, and I'm going to get to the bottom of this once and for all.

Grabbing my hand before I can leave his room, Alex lowers his voice, his tone serious. "I know you're tired of hearing this, but please don't do anything crazy. You might care for Sebastian, but blowing up his family even more than it already is certainly isn't the way to go."

Swallowing, I nod. "I know what I'm doing. I finally see a way out of this mess that Mom has gotten me into, and I plan on attacking the problem head on."

He tells me that he loves me, and then I'm back in the hallway, walking back to my room with all sorts of thoughts cascading through my head. So much has happened in the last hour that I barely know how to comprehend it, but I'm still not going to back down.

My heart is racing as I lie in bed later that night, unable to sleep as I think about what's to come. It would be so easy for Sebastian's dad just to turn me away, but I don't think that he will. There's the fear that he might be too sick to talk to me, or that showing up might shock him and be a detriment to his health, but I know that I have to be brave. I have to face this head-on, no matter what the outcome may be.

CHAPTER 24

Julia

"He's here, Julia. I just pulled in and I see his car."

I blow out a relieved breath, holding my cell phone to my ear. "Thank you so much, Alex. I owe you."

"You always owe me," he responds, amused. "But I've got to go. The deer aren't going to wait on me."

We tell each other goodbye and I hang up, tucking the phone back into my small purse and gazing out the window of the car. Once again, I had to call a cab, since I don't want my mother tracking my movements all the time, but it's becoming tedious. I make a mental note to have Alex take me car shopping and help with some driving practice.

It's early afternoon and I'm already parked across the street from the Van den Bosch estate. A single cab sitting so close has to look suspicious, and with all the horrible things that have happened to the family lately, I know I won't go unnoticed for long. The iron gates are obviously closed, and the only way to get them open is to speak to the security on the intercom.

After heaving a long sigh, I get out of the car, and press the intercom button, not having much of a choice if I want those damn gates to open for me.

"Good afternoon," I hear from the speaker. "Who are you and what's your reason for visiting?"

"I'm Julia Van Dieren and I'm here to speak to Johannes," I answer just as mechanically.

"Very well. Do you have an appointment, Miss?"

I pause for a moment, an answer forming in my head. "No, but kindly inform him that I am aware of the true reason why he asked Sebastian to break up with me. I'm sure that information will trump any potential appointments."

I don't hear any other sound coming from the intercom, but after a few moments, to my surprise, the gates start slowly opening and I waste no time in getting back into the cab so that the driver can get me all the way to their house.

Sebastian's family estate is beautiful in the daytime—the sun is high overhead, casting its warm golden rays across the front lawn. It's in stark contrast to what the inside of the home must be these days, with just Sebastian and his father inhabiting it. The house is now empty, for sure devoid of the usual commotion and laughter that once echoed through its halls when his mother and siblings were alive.

My legs feel frozen, and getting out of the cab seems impossible, but I don't have forever. The hunt has begun, and I need to seize this opportunity. Today, I will confront Johannes Van den Bosch and uncover the real reason behind Seb's sudden departure from my life.

Before I can continue to second guess myself, I throw open the cab door and step out into the sunshine. With determined steps, I make my way to the front door of the grand Van den Bosch estate.

The towering double doors stand as formidable guardians, iron bars running down the front of them like symbols of the secrets they protect. Touching the button to ring the doorbell, I stand back, my throat tight and feeling more nervous than I can ever remember feeling. I have to put on a brave front, but that doesn't mean it's easy to do.

After a few minutes, the doors creak open, and the butler greets me with a reserved nod. He looks me up and down, his eyes lingering with curiosity. I gather my courage, knowing that the fate of my bruised heart and ego rests on the forthcoming conversation. Still, the words feel sticky in my mouth, and they're so hard to speak.

"*He's just the butler!*" I admonish myself mentally. "*If you can't speak to him, then how the heck are you going to speak to Johannes?*"

"Good afternoon, Ms. Van Dieren," the butler greets.

"I'd like to speak with Mr. Van den Bosch," I announce, steady despite the butterflies that flutter within me. "Senior, of course. I know Sebastian isn't home."

A flicker of surprise dances across the butler's face before he composes himself. With a respectful bow, he gestures for me to follow him. My heartbeat quickens its pace as I trail behind him, anticipation and trepidation intermingling within me.

The butler leads me through opulent corridors adorned with timeless paintings and intricate tapestries. Each step reverberates with the weight of the unknown, the air heavy with anticipation. Finally, we arrive at the grand library, a sanctuary of knowledge and hidden truths. But more striking than that are the memories of first meeting Sebastian here during the ball, and how I was so enamored with the mysterious, bearded man from the very beginning. It makes my heart lurch to think about it. God, I miss him so much.

"Wait here, Miss, and I will fetch Mr. Van den Bosch, if he deigns to see you." Then, the man lowers his voice. "I will remind you that the senior man of the house is ill, and anything that may cause him undo stress is unappreciated."

The audacity of the staff member shocks me, but I shake myself out of my surprise and frown. "Noted. I'll wait here."

The butler departs and I find myself standing amidst the shelves lined with books of forgotten tales, sordid histories, and epic adventures. The room is bathed in a soft glow, the sunlight filtering through the heavy drapes. This is where it all began, where my heart first faltered under the gaze of Sebastian. Memories of stolen glances and breathy promises flood my mind, both a comfort and a curse. It almost makes me feel greedy. I want more of those memories… for the rest of my life, if I have the choice.

Moments pass, the silence stretching. I pause in my exploration when I hear the soft sound of footsteps on the carpeted floor near the door, and hurry back to see that the butler has returned. Now that he's back from delivering my message, he stands by the door, his presence a reminder of the gravity of the impending conversation and a message… a message that tells me that the household staff isn't going to let me upset Johannes too much.

And then, with a gentle creaking sound, another shadow appears in the doorway, revealing the figure of Johannes Van den Bosch. He steps into the room, his demeanor poised and composed, trying to mask how sick and downtrodden he really is. I'm shocked by how much different he looks from the last time I saw him, how frail and gaunt the once powerful man has become. There is still a fire in his eyes when he sees me, but there is a hollowness there, too.

"Ah, Miss Julia," he acknowledges, leaning forward on an intricately carved cane. His words carry a hint of intrigue. "Margaret's oldest daughter and the woman who has stolen my son's heart. I have to say that your visit is quite the surprise, as well as the message you have apparently brought."

I can't be sure, but I sense that he's trying to cover up his nervousness with ill-placed humor. Nervousness is an advantage that I can't risk wasting.

"That's me," I confirm, tilting my head towards him. "Thank you for seeing me. As for what I know about—"

"Come, come," Johannes interrupts, waving me toward a sitting area dotted with sturdy leather and mahogany furniture. "My staff is bringing refreshments. No reason for us to stand here awkwardly while we speak."

Annoyed that he stopped me from making my point, I follow him as he moves slowly towards his seat. It occurs to me that he's asking me to sit because *he* needs to, a clear sign of his weakness, but he won't say that out loud. Pride, I assume.

I settle into a large armchair, crossing my legs and leaning forward as Johannes sinks down onto the leather loveseat with extreme caution. There's a pang of sympathy in my heart, but I have to smother it. This man is not getting any soft feelings from me, not after he played right into my mother's hand, and that doesn't even take into consideration the terrible truth that he's been lying to his own son for all these years.

I watch the staff bring in tea and cucumber sandwiches, one of them pouring and plating the repast for Johannes so he doesn't have to make the effort. I can see his hands shaking as he sips his tea, quickly handing it back to the server who sits it down.

"Now that we're comfortable," I try to start again. "I'm sure you're wondering why I showed up on your doorstep with such a huge declaration."

"There's no reason to rush, my dear. Does my son know that you're here? I'm sure he'll be disappointed that he missed your visit." Sebastian's father is trying to play a part, I realize—the part of the doddery old man that deserves all the sympathy in the world. Well, he isn't going to get it from me. Not when he played such an integral part in Sebastian leaving me.

"We're not talking about Sebastian today. At least not directly," I counter, keeping my shoulders straight. "Let's cut the bullshit, sir, and just get into it."

There's a sharp intelligence that shines in his eyes when I speak, despite his age. He smiles, but there is an edge of anger to it. He is nowhere near amused with me. "Indeed. You have piqued my curiosity. Please, enlighten me with the knowledge you possess."

I take a deep breath, summoning all the strength within me. "I know the real reason why you asked Sebastian to break up with me," I declare, my voice unwavering. "My mother blackmailed you, because she knows you have a bastard child."

A flicker of surprise dances across his features, quickly replaced by an unreadable expression. He must have thought that I either knew about the blackmail, or the bastard, but not both. I can't see the anger in him anymore, but I know it's probably right there simmering beneath the surface.

Johannes tries to laugh dismissively, but it rings false. "A bastard, huh? You certainly think you've discovered something of a bombshell, don't you? Well—"

"Enough," I snap. "There is no reason for you to deny this. I know my father has one too. We all do. Sebastian needs to know the truth, and if you don't tell him, I intend to."

The old man leans back in his seat, sitting his cane on the loveseat beside him and folding his hands. "Go ahead then, Miss Julia," he prompts, his eyes fixed upon mine. "Tell me everything you think you know. Let's put it all out on the table, since you're proving to be just as stubborn and problematic as the woman that birthed you."

I clear my throat, and launch into the explanation of the knowledge that I have. It isn't everything, not by a long shot, but I'm banking on it being enough to throw him off. With each word that spills from my lips, I recount the tales of deceit and hidden truths, painting a vivid picture of the love that was torn apart between his son and I. I keep things simple when it comes to the whispers of infidelity and the shadows that lurk within his past, but hold nothing back when I describe how much his son meant, and still means to me. Let him feel guilty for it, he deserves it.

As I speak, his eyes betray a mix of emotions, a storm brewing behind his calm facade. I watch for the slightest hint of confirmation, a confession that will unravel the web of lies that have been catching me for the last few weeks.

Finally, as the silence threatens to consume us, he breaks it with a sigh. "Miss Julia, you possess a tenacity that is admirable," he admits, his speech heavy with hints of remorse. "There might be some truth in what you're saying, but hear me very clearly: I have zero intention of telling my son."

I can feel my eyebrow twitch, annoyed. "That's the most selfish thing I've ever heard. You have to tell him."

In a flash, the calm demeanor of the man in front of me shifts into something much more raw and vulnerable. "For what? So he will stop talking to me? You have to understand, Julia. I have no one else anymore. Just him." He reaches up and massages his temples with unsteady fingers. "The last thing I need is for him to find out...."

"You do have someone else, even if you want to deny it." I let my words sink in before continuing. "Your other child."

Johannes barks a cruel laugh. "The other child, as you say, has no idea that I'm his father. And frankly, I'd like to keep it that way. The boy lives a comfortable life, in no small part because of the strings I've pulled for him, so—"

I shake my head. All I hear from him are excuses. "What's the point in keeping so many secrets? After losing so much of his family, I'm sure Seb would understand if you—"

He grabs his cane, and taps it hard on the ground, the dull sound echoing with finality. "Are you not hearing me, you frustrating child? I said no, Miss Van Dieren! I'm going to have to ask you to leave now."

"Wait." I hold up my hands to stop him from calling for his staff. "We haven't even gotten to the fact that you allowed my mother to blackmail you, and you bent to her will. Don't you see that it's because of your pride and ego that she was able to win?"

"Spoken like someone that has never seriously gone toe to toe with Margaret Van Dieren," Johannes mutters, sounding exhausted. "I'm too old, and too tired, and have experienced too much loss to survive going against your mother. Sebastian will get over this breakup, and you should too."

"I can't believe what I'm hearing?" My thoughts tumble around in my head, making it hurt. "My mother knows that you're so ashamed of this secret that you'd sacrifice your son's own happiness by making him break up with me, just so it won't get out. It would be so simple to take control of this situation again. Just tell the truth. Beat my mother to the punch."

Johannes taps his cane on the ground again over and over, much more softly this time. He looks away from me, deep in thought, and I take the opportunity to try and force my point again. "Don't let my mom blackmail you. She'll never leave this alone if she thinks she can use your secret information for her own gain. Sebastian might be upset at first, but I know he will forgive you."

"Oh really? How did that go with Hendrik, I wonder?" The older man scoffs. "Look at him, exiled like a pariah with no contact with his children whatsoever."

"This isn't about my dad, or what my mother did regarding his affair. It's about you and your son. Mr. Van den Bosch, you're all Seb has left. He *will* forgive you. Please just tell him the truth. He deserves to be happy, and I promise you that being with me is what makes him happy."

"Good God, you are one stubborn woman, you know that?" Johannes sighs heavily. I can see, right before my eyes, that he's losing energy and becoming tired. I don't think I've driven him to the point that his health is at risk right now, but I probably shouldn't push any farther.

"Your son means a lot to me," I say simply, pouring all of my heart into the words. "Otherwise I wouldn't be here."

"That much, I can see." He closes his eyes, knuckles white where he clutches his cane. "I'll think about it, but that's all I can offer you. Now, get out."

* * *

Stepping out of the Van den Bosch estate, I am greeted by the gentle embrace of the crisp air. The weight of the conversation lingers, intertwining with the whispers of the wind. Did I do the right thing by coming here? Will anything really change, now that I've shown my hand and put pressure on Johannes?

As I make my way down the meticulously manicured path, my thoughts race like a whirlwind. I might have just ruined things to the point that they can never be repaired again, or I might have finally found a way to bring Sebastian back to me. Still, I wish it hadn't come to this. The confrontation certainly didn't leave me feeling happy in any way. The revelation of Sebastian's father's past, the web of deceit that entangled Seb and me—none of it can be ignored now that I've put it all out into the open.

My cab driver awaits me at the end of the path, having been paid to simply wait on me in case I had to make a hasty retreat. The driver is napping when I knock on the window, and once he rouses and opens the door for me, I climb into the worn leather seat and finally let myself relax. I did it. I can't believe I was actually brave enough, but I really did it.

As the cab pulls away, the grand estate diminishes in the distance. My part is finished, and now I just have to wait and see how everything plays out. Either Sebastian's father will tell him the truth, or he won't, forcing me to do so. My gaze fixates on the receding image, reflecting upon the profound impact this encounter will have on the future.

The repercussions of my actions now unfold before me with each passing moment. I have unraveled the hidden truths, but with it comes the weight of responsibility. There's always a chance that Seb won't appreciate me forcing his father's hand like this, but even if he never wants to speak to me again, at least I will know I did everything in my power to get the truth to him.

Then there is the fallout that is sure to come from my mother. I have no illusions that she won't find out somehow, some way, what I've done. I've undermined her blackmail attempt, and in doing so, taken her power in this situation away from her. She's going to lose her mind when she finds out.

But her reaction to that news will be nothing compared to the firestorm she is sure to stir up if Sebastian and I manage to work things out. Having her master plan defeated and thrown back in her face is going to make it even harder for me to convince her to accept Sebastian, and maybe she never will. I can't imagine going through the rest of my life with my mother shunning me, but if that's the choice she makes, there's nothing I can do about it. All I can do is hope that her love of me will eclipse any hatred that she has for the Van den Bosch heir.

In the distance in front of me, I can see the landscape changing to the familiar sight of the area around my family estate. *Almost home.*

Unless Johannes called her immediately, there's no way that she will know this soon what I have done. So I just need to lay low now, and let things play out.

Still, I twist my shirt in my fingers anxiously. I don't think I'll be able to relax until this is all over with.

CHAPTER 25

Sebastian

It's been too long since I've had a chance to relax, even a little bit. The weight of my gun in my hand, the crisp morning air that caresses my face, invigorating my senses, and the sounds of all the other hunters and their hounds make me reminisce on simpler times. Times when a hunt like this wouldn't be such a rare thing for me.

These days, it's rare that I allow myself such leisurely pursuits, caught up in the relentless demands of my father's company. Well, our company, I guess. But today, I have finally granted myself this reprieve.

The hunting grounds are picturesque, a haven nestled behind the DeVries estate. The rolling hills stretch out before me, adorned with a tapestry of vibrant greenery.

Trees stand tall, their leaves nearly blocking out the sun, creating a stunning backdrop against the clear blue sky. As we get further into the forest, the tranquility is momentarily interrupted by the muffled sounds of conversations and laughter. We should all be quieter, but it's early in the day, and excitement is still running through the group.

As I take in the scene, a surge of anticipation courses through me. The atmosphere buzzes with palpable energy, a shared enthusiasm among the participants. The air is alive with the mingling scents of damp earth and fallen leaves, adding a touch of earthiness to the crispness of the morning.

This hunt is not just a mere pastime; it is a temporary escape, a chance to shed the weight of my responsibilities and immerse myself in the present moment. It offers a rare opportunity to connect with others, to forge new bonds, and perhaps, in the back of my mind, to catch a glimpse of her.

Julia.

She wasn't here when I arrived, to my secret disappointment. Not even in the parlor having tea with the other women when I excused myself to use the restroom before the hunt departed, sneaking a glance into the room. I had heard talk that some of the mothers and sisters of the men hunting would be having their own event, but while I did see a few women, Julia wasn't one of them.

Oddly enough, I'm now walking next to her brother, who is better company than I probably deserve. Trying to put thoughts of my ex out of my mind, I savor the freedom of just being out here, the fleeting respite from the constant demands that have consumed my days. For now, I am not the heir burdened with expectations; I am simply Sebastian, a man seeking solace and rediscovering the simple pleasures that life has to offer.

In the company of Alex and Jan, indulging in idle chatter about the day's events, I follow the main group but make no large effort to keep up with them. Today is less about securing a kill, and more about just existing. Although the trophy that the deer will offer wouldn't be so bad, either.

As the conversations ebb and flow, Alex and I find ourselves left alone amidst the vibrant energy of the hunt. There isn't any awkwardness between us, surprisingly, and once again I see no reason to rush and catch up with the others.

Still, I know we can't avoid the subject of his sister forever. We talk about cars, work, and everything else in between, but the inevitability of the subject of Julia hangs above the two of us.

There is a long stretch of silence, and Alex inhales, his jaw working. I can't stand the anticipation of it any longer.

Before Alex can even utter a word, I take a deep breath and break the silence. "I assume now's the moment where you are going to tell me I should go back to your sister?"

He raises an eyebrow, a faint smile tugging at the corners of his lips. "Nope, my sister made me swear not to say a word to you about it."

A mix of surprise and relief washes over me. I had braced myself for a plea, a desperate attempt to reunite me with Julia. But now, in this unexpected twist, a sliver of hope flickers within me. Perhaps there is still a chance, a glimmer of light in the darkness of our shattered relationship. Julia leaving her brother out of this is such a mature move that I can barely believe it. I had been so prepared to shut him down that I don't even know what to say now.

"Really?" I blurt out. "I thought… well, I don't know what I thought. But thanks for keeping as neutral as possible."

The other man huffs a short laugh. "Don't thank me quite yet, because I have to tell you my piece. Not because she asked me to, but because I'm her brother. And, Seb, I'd like to think that we could be good friends, and as a friend, I'm going to be brutally honest with you here," Alex continues, filled with sincerity. "If you really love her, you shouldn't put your dad's lack of approval first. That's absurd. This is your one and only life, and Julia might be the one and only woman you ever feel this way about, you know?"

The weight of his words settles upon me, sinking into the depths of my soul. He is right. Love should triumph over all obstacles, including parental disapproval. My heart aches at the thought of surrendering to the barriers that separate Julia and me, barriers that are fueled by my father's acquiescence to Margaret. At the same time, though, my father is ill, and he has been through so much tragedy in such a small window of time. Hurting him would very likely be the end of me, too.

"He's very frail, Alex," I respond, a touch of anguish in my voice. "He nearly died of a heart attack, all because I wanted to stand my ground about all of this mess with your sister. How can I possibly risk hurting him like that again?"

Alex's eyes meet mine, his gaze unwavering. "He should be happy for you that you found a woman you love, though. Not the opposite. Do you really think he had a heart attack because his son had found love, or do you think there could be something more to it?"

We've all but come to a complete stop, the rest of the hunting party, including Jan, gone in the distance. Catching up with them will be a pain, but I'm glad this is a private conversation. I'm not sure that there is a single other person I could tolerate talking about this with besides Alex. He is in a unique position to be able to understand everything going on between me and his sister, but also able to keep an open mind about it since it doesn't directly influence him.

"I just don't know, Alex," I sigh. "Your mother was talking to him just before the heart attack, you know. She asked him to back off Julia and for whatever reason, he decided to side with her."

Alex grunts, shouldering his rifle as we meander in the direction that everyone else was going. "You need to be thinking more critically about that interaction, then. Why would your father side with my mother over his own son? Especially when the two of you are all each other has in the world, it seems like. Everything suggests that he would want you to marry, settle down, and start producing heirs to carry on the family line since you're his only son left, you know?"

A surge of frustration courses through my veins. A markedly unpleasant idea dawns on me—could my father's actions not be motivated by genuine concern, but rather by self-preservation? Margaret's manipulation has clouded his judgment, that much is clear, but there is no way a simple chat between the two of them would have convinced him to tear down the potential of my relationship with Julia so completely.

I shake my head, running a hand through my hair in frustration. "What am I missing here? What could Margaret possibly know that would weaken my father's resolve so much? He may be frail, but his mind is sharp and he's never been one to back down."

Stopping dead in his tracks, Alex puts his hand on my shoulder and turns me to face him. "Julia and I…we know the reason."

My eyes widen in surprise. "You do?"

He nods, his expression somber yet resolute. "But it's up to your dad to tell you. Believe me, your dad is just doing this to protect his ass, not because he's too frail to handle a wedding. Seb, my mother… well, she's my mom, and I love her, but she is a snake. A shark, even, and she smells blood in the water when it comes to your dad and she's not going to let this go."

The truth hangs heavy in the air, a bittersweet revelation. I am torn between anger and understanding, between the desire to confront my father and the need to shield him from further pain. My love for Julia intertwines with the complexity of family dynamics, leaving me caught in a web of conflicting emotions.

Gosh, I can't believe it! What is Dad up to?

As the reality sinks in, I find a newfound determination rising within me. I won't let my father's misplaced allegiance, or fear, whichever it may be, dictate the course of my life. Especially if he is hiding something from me, and from what Alex is saying, he definitely is.

My throat feels tight, my pulse picking up as adrenaline dumps into my veins. "I won't ask you what this reason is, but… it's something big, isn't it?"

Alex pats me on the shoulder before letting go. "Yeah, man, it is pretty big."

With a renewed sense of purpose, I nod once at him, gratitude etched upon my face. "Thank you, Alex. You've opened my eyes."

He gives me a knowing smile. "No problem, Seb. I want the best for my sister, but for you, too. No matter what my mother says, I think the two of you are a brilliant match. I'll save the whole 'don't mess with my sister' speech since I think you're going through enough shit as it is, but I assume it's already pretty evident. Treat Julia right."

His words resonate within me, fueling a fire that burns brighter than ever. I am resolved to confront my father, gently but refusing to back down without knowing the truth. Julia and I deserve a chance at happiness. I, my father's son, the one who stepped up to run his company, the one who lost just as many family members as he did… I deserve a chance at happiness, and he needs to let me have it.

"I guess we should catch up with everyone, huh?" I suggest, and Alex makes a noise of agreement.

We set off at a faster pace, our talk over, and both of us ready to finish the hunt strong. Once this is done, I will encounter an even larger challenge: Facing my father and finding out the truth.

***

I step through the grand entrance of my home estate, the weight of the day's events heavy on my shoulders. At first, my head is buzzing with exhaustion from the day spent trekking through the forest, but it isn't long until something musical catches my attention.

The resonant strains of an opera float through the air, echoing in the hallways, just loud enough that I can pinpoint where they are coming from: the library.

I have a bad feeling about this. I head in that direction, and as I grow closer, the familiar scent of cigar smoke greets me, mingling with the aroma of aged leather and mahogany that permeates the library.

There, in the sitting area amidst all the books, my father sits ensconced in a plush armchair, a crystal decanter of amber liquid within easy reach. The flickering glow of the fireplace casts a warm red-orange light upon his face, revealing the lines etched deep. Just months earlier, those lines wouldn't have been there. They're new, just like the cane that rests beside him, and the pallor of his skin.

Despite how alarmingly weak he appears, he seems to be having a good time. Dad is surrounded by a small gathering of friends, their laughter and conversation reverberating through the space, all of them either drinking or smoking fat Cuban cigars.

My eyes settle upon the scene, and my heart clenches with concern. Caught in this act of indulgence, I cannot help but question the choices he has made, the disregard for his own well-being. A man that has just gotten out of the hospital, a man suffering from heart failure, should not be fucking drinking and smoking cigars!

"I thought the doctor asked you to stop all the smoking and drinking?" the words tumble from my lips, cut through with an undercurrent of disbelief. "What kind of fuckery is this, Dad? I go and enjoy myself for one single day and you're at home breaking every single rule that the doctor has laid out for you? Where the hell is your nurse?"

"I dismissed her for the night." Dad waves his hand dismissively, and his friends laugh. I see red.

"Bullshit!" I yell, fists clenching. "Do you feel good now, Dad? Fucking around with your health while I spend the majority of my time worrying about you?"

The room falls silent, the jovial ambiance shattered by the weight of my reproach. My father's gaze meets mine, his eyes glinting with a mix of defiance and resignation. Sensing the gravity of the moment, he dismisses his friends with another wave of his hand, their presence fading out of the library door until it is just him and me. Pulse pounding in my temples, I grab a full glass of scotch from one of the side tables, wipe the rim of it with the hem of my shirt, and throw the entirety of it down my throat. I don't care who it was meant for—I need it more.

Now that we're alone, he leans back in his chair, the flickering light casting shadows upon his face. "Sebastian, my son," he begins, already so weary that it makes guilt flare in me, unwelcome. "Sometimes, we find solace in our vices, seeking temporary relief from our burdens, you know?"

"Dad," I force out. "Enough with the waxing poetry. You're in the wrong here, and you know it."

He laughs hollowly. "I will die soon, anyway. At least let me enjoy my last days on earth, Seb."

I feel a mixture of frustration and compassion welling within me. The doctor's warnings, the fragility of my father's health, all collide with the realization that his actions stem from a deeper turmoil—a desperate attempt to retain a sense of control, to preserve the vestiges of a fading power.

I hate what he's saying. It makes a pit open up in my stomach.... and I'm afraid of the amount of truth in it.

Unable to face how miserable all of this makes me, I go on the offensive. "If you're going to die soon, then why did you bother with asking me to break up with Julia?"

Surprise flickers across my father's face, a brief moment of vulnerability betraying his well-guarded facade. "You spoke to her, then?"

"I spoke to her brother, Alex, at the hunt," I reply curtly. I find the seat across from him and sink down into it, reaching for the carafe of scotch and filling an empty glass as I begin my interrogation. "So, what do the Van Dierens know that I don't?"

My father denies it at first, dancing around the truth. "You're going to have to elaborate, son. I don't know what you're talking about?"

I'm so tired of his lying, and the way he keeps me in the dark just to protect his pride. "I think you do know, Dad, and you just don't want to tell me, so knock it off."

A heavy sigh escapes his lips, carrying the weight of his confession. "You know… after being with the same person for so long, sometimes you find yourself longing for something new," he starts, his confession full of embarrassed remorse.

The words hit me like a blow, the reality of his infidelity crashing down upon me. Shock and anger mingle within me, fueling the fire of my disappointment.

"So you had an affair?" I exclaim incredulously. The things he's saying are like electricity jolting through me. "Why am I not surprised by that? It seems like every man your age has zero respect for the sanctity of their marriages."

"It was during a business trip, a few nights at most," my father confesses, his gaze dropping to the floor. "But… she came to Amsterdam once she found out she was... well…" he trails off, alluding to the consequences of his actions—the child conceived in the wake of his betrayal.

I can feel the rage bubbling within me, threatening to consume my senses. I rise from my seat, unable to contain the tumultuous emotions coursing through my veins. "Are you fucking kidding me?!" I shout, my voice echoing through the room. "The fact that you had an affair, I could look past that. But that you were too careless to protect the family from its consequences? Fuck! *You* are the disappointment here, Dad. Not me!"

The weight of his admission settles upon us, casting a shadow over everything. My father pleads for my attention, desperation in his tone. "Sebastian, please just listen!"

I'm consumed by a whirlwind of anger and betrayal as I pace around the room. "Everyone knew it but me, the fool who broke up with the woman I love because I thought it was about your health."

"Do you not see that the stress of you being with that girl really was a detriment to my health?" he insists. "If it makes you feel any better, the boy never knew that I was his father and still doesn't to this day."

For some reason, that fact makes me feel even worse. "Oh, so you had an affair and then lied to everyone, including your child, about it? No, Dad, that doesn't make me feel any better."

"I did it for a reason! Like you said, to protect our family, Seb. It cost me, but his mom never told him. I made sure she wouldn't speak. We have an arrangement." The longer he speaks the more remorse I can hear in his words. It doesn't make me feel guilty for confronting him, but a part of me aches for how long my father, this man that I love and have looked up to, carried this burden for so long. Even if it was his fault.

Letting go of my anger isn't an option, though. If my father paid off this child's mother, what will happen once he is no longer a part of this world? "I hope your arrangement still stands, because I'm telling you right now that bastard isn't going to inherit one penny from us! None!"

"Seb, I'm so sorry…" he murmurs, his posture defeated.

The apology, though sincere, does little to ease the pain that thrums within me. The shattered illusions of family loyalty and devotion lie in ruins around us. My world feels torn apart, the fractures in our relationship too deep to mend.

"So Margaret knows who the bastard is and threatened to tell me if I didn't break up with Julia?" I inquire, resigned to the fact that my dad has lied to me for the majority of my life. The reality that I have an illegitimate brother is settling into my bones, and becoming a truth I can't even try to deny. So, okay, my father has a bastard… now I have to find out who else knows our shame.

"She does," he confirms, his voice barely above a whisper. "But that's not everything you need to know…."

Tipping back my scotch glass and taking a heavy drink, I let the burn dissipate in my throat before croaking, "Tell me."

Dad shifts uncomfortably in his seat, but to his credit, he continues with the ugly truths. "She also wants to tell your brother the truth, and that would give him a claim to the family asset."

At first, what he's saying makes my pulse in my ears the only thing I can hear. I'm not just mad. Mad barely even scratches the surface of what I'm feeling. Swearing under my breath, I clench my fists in frustration. The consequences of my father's actions threaten to ruin our family legacy and split our hard-won fortune into pieces.

"Fuck!" I blurt out, standing and pacing, my head in my hands. "This is a fucking *disaster*, Dad! How the hell does Margaret Van Dieren know all of this?"

"I have no idea, Seb. She's crafted a reputation that makes almost everyone afraid of the things she knows, and I guess I am no exception." With a groan, he leans forward. "It doesn't matter where she got the information from, in the long run. All that matters is that she has no issue shouting it from the rooftops if we don't do as she asks."

I scoff. "Great. Just great. I guess now, on top of everything else, I have to step up and do a bunch of damage control too."

I can feel the heat of the scotch in my stomach burning, softening the edges of my rage, but by no means washing it away fully. "Finish your drink and smoke, Dad, if that's what you want to do. I need to get the hell out of here."

"Wait, Sebastian," Dad's plea stops me in the doorway of the library. "Don't you want to know who your brother is? Aren't you even a little bit curious?"

The question hangs in the air, a tempting offer cut through with uncertainty. But as the alcohol and the sting of all his lies course through my veins, I am firm in my response. "Me? No, Dad. Not at all." Turning to face him again, I continue, biting out the words. "The only brother

I've ever had is Freddie, who died. That's all. Never ever call that bastard my brother again. Are we clear?"

There is a long, tense silence that follows, our eyes locked in a battle of wills. The truth may have been laid bare, but the wounds run deep.

"Seb—" Dad begs, but I cut my hand through the air to cut him off.

"I said that I don't want to know who the fucker is. Are we clear?"

He looks haunted, and unlike the man I've known all my life. The father I knew would have never begged for anything, and certainly wouldn't have had the sheen of tears in his eyes that I can see now. The bond that once held us together now feels fragile, teetering on the edge of collapse. I turn away, my resolve solidifying with each step, leaving behind both my father and the man I was before I walked into that room earlier in the night. I will never be the same again.

My feet move as if they know exactly where I need to go without my brain even being involved. One thought consumes me—who am I? I don't even know anymore. An hour ago, I was a man with one dead brother. Now, that is still true, but there is also a man out there that is technically my half-brother, even if I refuse to claim him. I was the heir to the Van den Bosch fortune and company, but now there's the fear that this half-brother could take half of that from me if he wanted to. I was a devoted son, doing anything and everything I possibly could for my father's health, but the entire time he was lying to me. So instead of that devoted son, I just feel like a fool.

I have to get some air… some distance from home.

Legs carry me to the garage, where I choose my fastest car and exhale in relief when my hands close around the firm leather steering wheel. This. This, at least, is familiar and true. There are no possible lies between the car and I. Just truth, power, and speed.

The 1961 Ferrari slides out of the garage and into the twilight, wheels meeting the black asphalt and smoothly taking me away from the house that is full of so much anguish for me right now. Beneath the moonlight, driving, my thoughts become clear, even if that clarity hurts in a different way.

There is a possibility that is tugging at the back of my mind, almost too disturbing to consider. But the more I pour over the facts, the clearer it all becomes.

I recall the countless times my father insisted that I treat Karl as family, urging me to take him under my wing. It was a strange request, one that I never quite understood until now.

Each recollection resurfaces and brings with them the undeniable fact that my father has been manipulating me into interacting with my half-brother all this time. My father's insistence, his unwavering encouragement to forge a bond with Karl, begins to make sense. The truth dawns on me like a striking revelation: Karl must be my father's secret, the hidden son, the result of an affair that I was oblivious to until a little more than an hour ago. The weight of that truth makes me feel ill.

My grip on the steering wheel tightens as I feel a burst of rage, betrayal, and disbelief. How could the man I so revered, my father, betray me in such a fundamental way? I feel a boiling resentment at the idea that he planned this intricate charade and manipulated my feelings. He even controlled the way I viewed and treated Karl, without me being any the wiser.

I replay the conversations, the moments shared with the up and coming salesman, through a new lens. The two of us talking on the balcony before the tragic hunt where we heard about the car explosion, Karl being the first one to come and see my father at the hospital…all of these moments that made me think of Karl as a friend. Is it possible that he knows, on some level, that he's more to my father and I than just a mere employee?

As the memories come together, the secret reality that I had been blind to is revealed. My father's wish for me to accept Karl as family and embrace him was not motivated by kindness or a sincere relationship. It was a planned action to keep his illegitimate son, the one that he kept secret for the child's entire existence, nearby and concealed within the fabric of our lives.

Memories of times spent with Karl that now have significant weight to them flash across my mind. Shared chuckles and talks with hidden meanings all mirrored a deceptively hidden truth. The realization that my father's emphasis on a bond with Karl was a subliminal request for me to accept my own half-brother shocks me. Dad would have never told me who Karl was, but he couldn't resist pushing the two of us together.

The weight of this newly acquired knowledge hits me hard as I travel through familiar neighborhoods and then out into the countryside. I guess I'm mourning the destroyed image of my father and the family I thought I knew. I hadn't even thought to ask my father whether Mom knew about

Karl or not, but I'm sure there's no way she did. There was distance between my parents at the end, but never the kind of distance that would have clued me into a long-ago affair having been discovered.

God, I miss her so much. I wish I could speak to Mom right now. She was the only one that would ever listen to me quietly and give me advice untinged by her own opinions. Now I feel utterly alone, with no one to even vent my tragedies to.

With my mother on my mind, and lost in the depths of anguish, I find myself drawn to a place that I haven't visited since the funeral—a solemn sanctuary that holds the remains of my beloved family. I might not be able to hear my mother's comforting words, full of love, guiding me in my decisions, but there is one way I can still speak to her, at least.

It isn't too far away, but driving those roads brings me back to the day we buried my mother, sister, and brother. It was early afternoon then, but even with the change in daylight, the route makes a lump appear in my throat. Saying goodbye to my family was the worst day of my life, and as Dad and I had been driven home, I remember thinking that I would never come back to the cemetery. That I would never be strong enough to stand in front of those grave markers again. Yet, here I am. I feel sorrow, so heavy and thick, but there is also a sense of relief knowing that I can return to the graves… that I've healed enough to do that, even if it isn't much.

The tranquility and silence of the cemetery stands in stark contrast to the raging storm inside me. I pull into a parking spot, clicking the engine off, and exit into the gloomy silence.

As I make my way through the rows of tombstones, a kaleidoscope of memories floods my mind. I recall the vibrant laughter of my mother, Dina, her warm embrace wrapping around me like a protective shield. The loss of her love still reverberates within me, an ache that refuses to fade. My annoying, amusing brother Freddie, who never seemed to experience any sort of bad days. And, of course, my curious, reserved sister Adriana. The lack of them, the space they left, will never be truly filled in my heart.

The grass of the cemetery is soft beneath my shoe as I seek out my family's plots. My footsteps slow as I approach their final resting place, the familiar names etched in stone before me. The graves of my family stand as a stark reminder of the void they left behind. A pang of guilt seizes my heart, squeezing tightly, as I realize the extent of my own flaws and mistakes.

Kneeling down before the graves, I feel the coolness of the earth beneath my knees, grounding me in this moment of raw vulnerability. Tears spill from my eyes, mingling with the soil, as I begin to speak, words coming out strangled with sorrow and grief that is still so fresh.

"I'm sorry, Mom," I breathe, the words carried away in the breeze. "I miss you. I miss Dad. I miss our family." The weight of my confession hangs heavy in the air, the truth of my pain laid bare before them. "I should be the one lying here, not you."

Images flash through my mind, fragments of memories that intertwine with my deepest regrets. The hospital room, suffused with the scent of antiseptic and despair, where my father lay weak and frail. His voice, soft and barely audible, pleading with me to look after Karl—the brother I never knew, the one who was deemed unworthy of our family name. I hate him, and at the same time, feel this distant sadness that I never knew him when we were younger and would have had a chance to form a true bond. It's too late now.

Kneeling beside their graves, a mix of anger and grief wells up within me. The pain of my father's betrayal, the weight of his secrets, and the knowledge that I'm the last of his legitimate children, and as such, the only one to carry the burden of his decades of lies.

How can the man that was the strong, unmovable pillar of strength my entire childhood be a liar, cheater, and manipulator? At the same time, he's dying, literally of a broken heart, and I still love him so much that I can't put it into words. Fuck, nothing makes sense anymore!

But amidst the turmoil is the thought of someone who does care for me, someone whose intentions are pure and who still hasn't given up on me, even when I let her go. The thought of Julia is like a fire inside me. It is a flame fueled by the love that still resides within me. I refuse to let the darkness consume me entirely. I will rise above my circumstances and forge my own path, regardless of the shadows that haunt my bloodline. Dad has put me through hell, and I'll be damned if I walk the path he has forced on me without the woman I love by my side.

In the quiet of the graveyard, I make a silent vow to honor the memory of my family, to find the strength within myself to navigate the treacherous waters that lie ahead, and to stop neglecting my own desires, wants, and needs. With a heavy heart and a renewed sense of purpose, I rise from the ground, leaving behind the memories of my confession in the wind.

"I miss you three so much," I say in place of yet another goodbye. "And I love you. Always."

I move away from where they are laid to rest with a renewed sense of resolve. I have to be fearless if I'm going to tackle the uncertain, difficult, and question-filled road ahead. I take comfort in the fact that I am not alone in this vulnerable situation. The spirits of my mother and siblings are with me in a way, but in reality, there is someone waiting for me, too.

My sweet Julia.

I take out my phone and dial Julia's number, my fingers trembling with a mix of anxiety and anticipation. The phone rings once, twice, and on the third ring, she answers. Julia's sweetness, a lifeline in this sea of chaos, fills my ears.

"Seb?" she says, her voice laced with concern. "What's wrong?"

Tears well up in my eyes, and I struggle to steady myself. The urge to spill my heart and soul out to her is strong. "Julia…" I manage to say, my words cracking with emotion. "Julia. I know the truth now. I know why my dad wanted me to break up with you."

There is a momentary silence on the other end of the line, as if she is absorbing the weight of my revelation. Then, she speaks, her words filled with sadness and hope as they come through the phone.

"Oh, Seb, I'm so sorry."

My speech is thin, forced out through my tight throat, as I pour out all the feelings that have been choking me. The floodgates open. The grief of our split and the knowledge that we were forced apart on false pretenses all come gushing out in a flood of words. In the midst of my confusion, Julia listens, her mere presence serving as a solid anchor.

After what feels like an eternity, I finally manage to regain some composure. "Julia," I say, wondering if she can hear the longing that is filling up every inch of me. "Can we meet? I need to see you."

There's a brief pause, and I can almost hear her contemplating the weight of my request. Then, she speaks, resolute.

"Yes, Seb," she sighs, sounding both tired and relieved. "I'll come to you. I need to see you, too."

As I hang up the phone, my heart races with anticipation. I walk to the entrance of the cemetery, thinking about all the spirits that must be watching our reunion, my mind consumed with a mixture of fear and hope.

I don't have long to wait before I see the shine of headlights in the distance. For a second I wonder who she must have convinced to bring her here in the dead of night, but as the car slides up alongside the cemetery gates, I see the familiar face of Alex in the driver's seat. He gives me a quick salute before kissing his sister on the cheek and letting her exit the vehicle. The sight of her approaching the entrance fills me with a bittersweet joy. It took tearing the life I thought I knew to tatters to have her again, but damn, for Julia, I have no doubt that it was worth everything.

Our eyes lock, and the world disappears for a split second as time seems to stand still. The intensity of our mutual suffering and need reverberates between us, hanging heavy in the air. I go cautiously toward her, but I'm moving with purpose.

I can see the tear streaks on her cheeks as I get closer; they are a reflection of my own sorrow. Her face is carved with real emotions that I know are probably mirrored on my own, reflecting the love that has survived the storm. And suddenly, as our arms lock around one another, a tidal wave-like intensity of our feelings sweeps over us. The embrace, a long time coming, provides the first ounce of relief I've felt since my father's revelation back in the library.

I bury my face in her hair, breathing in her familiar scent. This is what I've needed… what I've denied myself for far too long. At this moment, nothing else matters. The pain of the past, the uncertainty of the future, it all fades away, replaced by the simple truth that we are meant to be together.

I hold her tightly, feeling her heartbeat against my chest, and for the first time in weeks, I feel a glimmer of hope. We have been through so much, and yet, here we stand, united in our love and our determination to fight for our happiness.

We find comfort in one other's arms, watched only by the silent departed. Maybe even my mother is looking down on us, somehow. I know she would love Julia, and that she would approve without hesitation.

"I'm so sorry, Julia," I choke out the words. "I know leaving you makes me a coward, but I hope you'll give me the chance to fix things."

She pulls back to meet my eyes fully. "You really know, then? About the bastard child."

"I do." I lick my lips, which are almost painfully dry. "Do you know the identity?"

Her eyes are guarded as she tells me, "Alex and I have our suspicions, but I'm almost positive my mother knows, even if she won't tell us."

Tired of playing these games that my father and Julia's mother have forced us into, I tell her simply, "It's Karl. The young man my father hired and has asked me to take under my wing multiple times. He's my father's bastard son and… my half-brother."

Julia sucks in a breath of surprise. "I knew it! That's who we thought, too. It just made too much sense. Seb, I'm so sorry that you had to find out like this."

God, she's so sweet and caring. I've broken her heart and still she worries for me. "Julia, do you still love me?"

She's surprised, but there isn't an ounce of doubt in what she says next. "Yes, Sebastian. Yes, I still love you. Otherwise why would I have come to a *cemetery* in the middle of the night?"

Despite everything, she makes me laugh, and her assurance that the love is still there settles my soul. "I love you too, Julia. But if we move forward, your mother will tell Karl the truth, and that doesn't sit well with me."

"Would that be the worst thing, though? I thought you liked Karl," Julia says, her brow furrowing.

I shake my head. "I liked him when he was just an employee that my father had a strangely intense interest in me becoming friends with. Now, knowing what I know, it's not the same, and him knowing that he's a Van den Bosch bastard will give him an opening to take part of our family inheritance. It's not right."

She looks slightly torn, but Julia trusts me. "Okay. I'm with you then."

"Against your own mother?" I drag the back of my hand down her soft cheek. "If it's too much, Julia—"

"I said I'm with you," she insists, laying her hand over mine, making my heart swell.

"Okay. The only way we can silence your mother is by attacking her reputation. It has the potential to get ugly, and I would spare you if I could, but… I'm not sure if I can."

A heavy silence hangs in the air as the weight of my proposal settles upon us. I can see the conflict in Julia's eyes, the struggle between her love for me and her loyalty to her family. But then, a spark of determination ignites within her, and she looks at me with unwavering resolve. My strong, fearless woman. I don't deserve her. I refuse to give her up again.

"Do you have a plan?"

CHAPTER 26

Julia

It's been a week since Alex drove me to the cemetery in the middle of the night, and Sebastian and I rekindled our relationship that had been so unfairly cut short. My heart has never soared as high when he asked me if I still loved him, but the nerves I felt as he described what we had to do to confront my mother were almost as powerful.

Mother left this morning to run some errands, and I used her absence to my advantage, calling Alex home and also telling Sebastian to hurry over. We've been talking the entire week, going over how exactly we can approach Mom and win the argument, and now that it's time to put our plan into motion I can feel my heart in my throat.

I'm frankly shocked by my own bravery. If it was anything else at risk, I'd probably just back down and let my mother have her way. But it's been so difficult to be with Sebastian, and we've had so many things standing in our way, that I refuse to let her win. This is my victory, and I will take it, no matter how difficult the battle.

Thank goodness Alex is my ally. Without my brother, it would just be me and Sebastian. Together, the two of us are strong, but having my brother here will be a shock to Mom, while also showing her that the other people in my life approve of my love match with Seb. I didn't even have to ask Alex; he simply volunteered to help us, which almost made me cry right then and there. I don't know what I did to deserve such a loyal brother, but I am so, so thankful.

We've settled in the petit salon, scones, coffee, and tea on the table we're seated around, but my stomach is in too many knots to try and eat. I'm stirring my cold tea for the third time when I hear someone clear their throat, and our maid peeks her head in the door. "Ma'am, sirs, Lady Van Dieren has arrived back home."

"Thank you," I tell her, nervously standing to smooth my skirt, and giving Alex and Sebastian a smile of confidence that I don't really feel.

Time is up. Mom is home, and now we have to face her as a united front. Sebastian and I find ourselves at the heart of this intricate dance, caught between the past and the uncertain future.

As we wait in anticipation, the familiar surroundings of my estate home offer little solace. The grandeur of the petit salon, with its opulent furnishings and delicate decor, feels suffocating under the weight of unspoken things. Alex looks relaxed, his long legs crossed, but I can see lines of unease etched on his face. We share a silent understanding, a bond forged through years of shared experiences. Both of us know how our mother is, and he has every right to be nervous. Just like I am.

And then, she arrives. Her presence alone is enough to unsettle the atmosphere, her eyes darting between Sebastian and Alex, a question lingering on her lips. Sebastian, unyielding in his determination, meets her gaze with unwavering resolve. He stands from his chair, tall and strong in the face of my mother's sharp examination. From what he's told me, he's more ready to confront the secrets that have haunted his life for the last week. They've been hanging over him for decades, but it's only these past few days that he's been aware of them, and that makes it so much worse.

Mom's surprise is evident, her inquiries tinged with suspicion as she questions Sebastian's unexpected presence. "Julia, Alex, Sebastian… what an unexpected surprise."

Her eyes betray a hint of trepidation, the realization that two of her children may be a united front throwing her off her game. Sebastian's voice cuts through the tension, his words carrying a weight that demands attention.

"I came here to make amends," he declares, shoving his hands in his pockets and raising an eyebrow at my mother. "That is, if you're ready to accept them, and make amends of your own, Margaret." The room seems to hold its breath, waiting for his next words. "If you're willing to face the truth."

Mom recoils, her denial immediate. "Ha. Absolutely not. Does your father know you're here pestering me once more, Sebastian? He's awfully ill, shouldn't you be home playing nursemaid?"

But Sebastian, undeterred, continues. He's unbowed and quietly confident. "I know what secret you hold against my family, Margaret." He drops the bombshell without a moment's hesitation. "I know about Karl."

The room falls into an uneasy silence, each person frozen as we wait for someone to make the next move. My mother has gone pale, but her demeaning sneer hasn't changed.

Sebastian's words have shaken her, but she still has another ace up her sleeve.

"Does *he* know, though?" she challenges, crossing her arms. "Does Karl know that he's Johannes Van den Bosch's bastard son? Oh, what a revelation that will be for the poor man. To know that his father cared for him enough to bankroll his entire life secretly, but not enough to be there for him, or even acknowledge him."

Sebastian exhales through his nose, almost a laugh, as if he expected exactly how she would counter. "No, he doesn't. And he never will, if I have anything to do with it."

My mother tilts her head to the side, regarding Sebastian. "Don't you feel even a little bit bad? Knowing that you are denying your own flesh and blood his inheritance and a chance to have a real relationship with his aging father?"

Sebastian waves his hand dismissively. "Karl lives a good, comfortable life. He doesn't need any of that."

Walking further into the room, Mom bends at the waist and pours herself a cup of coffee, sinking into one of the plush chairs and taking an audible sip. She is unhurried, moving at her own pace, and I can see a muscle in Sebastian's jaw ticking in annoyance.

Finally, Mom clicks her tongue and sits the ceramic cup down. "Well, be that as it may… I can comply with keeping your father's dirty little secret just that—a secret—as long as you leave Julia alone."

I feel a rush of embarrassment hearing her talk about me as if I'm not right here in the room with her. I open my mouth to complain, but Sebastian isn't even close to ready to retreat, and he beats me to it.

"Wrong. Julia and I are together, and you're just going to have to deal with it. Even so, you aren't going to tell Karl shit, Margaret."

If these two people weren't arguing directly about my future, the exchange would be fascinating. Leaning forward and observing the unfolding scene, I can't determine which one is winning. Confrontations like this are my mother's wheelhouse, but Sebastian seems unruffled.

Seconds feel like hours while Mom and Seb are still facing off. What happens next depends fully on which one of these combatants wins the verbal fight.

But Mom, stubborn in her resolve, refuses to yield. "I'm afraid I can't do that," she replies haughtily. I hear Alex let out a soft groan, and I feel the same. So much for this going quickly.

Sebastian scoffs, his words sharp and cutting. "Really? You think being the alleged killer of my family members is a better outcome?"

What he's saying makes me want to be sick. I still can't comprehend that my mother may be a murderer, especially the one who killed almost all of Sebastian's family. But Seb seems so sure, and when he laid the evidence out for me, I found it hard to deny, too. Still, I wish my mother would just drop her grudge against the entire Van den Bosch family so we never had to speak of it again.

Mom blanches, and then all the blood comes rushing back to her face, leaving her flush. "What are you trying to say?" she retorts, denial and frustration coloring her words. She isn't giving enough away for me to tell if she's guilty or not, but her reaction is undeniably strong.

I stand, causing everyone's attention to shift to me. As I speak, I push away the love and fear I have for my mother, and say my piece with a fiery determination. "Gabi's father is a prosecutor," I interject, my gaze locked onto my mother's. "I'm sure there's enough evidence to make you a valid suspect. Especially in motive."

Mom's defenses falter as uncertainty seeps into her demeanor. "You have zero evidence," she barks, her voice betraying a hint of desperation.

Sebastian, latching on to the momentum that we're building, gives her no time to catch her breath. "We have people ready to testify against you, Margaret. Give it up. You're done."

Her eyes dart between the three of us, sharp with defiance. "Who?" she demands, her composure fraying at the edges. When no one answers her, her expression changes, disbelief taking over as she glances between me and Alex. The truth hits her like a thunderclap. "No. Absolutely not. I refuse to believe it. You both wouldn't go as far as incriminating your poor mother for a crime she didn't commit, would you?"

"There's nothing poor about you, Mom," I snap, the words dripping with bitterness. "And God knows if you are truly the person who gave the order to place the bomb in the car or not. If you're guilty, I doubt that you would dirty your hands committing the crime directly, but that matters very little in the long run."

"Julia is right," Sebastian rumbles, and I can hear the promise of victory in his tone. We are almost there, I can feel it. "You might think you can go ahead and tell Karl something only my father and I should have the right to tell him about, but if you do, you're going to pay a higher price than you could ever imagine. Not only will you lose your good name, but also your reputation. And finally, your two oldest children will turn against you publicly."

I see my mother raise her hand and lay it over her heart, almost unconsciously.

"Alex?" Mom breaks the silence that follows Sebastian's devastating speech, eyes searching her older son's face for some sign of reassurance.

Alex takes a deep breath, a momentary pause before he finds his voice. "Sorry, Mom," he begins, almost apologetic as she shrugs. "I actually like Sebastian, so… yeah. I think they make a fine couple, and if you could let go of your pride, maybe you'd see the same thing."

Alex's words make my chest feel tight, warmth suffusing me. His support is everything to me in this moment.

There's a flicker of hesitation in my mother's eyes, a fleeting battle between her desires and the acceptance of reality. With a sigh, she finally concedes, her words tinged with resignation. "Julia, you are an adult," she states, her lip curling like saying the words disgusts her. "You can elope if you want to. I see now that I can't stop you from making stupid mistakes anymore; I can only warn you against them. But let me tell you something." She pauses, studying my reaction, searching for any signs of doubt or hesitation. "One day, in the near or distant future," she continues, softer now, her index finger pointing out. "You will be in the same place that I am right now. Maybe not in your twenties, or thirties, but mark my words, eventually you will be. When that moment comes, I will be here for you because that's what mothers do. We do all that we can to help, even when our children are being idiots. And trust me, my dear, your children will have moments of idiocy, just like mine."

With her piece said, Mom sweeps out of the petit salon, turning so quickly that her skirt flares out behind her. I stand there, my mind buzzing with thoughts and feelings, as I process that the confrontation is well and truly over. It's done, and she said *elope if I want to.* Can this be real? Will she really not interfere? The room feels both empty and full with her gone. I hate that this ended on such a sour note, but I think it was always destined to.

"I have to follow her," I tell the two men, giving them an apologetic look. "Wait here."

I quickly follow my mother, my heart pounding in my chest. She might think that I'm an idiot, and she might hate the idea of me marrying Seb still, but I can't let her walk away without addressing the one question burning within me.

I don't catch up with her until we reach the garden, the scent of the flowers incredibly sweet on the breeze.

"Mom! Wait!" I call out, my voice filled with urgency.

Mom pauses in her tracks, her figure poised and rigid. She turns slowly and her gaze meets mine, weariness plastered all over her face. She looks…defeated. Like she isn't used to losing. Despite all of that, I know that she did all of this out of love, no matter how horrible her actions may or may not have been. And if she still loves me, her daughter, then there is still hope for our entire family.

"What else do you want, Julia?" she asks, her words full of resignation.

My words come out in a rush, the intensity of my emotions propelling me forward. "Everything you said back there… does that mean if I get married, you won't tell Karl anything? You won't tell him that he's Sebastian's brother?"

A flicker of something undefinable passes through Mom's expression, a fleeting glimpse of vulnerability.

She seems to weigh her response carefully, contemplating the consequences of her actions. "I won't, no," she finally replies with a note of sincerity. "I have no interest in my two oldest children testifying against me in a court of law. You and I both know that we would never recover in the eyes of the public, and the case would follow us for the rest of our lives. So no, I won't tell the bastard, even if I honestly feel like *someone* should, so you and your boyfriend can rest easy."

Her sarcastic tone makes my cheeks flush with embarrassment, but I don't back down, even when her confirmation makes my knees weak with relief. The secret of Karl's lineage will remain under lock and key. But there's one more request I need to make, one more bridge I want to build between us.

"Is that all?" she huffs, and I shake my head.

"One more thing, Mom." I summon my courage and speak. "If I get married… I mean, if Sebastian and I get married… would you still attend the ceremony? You've made it very clear that you don't agree with my decision but… it would mean a lot to me if you do. Really, it'd be everything to me, Mom."

Silence hangs in the air, and I even hold my breath with anticipation. Mom's gaze intensifies, searching my face for any signs of deception or hidden agendas. She ponders my words, her brow furrowing in deep thought. A heavy sigh escapes her lips, carrying the weight of her disapproval and the corner that I've backed her into. And if I'm not mistaken, notes of the love that she still has for me and all her children.

"I shall think about it," she finally responds, unmoved. "I will make no promises."

My heart swells. It's not a definite yes, but it's not a rejection either. In this delicate moment, I can't help but embrace Mom tightly, the barriers between us momentarily crumbling. "Thank you so much," I whisper with sincerity. "I know how much it cost you, Mom, but thank you."

A glimmer of a smile dances on her lips, a small acknowledgment of our fragile truce. "If I come," she warns, her tone firm. "Don't you dare go inviting your father."

A surge of understanding courses through me, the reminder of the intricate dance between my parents and the secrets they hold. "Of course not," I assure her, gripping her hands in mine. "I won't. I know perfectly the deal you made with him."

My mother nods, a subtle acceptance of my words. "Good. At least you listen to me when it comes to some things."

In this fleeting moment, the bridge between us extends a little further, fragile but present. It's not a complete reconciliation, but it's a step forward.

In the late evening, among the quiet garden, I leave my mother to return to Alex and Sebastian. The sun casts a warm glow, bathing the flowers in hues of gold and pink as I walk. It's beautiful here. I don't think I've appreciated that for a long time.

Approaching the petit salon again, I can hear the quiet buzzing of Sebastian and Alex talking. I'm glad that they waited on me, because I want to share this victory with both of them. They stop talking when I enter, and my words carry across the room as I speak.

"She's agreed," I announce, my words punctuating the air with a sense of triumph. "She won't tell Karl, under any circumstances. We did it."

Alex, ever the celebrator, wastes no time in requesting that Stuart, the butler, bring a bottle of champagne to mark this momentous occasion. The anticipation in the room grows palpable as we await the arrival of the sparkling liquid.

Sebastian, his eyes filled with gratitude, turns to my brother and expresses his heartfelt appreciation. "Thank you, Alex. You truly are the best brother Julia could have," he says, his voice brimming with sincerity. "And now I'm honored to call you a friend, too. Soon enough it might even be family, huh?"

Alex chuckles, slinging an arm around Sebastian's shoulders. "If you're lucky, man. If you're lucky."

But as the room fills with the joyous atmosphere of happiness, I find myself lost in thought, a wave of contemplation washing over me. I watch my brother and the man that I've been fighting so hard to keep enjoying the calm that comes after the storm, but my mind isn't quite settled. My concern doesn't go unnoticed, and before I know it Sebastian is in front of me. He puts a finger under my chin and lifts my face so my gaze is on his. "Are you okay?"

I take a moment, turning the words over in my brain before I finally speak. "I, um, I was wondering if you ever found out who planted that bomb in your car? I know I don't have any right to ask you that, but—"

Alex, who must have heard my question, interjects, his disbelief palpable. "Don't tell me you really think it was Mom who gave the order? I know there isn't any direct proof that it wasn't her but...come on, Julia. She's our mom."

Sebastian exhales slowly, the shadow of all the pain he's suffered clear in his expression. "I don't know who it was, no," he admits. "And at this point, I don't even think I want to know anymore. Knowing won't bring them back, anyway, and revenge just feels so hollow to me now."

Alex shakes his head. "I still don't think it was Mom."

Surprising even myself, I realize that I don't want to believe that she's that evil, either. "She does have a motive for it, sure, but let's not assume the worst. I can't comprehend the idea of her being so cruel."

My brother nods a single time. "Agreed. No point in speculating."

Sebastian's face is shadowed, and there is an undeniable sadness there from still not knowing who might have killed his family. But his willingness to let it go, so we can move on with our lives, is astounding.

In that moment, when I feel like my heart might explode from affection for this man, Stuart enters the room, carrying the bottle of champagne with graceful precision. Alex eagerly grabs it and expertly pops the cork. The sound of the effervescent bubbles fills the room, a tangible symbol of hope and renewal.

"To you both," Alex declares, his toast ringing with sincerity. "May these hard times bring our two families closer than ever." His words resonate within me, a shared sentiment of unity and strength.

"To all of us," I counter, my heart filled with pride. "None of this would have worked without you too, Alex. Thank you."

As a trio, we raise our glasses and clink them together, the sound reverberating off of the salon walls. It marks the beginning of a new era, a united front against the challenges that lie ahead, and a testament to the unwavering bond that is forming between the three of us as we speak.

While the champagne flows and laughter fills the air, we toast to the future, embracing the complexities of our past while holding onto the promise of a brighter tomorrow. I keep catching Sebastian's gaze as we drink, seeing the fire there and the powerful attraction that is so alive between us. It's hard to comprehend that, soon enough, he may be mine for good.

It can't come soon enough.

CHAPTER 27

Sebastian

The evening is somber as I return home. After the flowing champagne and jubilance that had taken over after we finally received tacit approval from Margaret, my own home estate feels quiet and grim.

I step through the door, and most of the lights in the house are off. I can hear soft sounds coming from deeper inside, and I breathe out slowly, recognizing instantly in what direction they are coming from: my father's bedroom. My stomach sinks. I haven't checked on him all day… I'll never forgive myself if I've been out scheming and celebrating if he's been here suffering the entire time.

The nurse, a constant presence in our lives now, meets me in the hallway, her voice quiet but dripping with concern. "His pulse is low," she whispers, trying to keep our conversation private. I take a deep breath, mustering the strength to face the truth.

"Is he awake?"

The nurse nods. "He heard you come home. I think he's been waiting to talk to you."

"Thank you. Go ahead and take a break. I'll spend some time with him."

She retreats, and I continue retracing familiar footsteps that lead me back to my father's bedside.

Like always, seeing him so weak in the bed makes me feel like I've been punched in the stomach. All the air goes out of me, and the sadness it brings seeing him so frail threatens to drown me. I hold it in, though, not wanting him to see how much his appearance disturbs me.

"Hey, Dad," I say, moving to sit in the comfortable chair next to the bed. There is still a grudge between us, and its name is Karl, but I still want to be with my father on these hard days. He might have lied to me for decades, but I love him still.

"Look who finally came home," he gripes, but the way he reaches out to pat my hand lets me know that he's just joking. "I figured you might have been mad enough at me that you weren't coming back this time, but here you are."

I muster as much of a smile as I can. "Yeah, sorry about that. I was taking care of some things. Let's not talk about… everything. The nurse said your pulse is low?"

Dad huffs. "Yes, and? I think we all know that I'm not in perfect health, son."

"Have you been taking your medication properly?" I ask, unable to hide the worry in my tone. Despite the lingering negativity that taints our relationship, I cannot help but be concerned for his well-being. At this moment, I am not just his exasperated son but a caregiver with genuine concern.

"Yes, yes. You don't have to worry so damned much about me, Seb. I can take care of myself." We both know it's a lie, but I don't correct him. It doesn't hurt me any to let him hold on to these little bits of control.

"I do worry about you, Dad," I sigh. "Regardless of what I feel towards you, and whatever lies between us, you're still my dad, and I'm going to take care of you, whether you like it or not."

A moment of vulnerability passes between us as I help him sit up in bed, offering a glass of water. The simple act of care bridges the gap between us, if only for a fleeting instant, reminding us both of the shared bond that persists beneath our surface conflicts.

Dad drinks, lying back down with a heavy exhale. "It's been an entire week since we last spoke," he murmurs, his tone carrying a touch of remorse. "Are you any closer to moving on from all of this? Or are you determined to be mad at me for the rest of both our lives?"

I pause, annoyed at how he just assumes it will be so easy for me to forgive and forget something as world shaking as having a half-sibling as the product of an affair. "I'm talking to you now, aren't I?"

"Yes, I guess you are, but you clearly don't want to be. Even the nurse is warmer to me than my own damned son." His frustration comes through so thickly that it makes me cringe. No amount of guilt will ever make me just 'move on' from the fact that Karl is my half-brother, but I also don't want that lie to define my father and I's relationship from here on out.

"You're lucky I'm even here." I find myself saying. "Not only did you hide your affair child from me, but you also wanted to avoid telling me so badly that you almost made me lose the love of my life. I'm here because I love you, Dad, not because I forgive you. So take what I'm offering, dammit, and stop trying to make me feel guilty!"

I can see the surprise on his face, and he lets out a dry laugh. "Forget but not forgive, huh? Fine, I guess I'll take what I can get. You're a better man than I am, I'll tell you that." His next words lack the acidity of the others, and they make me feel like a fist is squeezing my heart. "For what it's worth, I love you son. And I want you to be happy."

"What if it's Julia that makes me happy?"

Dad takes a few moments to answer, and for a second I think he's going to tell me just to move on again, except this time, to move on from the woman I love. But, he surprises me. "Then I believe you'll find a way to make it work, even if I've made the road more difficult for you. You've always been a stubborn boy, Seb."

His eyes meet mine, and for a moment, the barriers between us crumble. The sorrow of our shared history bears down upon us, the wounds still fresh, yet in this moment, we find a sliver of reconciliation. Well, I think we both can see that sliver, but whether we will both take it is yet to be seen.

"Margaret won't bother you anymore," I reveal, savoring the look of shock that rolls over his face, knowing that I did something to set him free that he never expected. "We took care of it. Your secret is safe with us."

Silence blankets the bedroom turned hospital as my father absorbs what my words really mean. "She won't tell?"

I shake my head, and take one of his hands in both of mine. "No, she won't tell. Even if I marry her daughter, she wouldn't dream of exposing you, so you can rest easy."

"Thank you, son," he murmurs, gratitude shining through as he pats our hands with his free one. "I'm almost afraid to ask how you did it."

"With the help of Julia and her brother," I tell him proudly. "Margaret Van Dieren is a formidable opponent, and I needed all the help I could get."

"Well..." he croaks, reaching for another drink of water before speaking again. "I guess that means you and the girl have reconciled."

"We have," I confirm, tilting my chin up as I tell him exactly how my future is going to play out now. "And I'm going to marry Julia, Dad. With or without your approval."

His eyes widen, intrigue dancing within them as he reveals a secret of his own. "She came here to speak to me, your Julia," he confides, his voice laden with newfound sincerity. "And she seems to be very determined to marry you, too."

I'm stunned. "Julia came *here*? When?"

"Last week. I didn't tell you because, at the time, I didn't see a way for this all to work out. I guess I underestimated you both." He grins, and it reminds me of the strong, sure father I've known most of my life. "I think you may have met your match with that one, Seb."

I snort in amusement. "I certainly hope so. Life would be boring with a dull wife, I would imagine."

Silence stretches for a minute before Dad speaks again, and there is sorrow hanging on each word of the declaration. "Your mother was like that, too. Quiet, but formidable. I... never deserved the years she gave me. I took her for granted. Don't you dare do the same with your girl, you hear me?"

I swallow past the lump in my throat, my eyes burning with unshed tears. "I won't. I cherish her already. Plus, those Van Dieren women… I'm learning that it's a mistake to cross them."

Dad chuckles, his eyes crinkling in genuine amusement. "Indeed, that is very true. But Sebastian… even if you hadn't managed to keep Margaret silent, I planned on telling you this, and would have dealt with the consequences later." He pauses, and I can feel the importance of the things he's about to say hovering in the air around us. "I want you to know that you and Julia have my blessing to marry. I can't ever make up for all the things I've done in the past, so all I can do is make the right calls going forward. Marry her, Sebastian. If she's worth all of this, marry her."

I'm infinitely glad that the bedroom is dark, because there are definitely tears in the corners of my eyes at this point, gratitude and quiet, simple joy growing inside of me with each breath. My father's blessing… I never expected to have it, but now that I do, I can't imagine going through with this wedding without it.

"Thanks, Dad," I force out through the tightness of my throat. "That means…so much to me."

He clears his throat, having an equally hard time speaking through his emotions. "Your mother would give you both her blessings, too. I know it."

I take Dad's hand once again and squeeze, feeling the tattered edges of our relationship starting to sew themselves back together. "I think so too, Dad. I think so too."

CHAPTER 28

Sebastian

The golden hues of the setting sun cast a warm glow upon the park, creating a picturesque backdrop for our sunset picnic by the tranquil lake. Spring is finally here and the weather has been good enough for us to go out to the park we first went to seven months ago. Gosh, time really does fly.

I watch as Julia spreads the blanket with care on the small wooden dock jutting out into the lake, arranging the delicious assortment of food that my household staff had prepared and packed up for us. Her tenacity and unwavering determination has astounded me.

She's stunning—so beautiful that I can barely breathe when she turns and the sunlight catches on her golden hair, making it seem like it's been lit from the inside. There's an adorable flush to her cheeks from the effort of helping me set up the picnic, and when she smiles at me, I'm sure that everything is right in the world for once.

Wearing a pair of beige pants and a white sweater with her hair loose, Julia looks like every fantasy I've ever had. Lately, though, she's the only fantasy I need. Just the idea of spending my future with her satisfies me in a way nothing else ever had.

A small, black velvet box sits in the pocket of my pants, impossibly heavy for its size. It holds one of the most important things I've ever owned.

I settle down on the blanket next to her, watching her fold her long legs under her and throw her hair over her shoulder. Gratitude fills my heart, and I turn to Julia, unable to contain the emotions that well within me.

"Thank you," I whisper just loud enough for her to hear me over the sounds of the water lapping against the dock. My confession is laced with sincerity and admiration. "Thank you for never giving up on me, for being the light that guides me through the darkness. Julia… without you, my father would have never been convinced to open up, to set aside his pride and embrace the opportunity for healing."

Her eyes meet mine, filled with a tenderness that melts away any remnants of doubt or insecurity. In her presence, I find solace, a sanctuary from the chaos that has plagued my life. With her by my side, I am whole, complete.

She reaches out and smooths the line between my eyebrows, where they are drawn together in thought. "Is there something else on your mind, love?"

I take a deep breath, summoning the courage to reveal a truth that has been weighing heavily upon me. "When I learned that Karl was my brother," I begin, my voice faltering for a moment before regaining its strength. "I was shocked, betrayed even." The words tumble out, the rawness of my emotions laid bare. “I didn’t need any more complications in my life, you know?”

Julia nods, pouring wine for the two of us and passing me a glass before she leans back on her elbows, enjoying the fresh evening air. “I understand. Do you plan on ever telling him? Maybe it wouldn’t be stressing you out to this degree if you just put it all out there.”

I shake my head, swirling the wine. “Definitely not. I hope that he never finds out. The dynamic would just be… well, to put it simply, a mess. Dad was his boss, and now I am. It would blow everything we’ve worked for out of the water if Karl knew who he was to my father.”

Julia shifts closer, her hand finding mine, offering silent support and reassurance. “Seb,” she says softly in a soothing melody, “You don’t have to worry. Just treat Karl as you always have—as a treasured employee. Your father has made it clear that’s all he desires.”

“As long as he doesn’t come to any family gatherings, I’m good,” I assert, my tone firm yet measured. Karl, my newfound brother, remains an employee in my eyes, and I have no intention of blurring the lines between family and business. It’s a decision that protects the delicate balance we’ve established.

Julia hums in thought, picking up a grape and popping it into her mouth, her tongue darting out to lick the juice from her bottom lip. “Don’t be too harsh on him,” she suggests. “None of this is his fault. I don’t expect you to welcome him into the fold or anything, but he’s pretty much innocent.”

“I’m not going to treat him badly,” I reassure her. “But for the outside world, I’m his boss, and he works for me. That’s it. I will always look out for him, just as my dad requested, but I won't treat him like a brother. That's out of the question."

Julia nods in agreement, her eyes reflecting a shared understanding. "We can agree on that." She then pauses for a moment, before revealing something of her own, too. "You know, I never met my half-brother. I know who he is—a certain Jimmy living with his mom in Amsterdam—but we've never met him. So I understand how delicate those things can be. Your secret is safe with me."

I let out a breath when she says this. The amount of similarities our families share is astounding. We both recognize the need to maintain boundaries, to navigate the delicate balance between family ties and their legal implications. Sure, the situation I have found myself in with Karl is unlike any other issue I have faced thus far in my life, but the plan that I've set out, to keep Karl at arm's length, is the only way forward I can see.

We eat and drink, listening to the ducks on the water and the wind in the trees. I feed her from my fingers, my blood thrumming hot in my veins when her lips graze my thumb, and it takes all of my willpower not to just throw all the food in the lake and pull her to me, crushing my lips to hers. It's been too long since I've kissed her to my heart's content. The small pecks and caresses since we reconciled aren't enough to satisfy my hunger.

"*Tonight isn't for making out,*" I remind myself firmly. "*We have other, more important things to do.*"

As we indulge in the delicious food, our conversation dances effortlessly, the laughter and shared stories echoing across the water. The memories of our first encounter here resurface, painting the atmosphere with a sense of whimsy and serendipity.

"Do you remember," I begin, a playful tone lacing my words, "when you bullied me into taking you on a date here?"

Julia's eyes sparkle with a mix of fondness and amusement. "Of course, how could I forget? Except I remember it a little differently. Instead of me bullying you, I seem to recall you showing up at my school, completely smitten with me, and begging me to go out with you."

I chuckle at the memory, shaking my head in denial. "That is absolutely not how it went! You were the desperate one, Ms. Van Dieren, not me. You must have been dazzled by my masculine charms, that's why your memory is messed up."

She leans closer, her hand finding mine, fingers interlocking with familiar warmth. "Well, whichever one of us is right, I'm still glad that it happened. Because it solidified my decision to keep you around, no matter what."

I can't resist kissing her now, but I keep it short and sweet, refusing to fall into the soft siren song of her lips. We sit in comfortable silence for a moment, savoring the beauty of the surroundings and the company we share. The gentle noise of the water against the dock creates a soothing rhythm, a backdrop to our unspoken connection.

After packing the food back up, we both watch the sun start to slip beneath the horizon. I pull her to me, my arm around her delicate shoulders, and hold her close. Julia leans her head on my shoulder and lets out a content sigh.

"Julia?"

"Hm?"

I close my eyes, breathing in the sweet scent of her hair. "I want us to tackle the problems like we did now, together, no matter how ugly they are. I'm confident that if we work together like this we can face anything that life throws at us."

Julia's smile lights up her face. "Together," she echoes, sounding just as determined as I feel. It's in these moments, when we stand as a united front, that I feel an unbreakable strength coursing through my veins.

As the sun continues its descent, casting long shadows upon the landscape, I am filled with a renewed sense of purpose. The challenges that lie ahead may be formidable, the road uncertain, but with Julia by my side, I know that we possess the strength and resilience to overcome anything that comes our way.

We lean into each other, our hearts beating in synchrony, as we embrace the unknown. Together, we forge a path illuminated by love, trust, and unwavering support. With every step we take, we grow stronger, braver, and more resilient. And as we embark on this journey hand in hand, I am certain that no matter how treacherous the road may be, we will emerge victorious, our bond unyielding in the face of adversity.

The sun dips lower still, leaving behind a canvas of deep purples and blues. We sit there, basking in the beauty of the moment, knowing that together, we have the power to conquer any challenge, to navigate the complexities of life with grace and determination. As twilight settles and the stars begin to twinkle above, I am filled with a profound sense of thankfulness for Julia's presence in my life, for the love and strength she brings, and for the boundless possibilities that lie ahead for us.

"How is your dad doing?" she asks quietly. "You haven't spoken about him for a while now. Is everything okay?"

I consider lying to her, but what's the point? If she's going to be in my life forever, I can't imagine what I would gain by painting a false picture. "That's because my dad's health has been the same," I admit, my expression deepening. "Some days he makes some progress, and I think he might be back on his feet full-time again, but then he has another setback. It makes me feel helpless."

Julia's eyes well up with empathy, and she tightens her grip on my hand, offering silent comfort. "Seb, I'm deeply sorry to hear that. It must be incredibly tough for you. I can't even imagine… how are you coping?"

I inhale slowly as I gather my thoughts. "I won't sugar coat it, it's exhausting. I want to be there for him, to provide support during this difficult time. Yet, having to be reminded about his mortality day after day is really wearing on me. If Mom and my siblings were still around, he'd still be his strong, normal self. But now…" I trail off, not knowing what else to say.

I look down when she doesn't respond, my chest going tight when I see that there are tears in the eyes of my sweet Julia.

When she finally answers, she astounds me once again. "Seb, we can't control the passage of time or the hardships that life brings. But what we can control is how we face them together. We'll stand by your father, and we'll be there for each and every step of the way."

Her words embrace me like a comforting hug, and I draw closer, seeking solace in her presence. "Thank you, Julia. Having you by my side gives me strength. Dad might act standoffish and stubborn at first, but I really think the two of you will get along once he thaws out some."

"Hmm." She kisses my cheek, humor sparkling in her gaze. "I don't think I can say the same about my mom. She might never like you. Is that okay?"

"I expected as much," I sigh, sounding more miserable than I mean to, and Julia giggles.

"We'll keep our time visiting to her a minimum, okay?"

"Our time, huh?" I pull back just enough to look down at her. "Does that mean you're considering us a single unit now, Ms. Van Dieren?"

Julia blushes, nibbling at her bottom lip, just like I want to. "Maybe…."

And then, as if guided by the hand of fate, I reach into my pocket and retrieve the small velvet box. My heart gallops with nervous anticipation as I stand, pulling Julia to her feet despite her obvious confusion before sinking to one knee. She audibly gasps, eyes going wide, the reflection of the starlit sky mirrored within them. Finding my inner strength, I speak the words that have been etched upon my soul.

"Julia," I begin, fighting hard to keep my voice from shaking. "I'm not perfect. Sometimes, I'm proud, sometimes I'm stubborn. But there's one thing I'm not, and that's a cheater like my father. I may be a workaholic, consumed by the demands of my career, but you will always come first in my heart." I laugh as I recall the past few months. "Hell, Julia, you already do come first for me. You have for months. Since the moment I first saw you, really. You've owned me, body and soul, this entire time."

With those words hanging in the air, I open the box, revealing a delicate ring nestled within its confines. It gleams under the moonlight, a symbol of commitment, trust, and unwavering love. This ring once belonged to my mother, a cherished heirloom that holds generations of love and devotion.

Tears well in Julia's eyes as she realizes the weight of the moment, the significance of the ring, and the promise it represents. I take a deep breath, my heart pounding with both trepidation and uncontainable joy, and ask the question that has been waiting on my tongue to escape for weeks now.

"Julia, my love, will you marry me?" I inquire, barely above a whisper. The air around us seems to hold its breath, waiting for her response.

A radiant smile graces her lips, illuminating her face with a radiance that rivals the stars above. Her eyes shine with a mixture of love, adoration, and belief in our future together. Without hesitation, she answers, filled with warmth and adoration.

"Yes, Sebastian," she says, shaking like a leaf as she holds out her hand. "Yes, I will marry you."

It appears as though time has stopped in this enchanted moment. As we celebrate our love, our commitment, and the promise of a shared future, the world around us becomes less important. It's an unadulterated blissful moment, proof that love will always find its way despite chaos, tragedy, and uncertainty.

I put the ring on Julia's finger even though my own hands are shaking, making our vows official with this glittering representation of our union. The ring is a tribute to the synchronicity of our hearts, and it fits flawlessly, as if it were always intended to be there.

"*Thanks, Mom,*" I think, sending up a silent prayer to the woman that I miss so much. "*The ring is perfect. She loves it.*"

I jump to my feet, holding out my arms to balance as the dock sways beneath us, causing Julia to giggle through her happy tears. Once the water has settled, I sweep her into my arms, soaking in the heat and weight of her in my arms. My sweet Julia. My fiancée. My future wife.

"I love you," I breathe.

"I love you too," Julia whispers back.

Under the twilight sky, we embrace, sealing our commitment with a tender kiss.

22 YEARS LATER…

CHAPTER 29

Julia

As I gaze out the window of my bedroom, my heart feels heavy with a mix of excitement and sorrow. The vibrant morning sun bathes the gardens in its golden glow, illuminating the flurry of activity as the staff meticulously arranges the final details for Andries and Roxanne's wedding. It should be a day of celebration, a joyous occasion that brings family and friends together. For the most part, it is! Yet, a deep ache settles within me as I have to come to terms with the fact that Sebastian is still absent. His disapproval of Andries's bride is keeping him away from this important moment in our son's life. I wonder if he knows just how much it's breaking me apart inside for him not to be here? This should be one of the biggest, most wonderful shared moments we ever experience as parents.

"*There's still time,*" I think, almost frantic. "*Please, Sebastian. Don't let me down.*"

I watch as the photographers and videographers move around, capturing every precious moment, freezing them in time. I imagine the laughter, the cheers, the tears of joy that will fill the air later, but a tinge of sadness creeps in knowing that Sebastian won't be there to witness it all. He should be here, standing proudly by my side, offering his support and love to our son and his new bride. But Sebastian can't accept that his oldest child is marrying a former escort, and because of his hang ups, we all have to suffer.

I wonder who is hurting more—me, his wife, or Andries, his son. I know both of us feel his absence like a sore tooth—impossible to ignore. The weight of his absence is like an invisible barrier between us, a reminder of the fractures in our relationship that still need healing.

When I left home to come to my mother's house, which had at one time been my childhood home, I knew that my choice could mean the end of my marriage. I kept my head high then, but now it's becoming so painful that it hurts to even breathe when I'm thinking about him.

I brush a stray tear from my cheek, my gaze fixed on the lake beyond the gardens. It's moments like these that make me yearn for the connection we once had, the love that brought us together. I long for the understanding, the shared dreams, the sense of unity that seems to have faded over time. The realization that he couldn't find it in his heart to set aside his pride and stubbornness stings, leaving me with a sense of emptiness.

We all had our doubts about Roxanne and Andries at first, our daughter Elise most of all behind Sebastian himself. But on the lawn I see Elise, wrapped in a silk robe and looking over the preparations with Dan by her side. El looks… happy. Content. Accepting. If she can be okay with Roxanne, why can't Seb?

Sure, there are reasons behind his resistance. For one, Roxanne is significantly older than Andries, and not to mention her past career as a madam and escort, but anyone can see the connection between Ms. Feng and my son. They fought for each other, almost to the point of ruin.

"Just like we did years ago, right Seb? Have you forgotten?"

But amidst the sadness, a flicker of determination rises within me. I won't let his absence overshadow the happiness and love that fills this day. I won't allow his disapproval to cast a shadow on our son's joy. I will be there, standing tall and strong, representing the unwavering support of a mother's love.

I take a deep breath, allowing the fresh morning air from the open windows to fill my lungs, grounding me in the present. There is beauty all around me, in the blooming flowers, the laughter of the staff, and the promise of a new beginning for Andries and Roxie. I'll cherish these moments, savor every smile, and create memories that will endure.

As the staff finalizes their preparations, I remind myself that love and unity can still thrive, even in the face of adversity. Sebastian's absence is a reminder that we are flawed, that we stumble and falter, but it doesn't define us. We can find strength in each other, in the bonds that withstand the trials of life.

I wipe away the last traces of sadness from my eyes, vowing to make this day a celebration of love. I will be there for Andries, for our family, and for myself. And as the festivities unfold, I will hold Sebastian in my heart, hoping that someday he'll find his way back to us, to the love that still exists within our story.

I'm shaken out of my reverie by a gentle knock on the door, and I invite the visitor inside. It's my mother who enters with a warm smile on her face, so much softer and happier than the expression she wore when she told Sebastian and I that we were free to elope. The years have made her more affectionate, maybe, but no one should ever underestimate Margaret Van Dieren, despite her age.

As she stands by the door, Mom takes in the scene happening outside my window, noticing my fixed gaze upon the gardens, and her voice carries a tender concern.

"Darling, everyone is downstairs on the terrace for breakfast," she informs me, her words containing a gentle invitation. "Don't you want to join us? The photographer and videographer have already started capturing the special moments."

However, I remain rooted by the window, my thoughts lingering on the past. I turn to my mother, a pensive expression on my face, and pose a question that has been weighing on my mind.

"Do you remember how, twenty-something years ago, you were just as opposed to my marriage as Sebastian is to his own son's?" I ask, hoping that she doesn't read the turmoil that is churning inside me.

Mom closes the door behind her, before stepping closer to me until we are side by side. Her eyes meet mine, carrying the weight of memories and understanding, and I feel her hand taking mine in a sweet gesture of comfort. "I do remember very well, yes," she replies, her tone guarded. "Why do you ask, love?"

A small smile tugs at the corners of my lips as I tease, "Sounds like the two of you have more in common than you thought. Isn't that funny?"

My mother's grin widens, a glimmer of amusement dancing in her eyes. She envelops me in a warm embrace, her arms providing solace in a moment of vulnerability. I feel her understanding and love radiating through the gentle touch.

"Oh, darling, I'm so sorry for what you are going through," she says softly, her words filled with empathy. "But if you must know the truth, Sebastian hasn't turned out to be as bad a husband as I once feared. And look at your beautiful family. He's just too stubborn and prideful for his own good."

A sigh escapes my lips, a mixture of resignation and longing. "I know, but after everything we've been through, I had hoped he would have grown, learned from his mistakes."

Mom's voice carries a hint of wistfulness as she responds, "Ah, well… Sebastian is a real piece of work, as I always told you. When are you going to realize that I'm always right, hm?"

The seriousness of the situation lingers in the air, regardless of our attempts at humor. I gather my strength and turn my attention back to my mother, an idea tickling in my brain that I can't ignore begging to come out.

"Speaking of Sebastian, can I ask you a favor, Mom?" I inquire, heart pounding with the risk I'm about to take.

Her eyes meet mine, filled with a mother's unwavering love. Just like the love I have for Andries, and all of my children.

"Anything you need, dear," Mom assures me, squeezing my hand once more. Older and thinner, power radiates from her nonetheless. It's almost like making a deal with the devil, except this devil happens to love me endlessly. "Anything at all."

CHAPTER 30

Sebastian

Alex: *Don't be silly, you know you will regret this! I'm picking you up.*

I sneer at the phone and throw it on the bed behind me, absolutely done with this entire situation a million times over. Why is everyone so fixated on me attending this hellscape of a wedding? I said no, Julia moved out, and now here we are. Everyone is getting their way except for me, so what the hell else do they want from me?

I hear the clearing of a throat from my bedroom door, and I turn, annoyed, to see my butler with his hands clasped behind him. "Sir, there is someone here to speak with you."

"Of course there is," I grumble, pulling my robe on and tying it tight at the waist. I'm expecting Alex, anger and resignation swelling within me. "Go ahead and send them in."

The butler disappears, and I walk out of my suite and down to the foyer, expecting to see my brother-in-law waiting for me. Instead, I see someone totally unexpected. Even after all these years, her presence puts me on edge.

Margaret removes her light jacket and hands it to the butler, smiling at me with a saccharine sweetness as she walks through the doors and approaches me. She smoothes down the navy blue sheath dress she's wearing, grinning the entire time. "Hello, Sebastian. How are you on this beautiful morning?"

"I was better before you walked in," I confess, raising an eyebrow. "Of all the people I thought would come to drag me to this shit show, you weren't even on the list."

"Well, I do love a surprise, don't you?" she teases, brushing past me. "Aren't you going to offer your mother-in-law some tea? Coffee, maybe? It is rather early."

My butler looks at me, slightly alarmed, and I give him a quick nod. Maybe if we give her a drink, she will disappear faster. Unlikely, but it's worth a shot.

I join her on the terrace, grimacing at how bright it is. Margaret doesn't seem in any hurry to speak, simply taking her seat and gazing out at the long expanse of our property, full of greenery and gardens.

Finally, she speaks. "Doesn't this just feel so familiar, Sebastian?" Margaret says wistfully, barely hiding her satisfied grin. "It's almost nostalgic. Twenty-two years ago, it was me that was up in arms about you marrying my daughter. Now look where we are—with you being the asshole, this time."

I snort, a complex web of feelings warring inside of me. Seeing her here has really thrown me through a loop, and I'm struggling to catch up. "Don't pretend for one minute that if Julia had been marrying an *escort*, that you wouldn't have done everything in your power to prevent it. Andries is your grandchild, so you get to enjoy the festivities without worrying what chaotic bullshit their marriage will create."

"Roxanne is a lovely girl, despite her... less than tasteful past. You, on the other hand, have always been a rude, ungrateful little boy." One of our servers comes out, pouring my coffee before doing the same for Margaret. She smirks at me above the ceramic rim of the mug. "Even now. So little has changed."

I feel my jaw tightening with anger, but rein it in. "Did you come here just to insult me, or did you have a point you were wanting to make?"

"My point is that Julia and I's relationship suffered after my refusal to let her marry you in the first place. There is no reason it has to be like that for you and Andries. Sure, I like knowing that you're in this empty house all alone and pissed off, but my grandchildren and my daughter are grieving the fact that you aren't going to be there for the ceremony. Set your pride aside for once and come with me." Her lips twitch up at the corner. "I won't even reprimand you on the way over."

"I'll tell you what I've told everyone else: no. Hell no. You all can celebrate my oldest son marrying a whore, but I'm not going to be a part of it. Just because they sent the devil incarnate to fetch me doesn't mean I'm going to obey." The words come out of me nearly in a growl, giving away just how frustrated and tired of this thing I really am. "Let me know when you're ready to leave, Margaret. I'll walk you out."

Margaret checks her fingernails, humming to herself between sips of coffee. I'm just about to ask her what the hell she's waiting for when she speaks up again. "I know you're going to find this hard to believe, but I'm the lesser of the two evils in this situation, Sebastian. I'm going to give you one last chance you get dressed and come with me before I have to take the next step. And I promise you're not going to be fond of the next step."

I stand to leave, pushing down the hurricane of feelings storming inside me. "Goodbye, Margaret. I'm going to take a shower. The butler will see you out."

She makes a disappointed sound, like the hiss of a snake, before pulling a long white envelope out of her bag. "Very well, my least favorite son, since it seems that I'm unable to convince you to put your pride aside, then I hope Julia will be more convincing."

This stops me in my tracks. I refuse to feel hope that maybe, just maybe, my wife has returned to me. "She's here?"

Margaret stands, walking towards me, her heels clicking on the tile flooring. "No, she isn't. She asked me to give you this. I'll wait here for you to read it, and then you need to make your decision, because you're wasting my time."

She hands me the envelope before returning to the chair where she was enjoying her coffee. I open the letter carefully, unfolding the paper and reading my wife's flawless, looping handwriting. The brief happiness I felt knowing that she wrote to me is dashed when the contents of the paragraphs start to sink in.

Sebastian,

I'm deeply saddened that it has come to this. We made a promise to be together forever, and yet, here you are allowing your pride to destroy us. It's disheartening considering everything we've been through, and a shame that you can't put it aside for the sake of our family.

If my threats of divorce or my decision to move out of the house aren't enough to convince you, then I'm left with no choice but to take this final step: you must attend our son's wedding. If you refuse, not only will I file for divorce, but I will also reveal to Karl that he is your half-brother and has the same right to the Van den Bosch wealth as you do.

Be cautious not to turn your only ally into your greatest rival.

Julia

Throughout all these years, my wife's loyalty has been unwavering. She never let a family secret slip from her lips, especially not this one. Do I really want a war between us? Is Julia bluffing? Would she truly go to such extremes?

My sweet, smart wife has always been forgiving over the years. I can't believe she won't forgive me simply because I can't bear to witness my son marrying my half-brother's whore!

"From the look on your face, I have to assume that my daughter's words have been quite *persuasive*," Margaret says, a hint of the sharp, frighteningly cunning woman she has always been in her voice.

I offer a mocking smile to Margaret, who, despite the passing of time, remains unchanged. She's dangerous, ruthless, and has proven to me once again that she will go to any lengths to take care of her beloved daughter.

"*This old bitch is getting a kick out of this, I'm sure,*" I think bitterly, the smile never leaving my lips.

Still thinking, I stretch, walking to the edge of the terrace and looking out over our gardens. The day is almost painfully beautiful, just as beautiful as Julia and I's wedding day. How fitting.

An intriguing idea takes shape in my mind, a wonderfully cunning, Machiavellian plan that brings a mischievous smirk to my lips. If Julia wants me to attend that wedding, then I shall oblige. However, I will ensure that she deeply regrets ever asking me.

Turning back to Margaret, who is still comfortably seated in her chair, I finally give her what she wants. "Indeed, very much so. Julia's letter has made everything very clear. If you can give me a few minutes to get ready, I'll go with you. I have a feeling it will be quite an entertaining affair."

THE STORY CONTINUES IN SEBASTIAN.

Don't have the next bundle yet?

Get the next bundle of the series at 10% off

SCAN ME

ALSO BY MELANIE MARTINS

Blossom in Winter (Petra & Alex's story)

A forbidden, age-gap romance between a young, finance heiress and her dad's business partner who also happens to be her godfather. A taboo read filled with twists, mystery, power games and much more!

1. Blossom in Winter
2. Lured into Love
3. Lured into Lies
4. Defying Eternity
5. Happily Ever After: Part 1, 2, 3, and 4

Van den Bosch

This series follows members of the Van den Bosch family as they fall in love with someone they shouldn't.

1. Roxanne.
2. Andries.
3. Elise.
4. Dan.
5. Julia.
6. Sebastian. (You are here)
7. Hannah. (February 14, 2024)
8. Johan. (May 14, 2024)

Melanie Martins crafts forbidden love stories, intertwining elements of thrillers, morally gray characters, controversies, and a hint of eroticism. As her protagonists wade through emotional rollercoasters, scandals, and complex inner conflicts, she guarantees that happy endings always shine through. As a firm believer in the power of love, kindness, and gratitude, she also often embeds these themes into her novels. When not engrossed in her writing, Melanie revels in globetrotting, reading, daydreaming, and chronicling her adventures on social media.

Born in France and raised in Portugal, Melanie's travels across more than seventy countries serve as a profound wellspring of inspiration, enriching her stories with diverse narratives, settings, and characters.

Find more at melaniemartins.com
Socials: @melaniemartins and @melaniemartinsblog